EINSTEINEE EVOLUTION

THE BEGINNING

JOHNNY McKENZIE

IUNIVERSE, INC.
BLOOMINGTON

Einsteinee Evolution
The Beginning

iUniverse books may be ordered through booksellers or by contacting:

iUniverse
1663 Liberty Drive
Bloomington, IN 47403
www.iuniverse.com
1-800-Authors (1-800-288-4677)

ISBN: 978-1-4502-8679-4 (sc)
ISBN: 978-1-4502-8681-7 (dj)
ISBN: 978-1-4502-8680-0 (ebk)

Printed in the United States of America

iUniverse rev. date: 5/24/2011

PROLOGUE

Her milky blue eyes changed to a raging red and her waist length white, white, hair began to turn to raven black. The wave of color flowed evenly from the roots to the very tips. She felt nothing but anger as she evaluated the best from which she had to choose. It was like choosing the best of a bushel of wormy, rotten peaches. She began to evaluate Earth, the world from which she was going to choose her seed. Surely there were some who could meet her standards of honor.

But choose she would because she missed her children, the A'chant. She doesn't like the descendents of the A'chant people who inhabit the planets today in many different bipedal forms. These forms are governed by the needs of their environment. The true A'chant people have long ago left this universe. They left behind the lesser of their kind on various planets; if they chose to stay. These descendents fall far short of the honor of their ancestors. The Creator that claims this universe, The Mist, saw that it was not good and the descendants of the A'chant race were filled with evil toward each other.

She, in her wisdom, decided to create a replacement for the A'chant race. She needed help to rule this universe. She needed a police force. She studied the descendents who remained on the planets until she was convinced that the humans were closest to what she needed to aid her in the return to the old way of honor.

She began to search for the seed-bearers of her new race. She would school them in the things they needed to know to become the replacements for her beloved A'chants.

She had made a conscious decision to choose from the world of humans who had been at war for the last thirty-nine years. The battles being waged on both the East and West Coasts of the United States are horrific. The ground war on the East Coast rages as ground forces seize small areas back from the enemy – only to lose the ground the next day. The battles consume lives like a giant tidal wave engulfs an overpopulated coastline. It leaves in its wake only death and destruction.

The United States has suffered but not as much as England; it no longer exists. The European Union took it about twenty-five years ago. Canada and the United States took all the refugees who could make it to their shores. They needed as many fighters as they could get if they were going to save their respective countries.

The bright side, if there was one, was the failed attack on the West Coast. Uncommonly high surf that day kept the European Union from landing at the same time on the West Coast, as they attacked on the East Coast. The United States had time to move enough troops to the West Coast and be waiting to repel the invaders. The European Union lost the element of surprise and as a result failed to secure a foothold on the West Coast; and that battle front is less active. It's fought with ships and planes in the ocean. Only a few soldiers die each day.

The European attackers try to get a firmer foothold on the East Coast and to get a foot hold on the West. It's insane chaos with no end in sight. The United States government as well as the Canadian government and what is left of the English government do their best to push the invaders back into the sea.

The North American continent is under siege. No one is making any headway; it is at best - a stalemate. The two sides have been fighting for almost four decades to gain farm land. A few feet fall to one side one day and the next it is taken back. The combat on the East Coast is fought man to man in an attempt to keep from fouling the land for crops that will never be planted. If enough land is taken to try to plant crops it's not secure. The harvest will never happen. All that the land behind the attackers did was give them a place to fall back and regroup. The land is fouled at the same time with the blood of the dead. One would not be picking up rocks to clear the field to plant. He'd be picking up the spent brass of the ammo; and it would be a grand pile.

The side effect is that a lot of the population is destroyed on both sides and the need for farmland is lessened. It would be nice if someone in power noticed that they no longer need the land they are fighting for because of the population decrease. They don't notice and the war doesn't stop. One can only guess that neither side wants to lose face.

As for the people, the war has become part of their lives. The powerful, the ones toward the top of the ladder, Level threes and up in the current caste system, are making a lot of money on the war. The caste system doesn't exist according to the government, but that's a load of crap. It's even defined in tax documents. The higher classes pay more taxes and that buys their children some exemption from the draft. They don't want the war to end. It's a business to them, a very profitable business.

The draft affects the other end of the caste system very differently. For those who live in the lowest level, Level ten, the war and the draft are just as ingrained in their lives. The draft is ninety percent for able bodied males over sixteen and seventy percent for able-bodied females over eighteen who are not with child. The females, who gain the favor of the government, by having children, are left behind to do just that – produce more cannon fodder. The more children they birth, the better their status. It's a way out of going to the war. However most say after they have chosen this life; or it has chosen them, that it might be better to go to the war and die quickly rather than watch your children taken as they come of age and never come back.

The people who live in this wretched way are what make up the 'Level ten' world. They have become callous to their world over the years. They know nothing else. The young do as they please. The girls don't worry about having a child because they stay alive longer and get money from the government. The boys know they are going to die; most likely before they turn seventeen. They don't plan for a future. They live in the here and now with little regard to the trappings of a family. The girls are for the most part willing to have sex with anyone. Some of them ask for credits. It's against the law but those who ask for payment usually get it. The boys of all classes take full advantage of the situation.

The people unlucky enough to be Level ten have little or no means and no status. They have no skills and no hope. The way the government sees it they are there to breed soldiers. They are well cared for medically and given enough to eat and a very meager place to live in crowded clumps of older multi-floor buildings run by the government. The norm is one family to a four room apartment and some families are large. The government wants their future warriors to be healthy and used to hardships.

In that same line, the abuse of drugs or over indulgence in alcohol is not tolerated. It would damage the future soldiers. This rule spans all levels. The price for using drugs or being drunk is to be drafted on the spot, regardless of level. To be drafted is near certain death. The government propaganda, or maybe truth, boasts that there is no drug problem at any of the Levels. It's easy to understand why.

People can be drafted from anywhere in the United States but they go to the East Coast army, the ground war, and they seldom return. The ones who do are in such bad shape they would have been better off if they had been killed. Hundreds of soldiers die each day.

The government allows anyone to test for the Air Force. It's their way of trying to prove they are being fair. Most don't test. They think it's a waste of time. The paperwork to even get a date to take the Air Force test is very difficult and few below Level six have the knowledge or education to pass if they do get to test. The Space Force test is even more exclusive and much more difficult. You have to be a member of the Air Force for one year to be eligible to take the Space Force test; and a letter of recommendation from someone of importance is required. The better the signer's position the better your chances. It goes without saying that the higher your families Level the better chance you have of knowing someone of importance. The regulations say these requirements can be waived but...

There are real exceptions to the draft, mental deficiency and physical deformities that prevent you from taking or carrying out orders. It's not a good way out. Those who get the deferment are sent to special government run facilities – never to be heard from again. The most used exception was to join one of the religious orders. It became such a problem that the government regulates the number of people who can be registered in a religious order. There is a test to determine who can enter a religious order. The test is very difficult. The reasoning is - If God wants you he'll bless you and let you pass the test. It's a stupid idea but something the religious orders can't really contest.

The better educated higher Levels have a much better chance of joining one of the religious orders than the lower Levels who are poorly educated. If they have any formal education at all they have a chance; but not much of one. God's hand would be needed indeed for someone from the lower Levels to pass the test. Some believe the wealthier levels may be paying God off. The widespread abuse of the system forced the government to enact new laws. The law now states that a religious person who is not living up to his or her vows falls into the same category as a drug or alcohol abuser. They go straight to the war. If there is a God, he'd better be watching out for them then; because they can't buy themselves out of the war any more.

In this system William 'Billy' Holt caught the eye of The Mist. He and his family are Level nine by virtue of his father being a baker. Billy's life is already charted to take a path that will make him a very fertile seed for what The Mist has in mind. She will just have to protect him from his appointed death so he can sprout and grow into the Emperor of her new people.

He is the oldest of seven children who live in six rooms above the family bakery. He'll soon be sixteen, draft age. Level nines face an eighty percent draft rate across the board, males and females. They are considered craftsmen and to have some intelligence. The government doesn't want their art lost; so some have to be left to continue in their father's or mother's footsteps and to breed more Level nines. That's the way the draft works. The higher your level the less chance you will be drafted. The less chance you will die.

But, let's get back to William 'Billy' Holt – the twinkle in the milky blue eye of The Mist. He's her first seed and she will watch over him, guiding him to become the honorable man she needs.

×

CHAPTER ONE - WILLIAM HOLT

Today is a big day for Billy. He combs his dark hair just right so it hangs just over his ears. He wears his hair longer for two reasons; he hates to sit still long enough to get a haircut and more importantly to cover the fact that he has no sideburns. He really wants sideburns to go with his mustache. It was his first try for facial hair and it was more hair than whiskers but it had filled in nicely over the last eight months. He was very proud of it. He doesn't know anyone else his age who has such a nice mustache. He smiled and winked at himself in the mirror and headed out to start this very important day in his life.

Today he is going to take the Air Force test. He has studied hard and his parents are better educated than most Level nines. He hopes he will score high enough to stay out of the Ground Forces. He is exempt by law from the draft because he's the oldest child of a Level nine baker; but he really doesn't want to be a baker. He wants to be in The Air Force. As an Air Force member he has a much better chance of returning from the war alive; his duty done, his two years served and free to live his life. The Air Force also returns the bodies of the dead so his parents can grieve if death is to be his fate. Billy believes it would be easier on his parents to have something to bury if the worst was to happen. The Ground Forces seldom return the dead. They just send a letter.

Billy is very nervous as he begins the fifteen block walk to the testing center. He has walked these streets many times. He knows the sights and smells of this borough. The four and five story buildings were built back in the 1990s. They were built cheaply and the shoddy workmanship is beginning to show. If they had been built better back then maybe maintenance would have a better chance of keeping them up today.

The sidewalks are clear except for the stuff stored close to the building. The people are starting to come out of their cramped living areas to try to sell some of their wares on the sidewalks; as they do everyday. They hope to sell something they have created and survive another day. And maybe have something extra.

He tries to remember the facts from the six thick volumes of study material his parents bought for him. He asks himself hard questions and then tries to answer them. More than once he discovers that he doesn't know the answer to his own question. This is very disturbing for him. It shakes what little confidence he has. The thought goes through his head that maybe he should just forget about the test. The thought is just as quickly gone. He's not a quitter and he forces himself on toward the test center; pass or fail he's going to give it a shot. The worst thing that could happen is he will fail. At least he has a chance if he tries.

Several people wish him luck as he walks to the test center. They know him from his deliveries of the bakery goods. He always speaks; acknowledging that they wish him well with a 'thank you.' No one wants their child to go to war and die. Most of these people have already experienced that very thing. They have lost a child or children to the war and don't wish that experience on any parent. They hope that Billy will pass the test so his family will have some hope of him returning. It would also give his family the option to have another of their children carry on their trade. If he passes the test another of his brothers or sisters could survive to have children. He tries not to think about how much passing this test means to him and his family.

He continues to walk and can soon see the taller building of the government testing center. As he gets closer he sees it is packed with other kids who are trying to do the very same thing he is; stay alive a while longer. He didn't think there would be so many. This appointment to test was made last year. He has been very careful with the paper that has his ID number and test date certified from the government; without it he just made a long walk for nothing.

He took the next place in line and looked around the lobby. It's evident to him by the dress of some of the testers that they are from higher Levels with extra credits for nicer clothes. It sort of makes him mad that he is going to have to compete with people who have a much better education. He remembers everyone in his family giving up a set of clothes so there would be credits to buy the study material for the test. His brother, David, had a fit about the loss of a set of clothing. In the end their mother and father just told him they were buying the books. The other children could use them to try to get into the Air Force when their time came to be drafted. It's not fair, but that's the way of things in this world and there is no sense in crying over something that he can't change.

Billy will do the best he can with what he has been given and earned for himself. He has studied very hard for this test. He keeps telling himself just how hard as the unanswered questions rattle around in his head.

The test was overly organized as most things in the government were. The door opened to the testing area and the line started to move forward. Billy presented his paperwork and was given a test booklet and assigned a seat. The group wasn't allowed to open the test booklet until after the doors were closed at ten o'clock. They were given two hours to complete the test and turn the booklet in at the desk. After that everyone would be forced to turn the test in; whether they were finished or not.

The test was much harder than Billy thought it would be. It was much harder than the sample questions in the books.

He wasn't sure if he had passed or not; but he was finished. He looked at the clock. He had thirty minutes. He went over the test one more time paying particular attention to several questions he thought he might figure out if he spent enough time on them. He decided to turn the test in to be graded five minutes before time was called.

The attendant announced that there were five minutes left. "Everyone should finish as quickly as possible."

Billy closed the booklet and walked to the desk. He handed the test to the man at the desk. The man stamped a number on his test and then the same number on a small piece of paper. He handed the paper with the number on it to Billy and directed him to stand against the wall with the others. He took the last place in the line of people against the wall as he was directed. He waited nervously as others turned in their test and took their place behind him on the wall to wait.

The man would take each test and put it into a machine to be graded. He would then fill out paperwork and enter the results into the computer. The test was now graded and recorded. He would call the name of the person at the head of the line. The man would tell the person how they had done on the test, pass or fail. Today it seems most are failing. The man at the desk would call the name and the number and if they failed he would say. "You are dismissed."

The person at the head of the line waited. Billy assumed she was consumed by fear just as he was. She waited for the results to be relayed from the man at the desk. Everyone in the room would know the grade. The man said to her "You are dismissed." She tried as hard as she could to move away slowly and not cry. She took a step and burst into tears as she ran from the room.

Billy was now at the front of the line he watched as the man put his answer sheet into the computer. The non-feeling machine would determine his entire future. It chugged away for less than a second. His fate had been determined by a cold, lifeless thing.

The attendant took his time reaching for the results after they finished printing. He said nothing as he looked at them. It seemed like hours. He filled out a few papers as he did with the other tests and then entered something into the computer on his desk. The man did nothing unusual to give away whether Billy had passed or failed. Billy was about to explode with anticipation. He had been watching and knew this was his test that had just been graded. He was also at the head of the line. He remained against the wall waiting to be called to the desk. He was hoping to be called and not just dismissed.

If he didn't pass the test the man at the desk was going to say "William Holt", in his case, "you are dismissed" and everyone would know – he had failed. The man had said that a lot today. The man at the desk feeding the test into the unfeeling machine would call a name and then crush the person with the words, you are dismissed. It's a death sentence as surely as hanged by the neck until you are dead, dead, dead.

If he passed he would be called to the desk. The man at the desk picked up the mike "Holt, William Holt, please come to the desk." He was all smiles. He was going to be allowed to join the Air Force. He was on cloud nine as he walked to the desk to sign the papers. He didn't notice the envy in the faces of the others in the room whose fate had not yet been determined. The crying girl who was dismissed in front of him was no longer in his mind either.

The man at the desk pushed a paper at him to sign and then told him to report to room 2203, up the stairs. He signed the paper. He was given a copy and exited the room. He entered the stairwell and looked up "2203, damn that's a lot of stairs." He passed several people on the stairs leading to the 22nd floor, they were out of breath. He was just in better shape because he walked everywhere to deliver bakery goods.

Room 2203 was a large administrative office that served several of the local testing centers. He signed in at the desk and took a seat. He sat for two hours and twenty seven long boring minutes. He tried to read the two day old newspaper he found on the floor. The crossword had already been worked and the news was so old that it wasn't entertaining. He was interrupted once, after about an hour, when a girl sat in the seat next to him. It was the only empty seat. He watched the other people signing in and was happy to be ahead of them.

Billy, a shy, skinny, boy didn't do well around strangers. When it came to girls he was very shy. Even he got so bored that he overcame his shyness and struck up a conversation with the girl sitting next to him. She must have been very bored too because she didn't hesitate to talk once he started the conversation. Her name was Heather Mars. They were both bored and nervous and just looking for a way to pass the time. They got along well and talked for over an hour nonstop about how they saw their futures.

It was soon William's turn and the lady walked in and called his name. "William Holt", a brief pause to locate him among the hundred or so people who were waiting and "this way please." Heather wished him luck. He returned the wish but he had to go. "I hope I see you again." She smiled, "me too."

He followed the lady to an office to wait in another line. It was an hour later when the man at the desk called his name. Billy offered his paperwork. The man took it and pointed to a chair. Billy sat. After a few minutes the man handed him a card and a stack of information. Billy had been in the office ten minutes before the man spoke for the first time. "This card is a deferment from the draft for forty five days after your sixteenth birthday; don't lose it. You're now an Air Force asset and will report to this office on June the fourth for transportation to training facility S-45. If you do not report you will be immediately drafted into the Ground Force. One way or another you will be in the Force on June the fourth. Next please." Billy thanked him and turned to leave; stuffing the card securely in his pocket and holding tight to the stack of information.

Billy heard the very same speech being repeated in several of the rooms as he left the area. He looked for Heather in the main waiting room but she was nowhere to be seen. Her name must have been called.

The report date was thirty seven days after his birthday which was eight weeks away; in just 93 days he would be in the Air Force. It was the outcome he had hoped for in his dreams.

He almost ran home. People along the way yelled, asking if he had passed. He yelled; telling them he had. They congratulated him on the run. He rushed in the front door of the family bakery and everyone knew he had passed by his excited state.

His family was just as excited, he now had a chance. His sister Carol was very happy and hoped she would do as well in two years. She now believes there is some hope and she will study harder. The entire community seemed to be happy about Billy's good fortune; everyone liked him. His father told him that he didn't remember anyone from the neighborhood ever passing the test. The only one who wasn't happy about Billy's good fortune was his younger brother David. He was between Billy and Carol in age and had always been trouble.

David didn't consider himself smart and as a result he didn't try. It wasn't hard to understand his position. He wasn't the oldest and as a result he will not be exempt from the draft. But now, now that Billy was out of the way he might get the exemption because he was the oldest not in the military. The sad part about that was that he wasn't a baker. He never tried to be a baker. He will not be able to pass the bakery test to take his fathers place. Carol was a baker, she can pass the test. David was still going to be drafted and die. His position in life hadn't changed and neither had his attitude; except maybe to get worse, at least toward Billy.

Billy got to live the dream, so to speak, for three days. He was going to the Air Force. But that was not going to be his fate. Fate has him going to the Ground Forces and to his death. The Mist has other plans for him other than death but he must still go to the Ground Forces. There are things she wishes him to learn.

The finger of fate took charge of him and began to execute her plan for his future three days after he passed the test. David had been on his case even harder than usual. Billy just tried to stay out of David's way and out of trouble. He didn't want any trouble with his brother or anyone else that might jeopardize his career. But; trouble was what he was going to get.

David was feeling the pressure of the corner where he had placed himself. He was about to explode and someone was going to get hurt. Nothing, in David's mind was ever his fault and so the blame for the mess he was in had to fall somewhere else. David chose Billy to blame.

Billy was delivering a birthday cake when David and four of his hoodlum friends stopped him. David tried to take the cake but he really just wanted to cause trouble. The trouble he caused was even more that he could have wanted. Billy had enough of David's crap and he resisted. The fact was their father would take care of this later and David would be in a lot of trouble. But right now that didn't matter to Billy. The eight year old boy that the cake was for would be disappointed if he didn't get it on time. The cake wasn't the main thing on Billy's mind. It's time for David to back off and him to take a stand. This fight was something that could no longer be avoided.

Billy was pushed out of the alley and into the street. He collided with one of the members of another gang. The cake went everywhere. The fight broke out immediately. Billy could take care of himself in a fight, the result of having a brother like David who picked on him all the time. It was a long time before Billy fought back against his younger brother. David just wouldn't let things go and Billy had to fight.

These types of street brawls are against the law. This time the cops were close enough to catch all but one of the boys, David. He ran down the alley and disposed of the knife he just used to stab one of the boys in the other gang. The stabbing was extreme even for David. Someone was going to get into real trouble because this had suddenly turned into assault with a deadly weapon. The cops took everyone to jail.

In the hours before the trial the boy who was stabbed – died. The trial took place less than an hour after the death. These types of street fights usually resulted in public service work of three days. But this time a boy had been killed. The entire group was dumbfounded when the judge sentenced them to the Ground Forces for "two years or until eighteen" to be transported within the hour. Billy was mortified. The life that he had worked so hard to make had just vanished right in front of his eyes. At that moment he hated his brother.

The story began to break the next day. Billy was gone and David's family knew he was to blame. Carol was the first to say what everyone thought. "How could you do such a stupid thing? Your jealousy of your brother caused him to be sent to the Ground Forces." She yelled at him right in front of the customers in the bakery. "He's going to die and it's all your fault." Mother and Father knew David hadn't intended for this to happen; but that which is – is. David didn't think of what might happen. He just did stupid things. Billy had a good life in front of him and David didn't. His family never expected to see Billy again; no one ever came back from the Ground Forces. David knew the same thing. He may, no he had killed his brother just like he did the guy in the street.

David was hurt beyond belief. He was madder at himself for his jealousy than he had ever been at Billy for his success. He felt real remorse for what he had done. He wandered, lost in his thoughts and indulging in self pity. He wasn't welcome at home although no one would say the words. He knew this time he had just gone too far and there was nothing he could do about it. He could confess to the crime but it wouldn't bring Billy back. It would just send him to the war to die just like his brother. He wandered into the path of a city transport. A priest grabbed him and jerked him to safety "you should be more careful."

David saw the cross on the church behind the priest. He thought to himself of the story of Cain and Abel. God works in mysterious ways. "Father, could I speak with you, please."

CHAPTER TWO – DEATH DEALER

Bill didn't find God. He found hell and maybe a devil or two. Training was six days long, mostly processing the new draftees into the force. During those six days they were yelled at and punished unjustly more than a few times a day. If one member of the squad messed up then everyone paid the price.

That first night the 'more aggressive' of the squad tried to punish the ones who had caused trouble. Bill tried to defend one of them. He was beaten for his trouble as the man he was trying to protect watched. Afterwards Bill told the other guys who were beaten to be more careful the next day. He hoped it would sink into their tiny little brains.

When they were called to attention the morning of the second day the leader of the more aggressive group started on the Corporal as soon as he saw him. The Corporal told him he didn't have time for his shit and tossed him in the brig. He shook his head as he passed Bill and the others who had been beaten. "You boys better learn to look out for number one or you are not going to make it." Bill didn't think he had much of a chance of 'making it' anyway. The Corporal continued in a very loud voice. "We're going to get a few hours of weapons training and a little practice on the rifle after we get you a uniform. Let's go."

After the morning roll call they were marched over to get a uniform. They were issued one uniform, a pair of dark green coveralls, and a pair of used boots. Bill guessed the coveralls were used too when he found a repaired hole that he believed was made by a bullet in the back of one of the uniforms.

That afternoon, they were trained on the use of a rifle, the one they would use. Six hours and forty rounds fired from a rifle isn't enough to be called training but that is all they received. Bill ate the one meal they were served at the end of the day although he didn't feel very well. He knew he had to eat.

The next three days they just ran from place to place carrying heavy things. On day five they were pronounced soldiers. The ones who were tossed in the brig for various infractions of the rules during the training period were now soldiers too; even though they had not received much training. They were tossed in the brig the first or second day and they stayed there. It didn't change the fact that they were going to the front. They just didn't get any training.

The group of replacements, including Bill, shipped out on the sixth day. The people who had been tossed in the brig were brought to the transport in chains. They were unchained and told to have a seat. One of the boys snapped back at the Corporal and was shot dead on the spot. He yelled at the others "Now take a seat!" He told the two guards who had brought the prisoners. "Get this shit off my deck." The two Privates took the dead boy away almost as if they knew this was going to happen before it did. It was like they knew somebody was going to die. But it sure got everyone's attention. The others didn't seem near as hostile after the death of their peer.

The flight to the battle field was rough and cold. Bill was happy when the transport landed. He was happy to be back on the ground. His pleasure didn't last long. They emerged from the transport and were given a box lunch. They were marched straight to trucks for an eight hour ride. They could eat on the way. The

Corporal told them they were going by truck because it was too dangerous to fly unarmed crafts too close to the front.

The ride was just as rough but not cold. Bill dozed off for a time. When he woke he heard the sustained thunder of the cannon. They got louder as they got closer to the front. Soon they could hear the rifle fire. They knew they were very close because the sound of rifle fire just doesn't carry that far. They listened as the rifle fire started to die down and then stop like a bag of popcorn that had finished popping.

When they got to the base they were ordered out of the truck and 'marched' to the chow hall. "Get in line. Get your food and eat. You have thirty minutes." The smell was nauseating. Not the food, it had no smell at all. The large tent to the right smelled of death. No one spoke to the new recruits. It was all the same to Bill. The soldiers all looked half dead; kind of like the actors in a zombie movie he saw once.

Lunch was over too quick and they were marched to a group of tents. They didn't get a tent. "Find yourself a place under that canopy. We'll be spending the night." After the Corporal left someone commented that they thought maybe the dead guy on the transport was better off. Bill smiled. He had dealt with the fact that his life expectancy now was four hours and he was going to make the best of it.

One of the soldiers from another group came by and reported the news. It wasn't welcome but it was all the news they had heard. As a new unit they would lead the charge, nine out of ten would be killed or wounded. "If you get wounded just keep fighting. We don't have any doctors and you'll be better off if you get killed." Bill guessed that was opposed to a slow death. Maybe in that tent he smelled on the way to the chow hall.

The trench warfare of the First World War was timid compared to this one. It was like that game where a big ball is pushed around a field by large groups of players as they try to get a goal. In this case 'the ball' was the next trench. And they were being taken with guns and knives. The battles were extremely vicious trench warfare as one group or the other tried to take the next trench from the enemy. The Air Force made strikes, bombing and strafing runs. Space Force kept tabs on the enemy aircraft to minimize the Air Force losses. But, ground troops had to secure the towns; or what was left of them. The other side played by the same rules.

Life expectancy was four hours on the battle field. Bill believed it was four hours because the rest and regroup time between battles was about four hours; very organized. That's when the dead were counted.

Several men came out of one of the tents; each had a slash mark on their upper sleeve, a half stripe. Bill thought that meant they were Class Three Private. They didn't spend much time in training about how to recognize rank. He knew one thing - they were wearing a stripe and they were to be obeyed. The men came down the line and each told four or five men "follow me."

The men were taken to a man called a Charmer; a tattoo artist that records your military history on your arm in little squares. What he did today in this mess wasn't art. The computer did the work. He asked for your name and then, "put your arm here." He adjusts it a little and then said "don't move." He pushed a button and the machine came down and with a thousand needles injected ink under the skin. The charm was stamped out on your right forearm. The first, for Bill was a forced entry into the service. He is in the ground forces from a criminal conviction. The charm was painful. The second was worse because you knew what was coming. The charm reflected your assignment to your unit, in Bill's case - Fourth of the Tenth – Zed6 squad. He was told that after it quit bleeding he would be able to see the charm. The guy behind him laughed as he added "if we live that long."

The new six man squad followed their leader to their post. It was a muddy ditch that they didn't have time to enjoy. Their leader told them to find a weapon as soon as they could. The cry came down the line "attack."

Men began to charge out of the ditch. Bill yelled "We don't have a weapon!"

The answer was uncaring and hostile "Find one." He charged; he knew it was the only reply he could expect.

Men began to fall all around him; he didn't have any trouble finding a weapon. He felt a bullet tear through his clothing. He didn't know that that bullet was to be his death. But The Mist had willed different.

Soon it was out of ammo and he found another weapon. He kept his eye out for ammo but there was little to be found. He shot anything that raised arms against him, anything and everything. He found a knife and when he was out of ammo he fought with it. He fought hand to hand and he was going to stay alive. He felt a presence around him and somehow he knew he wasn't going to die this day. He took the weapons of the men he killed and fired them until they were empty. Then he looked for another.

The battle seemed to last for hours, how long it really lasted is hard to say. When it was over Bill was still alive. They had moved forward twenty feet to the next ditch. A Sergeant came down the line yelling for the squads, "Fourth of the Tenth – Zed6 squad." Bill yelled, "Here." No one else answered. The Sergeant nodded to Bill. "Collect your unit designators and the stripe is yours. You're the Third. See the charmer. Better find some ammo and weapons for your new squad." Bill asked about the dead and was told. "They'll be picked up."

Bill collected the designators of the dead and mangled, the charms were the only identifiers he could see on one of the dead; half the body was gone but the charmed arm told who he was. He found the leader of his group and took his half stripe and designator. Maybe he would be next. Who would pick these things off his body?

Bill reported to the charmer and received the promotion charm to Third Private. He found some water that was more water than blood and cleaned his self up, as best he could. Then he went to eat. The smell from the tent wasn't nearly as bad as it was the first time he was here. He didn't really believe that, it smelled the same. He was just getting used to the smell.

Four hours later he relived his first day when he was chosen except he was now the Third and he was the one picking from the new recruits. He knew that most of them were dead men just waiting to be cut into small pieces.

He and two of his new recruits made it through the next attack because he found them weapons and ammo. He took the weapons with him when he went to see the charmer. They had gained almost twenty five feet, taking the next trench. They held until the replacement force secured the trench. The replacement force prepared to attack. It would be four more hours before Bill and his group would be the ones to secure and prepare to attack again. A different Sergeant came crawling through the ditch, "Fourth of the Tenth – Zed6."

Bill answered "Here sir."

The Sergeant asked "How many are you?"

Bill said sadly "Only three sir."

The Sergeant nodded, "that's very Good," he pushed a pair of Second stripes at him. "Second, give your Third stripe to one of your men and come with me." Bill didn't know either of the guys, but one of them wanted the stripe and the other didn't. The one who wanted the stripe got it. Bill had already ordered them to find weapons and ammo for the next attack.

He followed the Sergeant as he yelled "Fourth of the Tenth – Zed5." The answer came from the only survivor. She was given the same instructions Bill had been given earlier, "collect your unit designators, the stripe is yours; see the Charmer."

The Sergeant and Bill the new Second moved on, "those are your men, Second, Zed 5 and 6; see the Charmer." Bill felt some relief in the fact that he wasn't going to have to choose more men to die. He was just going to have to tell them to charge.

The Charmer remembered Bill. "Back again, I see." Bill told him what he wanted and the Charmer checked the computer; and did the work. He added another Third of the Private Charm making bill a Private Second in command of Zed 5/6. He smiled, "in case no one told you; Seconds can use the cots in that tent if you can find one empty." Bill looked and saw a tent marked with two half stripes and nodded. "Thanks."

The next bloody barbaric battle would take them to the edge of what was a city at one time. Today it is just a field of rubble with a few walls of destroyed buildings standing. It wasn't worth fighting over. Bill was very upset, he was tired of the death and he was going to do something about it or die in the process. "When is somebody going to start thinking?"

Two days later Bill was a full Private and in charge of Zed5-10, 30 men. The next battle he was ready to die or do something to change the status quo. He decided to act. He fought harder than normal and tried to protect his men even more than he had been. It turned out to be a big day for him. He lucked out, he lived and so did sixteen of his thirty men.

The men who survived were given other commands and Third stripes. They had learned from Bill and they carried it to their next command. The survival rate, among the men that Bill and the others of his first command had trained by example was up from 9 percent to 28 percent. Bill was starting to gain the respect of many men.

Three days later Bill had made Private First when they were ordered to take the city back. The command expected to take the northeast corner of the rubble, again. Bill was tired of the charge and hold tactics. It was time to 'go for it.' He took the ninety men he was in charge of as a Private First all the way through the town. He picked up other troops along the way and in less than half a day the entire town was secure and fortified. It gained him a full Corporal stripe and the command of units M-Zed of the Tenth; a total of 840 men which he ran with better results and fewer losses than any of the other units. The Charmer was very surprised to see him alive. Bill asked for a special Charm on his left arm just above the elbow. The Charmer was happy to do the work he didn't get much call for such things and it required art work. The Charm was four inches tall – a Grimm Reaper holding a sickle with the words DEATH DEALER in an arc over the top. It was placed just above the elbow on the left arm.

The pure aggression of the Death Dealer and his forces quickly became 'stuff of legend.' He transformed the beaten group just waiting to die; into warriors.

The legend grew as he put on Sergeant Third and then Second, the Sergeant's stripes came with less than six weeks in combat. He was 'the Sergeant' as far as most were concerned. That put him in command of the Tenth, about four thousand men. His tactics made him a 'General and a savior' to his men. Causalities were down and he had recruited medical techs to help the wounded.

He took a radio from a dead officer and started to contact the top cover pilots directly. The first pilot he contacted was Sure Shot. The Death Dealer was pinned down at the time and he wasn't very nice. He told Sure Shot where he was and that he wanted cover now so he could move forward. He hoped he did the math right. It was on the test – one of the questions he wasn't sure if he got right. Sure Shot wasn't going to take any orders from an enlisted man.

Bill got mad because he wouldn't just do his job. "Listen to me Sure Shot; if I have to retreat I'm coming for you and I will kill you when I find you."

Sure Shot laughed, "I don't think you can do that but I believe you would try so where do you want the cover and who is this?"

Bill still wasn't happy "This is the Death Dealer and I want cover from Gram Charley 34 on a line to Fox Charley 39; burn'em."

Sure Shot laughed as he closed the comm. "I got to go fly, boys, we got a gutsy one out there calling himself the Death Dealer."

One of the other pilots, "I've heard he's a nasty enemy."

Sure shot laughed, "He sounds like it. Let's get this done."

The Death Dealer charm became popular and the Charmer suggested that Bill put his name under his, William, Wild Bill

Holt, sub titled with the original. He patented the changes. There would be only one. And all other Death Dealer charms had to be Ok-ed by him

The Sergeants of the First thru the Ninth looked to him for orders. In less than two months he controlled all the force solders either by rank or their willingness to follow. His superiors, the well off, the officers, were a little scared of him. He countermanded orders and made up new ones. He called in air strikes that Sure Shot was happy to give him with or without official orders. Death Dealer and Sure Shot developed a symbiotic relationship, they depended on each other. Death Dealer needed the fire power and Sure Shot liked being able to tell his superiors to go to hell knowing there was nothing they 'would' do about it.

Death Dealer stepped between Sergeants and officers more than once and always won; right then or in the next battle when the officer would die. He even helped Sure Shot out with a troublesome superior. No officer would go against him and Command was looking for an answer. The answer was to put him in an official command position so failures could be blamed on him. He was given the order to turn a pair of sergeant's stripes upside down and place them over his Sergeant's stripes. The rank of Administrative Sergeant was created just for him. He outranked every enlisted in every force, Ground, Air and Space.

The failures didn't come and within three weeks the other side was reduced to just mop up and the battle pushed back into the sea. This part would last years if it ever ended. But not a lot of ground troops were required any more. The East Coast of the United States was no longer occupied. The battle was now, like the West Coast, mostly in the sea. Command didn't know what to do with The Death Dealer and his 800,000 loyal troops. The ground draft was stopped and the numbers in the force would be allowed to wane. The wounded were shipped home after they were given better medical attention.

A Lieutenant found the answer almost by mistake as he was looking for an opening in the Air Force. He got a promotion for the discovery. William Holt becomes an Air Force asset as of June the fourth. He would become a Third Lieutenant in a totally different type of force. Bill would be out of the Ground Forces. He was awarded the highest medal the Ground Forces could bestow, the Cross of Valor with ten counters, plus all the awards he was otherwise entitled. The Charmer added, Ground Combat Commander – in charge, tactics officer - trainer, letter of merit – with three marks, letter of hero – ten counters, Letter of Block with ten counters, Conquering Commander – four counters. These were in addition to the weapons training and other charms he already possessed. He would carry them to the Air Force entry class, fifteen Charms on his right inside forearm or record arm. The Air Force Charmer would be honored to add the rank of Third Lieutenant to The Death Dealers very impressive record.

Bill was ordered to report to the induction unit in proper uniform on the assigned day. He was given five days leave and back pay. Payroll had a difficult time figuring out how much to pay for eight hours in the rank of Corporal Second.

Troops had been coming back from battle for the last three weeks. It was a happy time. The sight of a uniform was becoming common place as more and more of the soldiers were excused from the force. Most of the troops knew the Death Dealer by sight and often saluted him. He always returned the salute. The salute and the return are not required by regulations and few received one; and then only by people who knew of their achievements personally.

The Death Dealer logo on the uniform wasn't common place. It had to be authorized by the Death Dealer. He handed them out like medals to the bravest of his men. The charm on the non record arm was personal but it couldn't have 'the original' attached to it. Bill was the original and the only one to wear that part of the charm. The ones he awarded he added the persons name and the word "authorized."

The transport from the front was slow and rough. The four men who were riding with him were in awe of their traveling companion. One of them asked, "Are you leaving the service sir?"

He smiled. "No, I'm going to go put the Air Force in order."

They laughed and he added. "The war is about over here and they need fighter pilots to take the battle to the enemy on his ground." The men nodded in agreement.

Bill got to the airport as a group of Third Lieutenants was arriving to go to the front. They waited unnoticed as the truck unloaded. Several dozen solders were starting to gather; more than could fit in the truck. Bill set his foot on the ground. The cry scared him, "Group attention, hand salute!"

Bill couldn't help but smile. He returned the salute. "What are you boys doing?"

The Private Third said, "Just paying our respects SIR."

Bill laughed as the Lieutenants stood back in shock. "Well, how much is a keg of beer?"

"Forty credits" came the answer.

He laughed, "Show me where and I'll buy two. If you'll join me?"

The load master interrupted, "Sir, the plane leaves in twenty minutes."

Bill smiled. "Tell them The Death Dealer said hold it until we're done."

The load master laughed. "I think we just developed engine trouble, Sir." Bill was placed on the plane drunk, four hours later. The engines were "fixed."

The plane landed and Bill woke but he wasn't yet sober. "I didn't say this plane could land. This is my plane and I didn't say we could land. Where the hell are we?"

Bill looked up to see the man sitting across from him, a Major who was shaking his head. He introduced himself. "My name is Benton."

Bill reached over to shake his outstretched hand. "Bill."

The Major laughed. "Death Dealer." They smiled. The Major continued. "What are you going to request at the entry unit?"

Bill sat up in his seat. "Fighters, I think, war seems to be what I'm good at." The Mist smiled as she watched over him.

The Major smiled. "Good, it's hard to get into fighters these days. I have written you a letter of introduction. It'll help."

Bill heard something in the voice. "Do I know you?"

The Major smiled. "Not directly, I'm Sure Shot."

Bill laughed. "Well, it's nice to meet you in person." They shook hands again, this time in earnest.

They talked a while longer before they parted. The Major, Bill, told him as he left the plane "I'll see you in six weeks in Florida."

Bill nodded, "Yeah." Sure Shot was Bill's most dependable top cover pilot. He was always on time when Death Dealer called. He owed him a lot and now maybe more. They had become good friends over the radio and he seemed the same in person

The further Bill got away from the base the less he was known. He liked it much better. The street car he had boarded to take him the last hundred blocks to his home slowed and stopped. He was two blocks from the bakery and his home upstairs. He stood quietly and smiled as he looked around the neighborhood. It hadn't changed much. He picked up his bag and started down the street.

A boy about seven stopped him, "Excuse me sir."

Bill stopped and smiled. "What can I do for you?"

The boy answered quickly. "Are you a real Death Dealer?"

Bill laughed, "Yeah, I guess I am." The boy went on to explain that he was the only Death Dealer in the neighborhood and asked if he would sign his comic. Bill took the comic. "Are they putting comics out about the war?"

The boy was pushing a pencil at him. "No sir, just The Death Dealer and his Death Dealers, he stopped the whole war. He's a real hero." The boy stopped to think, "I didn't mean that you weren't. But The Death Dealer is what the book is about and you're the only one I've ever seen. There aren't very many real ones. So would you sign it please?"

Bill squatted down and smiled. "What's your name?"

The boy smiled "Larry, sir."

He nodded. "Well Larry, I'll sign your book. But you must remember that all of the Ground Forces did a very good job of stopping the war." He smiled "Just because this book is about The Death Dealer doesn't mean that he's the only one who stopped the war."

The boy wanted his autograph and agreed. "I know, sir."

Bill held the comic up so the boy could compare the drawing on the cover to him. "How would you like this signed?" The boy did notice the stripes but was too excited to think straight.

The boy thought a minute. "I don't know sir. Maybe 'A Death Dealer' and then your name, if that's alright; sir?"

Bill smiled "ok." He signed the book and handed it back to the boy.

The boy thanked him and ran away with his prize. Bill just smiled. The boy went straight home to show his older brother. His brother took a look at it and laughed. "For Larry, a fine boy I met today on my walk home. The Death Dealer, William, Wild Bill, Holt." The 'The' was underlined. The brother laughed "and I suppose he looked just like the cover."

Larry had to think but soon smiled. "The uniform did; stripes and all. It must have been him, The Death Dealer." The boys were very excited now and went to find The Death Dealer.

Bill set his bag down just inside the door of the bakery. Carol was behind the counter. He was very happy to see her. There were several customers ahead of him. He took a number. One of the customers saw the uniform and offered to let him go ahead, Bill declined. "That's all right. Thank you." He watched Carol as she helped the other customers ahead of him. She looked up several times. She was filling an order when she just stopped. She looked up with tears in her eyes. "Billy, BILLY'S HOME!" She was around the counter and in his arms as the tears started to build in his eyes. She was still yelling "Mother." By this time the boys had caught up and had several friends with them. It was grand chaos as the family began to join them. The news spread fast over the neighborhood that Billy 'Death Dealer' Holt - the baker's son was home.

That afternoon Bill and his family sat on the sofa talking about all the news in the neighborhood. Bill asked about David. "Will he be coming to dinner?" Father told him he doubted he would come by. Bill asked "why?" He was told it was because he was home and David surely knew by now and probably felt he wouldn't be welcome. Bill laughed. "What if I invited him?"

Carol smiled. "I can show you where he stays."

Mother smiled. "You wouldn't believe it if we just told you."

Carol showed him the way to the back of the church where David lived and studied for the priesthood. He was sitting on a bench and seemed to be in deep thought as he contemplated a hedge. Carol rang the bell and he started toward the gate to see what the visitors wanted. He recognized Carol from ten feet or so away. "It isn't any use Carol. I don't think I can come to dinner tonight. Bill has gone through enough without having to see the one who put him in that hell."

Bill laughed, "And what if Bill wants to see that person to tell him thanks for teaching him to fight." David took a step back. Bill laughed. "I have seen enough hate for a dozen life times. All I want is my family back together. Please come to dinner."

There was a long silence. Carol smiled, "Please."

David looked up and nodded. "Will we be saying grace?"

Bill laughed, "Not a snowballs chance in hell."

David nodded. "Then I will say it before I leave."

They had birthday cake that night to celebrate Bill's sixteenth birthday.

CHAPTER THREE -
THE AIR FORCE

On the evening of June the 3rd the Holts received a visitor, an Airman with orders for Third Lieutenant Holt. He thanked him and started to close the door... The Airman stopped him. "Sorry sir, but I'm supposed to take you with me, sir."

Bill looked at the orders and nodded, "Let me get my coat." As they drove to the induction center Bill asked. "Do you know what is in those orders?"

He replied "Yes sir, I typed them."

Bill asked "What do you think?"

He didn't want to answer but Bill forced the answer. "I think they're right sir, I would have hated to start classes knowing I was going to have to live up to someone like yourself."

Bill smiled, "but I might not be any good at this."

A laugh "I doubt that sir." The Airman paused and added, "I bet you're going to kick ass." Bill laughed.

Bill was processed into the Air Force that night; he was given his uniform and charmed with his new rank. The Charmer was very pleased to add the Third Lieutenant (TL) achievement to his record. Bill was granted fighter training and the letter did help. He couldn't help but think he was taking advantage of all the things he hated about the system by virtue of his status. Bill was returned home and told a transport would pick him up at 0730 in the morning.

Bill woke early the next morning knowing he was going to say good-bye again for a while. It was sort of sad. David came by and had breakfast with the family. Bill was very happy when the transport came and the sad good-bye could be ended. He was dropped at the side door and an Airman was waiting to open it for him. He took a seat and allowed himself to daydream a little and think about all the things that had brought him to this place and time. He wondered how he had ever survived.

The reporting recruits were placed in three separate processing rooms and as they were processed they were sent to the main lobby. Third Lieutenant Holt had been ordered to wait until some of them were released to the main area before he made his appearance. Bill couldn't help but smile. He never thought he would ever see this place again. "I wonder what it takes to get into Space Force."

The incoming recruits on this day numbered one-hundred and thirty. They would all want fighter training, only thirty-five; well, thirty-four more would get it. Of those only seven will get carriers. Those positions will be awarded based on your record in fighter training and volunteer status.

Now a leopard can be dressed in different fur and slipped in on a flock of lambs. But, underneath he's still the same as he was before; a battle hardened commander of 800,000 troops. Bill was no different; he watches everything like a predator. He had been at war too long and was having trouble relaxing.

Bill waited until several of the new Third Lieutenants were in the room. He made his way across the room to get coffee and something. He sat at one of the tables and looked around sipping his coffee. He was pleased that no uniform decoration can be worn on the uniform until after the six weeks of training was over; just your name and rank. He was enjoying his coffee and his anonymity in the very active room. He noticed her across the room just coming out of one of the processing rooms. He smiled.

One of the new recruits was headed straight for him. She stopped just short of the table and he stood. She said with a smile "Billy Holt do you remember me?"

He nodded. "Yes I do, Heather Mars. Or should I say TL Mars."

She laughed. "Thank you TL Holt." He asked if she wanted some coffee.

She nodded. "Where did you get it?"

He smiled. "This way Third, I need a refill myself."

They got coffee and returned to the table; she talked as Bill more or less just sipped his coffee. It was sometime later that a Sergeant come into the room and addressed the group. "Recruits, you are released for lunch. Be back at in this room at 1300 to begin testing and interviews."

Heather smiled. "There is a café just around the corner?" Bill told her only if she let him buy. They had a good lunch and a better talk – one where he got to say a few words. People watched them as they laughed and talked. They didn't care and were almost late getting back.

The testing was hard and on some subjects Bill didn't feel he did too well. However on tactics he did very well, it was based on his reports and writings. They were taken to a training base later that day and assigned a private room; Lieutenants get perks like that. Dinner was in the chow hall. Afterward they went to study the next day's lesson. At the end of the day Bill left Heather at her door just before eight.

The next two days were all about the same, with a lot of tests, physical and mental, very little sleep and very complicated instructions to follow. To Bill it was normal; to the rest he didn't know. On the fourth day they started flight school. They had two weeks to master the basics before they would be tested and allowed into the simulator. It was a hard two weeks with very little free time. However Bill and Heather were becoming close. They even shared a kiss; although both thought it wrong the second afterward.

The class was reduced by seventeen after the pre-simulator test. Those seventeen went to the enlisted ranks. There were only one hundred and four recruits left. The two weeks to master the simulator took another two recruits. Another eight didn't pass the simulator. The class that went for actual flight training was only ninety-three. The top thirty five, if they chose would be sent to fighter training. Bill had decided to turn down fighters if he wasn't one of the top thirty-five. The rest would go to heavies, bombers and cargo planes. Bill was number four in the class, Heather was number one but she didn't have a letter of recommendation. Although, she was never told of the letter of recommendation from the Death Dealer. She was told that a letter that assured her a place in fighter training was placed in her record. They went to fighter training together.

The real flying would prove to be another story. Bill would be first in the class in spite of his three demerits for excessively aggressive flying. Heather had dropped to number three. She was tagged once for overly aggressive flying when she and Bill were playing follow the leader. The carrier invitations came the day before graduation. Bill and Heather were invited and they accepted. That night she invited him to her room.

They talked a long while before anything happened. Bill told her he had secrets. She asked if he was gay. He laughed, "To tell the truth I don't think so but." He paused "but you have to promise to keep my secrets for a while or I'm going to my room."

She vowed to keep the secrets. He confessed that he had never done this before. She laughed. "Me either, I was hoping for a teacher, but I guess we can learn together." She told him if that was his only secret then it was safe and would soon not exist. He told her that wasn't all. She was most sincere when she told him his secrets were safe with her. He believed her. He told her "I don't think we'll have to keep them much longer anyway."

As they became involved the clothes began to come off and when his shirt was removed the action stopped. The charms told the story and she smiled. "The Death Dealer..." She laughed. "I've heard of you. Let's see how you do in bed Mister Dealer."

The graduation went well and they were transferred to the carrier. As they got off the chopper the group was met by their training officer, Major Bill 'Sure Shot' Benton. He welcomed them aboard and rooms were assigned, two man rooms. There's not as much room on a carrier. Heather was the only female and was given a room to herself. They were issued flight suits and told to put them on and report to the launch bay to inspect their birds. Bill was surprised to find the Death Dealer patch on his left shoulder and a ground combat commander patch over his left pocket, under his pilot's wings. The time of the secret was over. This is going to be interesting.

His roommate was just happy to be on the carrier. The charms that Bill revealed when he was putting on the flight suit really surprised his room mate. "Are you for real? I thought you were just a myth."

Bill laughed, "Sometimes I think I'm a cliché. But yes, I'm for real."

The roommate was getting a little nervous now. "Does anyone else know, well Heather would, but other than her? Does the Major know?"

Bill laughed, "Sure Shot and I are war buddies."

The knock at the door broke the conversation and Bill yelled "enter." Heather opened the door and smiled. "That was very commanding." She laughed as she saw the marking on the flight suit, "I guess the secret is out."

He smiled. "Guess so."

Bill's bird had The Death Dealer nose art already on it. The Major made a short speech about the nose art and told them if they had something they wanted to put on the nose of their bird he would 'look at it.' "Saddle up and lets take these birds for a ride."

They were airborne in a few minutes Bill never expected the drop off the end of the carrier. It was like the drop on a tall rollercoaster. Heather screamed, "Oh crap, what a ride."

Sure Shot was instantly on the comm "now that's what I like to hear - enthusiasm."

The next transmission was from the comm officer. "Keep the chatter down, this is a training channel."

Sure Shot was on again, "Squadron, a little follow the leader, Dealer take the lead and let's see some of that excessively aggressive flying, remember you have a tail and don't crash us into anything. Take us to twenty thousand before you start and TL Holt you have the squadron."

Bill was used to command and he wanted to know what these birds would do. "Squadron, we are going to try to break these birds. Make your checks for emergency climb in five-four-three-two-one." Bill took his bird to full burners and pointed it straight up. He recited a rather self serving line "Into the mouth of the horde rode the Death Dealers knowing only those fated would return. Each praying fate would be with him, just one more time."

A few seconds behind him he heard "or her. Move that pig or I'll run you down."

Bill put his plane through everything he could think of and the rest followed. Sure Shot took command back a little earlier than Bill wanted. But he was told he wouldn't run all the fuel out just to see when that would happen. Bill wouldn't land until all his squadron was on the deck and he and Sure Shot were the only ones still in the air. Bill contacted the tower, "Tower, dead stick test; shutting engines off now."

The tower operator was agitated "Negative, Dealer, a big negative, fire those engines now." The rest of the group were out of their planes asking what was going on.

Sure Shot was on the comm with Bill. "Fire your engines Bill you have never landed on a carrier."

He didn't like the reply. "Negative, I have to know what this bird will do."

Sure Shot was getting mad. "Damn it Bill you can be an ass. Tower this is Sure Shot we're coming in dead stick combat retrieval."

The tower was shouting orders. "I said No, fire those engines and bring those birds in normal."

Sure Shot smiled as he asked. "Dealer, are you reading the tower?"

The answer was what he expected, "No sir - nothing but static."

The tower warned. "I'll have your asses when you get back on my ship."

Sure Shot spoke into the comm. "Tower if you can hear us you better get ready, we're coming in hot and dead stick - combat retrieval."

As Sure Shot instructed Death Dealer on the hows and whys of this very dangerous landing. The tower raved. Heather and the other trainees watched. The fighters were coming in side by side. The last thing Dealer was told by Sure Shot was to "stay the hell on your side." The landing was flawless for what it was. Now they had to face the tower. The trainees were at the plane when it stopped. Heather yelled at Bill. "What are you thinking?"

He laughed. "Stuff of legend."

Sure Shot and The Death Dealer got quite a lambasting and a letter of counseling added to their record. It wasn't the first for either of them. They weren't grounded.

Two days of correct carrier landing later they received orders to the training carrier. They flew a strict formation to an older carrier. It was under manned and was strictly for training. They landed and it steered for a deep water training site.

The ship, Trainer one, was old and the crew was, for the most part, disabled in some way. They were a training crew. The ship was under armed. But it was in safe waters with air support twenty-four minutes away.

The training continued for two weeks. They loaded dummy ammo and rockets. The tension of the work was relieved on the third day of training when Jeff loaded a rocket on his plane backwards. It sparked the thought in Bill's head of aft rockets. They were having a good laugh at Jeff's expense when they were called down to report to class to study air battle tactics. Bill suggest some new ideas as far as tactics. He based them on a ground force charge. They were not readily received. He still believed they would work.

One month before graduation they were cleared for practice ordnance. The ordnance loaded on the plane included one five hundred pound dummy bomb, a hundred rounds of tracer ammo and one low yield short range rocket for the last target. Bill had been toying with the handle of Rocketman for Jeff. It was beginning to take hold and when he was about to load the live rocket on backward it stuck like hot glue to paper. Jeff is now Rocketman. That only left Heather without a handle. Dealer was still waiting for something to identify with her.

Dealer made a game of the mock attacks just like he always did and the squadron became very, very good at hitting even small targets with the rubber bombs. The tracers were only to allow the pilot to see where he or she was firing as the phosphorous was fired and burned in the air. The live, low yield rocket was not much more than to launch a rocket. It was almost useless for anything else.

The team become very close; not as close as Heather and Bill but close. They were three weeks into the weapons training and fifteen minutes off carrier when the trouble began. Head Case, one of the other pilots, he got his nick name because he was always seeing trouble. "I think there is an enemy ship down there." He got the usual response; disbelief and how can you possibly tell from here.

Sure Shot told him it was a freighter of some kind "but you can go take a look." Head Case tagged his wing man, Rocketman. Bill wondered out loud asking why air craft didn't have aft rockets.

He didn't get an answer. Head Case and Rocketman started down to check out the craft.

They peeled off and headed for the water and the suspected 'enemy craft.' It wasn't long before the radio crackled with a very excited pilot. "Sure Shot this is Head Case. I may have been right." The radio went quiet as the two planes got closer to the craft. Then Rocketman was on the radio. "Crap, confirm, confirm enemy. Is that a carrier?"

A second later Head Case yelled, "Confirm enemy Carrier. They've seen us and they are roll..." the radio went silent as the group saw the after burners fire as the two planes begin to climb straight up.

Sure Shot tried to contact anyone "trainer one, do you read; trainer one. Hell – we're being jammed." He asked if anyone could hear him and found the group could still hear him on local comm. The two planes rejoined the group. Sure Shot ordered the group back to the carrier. Dealer made the point that Trainer One couldn't defend itself against the planes from the enemy carrier and they would lead them straight to it.

Sure Shot didn't take long before he ordered "Dealer, Heather and John L; fly top cap and avoid the enemy. Give us as much time as possible before you leave. I'm taking these birds back to have a set of teeth put in them. Looks like you are going to see live combat a little earlier than we planned." Head Case was on the radio, "You mean we get real bullets and rockets. Cool."

Sure Shot told him to shut up or "I won't give you any toys." The planes left in a hurry. Sure Shot left Dealer with one order, "If it gets too hot up here, head home."

Dealer followed orders as long as he thought the enemy was going to buy it. That wasn't very long. "They have got to suspect we don't have any teeth by now." Heather asked what they were going to do. He didn't know. Then the light came on, the epiphany, and he knew what he had to try. "Ok pilots, I know this is like attacking a tank with a pocket knife but it's time to become stuff of legend."

"Follow the leader. I want their commutations and jamming off line. Those damn rockets might do the trick; Rocket only. Target the comm array." He started the dive for the carrier. The game was on, he was on a mission. He would not fail. The first pass gave him just what he wanted. The toy rockets took out the array with three direct hits. They could hear their carrier again and Sure Shot was pleased to hear them. Dealer told him they were about to kick a hornets nest and he better send a lot of help. Sure Shot laughed as he told Dealer "We have a fighter group coming twenty-one minutes out." Sure Shot laughed, "We'll see 'ya' in ten."

The pilots with Dealer were cheering about their success. Dealer was on the comm. "This isn't over yet. On me, we're going bowling." The dive started. "Let's all pretend that our rubber bomb is a bowling ball and the planes on the deck are the pins. If you get a shot at anything that might be holding fuel or looks like a fuel spill, take it. The tracers might set it on fire. Let's burn'em." It was a quick low pass and the flight deck was clogged with several damaged planes. But not before a dozen or so hornets got off the carrier. They or someone would have to deal with them later.

Dealer and his group didn't have time to think. The deck was being cleared and the airborne planes were beginning their attack. "Let's hit the carrier again folks; if there is one drop of fuel on that deck I want a tracer in it. Let's BURN that carrier!"

The second run at the carrier was just as quick, Heather's gun jammed. And for all the tracers they had fired at the deck of the carrier - they didn't get a fire started. Everyone's guns were empty except Heather's "My guns are clear and I have six rounds. Let's try one more time." Dealer asked if she wanted company. She told him no but he was going to lead anyway.

Dealer told John L, the pilot of the third fighter, to stay up top as long as he felt it was safe and then head for home as close to the water as he could. "On the deck, John L, do you understand?"

John L answered, "I understand, head for the deck and burn the water as I head home." He laughed "I think I'll play with them a while so some of them will follow."

Heather told him not to fool around there must be twenty enemy hornets in the air. There wasn't much time to discuss it with all the hornets in the air, but nothing else was taking off. Dealer ordered John L to get on the deck, as close to the water as he felt safe and high tail it back to the carrier. "And I hope you have a tail when you go."

Bill started the strafing run with Heather behind him. She needed to hit a fuel source at three hundred MPH and with only six tracer rounds. It was a big, big gamble. Bill told her to do the best she could and it would be enough. She was very nervous when she returned the radio message. "I guess this is the stuff of legend."

He laughed. "You said it wrong, more enthusiasm, STUFF OF LEGEND!!!"

She laughed. "We'll see." They didn't have time to look at much as they passed the carrier but Heather shot at what looked like a liquid spill on the deck of the carrier. It wasn't until they were in a climb that the fire started to rage and the dark black smoke plumed up from the carrier.

There was an explosion from the carrier and the flames burst through the black smoke and died back into them. The smoke became more intense and they knew they had succeeded in their mission.

The two planes, turned back toward the water. When they reached twenty five feet off the water they began to hug the deck staying very close to the water. The hornets wouldn't dare attack. If they put their plane in a dive and tried to shoot Dealer or Heather down they would most likely crash into the water themselves. Dealer and Heather were making a hard run back to the carrier and relative safety. They saw the enemy carrier in flames behind them and heard several more explosions.

They would have liked to take time to enjoy the win. But, they had their own problems some of the hornets were after them. All they could do was run as hard as they could for the force that Sure Shot was bringing. They did enjoy the secondary explosions.

It seemed like hours as they closed the five minute gap. They were on the deck and the Hornets were coming in to attack their six. Dealer again wondered why air craft don't have aft rockets. Dealer was out of tricks. They were sure happy when from above Sure Shot and crew started to open fire. Sure Shot ordered, "Keep the burners on boys; we'll get them off your six." Dealer and Heather or Pyro as Dealer was calling her, were headed home with burners on full.

John L reached the carrier and went in hot, combat style. He was yelling as he didn't get out of the bird. "Fill her up and give me some teeth." He was airborne again by the time Dealer and Pyro were close to the carrier and met John L's fighter headed back to the battle with a full set of teeth. Heather wished him "good hunting." John L answered, "We'll take it from here Pyro. Just get a beer and relax." It looked like the nickname was going to stick. Dealer and Pyro landed combat style –side by side and yelled for fuel and big nasty teeth.

The dog fight was over before support arrived. Dealer and Pyro were late to the fight but they both shot down a bird as they flew right through the enemy group like a ground attack. Dealer was sure this would work in combat now, it just had. They returned to the carrier very happy to be alive.

The support commander joked as he arrived too late to get into the fight. "Damn, guys, there was only one carrier. Why did you even call us?" They made sure the area was clear and witnessed the enemy carrier running for home slowly sinking into the sea. A rescue was mounted for the surviving POWs.

Pyro ran out of fuel before they got back to the carrier. Dealer cut his engines and showed her how to land dead stick. The landings were combat style, Dealer and Pyro were ready to hide in her cabin but the party was inescapable. The old guys on the carrier were very pleased to be in combat again. Pyro took up the cry "STUFF OF LEGEND!"

Training was over for them. They should have had another week but no one thought it necessary. Two days later they were helicoptered to a ground base for training in a new fighter which they were going to be the first to get. It was at a training base and the crew was watched closely. They had air to air kills.

They had received a Letter of Hero and a merit promotion to Lieutenant J G for their misadventure. Sure Shot awarded them a letter of stupidity. They liked it best of all. Bill allowed the use his patented Grimm Reaper as the squadron logo and nose art. They were now The Reapers.

The new planes were very plain. The first flight was a surprise to the tower and the commander. The trials were extensive and very aggressive. When they thought the planes ready Dealer told them, "Ok, paint'em up." The nose art and call signs were added over the next two days. They're excellent planes. Sure Shot turned the Reapers over to LtJG Holt and went to pick up another training group. It was a very emotional parting and everyone wished each other well.

They had four more days in the fighters before they were to ship out. Bill was doing everything he could to bring the Reapers to a joint fighting force, all for one kind of deal. They practiced his battle tactics. They were a close knit group and spent most of their time together. No one on the base had said much to them because they kept to themselves. The last night on base Bill took them to the charms club. He had to explain that there was no rank in the club and you removed your jacket at the door and let your charms speak for you.

They were in the charms club about to enjoy a steak dinner. One of the guys from their original class who had gone to the 'heavies', bomber training, came over and asked if he could have a seat. They told him sure. He asked the question, "How in the hell do you get to paint a carrier on your plane as a kill?" They told the story and bought a round for the club. Most of the people in the club had heard the tale or part of it but they didn't believe it until now.

They headed for their next base with their new planes the next morning. The true test of combat was about to greet them. In fact, it was going to greet them en route to the carrier, Hometown One. Hometown One was part of a four ship, not so sea-worthy group, which acted as an offshore stationary base. It was the Reapers new home

The Reapers were flying into 'The Zone' as it is referred to; and had a mouth full of teeth plus extra fuel tanks. When they were in range Bill radioed in for landing instructions. "Hometown One this is Reaper One."

The radio cracked the man seemed excited "Reaper One; battle status please."

Bill answered "Hometown One; a full set and over the top." The signal was just what Hometown One was hoping for, well armed and a full fuel tank. The commander had some reservations about sending a new replacement squadron straight into combat before they had checked in. But, he had little choice and the reports said they were battle ready. "'Reaper One - check your comm, beacon three-four-five. We have no friendlies in the air. If it's flying - kill it."

Bill smiled, "Yes sir. Reapers, the harvest awaits. Heat'em up!" They started to arm their weapons and proceed toward beacon three-four-five.

The tower Commander questioned the ship Commander. "Sam, there's only eight of them and I have over thirty bogies in that area."

The ship's Commander nodded. "I know Frank, but I have little choice and they have those new planes and the rep, god what a rep. Let's see if they live up to it. Then we'll feed'em."

The Reapers were far better than their rep. They worked like a well oiled machine. The bogies started to disappear off the radar screen. The chatter was over the top and the tactics were new. The radar screen soon only had eight birds on it. "Hometown One this is Reaper One; request rearm and fuel."

Reaper two/ Pyro kicked in, "And more targets. I need one more kill to be an ace." Female pilots were not the norm, female fighter pilots behind the lines, well. Pyro is the third at the front.

The commander smiled and said where the tower Commander could hear "I heard they had a female combat pilot."

The tower Commander smiled and said. "Reaper One approach south east follow the lights."

Dealer answered. "Yes sir." The comm continued as the tower monitored. "Odd Ball."

Odd Ball answered "Yeah, Dealer."

Dealer ordered "You're up; burn the sky and make sure whoever is running the show down there has what we need, we have your six."

"Sir," was the return indicating a 'yes.' The radar witnessed the single fighter pull away from the others as they assumed a top cap position.

Odd Ball landed and relayed their needs but ran into a lot of resistance from the weapons Sergeant and the fuel Sergeant. Both had been around a long time and Odd Ball was a newborn babe as far as they were concerned. It didn't matter that he had just made three kills. He wasn't going to give them orders. This didn't mean they weren't going to work the planes; but they weren't in as big a hurry as Odd Ball thought they should be. He relayed the information back to Dealer; who relayed it to the Captain. He didn't get what he wanted. "Sir, I'll be right down."

One of the officers in the tower smiled. "That sounded like a threat. Who does that guy think he is?"

The Captain laughed. "I don't know but if he can get Wormer and his crew to move faster; it's all right with me." The Captain got on the comm. "Reaper One, see Sergeant Wormer."

Dealer gave the orders. "Pyro you have the comm, keep the children safe, John L you're on me." They came in hot and side by side.

The tower commander, "Crap, DECK prepare for combat landing." He told the flagman to wave them off as he was on the radio, "One at a time."

The Captain laughed. "Maybe Wormer has met his match."

The call from The Dealer, "Sorry sir we are committed and short on fuel."

Wormer was a hard core, get things done kind of guy; that was the way he got where he was today. He thought all officers were pansy ass mama's boys. And none of them deserved more respect than a piece of shit going down the toilet. The men under him were of the same opinion.

The Captain ordered a six, no, twelve man security squad to the deck. This type of thing was normal for Sergeant Wormer; he liked to get his bluff in fast on new groups. Other new pilots had tried just what Dealer was about to try. It was the nature of a fighter pilot to do such things. If a fighter pilot wasn't inclined to act this way he is most likely not good fighter pilot material. But, none of the others pilots had succeeded in backing Wormer down.

The new planes hit the deck hot and came to a quick stop. The crew was gathering for the fight. The Captain was there to see that it didn't go too far; after all he had a war to fight. He could have his men busted up too bad. John L was a hard fighting brawler, that's why he was called after Mr. Sullivan. He was out of his plane quickly.

Dealer emerged more slowly and started toward the Sergeant and his group as he worked to remove his helmet. He removed the helmet just a few feet short of Wormer and raised his eyes to meet the Sergeant's. The expected didn't happen. Wormer smiled almost laughing as he yelled, "Group attention. Hand salute." Dealer laughed. "Hot Shot, I can't believe it; but I might have known." He returned the salute. "Thank you." Wormer smiled.

"Thank you sir, the planes will be ready in five minutes." He turned yelling. "Get to it boys."

The Captain told his aid to get the rest of those planes on the deck and find out what's going on with Wormer. The Captain went to meet the new pilots. "I want the cameras off those planes." He then turned his attention to Dealer and he reported. "Lieutenant J G Holt, reports sir." The Captain nodded "We can do this later; get something to eat and I'll see you and your second in planning; half hour. Ask anyone."

The rest of the planes were coming in by that time. Bill collected his guys told them to get something to eat. He told Pyro they had a meeting in half an hour.

The aid returned to tell the Captain what was going on. "Sir, the answer is you don't get a ten time Cross of Valor recipient called The Death Dealer landing on your deck every day." The Captain just shook his head. "Crap, I hope he can take orders."

War is one of man's most unattractive activities. It's also the one he seems to do the best. But even the best of warriors on the most noble pursuits gets bored with it sooner or later. Bill had been at war for almost two years when he lost interest. The Reapers were the best and in eight months of combat they hadn't lost a man or a plane. Bill's new tactics could not be stopped without the other side using the same tactics. They had three times the kills of the other groups and were always called to lead the attack. Bill continued to develope a fly through tactic that would just decimate the enemy.

The war was starting to slow and peace talks were in progress. The day the peace treaty was signed 'The Reapers' got a very strange invitation from Space Command. The invitation was to change forces. The change would include promotions to Lieutenant test pilot to test new space/atmospheric fighters. It seemed like a good idea at the time.

In the peace time force a successful fighter pilot can't stay out of trouble. It isn't in his nature. The down time is depressing and maddening. Cabin fever led to drinking to much and just plain laziness. The officers running the space program were too careful for even their supervisor's support. At one time or another all of the Reapers wanted to choke them almost to death; wait for them to recover and then choke them again.

Pyro was ready to retire and Bill wasn't far behind. They were only nineteen years old but they had accumulated enough points and rank to retire with a very tidy income - four times that of most workers. They figured that they could start a cargo shuttle for the construction materials to newly proposed Moon Base Alpha. They thought they could do very well.

The fighters when they were allowed to fly were exceptional in the atmosphere but in space they were like a sick dying snail; and almost as maneuverable as a voice commanded piece of cork in a heavy sea.

The Reapers were sitting down to their nightly card game and had just opened the first beer of fifty or more the group would go through before the night was over. A single drink was about all they would get to taste of that beer. "Battle stations, repeat Battle stations."

No one moved, they took another drink and moseyed slowly up to operations; not their battle stations. "What's going on?"

The commander was frantic. "You're supposed to be at battle stations."

The scientists and engineers were fighting among themselves. "We have bogies coming in from space."

The chaos in the operations room was unbelievable. Bill looked at the radar, the targets were changing course. They were not space debris. "Reapers, it's been a honor to serve with you." He looked directly at the lead engineer. A man he had fought with verbally a hundred times to make the crafts more maneuverable in space. "Let's get these turds out and see what we can do with them." He grabbed the engineer, slamming him against a wall, "If I lose one man or one ship; you better pray it's me because when I get back I'm going to skin you alive." The man was so frightened that he just slid down the wall sobbing and sat on the floor. Bill told the station gunnery officer to be ready. "You're going to get a shot at these things. We can't stop them all."

Bill got the turds in line and they waited. "At maximum range we start shooting." The force was reported to be thirty something by control. There had been no response to radio calls. They began to fire and were hitting the incoming targets well. The targets went through their line like a hot knife through butter. The turds were destroyed without effort. Pyro's last broadcast was to profess her love for Dealer; which he returned. He got a good look at one of the six remaining enemy fighters before everything went black.

If there is a book where the fate of all creatures is written and it is housed in some galactic library somewhere; then it sounded an alarm that a great change has been made to the fate of a species. It sounded very loudly. It sounded so loudly that The Mist was awakened. She had not told the others of her plan. She was very unhappy and summoned Earth Fate to her side with a blast that left Earth's Fate crumpled in her presence. "WHAT HAVE YOU DONE?"

The battle between 'gods' is a complex one and hard to understand. But The Mist had a plan for the first child Bill and Heather would produce. She made it very clear to Earth's Fate that she would not interfere again. She was also very, very clear who she wouldn't interfere with. Now, The Mist had to fix things because she wasn't going to wait another four thousand five hundred and thirty seven years, four months and three days, six hours and twelve minutes for the cycle of time to be right again.

Bill woke in the hospital and looked around. His vision was blurred and the room was dimly lit. He felt for the call button and when he didn't find it he tried to yell. He had no voice to speak. The bedside tray was within reach so he pushed it over. The noise brought the nurse. She wondered why the tray had tipped over and when Bill moved she gasped. He could barely make a sound. "water." She bent over to hear. "water." She went quickly to get the water. On the way she told the nurse at the desk, "He's awake."

It wasn't but a few minutes after Bill choked down the water that his voice returned. And he wanted to know what had happened. "Get me somebody that can tell me what has happened, RIGHT FUCKIN NOW!!!"

The doctor and an information officer arrived after only a few minutes. Bill was told the sad news that he was the only one to survive the attack. All of the enemy craft were destroyed, along with the space platform. He had been saved because the safety unit in his craft had remained intact. However he had suffered frost bite to the outside length of his left leg and a substantial portion of the frozen flesh had to be removed. The flesh would grow back but it would take about eighteen months. He had been kept in a coma-like state for almost thirty days and should still be in one. He, along with all the Reapers had been awarded the Star of Congress and promoted to Lieutenant Commander. It was the second highest award possible. And he was lucky to be alive.

Bill didn't feel very lucky. He had lost everything and was going to be in and out of hospitals for the next year or two. He didn't feel lucky at all.

Bill didn't know that The Mist had fixed her plan and that – William 'Bill' 'Wild Bill' 'The Death Dealer' Holt had a very bright future. But that wasn't going to happen until he was an Admiral selectee in command of the Science Vessel (SV) Einstein.

As far as the child of Heather and Bill that The Mist wanted, she'll never be. But, Bill's sister Carol's child would do just as well. Carol would give birth within the time frame.

Always have a back up plan.

Now The Mist just needs to assemble the rest of the players in her little drama.

CHAPTER FOUR -
CAROL (HOLT) FRANKS

The draft stopped. The Ground Forces have more people than they need. The Air Force never had a draft but it's now over manned as well. There just aren't as many missions these days. The war is over for the most part and a real peace seems just over the hill. With new hope in the air Carol accepted a marriage proposal from a man she had been seeing for several months. She married a pit fighter named Sam Franks.

The Mist smiles as she sips her tea. "I couldn't have picked better myself."

Pit fighters are like boxers. They are also Level Nine; but they operate more in the Level Eight world. They have an athlete star quality that gives them a perceived level boost. No weapons are allowed in the pits but anything else goes. The winner climbs out of the pit; the loser doesn't. The loser has to be helped out. Usually both fighters have to go to the hospital. It's a brutal sport. Although it is regulated by the government; it isn't watched that close.

Carol likes her new gypsy lifestyle. She enjoys the travel to a new town every three or four days to put on a pit fight for a weekend draw at a circus or county fair. She and Sam have a sweets stand they set up at the shows where she sells a lot of doughnuts and sweet rolls at a very good profit.

When she learned that she was with child she contemplated leaving the life. She and Sam talked it over and decided that their child wouldn't know the difference until it was at least a year old. They would continue in the pit fight game for a while longer.

The Mist took another sip of her tea and smiled. She knew it would be a female child and she would be named Sandra. Sandra would take the place of Eva, Heather and Bill's child that never was, Sandra will now become, when the time is right, the Warlord Queen of the Einsteinee Royal house of Dent. The Mist took another sip of her tea – her plan was proceeding very well.

Eight months later Carol gave birth to Sandra. Bill came to see her at the hospital. He was still on crutches but Sure Shot had just taken command of the Delta project and requested that Bill be assigned. He was en-route and made a stop to see his new niece and his sister.

The baby girl was so small. As he watched her sleeping in the nursery the lady came up beside him. He turned to look at her but turned back to the baby girl almost as quickly. The lady smiled, "I came down to see her in person, Dealer." Bill looked at her. "Do I know you?" The lady smiled, "Not really you were not doing so well the last time I saw you." He looked at her again and swallowed hard. "You're from my dream when I was trapped in my space craft safety unit." She smiled, "I wondered if you would remember. Most humans block such pain out along with everything else that happens to them at that time.

Bill took a step back. "You're, you're The Mist, I think you said." She smiled, "Yes and I have come down to see Sandra, she's as important to me as you are." Bill asked what this was all about but the lady just smiled as she looked at Sandra. "Oh, look, Sandy just smiled." Bill looked but the baby was still asleep. He looked back and the lady was gone. He heard a voice in his head "watch after Sandy; she is going to need your help." She laughed, "Often."

Sam came walking down the hall as Bill looked for The Mist. Sam told him they had decided to name her Sandra.

Sandra picked up the nick name Sandy before she left the hospital. She was raised in hotels. Her father, Sam, was at the top of the pit fighting game and he knew it wouldn't last. They reasoned that he would quit when he stopped winning. It's what they planned. Meanwhile, they had to save enough money in a few short years to support the family well on a much lower paying job when he could no longer go into the pit.

Sam was smart enough to take every advantage he could. He was paying into a government sponsored retirement plan that included life and disability insurance. They still had money left to do mostly as they pleased. They had a new transport and bought a new travel trailer when Sandra was two. It was a compromise so she would have a home and not grow-up in motels. Sam was still winning. It wasn't yet time to quit the pit game.

Carol liked the fights. She went as often as she could and always when Sam fought. She took Sandy. It was just after Sandy's fifth birthday that Carol lost sight of her for just a second. She looked franticly for her. Sam was yelling her name but she was nowhere to be found. They noticed several of the children of the other fighters around a pit that was to be used that night. They were yelling and cheering. They pushed their way through the children and in the pit they found Sandy, sitting astride a seven year old boy hitting him in the face, right then left, over and over.

Sam jumped into the pit and grabbed Sandy. She was screaming as he pulled her out of the pit. "Stay down David, I win and that's all there is to it. I want my money." This wasn't the first fight Sandra had been in but it was the first time she had gotten into the pit. The other fights were more of a sudden attack than a planned fight.

Sandy wasn't flinching as her bloody nose was cleaned and the break in her little finger set. The splinted finger and two stitches on her arm where she was bitten were badges of honor as far as she was concerned. She wore them with pride. Although Carol and Sam, as well as the other parents, tried to keep the children out of the pit; the kids always found a way. Sandy came home bloody at least once a week, with someone's money or without her allowance. Sometimes she lost; more often she won. She was dumb enough to take on a twelve year old boy when she was seven. She went to the hospital that time with a concussion. The boy went with her. She had bitten off the end of his index finger and swallowed it.

Sam was getting ready to quit. He was still winning but not as easily and Sandy was getting harder and harder to control. The fights were getting much harder and the competition much younger. It was time to do something else. They decided to go to the finals one last time. Sam had walked away with the purse the last five years. He was the man to beat this year and the Pit Fighters Union offered him a big bonus just to show up.

It was only a few weeks later at the finals that their life changed. Sandy was watching Father battle in a fierce battle for a large purse. It was the last fight of the finals and the winner was to take 50 percent of the purse with the runner–up taking 25 percent. The last quarter was split between the other fighters based on their win - lose record. In fights like this on very rare occasions a fighter is killed. The blow that killed Sandy's father wasn't a hard one. It was just one of those freak things that happen. He fell and didn't get up. He was dead.

Carol was devastated but the effect on Sandy was far more traumatic. She became terrified to do anything, afraid that she would move wrong and die. Although she was told and understood that it was just an accident. She was just paralyzed scared.

The Mist came to Sandy that night in her dreams. Sandy was sitting on a large dream rock when The Mist spoke to her. "I'm so sorry that it has to be this way Sandy. But I need you to grow up in a certain way." She paused as Sandy cried. The Mist held her and comforted her. "Someday I will try to make this up to you." The Mist was suddenly gone and Sandy woke quickly breathing hard. She tried to go back to sleep but her mind kept replaying the dream. She kept coming back to the words and wondered. "Grow up to be what?"

Carol's brother, Sandy's Uncle William 'Death Dealer' Holt couldn't come for the funeral. He was second officer on the escort ship Jersey City; guarding military cargo. He was deep in space with the first command of the newly finished Gamma station. Even nine years after the war the relationship of Death Dealer to anyone was used to sell papers. The headline read 'Death Dealer's brother-in-law killed in Pit fight'. The courts became involved and made sure Carol got the losers portion of the purse. Although it wasn't a problem, she got her share of the purse and more. The pit fighters are a close knit family. They took up a collection.

Carol applied for and received low income housing. It was part of Sam's civil servant's retirement package along with government life insurance and a pension for Carol. She would have a good income for the rest of her life. The money they had saved would allow them a very good life. But she had to be careful and she wanted the low income housing. She wanted a home and her status put her at the top of the list.

Sandy was meeting with the psychologist regularly and getting a little better. The doctors told Carol that she might never be the way she was. "Then tomorrow she may be back to her old self. She needs some kind of reason to begin to trust again." Given what had happened to her father Carol wasn't that unhappy that Sandy would be a lot more careful.

The low income housing they received was an apartment that had just become available in El Paso, Texas - Garden View 946 apartment D. She was at the top of the list and took the place, sight unseen. If she had known the reason it was open she might have not taken it at all.

Surely the crime tape and the blood will be cleaned up by the time she gets there. The apartment should have a fresh coat of paint and new carpet by then as well.

She would never know the part The Mist played in recruiting her next player from Garden View 946 apartment D.

CHAPTER FIVE – STICKMAN

It would be months before Carol would find out what happened to create the vacancy at Garden View apartments, building 946 apt D. But I'll tell you now.

Albert Van Smyth happened.

It started some years back with Ava. She was a strangely vindictive girl who had a habit of not doing anything her mother or father ordered or even suggested. She carried this attitude over to anyone who didn't agree with her. She fought easily and often. Well, she would listen to kids her own age. She got back at adults in many different ways.

She was always in trouble. Everyone agreed that her mother should have just killed her when she was born. Her mother; who was just as crazy as Ava, had tried to kill Ava. The Mist intervened. The Mist needed Ava's child with all of the mental problems she would inflict upon him.

The people who knew Ava couldn't think of anything more objectionable than Ava. But that was before she met Jane; then the trouble really started. Together they were much worse than when they were separated.

Eva and Jane saw eye to eye on most things. It didn't matter that they were mostly wrong. They had each other to reassure themselves that they were right. They dropped out of school and ran away. Whether it was in their nature or they just needed someone to hold on to – whatever it was, they became lovers.

Life on the street wasn't easy and before long they just wanted something to make it easier. Drugs were the easy answer and they always took the easy way out. The enforcement of the drug laws was much more lax than when the war was raging. The overuse of drugs led to addiction. They needed an easy way to get more. Prostitution was the next step. It paid the bills, bought the drugs and gave them time to themselves. They were happiest when they were stoned.

Ava gave birth to Albert Van Smyth eighteen months later, he was born addicted. It took a very long while to get him not to just cry himself to sleep. He was a horrible baby. But Ava, who the courts deemed an acceptable parent, took charge of him as soon as she could. The state paid fifty credits a month for the care of an addicted child. She never gave him any drugs. She kept them for herself. The child was also entitled to low cost housing. That's how they found their way to El Paso and Garden View 946 Apartment D. The courts liked to place addicted children with one or both of the parents who had addicted them. I'll leave that insanity for you to judge. But they are the ones who had the apartment before Carol and Sandy got it.

Albert was placed in El Paso, Texas, Garden View housing, a 1300 unit complex of quadraplexes development; building 946 apt D would be the place where Albert would try to survive his Mother and Jane.

His 'bed' from the time he arrived 'home' was a trunk and when he cried too much the lid was closed. The Mist came to comfort him often. Each time she would tell him how sorry she was but "I need the you that this life will turn you into." Ava and Jane 'entertained' a lot and the money went for drugs, not food. The other people in the apartments weren't interested in anyone but themselves. The cops were called often to Garden View 946 apartment D. They knew the place very well.

By the time Albert was four he was 'street smart.' He could feed and clothe himself from the street and stay hid. He was no stranger to a fight and winning by any means necessary. By the time he was eight his mother had found a new product for her to sell – him. The wiles of a street kid only go so far. Albert was caught, and rented to whoever had the credits for whatever purpose they chose. He remained captive for almost six weeks before he got loose. He was no longer under the control of Mother or Jane.

He gave in to his rage. He was pissed when he forced his way in the window. They were passed out on the bed. He had seen them in this state too many times. He knew just what he could get away with and he intended to push that just a little further.

He woke his stoned mother and told her that he had some drugs in the kitchen. That was all it took. He helped as she stumbled to the kitchen and sat in one of the chairs. He tied her to the chair securely. Jane was just as easy. He tied her very securely to another chair. Then he tied them again. He used an entire roll of duct tape on each one to make sure they were not going to get away.

He had stolen a package of hot dogs and some bread at the same time he took the duct tape. He cooked, ate and waited for them to sober up. He wanted them to know what was about to happen. He wasn't going to put up with any screaming either. He made a loop of fishing line and slipped it around their tongue. He tied it to a nail in the wall and if they tried to scream he would just pull the string. Maybe it would pull their tongues out of their heads altogether.

The police call came two weeks later. "Anyone in the area, Garden View 946 please see the lady in apartment B."

Officer Roberts knew the place so he and his partner took the call. "This is car twelve. We got it." They both wondered what had happened. They hadn't been called to the apartment in two weeks. It had to be some kind of record.

He knocked on the door of apt B and Julie answered. "Oh, hello Officer Roberts I was hoping it would be you." She paused. "This you'll have to see to believe it." She took them to the bathroom where she pointed to the ceiling. Something was dripping in the toilet. It was from apartment D above and was a red liquid. "I just noticed it this morning, but the water in the toilet has been tinted red for at least two or three days."

Officer Roberts nodded and checked the drip. He and his partner then went upstairs. Roberts noted to his partner that he thought the drip was blood. Apartment C had a small religious display outside the door with several incense burning. They didn't smell very good. They knocked on the door to apartment D and were starting to knock again. The door to apartment C opened. "Something in there smells very bad; like rotting meat."

Roberts asked. "How long has it smelled that way?"

He had to think. "It always smells but about ten days ago it started to get worse. I had to put these incense out here to try to cover the smell."

Robert's partner asked. "Why didn't you call the police?"

The man got a kind of crazy look, "The smell is better than the noise of the parties and the people coming and going."

There wasn't an answer at the door after the second or third knock. Officer Roberts didn't want to open the door but it was his job. He called housing security and waited. It was almost a half hour before Warden Smith arrived. He was a retired cop who lived in the complex and doubled as security. Roberts knew him well.

They had a brief conversation about the mess before the door was opened. Warden Smith unlocked and opened it about six inches. The cool rank air belched out of the room. It was the worst stench that Roberts had ever smelled; and he had dug up a shallow grave with a two week old corpse in it. This was out of his realm, he called for backup. Warden Joe Smith had stepped back out of the way as well. It was a nasty stench that tried hard to bring everything in your stomach out into the light of day.

When the major crime lab arrived the house had aired out some and the officers went in with them to make sure the house was clear. The first step onto the sticky, smelly carpet was unbelievably disgusting. The blood that squeezed from under the shoes shot four inches to all sides. It was all Roberts could do to hold down his lunch. One rookie cop had to leave quickly. He didn't make it to the door before he puked on the floor. The puke just splattered the blood and made it worse.

They found five men in the room immediately to the left. There were three men seated on one of the blood soaked sofas and two on the other. Each had his hands and feet duct taped together, they had signs of being tortured. But death was from their throats being cut. The sixth man was lying on the floor behind the sofa. He was face down and tied with his legs spread taped to a long stick. The small end of a bowling pin was stuffed up his ass. He had bled to death from that orifice over several days. The bloody prints of the soles of a tennis shoe were on the bottom of the bowling pin. It had been kicked deeper in several times.

Officer Roberts' partner checked the kitchen with Roberts close behind, he made a hasty retreat splashing blood on the other officers. Roberts was left to see what was in the kitchen. Whatever it was, it was so vile that a four year veteran of the force had lost his lunch. He looked around the corner and almost lost his.

The two women who he had visited – in an official capacity – were butchered. But worst of all the still oozing blood from their necks told the coroner they had been cut only about an hour ago. About the time the officers knocked on the door. Somebody kept these women alive for a long time. Whoever the monster was, he had cut pieces of them off as he or she saw fit over several days.

Further investigation would reveal the killer or butcher made meals and ate in the kitchen although no evidence supported the eating of human flesh. The rumors of cannibalism started anyway.

The Mist didn't smile; instead she just went on to find the last parts of her plan. She was glad it was almost over with Stick, she didn't like what she had to do to him. Now there was just Mouse and Brandy after Max. Her plan would be in play in just a few short years.

CHAPTER SIX -
MAX CRASH

The crash was horrible. The crushing of the car in which Max rode and the death of his parents were unavoidable as far as The Mist was concerned. She just waved her hand and the tire blew sending the Dent car into the path of the tractor trailer. The driver of the tractor trailer didn't even have time to touch the brakes.

Max was sitting in the back seat of his parent's car when it began. He was playing with his favorite toy solders. That was the way the nightmare always started. It was like he was watching the boy, himself, play. The boy was without a care. These dreams always made Max long for those carefree times. But Max, as an onlooker, knew the car was about to be involved in a head on crash with a tractor trailer. It won't be anybody's fault; just a bad tire on his parents car. The reason doesn't make a difference; Max would pay the cost in pain and suffering. He would lose everything and for the rest of his life there would be an empty place in his heart, his life and his soul. Although the hole in his soul is what The Mist intended. His soul, some would question if he even had a soul.

Max didn't remember the crash. He didn't remember the rescue squad cutting him out of the car. He didn't remember the coma that lasted six weeks. He didn't remember the pain. That was the good part. The bad part; he didn't remember his mother. He didn't remember his father. He didn't remember anything. Maybe that is why the faces of his mother and father are just blank when he sees them before the crash.

Well, he remembers how to go to the bathroom, but he couldn't get out of bed. His left leg was broken in several places. He had only one clear memory from that time. He remembered the strange lady, The Mist, who kept telling him, "It'll be alright Max." But no one else remembers her. He thought it funny because his name was Bartholomew, Bart; she kept calling him Max.

It would take many operations to repair the leg so he can, maybe, walk. His left eye was badly damaged. He wears a patch over it most of the time so it can rest. The doctors told him he'll be able to see out of the eye. But he'd have to wear the patch because when it gets tired 'it'd lie to him.'

The eye was for the most part useless; it would have been better if it has been totally destroyed. The more visible and worst injury is the cut that goes from the bridge of his nose almost into the left eye, outward past his high cheek bone and down the left side of his face to the point of the jaw bone under the left ear. It is also the most visible. There was going to be a scar, a bad one.

Now to a seven year old boy an eye patch and an ugly scar is not a big deal. Well, it wasn't to Max. The bigger problem to him was his broken leg. He worked very hard in therapy every day to make the leg as strong as possible. He wanted the leg to work just like it did before or at least as well as it possibly could. It took a year for the leg to get strong enough so he could walk with a cane.

If it hadn't been for 'old Jim' he would have gone bonkers. 'Old Jim' filled the void left with the loss of Max's memory of his mother and father. Jim was the first one besides The Mist who called him Max because he always did things to the max. He and Jim were confined to wheelchairs and they were the best of friends.

Things came to an end when the hospital received word that the insurance companies had paid out all the money they were held liable for by the courts. Max became a liability and things had to change. His leg was not completely ready for the outside world but the money was gone. He hated to leave Jim. Jim is the closest thing to a family Max remembers and he's old. Max considers him his Grandfather. Max knew he would never see him again. Max was released to an Aunt and taken to El Paso, Texas.

Max dumped the cane before he arrived at Garden View apartments, 946 B, in El Paso, Texas. Max thought it was the worst place on earth. Well, if you lived in the low rent neighborhood, with an Aunt that you have never met. But he refused to cry. Aunt Julie took Max because she needed the money the state would pay her to care for him. She's nice enough, but it's the money that she's keeping him for, not the Aunt, nephew, family thing.

Aunt Julie is a nice looking lady in her thirties. She has never been married or intended, and has no children. She is a slender, pleasant woman - irritatingly pleasant. She hovers. It serves her well because she waits tables at a truck stop. She gets good tips. The truck stop is close enough for her to walk to work; which she does. She has worse problems than money. She wants a husband or a man so bad that she makes terrible choices, just to try to find someone.

Max does have his own room at Aunt Julie's. It's small and the total furnishings are a twin bed and a small chest. The closet is full of boxes. He didn't remember what a real home was like, but he doesn't think this is it. Max wishes he was back at the hospital. He wanted to talk to his friend Jim. But he didn't cry.

Max was at the apartment alone in the afternoon. His Aunt worked from eleven in the morning to eight at night. He stayed in the apartment and watched out the window. The kids were ok, but there was one group that was mean to the rest. The lady in apartment D, Mrs. Franks was to watch him and feed him something during the day. He could go to her apartment if he needed anything. She asked him to call her Carol and he does. She has a daughter named Sandra; most people called her Sandy. She is a sort of outcast like Max. The kids liked her but she didn't have any real friends. Max decided that she was a good place to start to make friends.

Max wanted to go out, he was so tired of the apartment. He exercised his leg every chance he got. He could make the trip up stairs to Carol's without much trouble now. The leg was as good as it was going to get on level ground. He was scared. He didn't know how well his leg would hold up outside on the uneven ground. He kept telling himself. "You know you have to go outside sooner or later." When Max was at the hospital he had talked to old Jim a lot. Jim gave him a lot of advice. One of the things he had told him "you have to get your bluff in, when you go to a new place." Max spent the next two days looking out the window at the kids playing and fighting. He wasn't sure. He kept putting off talking to Sandy for one reason or another. He had never said much to her when they ate together at Carol's, her mother's. Sandy talked a lot but not really to Max.

The time to meet Sandy on different ground came the next morning. Sandy was sitting on the steps outside the apartment where Max could see her through the window. Max thought; this is the time. Max reasoned to himself, Sandy knew him because they ate lunch together, although they hadn't talked much. She was alone and not bothering anyone, just watching the other kids play. He gathered all his courage. After all, this making a new friend wasn't for the faint of heart. The meals didn't really count because her mother was there. But, with his guts boiling and his throat dry, he walked out and said.

"Hello Sandy."

She jumped and tried to run away. She stumbled, but she put some distance between her and Max. She got to her feet with a firm grip on a rock slightly larger than her hand. She exclaimed. "You scared me."

Max told her that he didn't mean to scare her. "I just don't like to play by myself. I thought you might want to play."

They sized each other up for a while. They had talked some at the meals and somehow that made the situation worse. They sort of knew each other but didn't. Max asked. "Why are you so scared anyway?"

She explained "I thought you were one of those boys."

Max thought he knew the boys she was talking about but he asked to be sure. "What boys?"

She told him "The mean boys, they hurt the littler kids and take things from them."

Max smiled. "I've watched them out the window. They are just bullies. If you stand up to them they'll quit. They may beat you up a time or two. But you'll get in a few licks and they'll get tired of getting hit. They'll quit." That was what Jim had told Max over and over, Max believed him.

It took the rest of the morning before Max and Sandy were almost at ease with each other. Sandy told Max that she thought he wasn't allowed outside.

He laughed. "No, I was a little scared. Making new friends isn't easy."

She smiled. "I know. It seems that just when you think you have someone figured out they change."

She asked him about his eye and Max told her the story. She thought it was sad about his parents and volunteered the story of her Father's death. She told him she was happy he had come to live with his Aunt. If he hadn't they might never have met. They never stopped talking after that.

Sandy's mother had been watching them off and on since Max had gone out to talk to Sandy. She didn't want to interrupt but it was time to eat. She called for them to come have something to eat. She let them eat their peanut butter and jelly sandwich with Kool-aid in private. She hoped that they would keep talking. Sandy's mother, Mrs. Franks smiled. She was happy that Sandy and Max had become friends. She hoped that Sandy's destructive tantrums, and violent mood swings would pass if she had a friend. But most of all she saw some of the old Sandy coming back. She wasn't as shy and timid with Max as she was with most other people. They clicked; they were friends by the time Max's Aunt got home from work. They had became best friends and anything that happened after that they were either both involved in together or had to tell the other one about it, as soon a possible.

The housing complex has several places to play, the woods, the playground, down by the bridge, or the open field where other housing was to be built. The money never arrived for that project. They liked to play close to the apartment in an abandoned flower bed. It could be anything but mostly it was a launch pad to go into deep space. They would play for a while and then they would build for a while. They liked to daydream and talk to each other about being in space and finding new worlds. They had gathered some small flat rocks to use as transports and a piece of iron pipe about ten inches long that was their rocket. They traveled to some amazing places, in their day dreams.

The base was always destroyed each morning and had to be rebuilt. Other kids tore up the base sometimes to be mean, but mostly it was stray cats. They liked the loose dirt and left gifts for Max and Sandy to dispose of the next day. Once the base was rebuilt they could talk about space. It had been a week since they started this game and they still enjoyed playing it in the flower bed.

It had to happen sooner or later and one day after lunch it did. Max was sitting with the pipe in his hand about to launch the rocket into space. He and Sandy were counting down for launch together. He caught something out of the corner of his good eye. Sandy started to crayfish back toward the wall. She grabbed one of the larger rocks they were using for buildings in each hand. She had a stern look on her face. This was as far as she was backing up.

One of the bullies was standing over Max. Another bully was standing a couple of steps away. The closer bully came up and scuffed his foot around in their base destroying their roads and launch pad. Another one of the group spoke. "Just in case you don't know it kid; this place belongs to us and you will do as we say or you will not like what happens."

Max's mind was racing as he identified the components of the gang. Just like Jim said "They'll always be the same." The two in front of him were the enforcers. The boss was the one who spoke and the rest were mostly just following the easy path. Jim and Max spent a lot of time together at the hospital. Jim had taught him how to judge people. Neither of them could move around very well; they were both in wheel chairs. They would sit for hours just talking about the people they watched. The old man said Max was very good at judging people. Max hoped so, because it was about to be tested for real.

Max also knew that he was about to be judged by these kids. He wanted them to leave him, Sandy and the rest of the kids alone. He had to stand his ground; win or lose. The words rang in Max's head, the words that the Jim had said over and over but it was a soft female voice that said. "It's better to be beat-up than to back-up." He had always found truth in what the old man told him. The voice was strangely reassuring. It was time to test the theory.

The boy closest was taller and heavier than Max, even if Max had been standing. The other enforcer who stood a few feet away was much larger, but mostly fat. A group of maybe twenty kids stood behind the leader of the gang. He was a tall skinny kid, Max thought he looked sickly and wondered how he got anyone to follow him. The boy taunted. "So, you will call me Boss." Max was still sitting on the ground. He smiled as his mind told him to "go ahead and launch your rocket."

Max's rocket, a length of pipe about ten inches long had just become a weapon. Max was about to launch the rocket. He hit the bully in the shin, as hard as he could with the length of pipe. Then he hit him again. Max was on his feet and the other bully took a step back; it was a good thing for Max and he knew it. His attentions turned back to the bully he had hit with the pipe. He was hopping backward on one foot holding his leg up to his chest with both hands. Max hit him in the side of the head with the pipe. The boy was larger than Max so he hit him with all he had. He didn't think he could hit him any harder. The boy fell like a big glob of mush, he was out cold. There was no time to think.

The other enforcer had regained his courage and was moving toward Max. Max knew that the correct move was to try to push the pipe through the boy's chest. But, could he do it? He gave it his best shot, he held on to the pipe as tight as he could. The center of the boy's chest slammed into the pipe as Max shoved it as hard as he could as the boy ran at him. By the look on the boy's face he was in a lot of pain. The force of the impact pushed the pipe through Max's hand leaving the length of the pipe lying along his fore arm. The words came to his mind again. "Step to the right. Elbow to the head." He followed the words; it was all happening so fast. He hit the bully as hard and as quickly as he could.

The end of the pipe struck the bully on the side of the head close to the eye and Max's elbow hit the boy full force just above the ear. The blood droplets seemed to hang in the air as if everything had slowed down. As the blood started to settle to the ground it fell on the unmoving boy, Max's first victim. The second boy went to the ground.

Max was sure that this fight was over. However in an unexpected turn of events; four of the other boys rushed Max. He got one of them with a straight blow to the nose. He hit him with a fist wrapped around the pipe. The wind whistled in the ends of the pipe as it was pushed through the air. One of the attackers was all he got before he was tackled. The three were holding Max down with their weight. He was being beaten.

Sandy had a rock in her hand and bashed one of the bullies in the back of the head. Max couldn't get loose and he couldn't get a clear shot at any of them. Then some of the weight was lifted as Sandy struggled to pull the boy off Max. She couldn't so she kicked him off. Max had a clear shot at one of them now. He was about to hit him in the head when he stopped; that's Sandy.

Another boy was watching and decided to take a part in the fight; he had been waiting for this day a long time. He pulled another one of the bullies off Max and started to beat him with a heavy stick; Leaving Max to deal with just the one. He had lost the pipe somewhere in the struggle but he hit him several times with his fist before the boy started trying to get away. Max grabbed him by the hair and held him. He kept hitting him until the bully finally managed to slip free leaving Max with a hand full of hair.

Max looked for Sandy. She had one on the ground hitting him in the head with the big rock she was holding between her hands. The boy was not moving. The other bully had his own problems. He was being beaten by the boy who joined the fight. Max didn't know him but he was hitting the bully with a long heavy stick. He swung it like a ball bat and then he would whirl around and hit him again. The bully fell to the ground and didn't move.

Max knew from what old Jim had told him that they had just taken out the enforcers, and the others who might fight. The remainder of the bullies would be the leader and a bunch of just followers. The leader might do something but the rest wouldn't do anything. The leader, the boy that liked to be called Boss, waited a few seconds before he stepped forward. He had to do something or lose his gang. He was taking a good look at these little punks who had just taken out his guys in seconds. He addressed Max. "I'm the boss."

Now; the scar and the eye patch made a difference. Max gathered all he had inside of him. He knew this was the time. "I'm the Boss. I just took everything you had." He smiled. "Why don't you come take it back?"

He heard Sandy whine "Oh boy."

The other boy who had fought with Max and Sandy smiled. "It's about time."

The leader of the bullies was a head taller than Max. He said. "I wish you had left me another way out." The boy pulled a switch blade knife. The followers stepped back. Max moved away from the building. He knew he needed room to move.

Max had only seen these things in movies. But he had committed to this stand and others were watching him. If he didn't finish this now he would just have to do it again later, he might anyway. He was going to stand. As he moved away his foot hit the pipe and he picked it up while watching the boy with the knife closely. Max twirled the pipe back into the right position. The words of the old man sang in his head. He would tell such stories. The punch line was always the same and Max heard it coming out of his mouth. "I hope you know how to use that toy." He laughed "Because now I can kill you and nothing will happen to me."

The adults from the building stepped in just in time. What would have happened, Max didn't know. He did know he wasn't afraid, and the 'boss' was. Everyone else knew the 'boss' was afraid too. One of the adults took the knife from the boss. Max had sense enough to drop the pipe. The boss turned and ran away. His bully boys followed. Max smiled as another phrase from the old man crossed his lips. "It's good to be the King."

This fight was over and the old boss was nowhere to be found. The kid with the stick warned. "He's got an older brother and he has a gang." He smiled. "This isn't over." He smiled as he added. "It sure is nice to have someone on the same side I'm on. It's hard for one person to fight a gang."

Max laughed and said. "I know. Thanks for the help."

Sandy had a big smile, "anytime."

Max walked over to Sandy and asked "are you all right?" She seemed a little scared now that it was over. Max was concerned.

She said "yes, I'm ok." She seemed to be talking to herself with the next statement, "I really am ok." Sandy's mother was beside them and the man who took the knife was in front of them.

The boy with the stick was gone. It was like he just disappeared. Max understood what he had done and why. But he was having a problem with what Sandy had done. He thought about it for a while and the only thing that made sense was that she had been pushed too far. All that rage had come out. The boys lying on he ground in their own blood were known to be the bullies of the neighborhood. The housing warden, a retired cop had taken the knife. He looked somewhat surprised that the bullies were the ones on the ground and not some poor kid that they were picking on. The warden took Max, Sandy, and Sandy's mother aside.

The warden is always a retired cop who doesn't get much retirement so they qualified for subsidized housing. They are also paid a little, usually the cost of the housing. This one's name is Joe. He looked at Max and in a cross way. "What's your name? I don't remember you living here."

Sandy's mother intervened. "He just moved in with Julie. She's his Aunt. His name is Bartholomew Dent, Bart I guess."

Joe asked Max "Is that right?"

Max remembered when the lady and then Jim had started to call him Max Crash because of how bad the crash was that brought him to the hospital. He smiled, "Max Crash at your service."

Joe said "Well Max, I'm Warden Joe Smith. What do you have to say for yourself?"

Max didn't like his attitude. "Veni vidi vici" It was a phrase that the old man used, I came, I saw, I conquered.

Joe laughed "a fan of the Caesars, I guess."

Max's face was without expression "it was just the best way this time."

Warden Smith sent the kids in the house. "You kids go inside. Mrs. Franks, could I talk to you a minute?" Sandy's mother stayed. Joe asked the bystanders if they saw anything. No one spoke up. It was what he expected. Several people were checking on the boys who were knocked out but no one was doing much with them. You can get in a lot of trouble for rendering aid if you don't know what you're doing.

Joe asked. "Carol, what do you know about that boy?"

She told him that Max was just out of the hospital from a car crash over a year ago "that's about it. But he seems a nice boy."

Joe shook his head. "That boy is dangerous. His eye was just blank." The conversation was cut short by the medics coming to care for the five fallen bullies. They got the onlookers back who had been watching. Joe had to go talk to them.

Carol went inside. When she looked into the kitchen, Max and Sandy were standing by the sink. Max was washing the blood off her forehead. "I think that's all."

Carol said. "Max, you got a little carried away. You hurt those boys."

Sandy was quick to his defense. "They were going to hurt us. Max is a hero."

Max, with some sympathy and an obvious lie on his lips said, "I was afraid and I knew I had to win or they'd hurt us."

The knock on the door closed the subject for the moment. It was Joe. He was almost white, and looked a little sick. Carol made him sit down. She got him some water and he sat there a while. Then he said. "I was a cop for 27 years, Carol, 27 years. I never had to shoot anybody. I never even saw a person who had been killed." Joe was in shock and rambling. Carol sent Sandy out to get one of the medics to come look at him. The medic came in and looked at Joe. Sandy followed him inside. Her mother went over to her and held her "Now honey, it's over now. You and Max go in the kitchen."

The medic decided Joe just needed a little oxygen. "I think he'll be all right. He's had a shock."

Carol asked "What's happening?"

Joe said "The boys are dead, all five of them." Sandy was a little shocked but Max just looked at the people in the room. He didn't understand what the big deal was; they started it.

Max didn't find out until much later that the warden didn't care that the boys were dead. It was just the sight of the bloody mess that got to him. Those boys had caused a lot of trouble and he told the police that they got in a fight with some of the other gang members. It was a common thing for gang members to turn on each other. The police accepted the story and filed a report. Sandy's mother didn't go into the kitchen until after the police left, about an hour later.

The warden was feeling better and went in with her to talk to the kids. What they saw was chilling. Max and Sandy were eating the snack that Carol had made for them just before this thing started. They watched the kids talking and laughing as they ate. Sandy shook her head to get her dark shoulder length hair out of her face. Max stopped eating and got a wet cloth from the sink and wiped the blood from the side of Sandy's face. When she had moved her head the blood was uncovered. He washed it away and then lay the bloody cloth down on the table. The warden said softly "I have always said; there is always a meaner dog. But those two together, I just wouldn't want to meet that meaner dog."

Carol asked the warden. "Joe, do you think Sandy is safe with him?"

Joe smiled. "Yes, that boy will protect her with his last ounce of life. But it may not be wise for them to be together too long. They're dangerous together."

Carol waited a short while before she went to talk to the kids. "Guys, I have some bad news; those boys died."

Sandy said. "We know, Max said the meat wagon only comes for the dead. Can I have some more to drink?" Carol didn't know what to say.

Max asked, "Are we in trouble?"

Joe said. "No, the police said it was self defense. There may be a hearing but you're not in trouble."

Sandy asked. "We're done. Can we go back out and play?"

Carol told her no, "Go play quietly in the other room." They went to play cards.

Joe was shaking his head. "That is one bad boy, it might be best if you could find a way to separate them." Carol smiled but she knew full well that her little angel was just as deep in this as Max. Joe and Carol talked for a while before Joe left. Joe went back to work. "I'll call if I need anything else."

Carol went to the kitchen to clean up. She was putting away the fresh washed glasses when Max and Sandy came into the kitchen carrying a bag of trash. "Mother, Max picked a yucky part of that boy off my dress and put it in the trash."

Carol said. "Did you change your top?" Sandy nodded yes.

Carol asked. "Didn't you have on that dress that buttons up the back? How did you get it unbuttoned?"

She nodded. "Max helped me."

The chill of the uncaring attitude over the deaths was eclipsed by this new development. Sandy was very modest. She didn't like anyone to see her skin and she had let Max see her back when he unbuttoned the dress. Her thoughts went back to when Sandy let Max wash the blood off the side of her head. Her little girl had a crush on a murderer - of course — she's a murderer too. It was unnerving.

As Joe walked back to his house he couldn't help but think about two weeks ago when he caught Sandy over in the woods. She had another little girl tied to a tree and was putting fire ants on her. The girl had lost one of the plastic shoes that belonged to Sandy's doll. For this loss of a shoe the girl suffered almost a hundred bites from the fire ants. Joe untied the girl and sent Sandy home. The girl refused to tell anyone what had happened. She was crying "She'll kill me. Nothing happened. It was my fault." Joe had not told Carol about the incident. But given today's events maybe he should.

The next day Max got into another fight and broke a boy's arm. It was a one on one fight. Joe couldn't protect him this time. The cops took Max away. They talked to him and studied him overnight, his Aunt Julie picked him up late the next day. Max didn't really care. It was better in the city shelter than at home - he ate better. But he missed Sandy even though he had only known her for a short while. Max was marked as a possible sociopath and his record was started.

Sandy's mother was a little concerned about Max and Sandy playing together. She watched them very carefully. The next problem came about three the next afternoon. Two boys from the bully group started to make sport of a much smaller kid. Max watched a second and then got to his feet and started in their direction, Sandy followed. Sandy's mother was some distance behind, but hot on their trail. She yelled for them to leave those boys alone. They just kept marching toward the boys. They were on a mission.

Max picked up a stick, he broke it in half and handed the stronger half to Sandy as he tossed the weaker end away. She took it and they marched rather quickly toward the boys. Max picked up another stick. Stick, as they had dubbed him, came from nowhere and was to the left of Max. Max offered him the stick. He laughed. "I already have one."

One of the boys turned to see them coming. He tried to run away, but ran into his partner, knocking both of them down. He turned back to see where Max was. Max hit him in the side of the head with his stick knocking him down. He jumped astride him and continued to hit him with his fist; first from one side and then from the other side, back and forth, over and over. When Joe pulled him off he was sitting on the boy's chest pounding him in the face with his fist – left, right, left, right. The other boy was being beaten by several kids, including Sandy and Stick, as he lay on the ground. Joe yelled for them to stop but he had to step in to get them to quit. Both boys ran away. Stick disappeared quickly.

Carol was on the scene soon after; these things can happen so fast. She escorted Max and Sandy back to the apartment. They got to play inside the rest of the day. Joe dropped by and asked them some questions about the other boy. They didn't know anything. Carol walked Joe to the door and he told her that the other boy was wanted by the police. "He's a runaway and they think he might be involved in beating and stealing from the bums."

Carol sighed. "We have a wild little crew here." Joe rubbed his mouth. "What do you expect in this neighborhood?"

Max was in trouble again. But it was let slide and his problems started to fade after a week. The bullies were not coming around. They were going somewhere else. The kids of the neighborhood had banded together. Any bully had to fight all of them. Max was there for the hard jobs. Max never picked on the other kids. He was just a very bad boy who was, well – as Sandy said, "very sweet on the inside." She helped Max control himself. It looked like they were going to have a very nice summer.

It was a few days later that Aunt Julie's new boyfriend pissed Max off. Julie tried to tell her new friend that Max was not like other children. "He's a little unstable." Max left the apartment, slamming the door behind him. He had already started to the bridge to find Stick. Sandy called to him from behind and came running up. "Where are you going?" Max told her he needed to see Stick. They stopped by the store to get some candy and then went to the bridge. Max called "Stick" and sat down to eat his candy. It wasn't long before Stick showed. "Can I have some of that?" He took the candy he was offered.

Max told him he needed a club "a good strong club." Sandy asked why and Max told her, "I'm going to kill Aunt Julie's new boyfriend."

Sandy nodded, "Oh, ok, do you have any more candy?" He had one piece left and he gave it to Sandy.

It didn't take much searching to find a good club. Stick knew where all the good clubs were. Stick helped him fix the club so it was easy to handle. They stayed and talked until dark. Max left the stick outside the door when he told Sandy good night. He went straight to his room once he was in the apartment. He waited for the new boyfriend to start to snore.

Julie's new friend had a habit of sleeping with one of his arms sticking straight out from the bed, palm up. It made a great target.

Max waited until he could hear him snoring before he went to get the club. When he brought the club down toward the man's outstretched arm he meant to break every bone in the arm. But the man woke and moved a little.

It didn't make much difference. The echo of the bones breaking resonated around the apartment. The man was on the floor and yelling. Max hit him again on the back and in the head. Julie was up and took the stick from Max. Max yelled "Don't be here in the morning, and if you are; don't go to sleep." Max's spent another night under observation and his record was extended by the police. He was sent home the next day. The man was leaving. He was scratching and cussing. Sandy greeted Max. "Hi, you might want to stay over at my house tonight. A bunch of fire ants got in your apartment." She laughed and Max smiled.

The summer was the best one Max could remember. In fact it was only the second and the last one he was in the hospital. They played down by the old bridge a lot. There was very little traffic in the daytime. The truckers mostly used it at night to bypass the city. Max and Sandy were safe and trusted. To the rest of the kids in the housing development they were the shadow of death. There hadn't been any trouble in weeks so they did mostly as they pleased in the peaceful time. There wasn't anyone to fight or protect because they were feared. All the other gangs were afraid of them and never invaded their turf.

When they went home for dinner they took Stick with them when he would go. He would always go on Sunday because there would be fried chicken. This Sunday brought a surprise. Sandy's Uncle Bill was in for a few days. Sandy, Max and Stick listened as he told stories about space and wars. They were all hooked and promised themselves that some day they would go into space. Bill left on Wednesday and things got back to normal.

To make money the three of them would collect cans and other stuff and sell it at the metal salvage place. They also returned the bottles that had a deposit. And anything else they could find to sell. If they couldn't find a way to buy the things they wanted;

they stole them. The old bums always had stories and would tell them new ways to get what they wanted for free. Stick, whose real name is Albert Van Smyth, would join them most of the time and as the summer went on the three became inseparable.

There were two bums who always traveled together. One day the two of them were the only ones under the bridge when the kids came down to play. They were drunk on cheap wine. One of the bums started to pick on Stick calling him Stick-boy. Stick didn't like it. The bum kept grabbing at Stick and he didn't like it at all. Stick walked behind the bum; he climbed up on some rocks. He hit him in the head so hard that he broke his stick. Max and Sandy laughed. The man screamed; Stickman tossed the smaller end of the stick away and jumped on him and hit him again and again with the longer end of the broken stick.

The man lay on the ground, bleeding. Stick was going to hit him again but Sandy stopped him. "Don't kill him. Remember how weird everybody was after we killed those boys."

Stick dropped the broken, bloody end of the stick on the ground. "Don't you ever tease me again old man or I'll kill you." After a few minutes Stick laughed as he started to relax. "Now I have to go make another stick." Sandy and Max laughed. Stick smiled. "I've got money for three drinks but we'll have to steal the candy." Max laughed. "I got some money." They all went to the store leaving the bum to be helped by his friend.

The bums didn't have enough sense to let it go. They went to the police. The police didn't have much use for the bums but they talked to the kids and their parents, not much came of it. The kids didn't forget about it either. It was two weeks before they saw the two bums again.

The kids were playing on the bridge when the two bums walked under it. Stick pointed them out. Sandy picked up a half of a concrete block and aimed carefully before she let it go and hit one of the bums in the head as they started under the bridge. Stick laughed "Good shot." It was about a thirty foot drop and the block was going very fast when it hit him. He folded up on the ground.

The second bum took off running and the three gave chase. Max caught him. He jumped on his back from a rock ledge knocking him to the ground. The man started to get up but Stick hit him in the face with his new stick. Sandy had arrived. She tried several rocks before she picked up the heaviest one she could lift. She got up on the ledge and threw it at the bums head. His head burst like a melon. She made a face "Yuck." They went to find the other bum; his head was busted open too. Sandy was matter of fact. "You shouldn't tell on us."

Stick went through their pockets and found some money. He laughed. "Drinks are on the bums."

Max smiled and said nicely. "Thank you bums." They went to get sodas. The police never even came around.

Max bought a box of Cracker Jacks with the money from the bums; he had been trying to find a box that had a ring in it for a while. The other two didn't like them so he got the whole box. The toy surprise this time finally was a ring. He couldn't believe his luck, and it had a red set and a diamond set. He put it in his pocket. Later that day after Stick left and he and Sandy were alone, well Carol was in the kitchen but other wise they were alone. They were sitting on the sofa getting ready to play some cards. Max took the ring out of his pocket and showing it to Sandy he asked. "Sandy, someday when we're old enough will you marry me?"

She smiled. "Yes, can I have the ring now?" Max gave it to her. She said, "We're supposed to kiss now." They hugged instead.

The end of the summer brought an end to the gang. Stick was caught. He's not only a runaway but also a, 'person of interest' in a torture and murder case. They also wanted to talk to him about the bums. He was sent to one of the juvenile units. Max and Sandy did get to go see him before he was sent off. They brought him some chewy chocolates. He likes the chewy ones the best. The trading card inside was of a scientist Albert Einstein. Stick,

Albert, liked it. He thought it was funny how they had the same first name.

Sandy's mother, with Bill's help, found a way to get Sandy away from Max; she was going to a state school for the gifted. She had scored very high on the placement test. The news was hard for Max and Sandy. They ran away that night. They didn't run far before it started to snow and the wind was very cold. They were both in jeans and a t-shirt. They had to find shelter from the cold and wet of the very unusual snow storm. They had to stay hidden and it just wasn't working out. They needed food and they couldn't get it without being seen.

The fourth night before they gave up and went home was very cold, below freezing. They huddled together holding each other under a ragged half blanket they had found. They must have dozed off. They were suddenly warm and comfortable. A lady spoke to them. "It's not yet your time, children." She smiled. "But, I have great plans for you, the both of you and they do not include you being found dead in this cave. I'm going to send you back." She paused and looked at Sandy "You do your very best in school." She looked at Max, "You learn all you can about surviving. Someday I will bring you back together. You will be blessed with six children of your own and two you will choose." She smiled. "And on top of that you'll rule as royalty over everything in the universe."

The next day they went back home. They were not hungry or having any ill affects from their stay in the cold wet weather that had left with the rising Sun. It was going to be a warm day.

Max got Sandy a big teddy bear and they even shared a small kiss and a long hug before she left. Sandy told her mother as they drove away; "It doesn't matter what you do, Mother. I'm going to marry Max and have six babies and be queen of the universe. The dream lady told us." Carol was just hoping that Sandy now had a chance to grow up and not to go to jail.

Max was alone - again. The bullies will be coming soon. Max decided to go for them, before they came for him; at least he would have the element of surprise. He caught the three leaders one by one over a weekend. When he had all three he took them under the bridge one at a time and tied them securely. It had taken a lot of planning to ready the traps, but they had done their job. He had already decided to dispose of the leaders; and with little talking he set about that task. He looped a small diameter cable he had found around their necks; two loops for one and then two for the next and then two for the last. He tied a makeshift hook to the end. He drank a soda and ate a candy bar. He waited for night and the trucks to come.

He watched his prisoners try to get their hands and feet untied. He didn't say much to them. He didn't feed them or give them water. He just waited until it was dark and large trucks were passing. He threw the hook on the truck, it didn't hook; the next truck didn't hook either. Max was determined. The third try worked. The cable pulled tight quickly and the boy's heads popped off. One at a time, pop, pop, pop. That should take care of that.

However this time Max was caught. If he had just thought not to anchor that cable so well. It jerked part of the load right off that truck. He pled guilty to every one of the murders. He didn't want them to come back on Sandy or Stick; after all he was already caught. Only the three Max had just done could be proven; but the rest were closed. He was kept in the juvenile unit until he was sentenced and… Max was on his way to a very tough school up state, just like Sandy. He was going to a school that would teach him to survive.

The Mist was very pleased that now Max, Sandy and Stick were in the place she wanted them; the place she needed them. She had another member of the crew to get ready and she was off to the stars to prep the newest member of the crew.

CHAPTER SEVEN –
TIME TO START

At 10 years old Max was sent to Anderson Detention Centre for young boys. He was not a model inmate. For the first two years, the time he wasn't in school, he spent mostly in solitary confinement. A very kindly guard would bring him things to read. It was all religious crap, but it helped pass the time. Sometimes he would feel a presence in the solitary cell. He always felt better afterwards.

Sandy wasn't doing much better at the boarding school. She had already been in trouble for fighting three times; all of which had resulted in broken limbs – not hers. She got away with the fighting at first because she excelled in Plant biology and how alien environments might affect them. But a tenured professor can only protect you to a point. He came to her at her 'solitary confinement', study hall. "Sandra, you are going to have to stop all this fighting." She just looked at him and he added. "You must have some very powerful friends or family to have gotten away with the fighting as long as you have." He shook his head. "But it's over. One more fight and you're going to be expelled." It didn't get through to her until he asked how that would make her mother feel. There was a lot more said but it didn't matter. Sandy buried herself in her studies to save herself from exploding. She was so mad that she couldn't even guess what she might do if someone crossed her. She missed Max. He understood her and loved her. She wanted to be with Max but not enough to chance being expelled and hurting her mother.

Sometimes she had dreams. She couldn't really remember anything about them but she was always more at peace after she had one of the dreams; maybe it was that lady.

Stick was sent to the Kernice Temple. It was a very old and dying religious order that believed in a deity they called TheFog. The Mist arranged for him to be put there for a reason, he needed to have a very stable mind and the monks would help him. The monks also told him they could feel the presence of TheFog all around him. He began to believe the same thing as several things happened to prove it to him. Once a large box he was helping to carry tipped over on him and he just knew he was dead. The monks pulled the box off him. He felt the stake-like wooden splinter pull out of his stomach and watched as the wound healed in front of his eyes. The soft voice in his ears told him 'it will be ok, Stick.' He had almost no trouble believing after that incident.

Max's case worker couldn't do much to help Max. He thought him a very stable young man who just didn't believe it was wrong to kill. The board considered Max unsalvageable at the age of twelve. He was released into the general population. His schooling would continue if he showed up for class; it was his choice.

A boy called Beau took him under his wing the same day he entered the general population of the prison. Beau was sixteen and a lifer just like Max. He was a kind boy at heart. He just wanted Max to help protect him and in return he protected Max. Beau had been in this place since he was twelve.

Max stood at the door going into the general population area a little too long and a guard pushed him from behind, "get in there boy." Max looked straight at him with killing him in mind. Beau laughed from the side and Max looked toward him. Beau smiled "So Max," he paused and walked a few steps toward Max. "I understand you have a special talent for killing." Max didn't answer. Beau had not missed the look in his eye concerning the guard. He had seen it before on many inmates. He laughed "Oh, yeah. I think that you are just as bad as I've heard you are."

Beau was in charge of the boys in the population and he knew it even if the guards didn't. Over the next two years Max was given large doses of testosterone from the illegal drug trade in the Centre, and steroids when they were available. He and Beau became friends as they exercised together every day in the gym. Max told Beau about Sandy and Stickman. He told stories that he couldn't tell someone who wasn't in prison for murder. Beau laughed but thought Max very, very scary.

Max took full advantage of his new status. He had free access to anything he wanted to read, listen to, or watch. As the drugs took effect he began to grow. He got bigger and bigger. He got stronger and stronger. He got meaner and meaner.

At age eighteen, Beau was taken from the prison for reevaluation. He was going to a military training unit or to another prison where he would be the new fish. Max might never know what happened to him. The only sure thing was that he wasn't going to return.

Max became defacto king. He stopped taking the drugs and started to exercise all the time he wasn't reading. Nobody challenged Max. He ran a tight ship, nobody picked on anyone or they had to answer to Max. They believed, with good reason, they would surely die. It just wasn't worth the chance. It was as Max had always been told 'It's good to be the King.'

Max was very unhappy four years later when it was time for him to leave. He had been in this place for six years, and while he might not like it sometimes; he knew what to expect. His thoughts went to the idea that he might see Beau in some adult prison somewhere.

He also knew that this place was going to go back to a dog-eat-dog world and his kingdom would only live in memory. He had no choice and the new King was going to be one of his people. His replacement was power hungry and a little crazy. He was not going to be an honorable leader.

At eighteen years of age Max was put into a social rehabilitation program and moved to somewhere in Florida. It turned out to be a brainwashing kind of deal and Max soon failed the course. But the secret government has a special place for boys like Max. He'll be treated well and taught to do the bidding of the secret government.

He was sent to a training camp in Utah. He turned out to be a very good soldier. He was placed in a special unit that took care of 'problems.' He spent the next three years in training and on missions. He was very highly-thought-of by his handlers.

The program was disbanded just after Max turned 21. The government no longer wanted to be in the assassination business. Max had nowhere to go except back to the job he was officially trained to do. Max was trained to be a power control technician. He had been assigned to ships at sea in his cover job and received several awards for his exceptional knowledge of the power units. He had also been in several power unit runaways or cascade situations as they are called; the fact that he survived was extraordinary, most don't get out of a single cascade alive. Max had survived three. One of the cascades happened very fast and Max was the only survivor. That weird lady was there. Max believed he had died in that cascade, he was almost sure – but here he was – alive.

With a little help from friends and his power unit expertise he was asked if he wanted to volunteer to be posted to the control team of the Science Vessel Einstein that would be launched in six months. It was a deep space probe and the mission would take three years. He would be power unit control, security augmentee and a test subject. He jumped at the chance. He was almost twenty-two years old and he was going to really get to go into space. It was what he had wanted since he could remember. Max was promoted to Sergeant; top of the game for a power unit technician.

However, he remained the lowest ranking member of the control team of six. Sergeant is also the top of the game for a security man. Four of the others have more time in grade and out ranked him. The Lieutenant is in charge. In Max's opinion the Lieutenant seemed a nice guy and runs a tight crew with a loose rein. Just like Max liked things. The members of the control team became friends quickly.

Max was the largest member of the control team, at six foot four, two hundred and eighty pounds of well trained muscle. He might kill you by breathing on you. Well that's after he has had his favorite pizza – anchovy, garlic and jalapeño. Max and the other five security agents were allowed to train together for four weeks on Earth before they were transported out to the launch site, Moon Base Alpha.

Max enjoyed the eight hour flight from Earth to the Moon. He watched out the small windows at the stars and empty space as they passed. He couldn't help but smile. His new friends on the control team kidded him a lot on the flight to Moon Base Alpha. The Lieutenant smiled at how happy Max was. It reassured him that there really was a human being somewhere down deep in the mountain sized killing machine. His friends kept kidding him about hogging the window. He would let them look out the window for a while all the time knowing they wouldn't want the use of the window long. It didn't matter he was still in space and headed for the moon; as soon as the window was unoccupied he was back looking out. He couldn't help but smile.

Max was ordered to take a seat and buckle-up before the cargo craft docked at Moon Base Alpha thirty minutes early. The Lieutenant told them they would take care of their cargo before they went to any of the establishments on the base. Max could hardly wait and he pushed his friends to hurry. They were all teasing Max about his boyish enthusiasm. He didn't care; he was about to set foot on the moon.

Within a few hours the cargo was stored and the control team was released.

CHAPTER EIGHT -
MOON BASE ALPHA
TO MARS STATION

Max's friends were in a hurry to find the bars and relax a little. Max wanted to take things a little slower, to savor the moment - so to speak. He was on the moon and he was very happy to be where he was. His whole life he'd wanted to be in space. He had held onto the idea when he was put in the Anderson Rehabilitation Centre. But when he was put in the general population the idea became much harder to hold onto so he forced it to the back of his mind in hopes of retrieving it some day. He also put the thought of a life with Sandy in the same place at the same time. He wondered where she was now. He wondered if she ever got to go into space like they had pretended. He hoped she had.

He closed his eyes as he thought, 'you have to get past this.' Stick came to mind and he repeated the thought out loud. "You have to get past this." The thoughts of his childhood were stronger than they had been in years. The thoughts of things he would never have were brought to mind just as he realized he was in space. The thought almost formed that if part of a dream could come true then maybe all of it could. He pushed the hope from his mind. It came right back.

He wanted to drown the thoughts in alcohol. This had happened before but it had never been this strong. He needed to find that bar. He followed in the direction his comrades had taken. This was a small place and surely he could catch up.

He stopped at a plaque that marked the main entrance from the port to the base. It told of the building of the Moon Base and it's completion as a military complex that started to build spacecrafts 15 years ago. It credited the success to the transporters that brought the building supplies uninterrupted from Earth. It made special note of the exceptional contributions of Commander William 'Death Dealer' Holt.

Max's mind stopped for just a second, "Didn't I meet him once, yes, when I was in Texas." Sandy and Stick were in his mind in a second and he wanted a drink very badly to hopefully take the edge off the thoughts. He needed a very large drink to get rid of the taunting memories that were just memories and would never be anything else.

That's why they haunted him they'll never be anything but memories. The times that summer in Texas were the ones he remembered when he wanted a very happy feeling. He replayed them over and over when he was in solitary. Their loss was also the source of great despair. It doesn't matter what the weird lady keeps telling him in his dreams. "She's just in my head anyway."

The base was a rough place with hard men and women who made a living building spacecrafts and structures in inhospitable places. This was where they built Mars station in four 25,000 square foot three story sections. Then Commander Holt 'herded', as he described it, those sections to Mars to be put together on the surface. Moon Base Alpha was a hard place.

Max shook his head side to side to clear the thought from his brain. He remembered that his friends were looking for the best place to have a good time and it was reported to be a brothel called Bertha's. It was said that the new brewer, Robert Kirkland, who arrived a few years back owns most of the civilian part of the station. The Kirkland brewery exports several kinds of beer to everywhere – including Earth.

They say it's the best in the system. The whiskey is reported to the very best anywhere. But current laws prevent it from being legally shipped off station. It's widely smuggled and Kirkland himself must have a lot to do with the smuggling. Why else would he own a fleet of very fast cargo crafts? The fact that the whiskey could be bought everywhere his beer could; should attest to the smuggling. The large number of credits he has is just another witness to his business sense.

Max paid the three credits to get into the bar as he looked for his friends. The attendant told him the cover was refundable for drinks. Max saw his friends and started toward the table.

It didn't take but a second for him to notice the blonde bombshell leaning on the balcony rail. He looked at her and wondered if she could possibly be worth what she was going to want to have sex with him. He didn't have to think long before she was joined by an older man. As she stood and turned to hug the man Max realized she either had a very large beer belly or she was about to drop a baby at any second. Max thought she might be the man's daughter but the kiss they shared on the lips told him she was a lover or possibly his intended. She might be his wife.

The Lieutenant came over to collect Max. "That's Kirkland and his wife. They say he'll torture you almost to death several times before he kills you if you even think of touching her."

Max laughed, "I would too."

The Lieutenant laughed, "me too."

He and his friends drank too much and spent every extra cent they had on the available ladies. Max bought every one of them he could. He was about to go on a three year mission. He wouldn't have any place to spend the money anyway. He and the team had already laid-in as many extras as they could get; it might be enough to get him to the next stop. Max and the rest of the crew had private stashes but the majority of the cargo they brought in was put on the ship under the guise of security - top secret. The contents were really for resale on the black market. It had been done this way for years. The simple fact is a black market cannot exist without some help from ship's security.

The Science Vessel (SV) Einstein was in orbit and could be seen with a telescope and on a closed circuit monitor. Max and his friends watched the S V Einstein on the monitor. Between women and as they drank they talked about their experiences to this point in their career. They showed off their charms. The half by three quarter inch tattoos on their right forearm that mark them with what they had done and what they had been trained to do. The S V Einstein was going to be their first ship. The Lieutenant was the only one of them who had been in space before. They looked forward to being awarded the first space mission charm.

They smiled as they watched their ship. It's the shape of a mushroom before the cap opens, the engines are in the stem and the cap was the crew habitat. The labs were located in various places through out the ship. Security, where Max will work, was centrally located for the best response times. Max could hardly wait for the call to go aboard the ship. The Lieutenant called their attention to another ship that was posting next to the Einstein. "That's the scientists arriving." Frank, one of the security guys asked if the scientists were going to come down to the Moon Base. The Lieutenant laughed and told him "No, they're not allowed. The force has too much invested in them to take a chance on them getting killed."

Max was half drunk the night he reported in for transport to the ship. The rest of the people in the transport were in just about the same shape. The Lieutenant was assigned a group of quarters and in turn assigned them to his men. He told them to be ready for duty at 0500.

Duty began the next morning. The ship had to be secured and checks made. Their cargo was another thing. It had to be cleared by the Lieutenant because of security reasons. A cargo man asked the Lieutenant why they had so much secret cargo. He told him that security wouldn't allow him to talk about the cargo. He accepted the answer or at least stopped asking questions.

Their day ended about seven that evening and they went to eat. After dinner they played cards and had too much to drink again but they had to get rid of the alcohol before the launch. No known alcohol except medical alcohol is allowed on ship after launch. That's the rules and they are sort of obeyed. If you have alcohol, don't tell anyone and don't get drunk; or that's how the Lieutenant told them it worked.

Max got into bed late and the last thing the Lieutenant told them before they went to their quarters was "Report to the launch room and find yourself a seat on the left side as you enter the room. Launch will be at 0530."

The computer woke him at 0400. It's too damn early. Max didn't want to move, until he thought about the coming launch. He had only gotten three hours sleep but it really didn't matter. He was now wide awake and excited about the launch. He did wish he hadn't drunk so much the night before. He took a deep breath and got to his feet. He dressed in his uniform and went to the launch room.

The small auditorium off the chow hall doubles as the launch room. It's the room that has the strongest flooring. The seats are bolted to that floor and are laid out like a commercial aircraft.

Max looked around a few seconds before he found a seat on the left side aisle, as instructed, and sat down. There weren't any seats next to his friends so he took a seat in the next row. He watched as the rest of the groups came in and found themselves seats. The seating was in rows, three wide on each side with four in the middle. There are six such rows open. A mild mannered slight fellow took the far seat next to the wall, leaving the middle seat open and Max in the aisle seat.

Max went over the crew list in his head as he looked for the Lieutenant. There are sixty people on this mission, twenty scientists, four flight crew, six members of the security squad, ten in the command crew that form the Command and Control board (CC). The medical crew is only two doctors since most of the members of the crew are well versed on the subject. They know what to do - if not the why. The rest are miscellaneous crew needed for more than one purpose.

Other crew members will be picked up on the trip, twenty scientists from Mars Station and thirty other crew members from Beta station. It's after Beta station that the mission really begins.

The scientists were the last to board. Max noticed that he was staring at one of the female scientists. She was the prettiest thing he had ever seen. She reminded him of somebody but he just couldn't place her. She looked around the room. He was staring. Where had he met her before? She stopped and stared in Max's direction. She smiled and headed straight toward him. Max knew better. Stuff like this never happened to him. She was smiling at someone else.

She stopped in the aisle next to Max. She asked "Who are you saving that seat for, Max?"

Max stood and asked "Do I know you?"

She smiled, she was not surprised. The weird lady had told her that Max had not held as tight to the promise as she had. She had been told that he might not recognize her because it would be too painful for him. The weird lady told her that Max believed he would never see her again.

Sandy smiled. "That weird lady told me you would be here and showed me an image of you. Yes, we know each other but when we last saw each other, you had an eye patch."

Max was thinking to himself as he spoke softly. "I had a computerized version put in a few years back. Who are you?"

Sandy smiled. "Remember when we ran away and froze, she said our day would come."

Then he figured it out. "Well, I'll be damned; Sandy." She smiled. What came over him next he couldn't say, but he kissed her and she kissed back. It drew a grand round of applause from the room. They were both embarrassed. They sat down and started to try to catch up.

The launch wasn't as forceful as it could have been. They weren't going to go to top speed because they couldn't slow enough to stop at Mars Station if they did. The speed chosen would take them to Mars Station in forty-six hours. After the launch the flight settled into a steady run for Mars Station. Max and Sandy were both pleased that they were finally in space, together. But, they had work to do.

This was the maiden flight of the S V Einstein and most of the crew was new; everything had to be watched very carefully. The Einstein was a new design and might have a few bugs. The problems with a new spacecraft or any other craft can be as simple as a badly routed line or as bad as a major design flaw. Max hoped this ship wouldn't have any major design flaws. Sandy was on board and he was looking forward to spending the next three years with her.

Those dreams were coming true and at the back of his mind was the Lady, the things she had said when he and Sandy had run away. How were they going to become so powerful? He didn't remember the exact words but it had something to do with King and Queen of the universe.

Max's mind got back to business; he knew the power units were going to be a problem. They always were. They are the same power unit used on Earth sea-going and near-orbit crafts. Officially they have a good record on Earth and have a few more problems in space. The unofficial record is much worse. In space, according to the power unit techs who Max had spoken to, they are just dangerous. They have to be watched all the time. Max had pinned several power units on Earth. But on Earth they had an out. They could abandon ship. In space, he didn't think that was a very good idea.

The power units themselves were the problem. They are a relatively new technology and just not right yet. The inner cylinder was a secret, Max wasn't told what was in it and he didn't believe the government knew either. The secondary shell had dozens of electronic metering and control devices. It was a very complicated electronic system. The black boxes were replaced and sent back to the factory for repair when they failed. Max didn't like the design at all. You never had any idea what was going to go wrong with the damn thing. The only way to stop it from exploding was to bleed off excess electric power so the computer could activate an onboard shut down system. Max was just happy they were not nuclear reactors. Although he would like to know what was used to produce the energy in the form of electricity.

Max and Sandy made note of how they could find each other and went their own way, to work. The parting kiss was a lot more difficult that the first spontaneous kiss after they had met again in the launch room.

Sandy knew she was going to face a world of questions from her two lab partners. It didn't matter; she still had to go to her lab. Her lab partners, James and Karen, were waiting for her to explain her action on the launch deck. In a way she was looking forward to explaining. Karen asked Sandy as soon as she walked into the lab. "So who's the hunk? I thought you were in love with some criminal." It was all in fun. The three of them knew each other well. Sandy laughed. "I'm going to marry that hunk, and he is the criminal I love."

James was shocked "That is the boy that you talk about." He made a quick 360 degree turn spinning on the toe of his left foot saying "Lord, help us."

Karen was very pleased "Maybe he could join us for dinner." Sandy nodded "Yeah, as soon as we have a schedule."

There was a lot to do on this leg of the mission. Max was busy most of the time and Sandy didn't have much time either. Max dropped by the Biology lab and talked Sandy into a late lunch, or coffee or a walk as time allowed. Neither of them had a lot of free time but what little they had they considered well spent as long as they were with each other.

Several problems occurred as they were in flight toward Mars Station, none of them big problems. However there were several problems with receivers and transmitters mounted on the outside of the hull. The posting at Mars station in twenty hours will be just in time to fix several small outer hull problems before they get bigger.

The Einstein's mission at Mars station was to drop off some food stuffs and other supplies and pick up crew. Some of the things to be dropped off were biological experiments. Sandy begged her boss, Professor Kent, to go down to Mars Station. He refused, "You're a scientist and we can't have you in harms way." She asked how going to a force station was in harms way. It was explained that the station had 140 men who hadn't seen a woman in two years. "It would just be best not to tempt them."

She was raving mad when she found Max. She told him that she hadn't gotten to go down to Moon Base Alpha and she wanted to go down to Mars Station. She reasoned that he was security, he was going down and she would be safe. He told her he couldn't take her down to the station. It was against dozens of regulations. "I've just found you again and I'm not going to take a chance on us being separated because I disobeyed the rules." He added "I'm not even sure whose permission you'd have to have or I'd ask."

Max was making arrangements with the team to go down to Mars station in just ten hours. The Lieutenant came over to him. "Let someone else do that I need you to give a small arms training class."

Max looked at him and smiled. "Are you kidding?"

He laughed, "No, Max, you're my certified trainer and the Captain ordered the class completed before we get to Mars Station."

Max smiled. "Well the class is four hours long so I better get started if I'm going to get finished before I go down to the station."

The Lieutenant handed him the list. "You better get to it then. The trainees are to be in the training room in a half hour."

Max looked at the list. "Lieutenant, why is there a scientist on this list?"

The Lieutenant laughed, "I was hoping you wouldn't notice. But it's the Captain's orders, all personnel are to be small arms certified."

Max shook his head. The Lieutenant asked what was wrong. Max smiled, "Sandy is on the list." The Lieutenant didn't understand. Max clarified, "She the scientist I've been talking too."

The Lieutenant laughed "Better you than me. Maybe you won't kill her when she starts asking for more information than necessary. You know how hard headed scientists can be about simple things." He left telling Max to "just take care of business."

Max nodded and said sarcastically as the Lieutenant walked away, "I will, sir."

Sandy was sitting at one of the tables as Max walked into the training room. He smiled and started the lesson. He called roll and started the training. Sandy was a good student. She didn't try to get too deep into why a weapon fires but just accepted the fact that it did. Things were going much better than he had expected. At first break she came up to his desk. "Thanks, I don't know how you pulled it off, but thank you very much." Max looked at her, he didn't understand.

She said. "I get to go down to Mars station if I can qualify."

Max looked at her, "Sandy, I didn't have anything to do with this." She just smiled and he knew she didn't believe him.

The class went very well and Sandy passed with 91 percent. She was whining that it was the worst grade she had ever received. Max just told her the report of the class just has pass or fail "There will be no grade."

She said, "But you gave me a 91."

He told her it was the number of rounds she put in the target - 91 out of a hundred. She laughed, "I hit it that many times."

Max laughed, "Yes, you're really very good." She kissed him. He smiled, "I don't give extra credit." She laughed.

Sandy was very pleased that she was going to get to go down to Mars Station. The mission had its tense moments. But she was armed and it went very well. She explained how the experiments were to work and what was to be reported. She did have some trouble getting the scientists to keep their eyes on her and not her weapon. The eyes of the other crew were not on the weapon but other parts of her anatomy. It was a good outcome and although the men were very attentive and tried to do everything for her, she never felt she was in any danger. One guy did ask her if she had a boyfriend; she pointed toward Max. He just nodded. "I figured you'd be taken."

They left the Mars posting on schedule ten hours after they arrived with everything fixed. Sandy was very happy. She was greatly admired by her fellow scientists. She had gotten to go on a dangerous mission and been given a weapon.

The Einstein moved slowly to launch point as everything was readied for the launch to Beta station. It was two days of getting the Einstein ready for launch before there was more than a stolen moment to talk. Over the two days, Max and Sandy ate together when they had a break at the same time. They went out of their way to see each other and talk everyday.

Before they could launch for Beta station, everything had to be tied down and long term experiments had to be stable. It was going to be a full power launch. Max was getting everyone certified on small arms, as the Captain ordered. The training was going much better than he thought it would.

When everything was stable and ready the Captain set launch for the next window, twenty four hours later. They had to check everything one more time. It didn't really matter to Max or Sandy, they were looking forward to dinner – together - tonight.

CHAPTER NINE – DINNER, DANCING, DUTY AND ...

Sandy was more than a little nervous as the time for the dinner date got closer and closer. Karen asked "What's wrong, Sandy?"

She smiled very nervously. "I know how I feel about Max but, he has never told me how he feels."

James smiled. "I think he feels the same way. It's just that he's a soldier. You know they're trained not to say four letter words like love."

Sandy nodded "We were eight years old the last time I saw him. Now he's a soldier and I'm a scientist. What are we going to talk about?"

Karen smiled "You guys talk all the time." Karen realized this was different, "Oh, the things you talk about when you're by yourselves are well... You're afraid he'll feel out of place, you know three scientists and one soldier."

James said. "I guess we could wait until later."

Sandy thought for a while and said "No, the Max I know can do anything. I need to know now the things he can't do. He's not perfect even if I do think he is. And besides he'll have to fit into my world just like I'll have to fit into his."

Max was feeling a little nervous too; although he didn't really understand why. He had met her friends and the dining was limited on the ship, the chow hall. The chow hall personnel did the best they could to decorate the place and make it more than a chow hall. He was just going to have to do this. Max picked Sandy up at her door at 1700 just as he was asked. The door was open. Karen and James were already there. Max asked "Am I late?"

Sandy smiled "no." He handed her some roses.

She said "Where did you get these on the ship?"

He laughed. "I made them. They're paper."

James asked "Where did you learn to make something so beautiful."

Max sort of laughed. "I spent a lot of time in solitary when I was in prison. I had to do something to pass the time. I learned how to make paper flowers." They laughed at the thought of a convicted murderer in solitary making paper flowers.

Max was the one dominating the conversation at dinner. He had some wild stories, most of which were true. He had been just about everywhere 'to kill someone or other.' Sandy confided in Karen. "I'm the one feeling a little like I don't have a life."

Karen asked James to get her a drink. James wasn't listening. He said. "What, sorry, I was listening to the story."

Karen laughed "He always wanted to be a soldier."

Sandy laughed "Well, as much trouble as Max seems to get into, he might get his wish."

It was 2100 when the mood changed in the dining facilities. The computer started to play some soft music so everyone could relax. Max reached for Sandy's hand. She said "What?"

He asked "Do you dance?"

She was at a loss, "Not very well."

Max joked "Good, neither do I." He made her get up and they danced.

She smiled as she realized he did know how to dance. "You lied to me. You dance very well."

He smiled "Sorry, I was a dance instructor in Turkey." She moved back a little and he said "It was a deep cover kind of thing - I can't really talk about it." She started to laugh and then he did.

Another of the security men was suddenly behind him. "I hate to interrupt this but we have a Code Silver."

It was easy to tell that Max was irritated with the news. He smiled as he nodded. "I knew this was going too well. I'll be right with you." The security man stepped back. Max said "This won't take long. I'll be back in a half hour." Max escorted Sandy back to the table excused himself and left with the security man. The security man was feeding him a lot of information. This was going to be the first time in a real situation that Max had worn a 'White suit'. It was going to be the first power unit he was going to try to pin in weightless space. The White suit isn't really white it's more of a light orange. The suit itself is designed to operate in the Jim White gravity fields. White also designed the suit, thus the name. It allows the wearer to operate just as if he is in gravity.

Max had worn one before in training and he didn't really like it. The suit does let you operate just like you're not in space but it feels like you're floating and tied in place at the same time. It's a very weird feeling and he had been told it was sort of nauseating the first few times. He had heard it described as getting use to line bifocals. He didn't wear glasses but in training they had performed the experiment and they were close to right about the feeling. However the bifocals were for just a second. The feeling in the White suit continued as long as you were in the White Gravity fields.

White really didn't invent anything. He just put the north pole of an electro magnet in the floor and the south pole in the ceiling. The walls being negative as far as magnetism are non players. It's a good working system and better than floating around trying to fix something. Max just wishes it had been one of the power units on the spinning gravity area that failed first. He would have felt better about his chances to stop it from exploding. This is a new game for him.

Max preferred the rotating spinning motion that the habitation ring used to produce gravity. You didn't have to wear one of these White suits and it just felt more normal. But he would deal with what he had. That which is – is.

The magnetism is disruptive to AC and DC electricity; special shielding had to be developed to fix the problem. It turned out that the shielding was a lie. White just housed the outputs and conduits in a version of his gravity room and set it to normal gravity. It works but the DC outputs are much easier to understand. White Gravity rooms are very interesting. Max always thought it should be a carnival ride.

White gravity areas are restricted. No material that reacts to magnetism is allowed unless cleared. The White rooms were equipped with everything you needed. Max found the coffee cups intriguing. They would sit on the tables and other furnishings but they had a straw that came from the bottom of the cup and any liquid had to be sucked from the cup. The funniest part of the cups was that you have to blow back into the straw or the siphoning action you created to get the liquid out would continue and empty the cup. The liquid would float in the air. Then you had to chase the floating blob around until you caught and contained it. Max had to smile as he remembered the video they had shown them. The guy had let the cup empty as he laughed at the odd happening. He didn't have near as much fun catching the blob. Food in the area was limited to finger foods.

Sandy watched them leave and then sat down at the table with James and Karen. Professor Kent came over and sat down. "Ladies and James," They laughed at the very tired joke and he continued. "We need to go quietly. The power unit in White room six is going critical. There is an expert headed that way right now but we need to be there to shut the computer down when he gets it back to a safe point." Sandy smiled. "Max." She laughed.

Max was just finishing getting into the White suit when Sandy came into the outside room. He laughed. "So this is your bag too."

She laughed "Yeah, aren't you nervous?"

He shook his head "nah, if I don't get this right no one will ever know because this whole ship is going to blow. If I get it right we won't tell them." Sandy thought it disturbing; but he was correct. He went into the room.

James asked. "Professor, what does he have to do? I know what we do out here but I have never thought about the guy inside. I never knew the guy inside."

The Professor said, sort of tongue in cheek, "Well, James, as we know the main voltage regulator inside the power unit has failed and the secondary one is going to fail very shortly. He has to run a sixteenth inch diameter tungsten wire through an eighth inch diameter hole that is four inches long. And connect it to a ground on the other side. The wire can't be there in normal operation; the power unit will not fire if it is. He has to do that without touching the wire to the sides of the hole."

Sandy added "if he touches the sides he gets a bad shock. It is not strong enough to kill him and it will cause the power unit to fail faster and… well, we won't have to worry about it."

Professor Kent continued. "Once the wire is through and grounded; the power unit bleeds off the excess power through an external larger voltage relay box that he took in with him. When power levels get back to the safe range we can use the computer to shut it down. If he doesn't get the wire connected correctly then the safety device turns into a detonator and will drop and touch the case and the power will be shifted too fast." He checked the readouts before he added. "The wire is strong enough to hold the safety device above the case ground for a short time. After that it'll break and the power unit will explode."

The professor began to babble as much to himself as the others because they already knew what he was telling them. He was watching the readouts as he spoke. "The obvious question here is why don't they put the larger voltage regulators in the case to start with? They won't fit and that is why the safety device can reach the bottom of the case as well. The other reason is because, it is a progressive type failure – the first regulator fails at a certain voltage and the second takes over at the same voltage that is still getting higher. That sounds an alarm; a heavier duty external regulator is then attached to the connector and that hopefully gives the computer time to shut the power unit down so the regulators can be replaced. The external regulators are always damaged and have to be rebuilt." The Professor paused and then asked. "How many times has he done this?"

The Security Lieutenant smiled "Relax, he's the best, he's done this dozens of times in practice and." He clicked on the mike. "Max, how many times have you done this for real?" Max answered "This'll be thirteen. Some people say that's an unlucky number."

The job was done in less than twenty minutes. The computer shut the, now under control, power unit down in about the same amount of time. Max told the Lieutenant "You owe me. I told you it wouldn't be a week."

The Lieutenant laughed "They're on the way to your quarters as we speak." He added. "I guess I may as well pay off the other bet too."

Max smiled "No, I'll pay off on that bet. I'll bring it up tomorrow."

The Lieutenant smiled. "ok." He could only guess why.

After the power unit was shut down, only the clean up work remained. James and Karen told Sandy they'd take care of the clean-up. Max was finishing up the paper work when she spoke to him from the security office door "Are you about done?"

He smiled "Yes, are you?"

She smiled "They told me I could go."

He smiled "We're supposed to be passing close to some nebula. It's supposed to be beautiful. Do you want to go have a look?"

Sandy smiled as she nodded. "I think so. Can you tell me about the other bet, the one you said you would pay off?"

Max laughed. "I can do that." As they walked Max asked "What would you like to know?"

She asked "Was I part of the bet?"

Max said "In a way. The bet was who would get laid first." If the lights had been brighter Max would have seen Sandy blush.

She said "And somebody else already has."

Max laughed "Probably, but not that I know of, or the bet applied too."

She said "So, why are you paying off the bet?"

Max stopped, he turned and looked at her "Are you saying you want to be part of a bet."

She smiled. "I'm not going to be part of a bet, Max. That's not what we have. But since I'm planning on staying the night with you anyway..." She paused "and I know about the bet." She paused again. "I wouldn't mind helping you win."

Max smiled "Let's go look at the stars."

She asked "Is that a no, Max?"

Max spoke softly "I still want to see this thing and then I'll show you my quarters."

She held his hand and they walked. Max spoke softly "You know I have been engaged to this girl for fourteen years."

Sandy laughed and retrieved a chain that she wore around her neck. She pulled it out of her top and showed the Cracker Jack ring to Max "And she still has the ring you gave her." They laughed and she added "It's too small now, and it turns my finger green, but I still have it."

They walked on to see the stars. The observation area only held ten people and they had to wait a few minutes to get a look. The computer spoke. "Please limit your viewing to ten minutes so others can view the nebula. Thank you." After a while they were allowed into the observation area. As they watched the computer spoke "no one else is waiting to see the nebula, please take your time." It wasn't long before they were the only ones in the room.

Sandy sat on Max's lap and kissed him "Can we go see your quarters now? I'm getting a little nervous."

Max smiled "You need to be sure about this. You know we can't take it back."

She smiled "No, I don't know."

Max said "Sandy, I'm not real sure about this." She wasn't happy to hear that. He sensed her anger "What I mean is this time it matters to me. The other times," He paused in thought "The girls were just something to do. This time it's different. I…"

She smiled "You feel something."

He nodded "Yeah."

She smiled. "I'm sorry I was getting mad about the wrong thing. I thought you didn't want me; not that you WANT me."

Max was concerned. "Sandy, is this love? I don't know. I've never felt like this, except with you; and that was a long time ago. It started again as soon as I saw you."

She kissed him again and said. "When it comes to you I have always loved you."

Max smiled "So I guess I love you. This is scary."

She laughed "I scare you."

Max laughed "Yes, very much."

The mood changed to a more serious tone. "Max, I'm going to scare you worse." She took a deep breath. "I just kissed you for the fourteenth time."

Max didn't understand. "You keep count."

She smiled. "I have never kissed anyone more than once."

Max thought for a second "You're twenty two years old and you have never." He realized what she was saying. "Never."

She sprang to her defense. "Max, I'm not weird or anything. I just never had time." Max kissed her again and run his hand up her side and to her breast. She pushed it away.

She was breathing heavy. "Max, let's go to your quarters." He kissed her again. She said "Now Max, before my legs pop apart and we have to do it right here."

Max smiled "We would get higher odds on the bet that way." She laughed. Then Max started to laugh. They made it back to his quarters.

She teased "What happens to the odds when you find a virgin?"

Max kissed her. "I don't know. You're the first."

Max showed Sandy many ways to do things before they finally won the bet if they had been playing. Sandy was lying cuddled up to Max. She said. "I sure hope there are some abbreviated versions of what we just did, or we are never going to get any sleep."

Max laughed. "I love you Sandy, God help us both."

She laughed. "I love you too, Max. Do you know what?"

Max didn't "no, what?"

She was serious. "I always knew this was our destiny. Max, do you ever think about that night when we had that weird dream. Do you think we were dead and that lady made us go back?"

Max smiled. "You told me the lady told you I was going to be on this trip."

She was a little upset. "Yeah, she talks to me a lot. Do you think I'm crazy?"

Max laughed. "No, she talks to me a lot too." Sandy kissed him and he laughed as he grabbed her. "I'm just glad I didn't get killed before we got to this destiny." She giggled.

The computer woke Max at 0400. "Good morning Max. You have duty starting at 0530." Sandy asked about her duty schedule. She was told 0700. They had been asleep but a few hours. Within a few minutes there was knock on the door. Max answered it. It was the Lieutenant. He handed Max the dozen eggs "here you go." Sandy was still in the bed. She turned over and adjusted the cover. The Lieutenant smiled. "I guess you won that bet too."

Max said "no, I told her about the bet so, I'll pay up. Just a minute." He went over to get the pint of Kirkland's best whiskey from his dresser drawer.

The Lieutenant laughed as he took the whiskey. "Ok, see you at 0530."

Max closed the door and put the eggs on the desk. He dug out a hot plate a skillet and some bacon. Sandy was starting to doze back off when the smell of the bacon found its way to her nose. She sat up in the bed sniffing. "What is that?"

Max said "Bacon and eggs." He got a toaster out and plugged it in to toast the bread.

She warned "You're going to have the cops over here in seconds using all that power."

Max laughed. "I, ah." His beeper went off. He answered the mike "Dent."

The voice on the other end of the line, "We have, an electrical surge, somewhere on seven. Please check it out."

Max answered. "I'll check it out." He turned on his monitoring equipment,

It began to look for the surge. The equipment began its automated search. Max continued to cook. When he was done he turned the hotplate off. The equipment looking for the surge stopped. He called in. "The surge has disappeared. I was unable to locate the cause. I'll monitor the circuit." Sandy was laughing.

Sandy put one of Max's shirts on and was in awe at how easy Max had gotten away with the over use of power. Max said "There are some plates in that drawer and silverware in the one under it." He added "oh, and little packs of jelly and butter in the silverware drawer. Get me a couple of grape, will you please?"

She started to laugh. "I always thought we scientists had the good stuff. Max, I haven't seen bacon in years."

They had a very nice breakfast. Max told her he had to go to work. He kissed her "You look nice in my shirt. But, if you want you can push some of my stuff together and keep some of your stuff here."

Somehow she knew that this was the first time Max had ever invited anyone to do that. She smiled. "I might just do that." He told her he had to wash her plate if she was done. She told him. "I'll take care of the plates." Max kissed her, closed the door behind him and reported to work.

Sandy smiled "Mom always said good things come to those who wait." She almost laughed. She cleaned the dishes, and started to her quarters to get ready for work. Then she noticed that her necklace was missing. She looked for it for several minutes but finally had to give up. She planned to spend a lot of time in these quarters. "I'll find it later."

CHAPTER TEN - INSPECTIONS

Sandy was almost ready to leave for work from her quarters when there was a knock on her door. It was Karen. "I guess you had a good night!"

They laughed. Sandy told her "I had the time of my life."

Karen said. "I think it's about time. I was beginning to worry." She paused. "Now, I know you're in love but is he?"

Sandy was happy to share the great news. "Yes, he told me so."

Karen was very happy for her and they hugged. "I'm so happy for you. Now what happened this morning? Did he do something special?"

Sandy said. "I don't think so. I mean it was special for me but I think it was just normal for him."

Karen asked. "Would he have known it was special for you?"

Sandy laughed "He cooked real bacon and real eggs with toast and butter and jelly. Yeah, he would have known it was special."

Karen was awestruck and said with a bit of envy in her voice "real bacon and real eggs."

Sandy smiled. "I even cracked one of the eggs." Sandy told her some more of the story as they started to work.

Karen said "You forgot your bag."

Sandy smiled "That's for later I'm moving some stuff to Max's"

Karen cautioned "You should be very sure about something like that."

Sandy said. "I have never been more positive about anything." They walked on to work and talked.

Max came by about ten, he was on break. "Do you get a break?"

She smiled at the sight of him. "Yes, this is going to take a while, so how about now."

Max handed her the necklace. "This was hooked on my belt somehow. Those guys didn't cut me any slack either."

They laughed. She said. "We have coffee, well, instant."

Max said. "Just hot water and I have four donuts. James, Karen would you like to have one?"

James was the first to answer "Yes," he paused "You wouldn't happen to have a raspberry filled in there would you."

Max looked at James. "What do you think I am, a magician?"

James sort of smiled "Well, I'll take whatever you have but - you know."

Max handed him a raspberry filled doughnut. "I am a magician."

Sandy said. "Well, you better have a chocolate glazed in that bag then."

Karen said "two would be better."

Max took the lemon filled out of the bag and said as he handed the bag to the girls. "Yep, I have two chocolate glazed left."

Professor Kent entered the room. "Max, I thought I heard you in here."

He smiled and continued "Well, those doughnuts are black market. They only make 24 a day. They're not cheap."

James reluctantly said "You could have part of mine." Kent laughed. "That's all right. I don't like them."

Max opened the Earl Grey tea bag and put it in the hot water. Max said "Professor Kent, could I talk to you a minute?" They stepped to the side and spoke quietly.

Kent smiled "What could I possibly have that you would want to trade for some of that tea?"

Max smiled "Access to some equipment I need to use."

Kent asked "And what do I get for the trouble?"

Max handed him a small bag "One of these each day for the next 24 days."

The professor opened the bag and looked inside to find an Earl Gray tea bag and two packets of honey. He laughed. "Who do I have to kill?" Max took him out of sight of the others and handed him another bag, and an envelope. He whispered so the others couldn't hear. The professor laughed "and if I need more?"

Max said. "I'll do the best I can." The professor left after getting a cup of hot water. The four finished their break and Max told them he had to leave. Sandy followed him to the door. He kissed her and then gave her a small box. "This is really hard to get, and it may be stale. So, I hope you enjoy the effort I put into getting it; if not the product."

Max left and Sandy opened the box. She laughed out loud. She took one of the four pieces of bubble gum out of the box and put the rest in her pocket. She told James and Karen. "This used to be my favorite. We were just eight and sometimes didn't have any money. Max would steal it for me." She laughed. "He always was a criminal." They went back to work. The bubble gum was stale but after a few very hard chews it started to soften.

That afternoon Professor Kent came into the lab. He gathered the three around him. "I was just invited to a meeting tomorrow at ten. I need each of you to form your thoughts on shutting the auxiliary power units down and checking them to make sure they are all to specs. Security or power unit control, Max I think, wants to try to stop another power unit breach if possible. It would mean some inconvenience on the part of the labs. Check your mail for the proposed schedule. I think we are going to be stuck with the inspections so this meeting is more to minimize the impact."

Later that afternoon Professor Kent called Sandy into his office. "You are excused to go make the Earth call you requested." She was hoping it wouldn't be her turn until tomorrow. But today was as good a time as any to tell Mom about Max's return. "She's going to have a fit." She muttered to herself as she went to make the call. Sandy was glad that the calls were one way, more like a letter than a call. She had ten minutes to talk and then at the last seconds tell Mom about Max. Yeah, that's a good plan. And it would take a week to get an answer back. Her mother had never answered before but the news of Max's return to her life just might get her to call back.

The professor was right about the inspections, they were going to happen. The schedule was changed to make the best of things. It would take six weeks to finish all the inspections. They will be over the asteroid belt between Mars and Jupiter and almost to Beta station at the edge of the Kuiper asteroid belt by that time.

The only good thing about it was Sandy and Max would be on the same schedule for that six weeks. She would be assisting him. Max arranged for the use of larger quarters and they moved into them. He told her. "We may have to give these quarters back when we pick up more crew at Beta station in a couple of months."

She was surprised. "I didn't know we were going to stop."

Max told her they were but it was a secret of sorts and she shouldn't say anything. "It's best if it just stays a rumor for now." She agreed and told him she would keep it to herself. He explained to her it was to be a kind of upper. Everybody is going to get cabin fever, so about two weeks out of Beta station; it'll be announced ship wide.

The inspections went well until, there is always and 'until.' The reserve power unit in the game room was checked expecting to find nothing just like the rest. Sandy shut it down and Max made the inspection. Max laughed "It's a good thing this one is down." He showed Sandy the bad pin placement. It didn't mean the power unit was bad but if it went bad it couldn't be stopped. It would explode. The safety apparatus was installed incorrectly. They tagged it out and made note not to return it to service. They even removed the hot wire and fuses from the unit. The rest of the power units were ok, the project was deemed a success because of the one bad unit. But everybody knew that it didn't mean they were out of the fire - just safe for now.

There had been two power unit failures over the six week inspection period. The week after the inspections were finished the next reactor failed. It almost started a cascade. Max didn't have to explain how dangerous a cascade could be. The ship would explode. No one had ever stopped a cascade once it started. They as well as everyone on board knew that a lot of people die in a cascade on a sea craft on Earth. In space it was a death sentence for the ship and all aboard.

Six months after leaving Earth the Einstein was now two weeks out of Beta station. Everyone was getting - just a little nuts. The plague of bad power units had settled down to a failure about once a week. Max and Sandy seemed to always save the day, but it was not fun having a constant possibility of death. They didn't notice, they didn't notice much of anything. They were just getting deeper and deeper in love. Sandy's mother hadn't written back and from what Sandy told Max it wasn't unusual. Most of the goodies were gone because two people were enjoying them. Max told her it would never happen again. It didn't change the fact that they had to eat in the chow hall like everyone else. In fact, the security personnel were all just about out of everything. It was going to be a long dry spell until they got to Beta station. The good thing about it was they weren't disgusted with the chow hall food because they hadn't been eating there.

CHAPTER ELEVEN –
BIG CHANGES

When Max got to work the next morning he was called in to see the Lieutenant. He started to report in but the Lieutenant just told him to have a seat. "Max, I'm going to be getting off at Beta station. I'm being assigned to security there. I knew this when I signed on for this trip, so it's no surprise." The look on the Lieutenant's face told Max there was a 'but.'

He waited for the other shoe to drop. The Lieutenant continued. "I'll be replaced by another officer. I know her by reputation and talks with friends who have had to deal with her. Let me just say that she is a stickler for the rules."

Max nodded "Just what does that mean?"

He laughed. "What it means is this. You're going to have to be more careful. She will not put up with you and Sandy shacking-up in confiscated quarters. I suggest you file intent with the girl and file for the quarters. That should solve the problem. My replacement will not like it but there'll be nothing she can do about it."

Max told him. "I have been thinking about that." A knock at the door broke the conversation. "Max, I have to take this, you watch yourself with my replacement. She's a real bitch."

Max stood and the Lieutenant opened the door. It was the ship's Captain and his aide. "Attention!" The room snapped to.

Captain William Holt stepped in and mumbled "As you were" like it was an unpleasant duty he would like to avoid. After talking to the Lieutenant for a few seconds, he turned his attention to Max. "I understand they call you Max instead of Sergeant Dent."

Max had never talked to anyone of this rank before. "Yes sir."

The Captain smiled "Well, be that as it may, I want to tell you how pleased I am that you're in your current position. It seems that you have kept this ship from exploding at least a dozen times. There will be an awards ceremony as soon as they get the broadcast systems ready. I want you to know we have noticed your effort." He looked around the room and said to the Lieutenant. "Could you excuse us please?"

The Lieutenant left and in just a few seconds Max and the ship's Captain were alone. Max was going to have to talk to him. The Captain smiled. "Max, please sit." Max did and the Captain did as well. "Max I need to know what your intentions are toward my niece."

Max was surprised. "Sandy is your niece. I mean sir, I didn't know." The Captain laughed. "Just relax, Max. We met when you were just a boy but I doubt you remember. And please answer the question."

Max was sort of in shock. "Well, sir, I was thinking of asking her to file." He paused and added, "I sort of remember meeting you but I wasn't sure it was you until just now."

The Captain smiled and disregarding Max's memory, continued. "I'm sure she'll agree, and I'm equally sure that your intentions are honorable." He laughed, "toward Sandy anyway."

He stood. Max started to stand. But the Captain told him to remain seated. The Captain sat down on the desk. "Max, you should consider that we have removed our rank. What I am going to say now is off the record."

Max said "Yes sir."

The Captain asked him to call him "Bill."

Max said. "I think I will stick with sir, sir."

Bill laughed "Very well. We're getting a new Lieutenant at Beta station. I don't like her and she is being shoved down my throat so I need some leverage. I need a man on the inside." Max had heard about this kind of stuff. The new Lieutenant is an administrative spy. She is not here to do the job she is assigned, but to check up on the command crew; something no Captain likes.

Max said. "I'll do whatever I can, sir."

Bill told him he wanted him to keep the "special services" going and gave him the name of a third in command who would help as much as possible "The black market is essential to the morale of a ship, especially on a trip of this length." He added. "I do have some reservations about the latest development." He laughed. "Why are you requesting that fertilized chicken eggs be made available to you at Beta Station?

Max said. "How did you find out about that?" Bill looked at him. Reluctantly Max said "I was going to hatch them so there would be eggs available for the entire trip."

Bill asked "Where are you going to keep them?" Max told him there would be enough room in the hold as supplies started to be used. Bill studied a while. What are you going to feed them?"

Max sort of smiled, "I was hoping to get scraps from the chow hall. I'm told they will eat just about anything."

The Captain nodded. "They will and I think that's a good idea. When will they start to lay?"

Max said "I'm told this species will start to lay eggs at ten weeks."

Bill laughed "What the hell. This is my last run anyway. Max, you and Sandy need to come by administration and file intent. It'll make it a lot easier." Max assured him they would. Bill nodded "rank back on." Max nodded. The Captain said "This is an order. My niece is not to know of our relationship. She doesn't remember me either and I want to keep it that way for a while. That may not have been clear. She is not to know that I am her uncle."

Max responded "Yes sir."

The Captain opened the door and asked "Are they ready?" "Yes sir" was the answer.

The Captain walked out and his aide told Max to wait. It was just a few minutes before three other people arrived, Sandy, James and Karen. Sandy said. "Max, are you getting an award?" Max said. "I think so."

She took him aside. "I was told in no uncertain terms that we need to go to admin and file intent."

Max nodded "Me too, so would you marry me?"

She smiled and said "oh, yeah. But let's just file intent first."

The room was small and the aide heard. The aide said. "I'll inform the Captain." Karen and James were very pleased and everyone hugged. Max didn't care for the hugging but he was polite.

The door opened a few minutes later. The group was escorted to their places. The room was called to attention as the Captain came in and the meeting began. The first order of business was to announce the plan to stop at Beta station. The rumors now confirmed; cheers could be heard from all over the ship. The awards were next. The scientist received a Legion of Merit. Max couldn't expect anything that prestigious; he was too low in rank. He was going to get a certificate of some kind.

The Captain put the room at ease. "Sergeant Dent, as much as anyone else on this stage, has done unbelievable things to keep this ship in space and not spread all over space." There was a short laugh. The Captain continued. "I have two awards for Sergeant Dent; they will be bestowed on him at the same time." The call came "Attention to orders, this citation is to accompany the award of the Legion of Merit to Administrative Sergeant..." Did Max hear that correctly? Did he say Legion of Merit? You have to be a level six to be eligible for a Legion of Merit. Wait a second, did he say Administrative Sergeant? What is that? The next he realized Sandy was on one side of him and the Captain on the other. They were pinning on his new stripes.

It's an old custom to have ones spouse help pin on your new stripes. This was getting weird. The CC3 Mike Hall congratulated Max. "Max, I'm to help you in your special mission as much as possible."

Max smiled "Thank you sir. I'll try not to have to call on you."

CC3 Hall laughed "Anytime A S Dent." Sandy noted that they were now the same level, level 6. Max was still having a hard time with the promotion. He asked CC3 Hall "I didn't know that a power unit technician could be promoted above Sergeant."

Hall smiled. "Administrative Sergeant is a special rank. You are the fifth A S in the Force, the only one active in that rank and the first A S just pinned it on you." Max smiled, "The Captain?" He was told that was correct. Max's mind flashed, the first A S was the Death Dealer. He remembered for sure now. He had met the Captain before.

Over the next few days Sandy and Max filed a three month letter of intent. That amounted to a practice Marriage, three months was as long as they could extend the first practice. Max was still full of questions about his new rank. The Lieutenant helped him set up his office, get him enrolled in some classes and start his flight training. This was what the Captain meant by a man on the inside.

On the first night of the training Max brought home nine technical manuals. He and Sandy were working a split shift. It was twelve hours in which Max worked eight and Sandy worked eight, there was a four hour overlap when both Max and Sandy were on duty. Max was asleep on the bed with the books scattered on the floor when Sandy came home. She woke him with a kiss. He grabbed her and rolled her over in the bed. She squealed. He kissed her again. She said. "I thought you were studying."

Max said. "I'm going to read them again, but I think I know what's in them now."

Sandy sat up in the bed. "Max, this is important."

Max seemed surprised "What's wrong?"

She said "You can't tell me that you know everything in those books after reading them one time." She looked at the nine thick books "In fact I don't believe you could have read them all even one time."

Max laughed "Why would I lie?" She picked up one of the manuals and opened it. She's a very quick reader. She read a couple of paragraphs and asked Max a question. Max answered it by telling her there was a problem between two of the books. "That manual over there on page 345 paragraph 3, third line down doesn't say the same thing as the one you're holding."

She stopped him. "Max, how can you remember that?" She checked the book. "Damn Max." She stared at him.

She laughed when he asked "Doesn't everybody?" She said "No, what you have is a photographic memory. I knew a girl in college who had one. But she could just remember facts. She couldn't link them to other things she had read."

Max took his time answering "So, if I'm some kind of freak let's not tell anyone, ok?"

She shook her head "How many books do you have in your head?" What she expected and the answer she got were very different.

Max answered very quickly almost without thought. "42,897 although some are incomplete from around the time of that summer we met."

She sat without saying a word. She took a deep breath. "Max, how many normal steps is it from our front door to your new desk?"

Max again answered without thought. "931, why?"

She sat quietly for a while. "Max have you ever had your IQ checked?"

Max laughed "No, it's not something they looked for in my line of work. Are you sure that everybody can't do this stuff." She assured him that he was the only one she knew who could do 'this stuff.'

She asked "Do you remember the book that you gave me when we were eight?"

Max smiled. "Yes."

She said "It was about three horses."

Max nodded. "Yes, I remember." She asked him to read it to her, and he did, every word.

When he was finished she told him that "It might be a good idea not to tell anyone about your gift."

Max said. "You bet I won't. I didn't know everyone couldn't do it and I damn sure don't want to be weird." They laughed. Max said "You're not just feeding me a line are you?"

She laughed "No Max, you are very special."

He said. "I knew that." He kissed her and they found the place they were, before the conversation started. He noted once more after they started to kiss. "This photographic memory thing does explain a lot of things." She just told him to kiss her.

Max had no trouble completing the course of study in the minimum time. The shuttle simulator was a little different, he figured it out after three days, and finished the course. He would receive training on the actual craft when they reached Beta Station. He also taught Sandy, James and Karen to fire other weapons than what the Captain had ordered them trained to fire. To James it was a great adventure.

A week out of Beta station Max woke from a sound sleep. He lay there quietly for a while. Then Sandy woke. She was quiet for a while as well. Then they felt it – The thing that had wakened them - a burst of speed. Sandy exclaimed "damn, a cascade"

Max blew out a deep breath. "I love you Sandy with every fiber of my body and mind."

Sandy assured him "and I love you Max with all I have."

The calls started. It was a scary call "Code Gold, all technicians to their station." Then the scariest part, "This is the Captain. We are in cascade failure. All crew to their appointed place and shut this thing down." Max and Sandy were out of bed and dressed in seconds and away to their stations. They kissed at the door telling each other "see you later." Hoping there would be a later.

Max could still feel the ship accelerating and then slowing. He went straight to the main power flow and shut it off. It wouldn't stop the cascade but it did shut the flow of electrical power between the power units off and only allowed the fuel the power unit was generating to be used. The computer techs were shutting the non-critical power units down as fast as possible.

Cascades are a death sentence for any ship. But, in space it's a death sentence for the crew as well. Max had been in two cascades on Earth. The standard procedure is to abandon ship. But that was a ship on the sea. Max was almost sure it didn't apply to a spacecraft. It was a very intense twenty minutes before the power units that could be shut down had been. There were four left and there was no time. This is when the order to abandon ship would be given on the sea. Three were going into failure and the main unit was building to an explosion. It would take longer for the main unit to explode now but it was going to happen unless someone stopped it. Max yelled on the talkie to contact the other members of his crew. He was short two men to do the pinning. He remembered the Captain was charmed with an angel. He had pinned a power unit before. He hoped Sandy could take care of the other one. "This is Max I have three units that need to be pinned. I don't have time. Bill could you get the one on four. Sandy pin the one on six and I'll take the one on seven. Sandy it is just like threading a needle." Sandy was right back. "I'm on my way." Bill was on the talkie soon after. "I thought that was Captain." Max laughed. "I figure we're going to die and I just wanted to call a Captain by his first name one time." Bill was back on the talkie laughing "On my way Max and may the Angels watch over us all." Sandy smiled and said softly to herself, "and The Mist be with us."

Professor Kent went to help the Captain, Karen to help Sandy and James to help Max. No one thought they were going to fix this. It had never been done before. There was a lot of chatter over the talkie. It had been a long time for Bill and this was Sandy's first live show. Max began to sing a round as Bill and Sandy listened "row, row, row your boat." He yelled over the talkie for the others to join in and they reluctantly did. The power units were pinned without much of a problem. Although it was an intense twelve minutes. The computer technicians were left to do their jobs.

Max ordered everyone to the main power unit. They ran down the hall and cussed the slow elevators. They arrived in the main power unit room almost at the same time. The computer technician on duty was sitting on the floor. "It's too late. It started to feed on itself." The secondary alarm was already going, screaming in a wavering tone. This would be the time to abandon ship and swim like hell on the open sea but... Bill was first to see the pin was dropping. "It looks like this is over. Good try Max." Max said "It's not over till the damn thing blows."

Sandy had almost lost one of her shoes and she was trying to put it back on but instead she threw it at Max "Damn, don't you ever give up?"

Max laughed. "Bill, ah Captain. Would you be interested in performing an old fashion until death do you part marriage this afternoon?"

He said. "Captain, I hope that means you figured a way out of this."

Sandy threw her other shoe at Max. She laughed. "until death do you part? This afternoon, ok."

Max was sitting on the floor taking off his shoes "give me your shoes."

The Captain started to take off his shoes as he laughed realizing what Max was going to try. "Until death do you part this afternoon?" Max burned one of his hands pretty bad stuffing the shoes into the power unit. The shoes were fire proof, they would insulate the drop and maybe, just maybe they would hold up long enough for the computer to take hold and shut the thing down.

It was a tense few minutes as Max pinned the power unit while the shoes were keeping it from exploding. The time stretched to twelve minutes before the alarm changed from red to yellow. They held their breath as the temperature dropped and the readings came back to norm. The alarms stopped and the light changed to green. It was a few minutes later that the power for the entire ship shut down. It was quiet as death in the ship until the echoes of the crew yelling that they were alive. Max, Sandy and Bill were sitting there in the dark and they started to laugh. It was a nervous laugh. Bill said. "I haven't felt so alive in years."

Sandy said. "Max, are we still getting married this afternoon?"

Max laughed. "You damn right. Until death do we part?"

The Captain laughed. "I have a book on how to do that, 1600 ok. We should be on reserve power by then"

The Captain ordered the ship into recovery mode as the emergency lighting began to illuminate the halls. Max was ordered to sick bay for his burns. But he wrapped his hand and went to check on his crew. While he was wrapping his hand Sandy noticed that the Captain's hand was bleeding. She asked if he had cut his hand. He laughed as he looked at his hand and told her that he had lost part of a little finger 'somewhere in this mess.' Max told her to go to sick bay. She had burnt the side of her head. She didn't go to sick bay either. She went to check on her crew. The Captain wrapped his hand to stop the bleeding and got back to running the ship. It was some time later that Max went up to get Sandy and they went to sick bay.

The wedding was the best. They dined on cold sandwiches and water. That's all there was. They were glad to be alive. They made solemn promises, "until death do us part." Max even had a ring. It was just like the one she wore around her neck. But it was gold, not gold colored. He had traded professor Kent twenty-four Earl Grey tea bags with honey to take the plating off several pieces of jewelry to make the gold ring. It wasn't going to turn Sandy's finger green. The jewels were not real. He explained that he was going to get the real ones when they got to Beta Station. She told him it didn't matter.

It took twenty-six hours to get the ship back under full control. But, they were two days ahead of schedule. Max and Sandy were not scheduled for duty the next day. They spent most of the day in their quarters. Late in the afternoon the Captain came by. The knock on the door was a surprise. But to open it and see the Captain standing there was almost enough to take your breath. Max invited him in and Sandy said "It's nice to see you again, Captain." She smiled "Did they find your finger?"

He laughed. "No, I guess I'll just have to get along without it." He smiled "I brought a bottle of wine. I'm told it's custom." He smiled, "and there is no alcohol allowed on board so I think we need to get rid of it." Max took the wine and sat it on the table.

The Captain asked. "Max, could I speak to Sandy a few minutes, alone?"

Max smiled "Of course. I'll go check with the office."

After Max left Sandy asked Bill to sit down and he did. He put an old candy box on the table. "I have something I'd like to show you." He opened the box and took out some pictures "people say I should put these in an album but I like them in the box." Sandy wasn't at ease. She didn't know what was happening and she didn't like it. The Captain picked through the pictures and found one. He smiled and handed it to Sandy "This is me when I was two, I'm holding my new baby sister, Carol." He had several school pictures. He explained as they looked at the pictures. "These are of me and my sister as we grew through school." He handed her another picture "This is the last time I saw her." Sandy thought the woman looked familiar. He continued "Before I went back to the Space Force to haul cargo. She married some guy named Sam Franks." He looked at Sandy and asked "You ever heard that name?"

She was a little scared and kind of stumbled over the words "Yes, my father's name was Sam Franks, but I don't remember him as well as I would like."

Bill said. "My sister's name is Carol, as I said and we used to write. She lived in El Paso, Texas." He handed her another picture.

She laughed just to look at it. It was her and Max sitting on the steps of the apartment in Texas.

She said with some question "So, you are my uncle."

He said "If you'll have me."

She asked "Are you the one who got me into that school, the Death Dealer?"

He smiled. "I was called that once and I did what I could. But you were smart enough on your own to get into that school. You just needed a sponsor. I must add that the fighting was not helpful. I had to call in a lot of favors to keep you in school." She laughed.

Max opened the door slowly and said. "I'm back. Is that ok?"

Sandy laughed "Come look at these pictures."

Max went over and sat down. She said "You knew, didn't you?"

Max questioned "Knew what?"

Bill said "It's alright Max, I told her." Max opened the bottle of wine that Bill had brought and poured the contraband liquor into some glasses. They talked and reminisced for almost an hour.

Bill didn't want to leave but he had put off business as long as he could. "I'm going to have to get back to work. But before I leave I wanted to tell both of you something." He paused a minute and then started. "Well, here it is. This thing we just went through is going to cause some problems. It's never been done before. Everybody wants to reward us in a very special way. As a result I've been put on the Admirals list. I'm now promotable." He paused. "Sandy, you are now eligible to take the Professors test." He laughed "Max, well, I don't know just what to tell you." He reached over and touched Max's shoulder, "Boy, you may be promoted to Ensign. You would have to pass the test, but from what I've seen that's not going to be a problem. We don't know just what is going to be done but, it's going to get strange. In the Force they like things to go smooth, and this is not." Bill added

"I have work to do and I know you both have first watch. So I'll say good night. This is just a heads up." The Captain left.

Max told Sandy that he didn't want to be an Ensign. She laughed. "Well, I want to be a Professor and if I go up a rank it would be best if you did too."

Max shook his head "I don't know if I even like Class Six yet."

She laughed "Poor baby, is your career going up too fast?"

Max laughed "As long as I can still work on power units then I'll be alright."

She laughed and added in a sexy tone "Well, I have a power unit that might blow. Do you think you can pin my power unit?" They laughed.

The next day Max was at his desk trying to get some more of the never ending paperwork filed. It was a lot easier than the paperwork he had to fill out on the cascade. Max was making up the rules as he filled out the paperwork on the cascade. It wasn't easy. There was no precedent for what he had done. It was just not right. Plus he had to make a full report and the shoe deal; it just didn't write well. Just the thought of that report made him happy it was done. This time it's just a standard weekly report. He has rules to go by that are in the book. He checked the space 'one cascade' see report Sept 4, 1400 this year

Sandy came down at lunch and asked "What did you get?" Max asked what she meant. She said. "The charms are out." Max needed a break so he took Sandy up to check the charms list.

CHAPTER TWELVE, BRANDY AND BETTY

Four years earlier.

The Mist waited quietly as Betty gave birth to Brandy. They are the last two main players in her little melodramatic version of the birth of a new people. She smiled as she waited and remembered when she told the world about Betty. It was 17 years ago. And now Betty's daughter Brandy, the last major player in The Mist's plan, was being born. The Mist was very pleased that soon, very soon, her chosen people will be in place to create the new race. As any mother would The Mist has big plans and high hopes for her children.

Just four more years and it will be time to start the final phase. The prep work will be done and it will be time for her to just sit back and watch. She smiles, knowing there will be times when she will have to point them in the right direction. She hopes she will not have to intercede too often.

She let her mind run back and relive the time when she claimed Betty seventeen years ago.

Betty Jacks was a mere four pounds and twelve ounces when she came into the world. The Mist knew the moment she was born and took her first breath. She was born to an asteroid miner and his wife. She, her two brothers and three sisters lived on a mobile miner with seven other mining families. They made a good living and were for the most part happy with their lives. All the miners looked forward to the two weeks break they took between loads on the place they called home. They were given a house in the Delta-5 system by contract with the company.

Betty, however, was born on a miner in space. She was five days old when they went to deliver the ores they had amassed over the last two months. The trip hadn't looked very profitable just before Betty was born. They had found a lot of asteroids but they contained very little ore that anyone would buy. The storage units were only one third full.

After Betty was born things changed. In fact the second she took her first breath the discovery was made; the very rich field of greatly desired ore. They filled the storage compartment within two days. This cut two days off their scheduled flight and promised a big payday. Dinner the night they turned to deliver the ore was much more elaborate than expected because they always saved extra supplies for the turning celebration. This time they had more because the trip was shortened by two days. Everyone was looking forward to a couple of weeks off on their home moon after they sold the ore.

It's the custom of the miners to take newborns to the seer as soon as possible to discover whether or not the child is going to be an asset to the group. The seer they are going to see is on the cargo transport where they plan to sell their ore. She has a very good reputation for being very close to right; most of the time. She's well respected.

Betty's family had to wait in line for a reading. It was a public forum and several new parents were there from other mining groups for the same reason. Because the presence of the seer was considered holy, everyone was on their best behavior.

They watched the seer as she entered the room. She was a beautiful sight. Mother noticed the seer seemed a little dizzy just as she passed them. She looked directly at them and mother was a little alarmed at the look she gave her. Something was wrong with

Betty. Others noticed the contact as well and now they refused to look at Betty's mother. What had happened almost always meant a vision and a report of the death of a child at a very early age. Sometimes the seer would refuse to read the child.

This seer was amazing as always. She had predicted the marriage, work, and children of the babes she had examined for over thirty years. Her mother before her was as well respected for she was seldom wrong. The crowd waited very quietly for her to begin the readings of the children present.

She motioned for the first child to be brought to her. She always knew the name without being told. She took the child in her arms and smiled "Hello James Martin." It was always amazing and the crowd gasped as his parents lowered their head signifying she was correct. The seer got another name correct. This act always made the reading more believable. James' mother smiled, the seer knew her child.

The seer continued. "James will be a miner and marry the first daughter of Mark and Hanna Wills." That reading in its self told another future. The Wills currently only had two sons. Someone in the crowd congratulated the Wills. The seer smiled and congratulated them as well. She continued "They will have only one child, a son." She paused. "James will die in an accident in his 34th year." The group was already grieving for a child that was just born.

This was a normal reading. Most newborns in this group could expect to become miners or miners' wives. Those that were to become something more could only expect to be the commander of an ore harvester or possibly a foreman. To expect more was not a good idea and seldom ever happened. Mother and Father hoped to find out who Betty would marry and about the grandchildren. That was before the seer noticed them. Now they just hope to have some time with Betty before she dies as a child.

The female child, Freda Gotton was told she would become a leader of her group. It was a very unusual reading for a female. She was also told she would never have a child but be the mother figure of twenty-three children. This could mean only one thing she would become the religious leader in her group. She would not die until she was very old. This too proved the caste of religious leader. Her parents were very proud.

The seer always knew the order of the parents requesting a reading and only skipped a parent under very special circumstances. She skipped Betty's mother and father. She told everyone to wait for all to be called before they left.

Soon there were no more newborns to be called when the seer took a deep breath and waved to Betty's Mother and Father to come forward. They were very nervous. Mother knew the seer was going to tell her of Betty's death in just a few short years or maybe just months. She hoped it wouldn't be weeks or days. They started toward the seer and she had to sit down. "I'm a little dizzy."

She held up her hand for them to stop. They stopped and waited for her to motion them forward again. She regained herself and motioned for them to come forward. They started again and the seer held up her hand, "please get that child away from me." They backed up. What was wrong with Betty? What will Betty do? Is she going to be a problem for the group?

The seer told them to please wait. It was something she didn't have to say. They would wait. Everyone was curious now and no one was leaving until the reading was finished. The seer left quickly saying she was going to get her mother, promising to return in a half hour. There was a lot of talk about what was happening. No one seemed to know and no one remembered this ever happening before.

Betty's parents started to leave but the others wouldn't allow them to go. One of the old ones remembered the child Mitchel from two generation back. His actions had killed many, many miners. Betty's mother and father were very nervous. The things Mitchel did were not spoken of and for his name to be mentioned at all was scary. Mother and Father were being watched closely and the thought was in Mother's head that maybe Betty would be worse than Mitchel. The seer knew the crowd was going to kill her as soon as the reading was done. They tried again to leave but the crowd wouldn't allow them to go. If this was another Mitchel then they wanted to know. Mother was in tears. Betty was just a child.

Within the half hour, the seer and her mother stood together holding hands on the stage. This was not a good sign. It meant that one seer couldn't receive all the information that was about to be revealed. During the worst of times was the only time it took two seers to relay the message. It was another ten minutes before the mother of the mother of the seer joined them. She slowly made her way to her daughter and granddaughter. She could barely walk. She was very old. They joined hands and the seer said. "Please bring the child forward." By this time the story had spread to everyone. Something very special was happening. The question on everyone's lips was, is this a good thing or a bad thing? It seemed the entire port had come to hear the reading of this very powerful child.

Mother and Father were very nervous. As they were forced toward the seers they began to speak as one. "This is the most powerful child we have ever encountered. She, Betty Jacks Holt," They paused as if looking for the right word, "Goddess of the Universe. She will bear six children by the war god Death Dealer; who she loves more than herself. This love is returned in full. She will hold the life essence of the universe in the palm of her hand to crush or nourish as she sees fit. She will become the basis of a new species when she is transformed into one herself. Her firstborn will not be a goddess born but make one of herself by her own hand just as her mother did. The life span of this child is tens of thousands of years. We do not see her end. She will become a legendary warrior and a beloved ruler with great wisdom. You are in the presence of one of the rulers of all that is now and the vast universe that will be known. She will discover much and conquer all that she chooses. She will live with honor and be greatly blessed by The Mist."

The seers fell to the floor.

The crowd began to move toward Betty's mother and father almost before the seers hit the floor. The flash of light and the sudden appearance of The Mist as a floating golden ball of light stopped them in their tracks. The boom of her voice shook the room. "You will stay away from my child." The crowd stopped. Mother and Father left quickly through the path that opened as the crowd moved aside. They walked quickly to the mining craft and boarded hoping to get away with their lives, not just from the crowd but also whatever had claimed Betty.

This wasn't the normal reading her parents had hoped for and they were overwhelmed. Betty took it all in stride. She smiled a funny smile and filled her diaper. Over the next few days Mother and Father didn't mention the event. Some weeks passed before no one remembered what happened but them and their family.

Betty's status as a future Goddess didn't help her much as she grew. Some of her family picked on her because of it but all in all she grew up normally for a miner's child. She was caught up in a major problem when she was fifteen. She believed she had no way out and ran away with a boy she knew she didn't love but was convinced loved her. They didn't re-board the miner at Beta Station. They both found work and had a fair life until she became pregnant, then he left.

The Mist shifted her mind back to the here and now, she would be needed soon. Brandy would need her. Brandy was the last player in The Mist creation of a new species. No harm would come to her now, no matter the intent of the government. This baby born in prison would live no matter how they tried to kill her. The time of the change was so close. The Mist would protect her from the self-serving intent of the government.

Betty was very happy that her child was now in the world. The Nurses went right to work on the child. It was scary for Betty. She waited for the cry of the child. It didn't come. One of the nurses looked sad and said "I'm so sorry." Betty began to cry She knew her baby was born dead just like many in the prison system.

The Mist was expecting this; she knew Brandy would be killed at birth just like forty percent of the babies born to prisoners. The government didn't want to pay the cost of raising the child. The Mist appeared and smiled as she took Brandy. "Not yet my child; I have waited a long time for you." Brandy began to squirm as she was wrapped in the blanket and then cry. The Mist laid Betty's living daughter beside her. "I think she'll be alright now."

Betty smiled and was very pleased to have Brandy, alive. She was too happy to wonder how the Nurses had been mistaken and thought her daughter dead. The Nurses were stuck now. They had done something wrong and Betty still lived. They would just get the forty percent with the next child.

CHAPTER THIRTEEN, CHARMS, CHARMS CLUBS, IRONMAN JIM AND MOUSE

Max walked with Sandy toward the Charms posting board. Charms are, in Max's mind, the single most important thing the Force has ever done. Most military personnel can read them very well. Their life could depend on knowing what someone had been trained to do. They would know in a glance how well you had been trained and know how brave the person had been in the past. Charms are tattoos one half an inch wide and three quarters of an inch long that are applied to inside of your forearms. The computer automatically adjusts for future adult size.

Some of them are placed on the right forearm. They are your career. Anyone who knows what they are can see the person you have been. There are no lies. It's billed as a security aid, less chance of blackmail if you wear the truth on your arm. Although no amount of charms can tell the entire story of one's life.

The arm is divided into several areas. The inside of the right forearm is for personal achievements, promotions, medals, and other things of that nature. The sides as defined by the wrist bones and the elbow bones are for the ships on which you served. The back of the right forearm is for group achievements. For example the cascade, could generate three separate awards, one on the back of the arm to show that you have been involved in a cascade. The second and third would be placed on the inside of the arm. You may be entitled to both; one for having a back-up role in shutting the cascade down and another for being in the front shutting it down. The back of both hands is reserved for very special awards.

The Captain for instance has been awarded the Star of Congress for his actions in the first space battle in which the Earth had been involved. It's the second highest award that the government can award. The highest is the Cross of Congress. Other awards that are put on the back of the hand in certain places are like the Angel award for pinning your first power unit. It is awarded by the Captain of the ship where the pinning took place.

Max wanted to see what charms he was to receive as much as Sandy and they went to the posting area. They stood in line and waited their turn to print the list of their new charms. They would have two days to have it changed or it would stand.

James and Karen were in line ahead of them. "Max, Sandy, come join us." Max and Sandy went over to where they were. They talked as they waited their turn to print their charms.

Max and Sandy were both looking over their respective list. James asked. "Max, what does the small arms charm look like?" Max wasn't listening. James repeated. "Max, what does the small arms charm look like?"

Max described the charm "It's just a pistol at forty five degrees so you can add the large weapons to the charm later. You should get both weapons."

Sandy said "Show him Max." Max pulled up his sleeve and showed James the small arms award. That led to the Cascade charm and several other people wanting to see what a certain charm looked like. Somebody had one of the charms that were asked about. The easier charms for someone to get, like first space assignment were still important to them and they wanted to see what they looked like. Everyone was happy to show off their charms. The harder ones to get were sometimes not available for show.

Max received twelve awards. Sandy was looking at eight. She wondered asking Max. "Why are you getting more than me?" James and Karen were getting six, the rest of the crew five. The Captain was just getting three. It's a lot for a Captain to receive. After all, charms can't be duplicated. Most, if not all, received the first space flight, it was a new crew. The cascade generated one for everyone, two for some and three for – three well, Max only got two. He already had the one for being on a ship that had a cascade. There were the small arms, blade weapon training and marshal arts basic charms, for James, Sandy, Karen and several more. There were the promotions and awards. Max got extras because he was outside his field. Some of the charms he got - the rest of his group had already, like the shuttle wings. Max received a gold coin charm for his security work, notable achievement.

The quarantine time at Beta Station will be used for tattooing. When it's done James will have a massive ten charms. Well, massive for his age and rank. Karen will have eleven. Aside from the ones they received from this trip, the charms were for educational work. Sandy was very happy with the Angel charm that the Captain had authorized.

The Angel charm is given for the first actual failing power unit that you successfully pin. Few scientists would ever pin a failing power unit. It's placed on the back of the right hand between the thumb and index finger for everyone to see. She is very happy to carry the fifteen charms. It's more than she expected at this point in her career. Max is carrying twenty eight, but his career was a lot more active than the others. Some of the old salts carried as many as forty, Bill now has thirty eight.

Max has more charms than most of his peers because he was able to change levels. Most solders never made it to Level six, they stayed a Level seven their whole career. Max questioned why he was so special as to advance. Only .5 percent of those who enter the force as a Level eight ever make Level six. Officers and scientists came into the force at Level six.

The Einstein will port at Beta station tomorrow at about ten o'clock. Meanwhile there is a lot of work to be done. The radio to the station is busy all the time. A simple call is a four hour wait and that is for five minutes only. Max went to see CC3 Hall; Max told him "It's impossible to do business five minutes at a time." CC3 Hall arranged for Max to get special access to the priority line. It didn't take but a couple of hours for Max to get things put in order with the uninterrupted secure comm line. As he left the room, Mike the CC3 asked "Are we set?

Max laughed. "I hope so."

Mike reminded him that they were early and to "get things done before the new Lieutenant gets here."

Max smiled. "Sir, I have done this a lot. I'll take care of it." Max laughed again. "But, something will come up so expect my call."

Mike smiled. "The Captain said this is going to be a learning experience."

Mike laughed. "See you guys at The Charms."

Max smiled "We'll be there."

There is always a Charms club in port, on Beta station there are two Charms clubs. Charms clubs have different names at each port, but it's always close to the same on the inside. These clubs operate by the same set of rules but the interpretation of the rules varies. When you go into the club your charms speak for you. You leave your rank with your coat at the door. And you better have a sleeveless shirt on under the coat that will let the world see your charms.

Unofficial Charms are not available on board a spacecraft. They can only be gotten on station from a certified Charmer. The crew is allowed access to a quarantine area for the first twenty four hours after they arrive. The Charmers usually set up office in that area. Those wanting a charm have to prove they are entitled to the charms with a registered Charmer and be entered in the computer as having taken the charm.

Personal charms are available if the Charmer has time. Max wanted to see if Sandy wanted to get one to commemorate their wedding. He had in mind a double heart that would cover the space on the left arm where intents were placed. Sandy was willing but she wanted to add their names across the hearts in dark black and make the hearts bright red instead of just an outline. Max was willing. The charm maker helped them add the wedding date and the words under the hearts "until death do us part." Sandy insisted on leaving three fourths of an inch under the words. Max asked. "Just in case?" She kissed him. "No, so we can add the names of our children" Max laughed. "We're really going to have to talk about that." She didn't budge "No, we are going to have eight. That's what I was promised and that is what is going to happen" The Charmer laughed. Max and Sandy laughed too, but Max was almost sure she was serious.

After thirty hours in port the crew was allowed ashore and out of the quarantine area. Max had taken full advantage of the quarantine and finished his flight training. He flew second chair for the first two flights and then first chair for the next five. The last flight of the day was his solo. He was the only one aboard and he had to make several difficult maneuvers. He did well and was certified. Sandy was waiting for him when he got back to the ship. She wanted to go to the Charms club. Max told her that's what he had planned. He asked if James and Karen were going with them and the answer was "Of course, you think a scientist would miss a chance to go to one of those places." She held up her arm showing her Charms. "Besides I want to show these off."

They got ready to leave the ship for the club. Karen asked if the place would be as rough as she had heard these places were. Max told her it was still a military place and if any of the men gave her a problem in that way, just to show their intent space on their arm and "They'll leave you alone. Other wise call me." Sandy asked sarcastically "Married counts too, right." Max smiled. "Yes, but call me anyway."

When they got to the club James was smiling at the night that he was planning on having. The club was called 'SlammerS.' They dropped their coats at the door and went inside. Max found them a booth and ordered drinks. A waitress brought the drinks. Max paid for the drinks, a four credit tab, with a hundred credit slip "Keep the change."

She smiled "What are you looking for?"

Max said "Wild Jacks."

She nodded. "I'll let them know."

After she left Sandy pried. "What was that all about and where did you get a hundred credit slip?"

Max smiled. "Business money and I need a bank. I'm short on cash."

James questioned. "You're looking for a game of chance?" Max told him that was right. They talked and drank a few more drinks. Max and Sandy even danced a few times. They ordered dinner; fried chicken served family style, while they waited. It was early and the real party wouldn't begin for two or three more hours.

Max noticed the waitress talking to a man and then the man came over to their table. "Wild Jacks? How long? You'll need two grand minimum to open."

Max nodded. "Wild Jacks, three hours, five grand to open." The man nodded. "I need to see the five." Max laid the five thousand credits on the table.

The man made a quick count. "Top of the stairs first door to the left, just show them the money."

The man left. Max told Sandy. "I'll be back in three hours." He left.

Karen asked. "What is Wild Jacks"?

James was happy to tell her. "It's a card game, the better your memory the better chance you have to win."

Sandy smiled as she remembered Max's photographic memory "Oh I get it, he's going to the bank." She laughed and ordered another round. Three hours later the place was just starting to wind up. Max tapped Sandy on the shoulder and asked. "Want to dance?"

She accepted. As they danced she asked. "Did you do ok?"

Max smiled "Of course. Turned five into thirty, I think that should get us through."

She laughed "You're a criminal."

He laughed. "If I was I would have a hundred grand." He laughed "But if I did that I could wind up dead."

They had a snack tray and a few more drinks. About 0100 Max started to 'get right;' he was a little drunk. He went up on the stage and started to play songs by an old time singer. He played the guitar, harmonica and sang. He was a real crowd pleaser. He played an entire set, 45 minutes. He left the stage with a lot of folks yelling for him to do "just one more song."

The exact order in which the next few things happened, well it's hard to say. First the guy was thrown down the stairs, I think. He made somebody mad in the Wild Jacks room. He slammed into the floor. That caused the drinks the waitress was carrying to be spilt on two other guys. The bouncers stepped in and somewhere about that time the whole damn thing went to hell. It was the worst brawl that had ever been. Max saw Sandy deck a guy with a chair and then she got hit in the side of the head. Max saw stars about that time and the next he knew he was picking himself up off the floor. James and Karen were just pounding on a big guy. He was going down for the count. Max found Sandy. She was beating on a big guy and wasn't having much effect. Max walked up to them and asked. "Do you want some help?"

The guy pleaded. "Just hold her a second so I can get out of here."

Sandy yelled "He grabbed me and I didn't like where he grabbed me. Just kick his ass." Max hit the guy in the face. Down the guy went. The suppression water came on about that time and the bouncers were trying to stop the fight. It took another half hour before the last punch was thrown. Sandy threw it and decked a bouncer.

Max was almost laughing as the four limped out of the Club. Sandy started to yell at him but wound up laughing. "You lost a tooth." Max smiled and James and Karen started to laugh. They had found just what they were looking for, a pressure release. They grimaced with a new pain each time they moved.

James smiled. "I have never had so much fun in my life."

Karen laughed. "Thank you Max for a most enlightening night."

Sandy was still laughing as she hung on him. "Max, you look so funny with that tooth missing." They were laughing as they found their way to a shuttle marked Einstein and asked. "Could you take us home, please?" There were several others in the shuttle. They were in a lot better shape than the group with Max.

Max asked Sandy a little loud "Is your eye swelling shut?"

She answered, "I think so; damn, that guy could hit."

James was just laughing. Karen told them. "He is really going to have a head in the morning."

The next morning came with all the aches and pains of the past night. Sandy was up first and was in the bathroom when Max rolled out of bed. He walked into the bathroom and plopped down on the toilet. Sandy was looking in the mirror. "Damn it, Max, look at my eye." She turned around and Max saw the side of her face was bruised and her eye was turning black on one side of her face and on the other side he could still see the slight redness of the power unit burn.

He smiled and she laughed. "Oh my, we have to get that tooth fixed." She laughed some more. She bent down and kissed Max.

He kissed her and advised. "You don't even want to start that."

She smiled. "Yeah, I do Max, I had a great time. Scientists don't get to do stupid things like that."

Max laughed. "I wonder if James and Karen are still alive this morning."

Sandy laughed. "I bet they wish they weren't." Max laughed. They were soon ready to start the day.

They walked down the hall to the chow hall. They met a lot of people; some of them had been beaten. They stared at them and Max would smile at the people until they started to laugh. It was great fun. Max stopped at sick bay and the doctor set him up an appointment at two that afternoon. She gave Sandy a cold compress. The doctor was overworked that morning. "It must have been a hell of a fight. You wouldn't believe how many of the crew have stopped by this morning."

As they went into the chow hall the Lieutenant smiled. "Have a good time last night?"

Max laughed. "No sir, we had a little lover's spat." Sandy started to laugh, she dropped her compress and Max picked it up.

The Lieutenant said, "That's all right, other people had a good time." The laughter was contagious. Breakfast was a trip down a bad road, in an old car. Everybody was still slightly intoxicated and enjoying the ride. They watched as several people limped in or out with one sign or another of a beating.

James and Karen came into the chow hall. They got food and sat down with Max and Sandy. James was still on a high "I don't believe how much fun I had last night." He had to recall the entire night minute for minute. Max didn't even remember some of the things. But it didn't matter. Karen was smiling even with her black eye. It wasn't as large as Sandy's but you couldn't miss it.

She asked softly. "Thank you very much for last night but can we go to a quieter place tonight?"

They laughed and Sandy volunteered "There is a nice dinner and dance club I heard about, do you want to go?"

James added. "Do they have a stage so Max can sing?"

Sandy smiled. "I hope so."

Max laughed "Maybe they have one of those machines that plays music back without the words."

Karen laughed. "Oh, no not me…"

The day was busy; there were more things to do than time to do them. Sandy made Max keep the appointment to have the tooth fixed. It didn't take ten minutes to have the old fake tooth part replaced with a new fake tooth. While they were in sick bay the doctor checked Max's hand to see if he had caused more damage to the burn, it was ok. Sandy's burn, on the other side of her face from the black eye, had been scraped. Doris, the doctor, was a little concerned. She told Sandy to be careful or it might scar.

The four left for dinner about 1800. They went to the other Charms Club on Beta station. It was reported to be a nicer place. It was called Diamond Jim's. It turned out to be a very nice place. Max commented, "We might not get into a fight tonight."

James hopefully joking said "damn." He tried to snap his fingers but they didn't snap. They were seated and ordered a cheese and cracker plate that Karen wanted. It was better than Max expected.

They drank beer and talked about last night. Max noticed a girl who came in and sat at the bar; she ordered a drink and was sipping it very slowly. It was obvious to Max that she just didn't have the credits to be there. She was a slight little thing, small and short. Sandy asked "About to pick up another stray?"

Max smiled. "She looks so lost and lonely. It couldn't hurt to ask her to have a drink with us. I remember what it's like to be lost like that."

James smiled, "I do too." The girls gave in and Max went to see if she would like to join them.

The girl was watching the room. It was like she was off in her own dream world. Max believed she was dreaming of really being part of the group. He could see the line of charms, well, the three charms.

The forced entry into the force and that she was a scrubber. A scrubber is the lowest, they are Level nine. They are paid almost nothing and they work hard. She has to be stationed at Beta Station because ships usually don't have scrubbers. They're contracted to the ships that are in port. The enlistment charm was for forced to enter. That happens usually when you are in trouble with the law or have been. Max could tell because it had a black border around it. Max asked "Are you alone?"

She stammered "No, well yes, but I'm not one of the girls. So if that is what you're looking for, then I'm not alone."

Max smiled. "Well in that case, would you like to join my wife and our friends for a drink?"

She asked very flatly. "Why?"

Max smiled and turned his inside forearm so she could see his enlistment charm. "You looked lonely and I have been where you are. If you would like to join us you are welcome and I'm buying the drinks and dinner."

She almost smiled recognizing the forced entry charm "and dinner." Max offered her his arm "and dinner." She needed to be reassured "no strings."

Max laughed "no strings, you're safe."

She reluctantly took his arm. "Ok, but I have to leave by eleven. I have a curfew."

Max introduced her to Sandy, "This is my wife Sandy and these are our friends James and Karen."

She was nervous. "Hello, my name is Betty, Betty Jacks." They all said hello. She sat down.

The waiter came by a few minutes later. He asked if they were ready to order.

Max asked "What's good here?"

The waiter laughed. "What's good is a matter of opinion. But the meatloaf, the beef tips and the fried chicken are bad." They laughed and then he added. "There are several other choices on the menu."

Max looked at the menu. He asked "do you have T-bones, I mean real Beef now."

The waiter nodded. "They're not on the menu but we do have several. They are fifteen credits each with a real baked potato and all the trimmings.

James asked "Do you have cheesecake with real cherries?" The waiter acknowledged. "We can make one. It will take about an hour. The entire cake will cost twenty credits. That's the only way we sell them." Sandy asked for green salad. She was told yes.

Max was ready to order "So it's settled. Make my t-bone medium and I want extra sour cream on the potato and French dressing on the salad."

James nodded. "That sounds good, make it two." Sandy wanted hers well done and Karen wanted hers rare.

Max asked Betty "How would you like your steak?"

She was lost. "I don't know. Am I going to have to pay for this?"

Sandy laughed. "No, Max is going to pay for everything." Sandy told her. "Medium is a little red in the middle."

Betty looked a little sick. "I think I want mine done."

They laughed as Sandy said. "Now that's a girl after my heart." They helped her with the rest of her order and the waiter left.

It didn't take long after that for Max to ask about her forced entry charm. "What were you in for?"

She was getting more at ease, but not that much. "What were you in for?"

Max knew it was a matter of public record anyway. "Murder, three counts."

She was surprised. "Damn, I was just doing a little second story work to feed myself and…" She paused. "What were you guys in for?"

Sandy smiled. "Nothing, we were in college. Max is just trying to show us the error of our ways. He got us into a hell of a fight last night." She turned her head so Betty could see the bruise. Betty cringed, "That looks bad; but…"

Sandy smiled. "Oh, this side is a power unit burn, Max burned his hand." Karen was deadpan. "I had already sent my last will and testament to records when he pinned that damn thing. I was sure we were going to die."

They talked back and forth for the rest of the night and the guys found out that a second story man was a cat burglar. At ten thirty she had to catch the bus.

Max walked her out and when he came back Sandy met him on the dance floor. "Alright Max, picking up strays is entertaining and you feel good afterwards. But what was in it for you?"

Max kissed her "That's the way I feel about it. Would you like to dance?"

She laughed. "I thought you'd never ask." They began to dance to the slow music.

Max asked. "How would I go about getting a scrubber assigned to the ship?"

Sandy asked. "Why?"

Max smiled. "I need a thief and a small person to help me map the nooks and crannies on the ship. That way we'll have more places to hide stuff."

Sandy smiled "That's a good idea. But I don't know – I'll see if I can find out." She added. "Maybe James does; he keeps his eye on strange things."

Max nodded. "We should ask." They finished their dance and went back to the table.

Max asked James "Do you have an idea what it will take to get a certain scrubber assigned to the ship?"

James was trying to think "You mean Betty, I don't think so... Wait a second." He asked Karen "Didn't the controller at our first station, yeah, he wanted a certain cook and pulled some strange stuff to get him?" Karen didn't remember. James did "A dinner party with several cooks and then one stayed over... or something like that?"

Karen laughed. "Yes, something along that line." They slowly remembered how it was done. Max would start the process tomorrow.

It was midnight when the bell started to ring; a man came out on stage. "Ok, Ok, here we go. Sign ups are now open for the fleet champion of the eight ships that are in dock today and will be here for the next ten days. There is no entry fee and all you need is proof that you are from the ship you want to represent. If no one else chooses to represent that ship you're in, otherwise you have to fight them first." James was very interested. The announcer continued. "The rules are. Bare knuckle and you fight tonight. The four winners fight in two days and the two winners fight seven days from now. The entry books are now open. As I call your ship you may come up to the stage and enter." He started to call out the names of the ships in port. There were four merchant marine vessels, two force vessels, a police cruiser and the science vessel, Einstein.

Everyone laughed when the Einstein was called. "Come on; who gets the bye." Before anyone could stop James he went to the stage and put his name in the hat. When he got back to the table he said. "I fight second, a guy named Short Stout."

Max smiled. "Short Stout is a ring name. The guy is a merchant marine and he is damn mean."

Karen didn't like the idea and was a little short. "Are you out of your mind?"

James smiled "The fight last night; I loved it." Max had mixed emotions about James - did he know what he was doing?

The first fight was brutal. Both guys were bleeding badly. One had at least one, maybe two broken fingers. The guy who won looked a lot like a loser. He was beaten badly. The round took four minutes thirty-one seconds out of a possible fifteen minutes. That was when one of the guys hit the floor and didn't get up. Max told James "James, these guys may not be pros but they do this a lot. Are you sure you want to get in the ring with one of them?"

James was wired. He asked Max if he would get in the ring with one of them. Max shook his head, "There would have to be a lot on the line." Max's reluctance didn't stop James. There was no talking him out of it. The glaze on his eyes told Max that his mind was clearly already in the ring "I'll be fine."

James was across the ring from Short Stout when the bell rang. James moved to the center of the ring and Short Stout hit him in the face knocking him back into the ropes. James slid down to the floor. Karen was happy it was all over. Everyone was laughing as they shouted things about scientists.

Then the surprise of the night, James got up. He yelled "Hell, is that all you got fat boy?" The fight ran thirteen minutes with both fighters pounding on each other. The crowd yelled and money was flying everywhere as the bets were made. Short Stout was almost done when James connected with an upper cut that picked him off his feet and laid him out on the mat. It was done; James had fought a great fight. The ring announcer counted Short Stout out and raised James' hand, "and the winner from the Einstein – Ironman Jim."

James was very tired just moments before; but now, he was laughing and spitting blood as it ran down into his mouth. He was jumping up and down yelling, "See you losers in two days!"

Karen laughed. "I think a monster has been released." It was hard to tell which he liked more, winning or being Ironman Jim.

The next day Max started the process of getting the scrubber. He went to see the CC3, Mike. He spoke to the clerk, "AS Dent to see Commander Hall."

She smiled. "I'll tell him you're here." She looked in on the office and then smiled. "He'll see you."

Max walked into the office and reported. Commander Hall nodded. "At ease, what can I do for you?" Max told him he wanted a scrubber named Betty Jacks assigned to the ship. He explained about the second story work and what he had in mind for the smaller areas of the ship. "The Commander called the clerk in and had her pull up the scrubber service. He selected five names off the list and told the clerk to have these people on board tomorrow morning to clean the chow hall vents. She left and he said. "Now maybe the cooks and sanitation will get off my back." Max laughed. Mike smiled, "Ok, when she gets here we are going to have her stay overnight to do some more work the next day. Right?" Max told him that was the plan and thanked him for the help.

Max was clearing cargo to be placed aboard that afternoon when the Captain came by with a tour. He excused himself from the tour and went to talk to Max. Max came to attention and saluted. The salute was not required but it was returned and the Captain asked. "How are things going?" Max told him they were going better than expected. The Captain smiled. "I heard you ordered a Mouse."

Max smiled "If that is alright with you, sir."

He wasn't sure. "How well do you know her?" Max told him about dinner. The Captain was cautious. "Ok, we'll get her aboard." The Captain laughed. "One more thing, Ironman Jim?"

Max smiled. "He is untrained and he loves to fight."

The Captain asked. "Has he got a chance of going all the way?"

Max told him "I just don't know. He is going to fight again tomorrow night."

The Captain nodded. "Maybe I'll drop by and see. I have to get back to these VIP's." Max smiled and the Captain went back to the tour.

It was nine o'clock that night before Max got home. Sandy was on the bed fully dressed, asleep. Max woke her. "How was your day honey?"

She laughed and whined at the same time "It was a living hell."

Max was spent too. "I'm going to shower and get some sleep."

She smiled "Want some help?"

Max smiled. "I do need a good ending for this day." They were too tired to sleep even after they made love.

Sandy was excited for her friend James. "You should have heard the guys from the labs cheering for 'Ironman Jim.' James is having a great time." Max told her that Bill had even asked about him. They laughed. They talked a while longer before they drifted off to sleep.

****

Recruit Betty Jacks didn't have a good day either. She was sent to the food processing plant. It's the worst job on the list and she always gets it. The 'sweeper' (that's her boss) and her don't get along. He wants special favors from her that she is not willing to provide. The other girls didn't have any problem providing the service. It left Betty out in the cold. When they got back to the shop Betty was told she had a job the next day. She was disappointed. It was to be her day off. She was very upset. The sweeper took great pleasure in her pain. "It's a special request from the science vessel Einstein. I don't and you don't have a choice. Be ready for transport at 0500. That means you will not be getting a day off this week. She was very mad, too mad to argue about something she couldn't change.

When the 0500 bus to the Einstein left she was on board. They had already been told that they would be cleaning the galley. It was going to be nasty. Max had made sure that an overbearing little ass of a cook's assistant, Private Jones was going to run the detail. The entire detail was female and he worked them hard. They didn't get a morning break and lunch was late. They finished at 1500. Max made sure that Jones knew what he was supposed to do. Jones went to inspect the work. He had been watching and knew where Betty had been working. He raised holy hell with the girls over the project and when he got to Betty's work he got even worse. Four of the girls were released. Betty was told she had to stay and redo the work the next day. She was almost in tears when the others smiled tauntingly as they left. A security guard was called and Jones told him to "take her to A S Dent in security."

As she followed the security guard she didn't know if she could speak. She took the chance "Who is A. S. Dent? Is that a rank?" The security guard, Frank smiled "He's the top ranking enlisted in the Force." She didn't know what to say. Frank volunteered. "He's a nice guy. He's never treated me bad." They arrived at the office and the guard told her. "Have a seat I'll tell him you're here." The guard knocked on the door and was told to enter. He opened the door. "I have recruit Jacks as you requested."

Max told him. "Give me five and then send her in."

Frank walked back out. "He'll see you soon, five doesn't always mean five." She nodded. Frank told her. "There's coffee for sure and there may be a donut left. Help yourself." She asked if she had to pay for it and was told "no." She poured herself some coffee and got the last donut. It was a little stale. But she had a donut so infrequently that it didn't matter. It was really good and she was really hungry.

She finished the donut quickly and was working on the coffee when Max buzzed Frank "You can send her in and if she wants she can bring her coffee. She can bring me a coffee too if she would."

Frank said. "Yes sir." Frank knew that Jacks had heard the intercom and told her "You don't have to but he would like coffee and you have to go in." She refilled her cup and poured a second cup of coffee. She went into the office, set the coffee on the desk and reported. Max was standing with his back to the door, "Close the door please." She closed the door and he noted. "Betty, you smell bad." He turned and took the coffee off the desk. She didn't know what to say.

He smiled. "It's Sergeant Dent when the door is open. It's just Max when it is closed."

She felt enormous relief and knew something was up. "So, Max what's going on?"

Max laughed. "First of all I would like to tell you how sorry I am about the way you were treated today. It was necessary, but I am sorry." He noticed she was watching a candy bar on his desk. He said. "Go ahead."

She asked "What?" He pointed. "The candy bar, you can have it." She took the candy. Max informed her. "We'll get you down to be fed in a few minutes. But I need to talk to you first." She was chewing the candy bar. Max asked her to have a seat and, "Do you have any ties to the station?"

She answered between chews. "I have a daughter, Brandy, she's four. She's really smart. I guess the way she had to grow up has made her wise beyond her years. I was supposed to get to see her today, but this job came up."

Max wished he had known that before. "I'm sorry about that too. I didn't know. You can go now if you want. We can do this later."

She shook her head no. "I could never get there in time."

Max smiled. "Well, let's get on with this then."

There was a knock on the door and Max told them to enter. It was Frank. "Am I cleared to go to the chow hall?"

Max asked "can you bring your food back?"

He nodded. "I could, would you like me to bring two more meals."

Max smiled. "Yes, thank you." He left.

Max asked "Do you know what a Mouse does?"

She smiled. "Runs around and eats cheese. But I've never seen one."

Max laughed "Not that kind of Mouse."

She shrugged. "Then I don't know."

Max explained "a Mouse hides things and remembers where the things were put; mostly in the open places in a ships hull. It helps a lot if that Mouse is small."

She asked "we're talking black market aren't we."

Max didn't answer "Your second story work has qualified you to be a Mouse. Your small size will help a lot in your work." He stared at her a second. "Now do you want the job or do I send you back to the cleaners?"

It didn't take a lot of thought on her part. "May I ask some questions?"

Max nodded. She asked. "Will I be assigned to the ship?"

Max smiled. "It'll still have to be approved but if you accept you'll be assigned to the ship effective midnight tonight."

She asked. "As what…" Max told her. "A scrubber, that will lead to a promotion to private in a week and then to a combo job of sweeper and security augment. When we launch, in two weeks, you will be a private with duties as a scrubber, a sweeper and have security access to the hull."

She asked. "Will I be able to bring my daughter with me?"

Max smiled. He got the idea from her voice that it was part of the deal or there wasn't a deal. "I didn't know about her until today but I'm sure I can get her on board someway. There are other kids aboard."

She nodded "Ok, if I can have my daughter. What would I really be doing?"

Max laughed "We can talk about that tomorrow."

She was very matter of fact in her next statement. "Max, I am not going to sleep with anyone to get this job and I will not sleep with anyone to keep it either."

Max smiled "That isn't part of the job description."

Max told her to wait a second and he made a call. "Yeah, the quarters are a problem. Let's put her in six – thirty four for a while." "Ok, thanks." The food was back and they ate and talked a while longer. When they were done Max told her to "stop by and see Sandy. We're in six –zero eight. We're planning an outing tonight to a club just across the way and you'll need to be there. Sandy will help you find something to wear." Max made sure she could find the place and then she left. "Tell my wife I'll be about another hour."

As soon as she left Max picked up the open line "Did you get all of that?"

Bill was on the other end of the line. "Yes, I want to talk to her in person. I'll come by the club tonight. Let's leave it as Bill for now."

Max said. "Ok, Ironman is fighting at 0030, that's the second fight. He'll be fighting the guy who won the first fight last time."

Bill laughed, "Maybe he can win. I'll see you tonight." Next Max called Sandy. She answered and Max told her to find out as much as she could about the girl. He also told her that Bill would be joining them for a while tonight. "Make sure that James and Karen know its Bill. I have to be at the gate in a few minutes. I should be home by 1800." She told him she loved him and he told her the same.

Betty followed the instructions she was given. When she got on the elevator the man who was there didn't like the smell. Although he didn't say anything he apologized anyway. "Oh my, oh, I'm sorry you must have had a bad day. I didn't mean to be alarmed by the smell, sorry." She didn't answer and he got off on the next level. She got off on six and found quarters zero eight. She knocked on the door.

Sandy opened the door. "Hello Betty, please come in and go straight to the bath I have run for you. I hope you like the bath hot. There is a bag in the bath room please put that smelly uniform in the bag. I'll have it cleaned."

Betty smiled. "I smell that bad?"

Sandy told her "Yes."

Betty asked "What will I wear?" Sandy smiled. "There is a robe in the bathroom and then we'll see if any of the things Max told me to buy for you fit. Karen and I had to guess at your size."

Betty started to the bathroom but stopped. "I'm not going to have to do anything I don't want to do, right?"

Sandy wanted her in the bath, "No. Now get to that bath, please."

Betty said. "Oh, Max said he would be about an hour."

Sandy smiled. "I hope that's enough time, the bath please."

Betty wasn't used to taking baths; she had always taken showers and only had five minutes. She bagged her clothes and set the bag out the door. The tub was filled with bubbles and Sandy had added a nice smelling bath salt. Maybe it would kill the smell. Betty took her time; she had to read the instructions on most of the products. This was a lot more than she had ever had.

After a while Sandy knocked on the door "Betty, I know you're having a nice time but we're running a little late." Betty wasn't long after that. The robe was 'a little' large but it fit well enough. She was toweling her hair when she came out of the bath room. "Does my quarters have a bathtub? My daughter will love it."

Sandy smiled. "Yes, all the quarters on six are made about the same."

Betty asked. "Do I have something to wear?"

Sandy took her into another room. "This will be the second bedroom in your quarters. We got those things on the table. Just see what fits and we'll return the rest." Betty asked. "Am I going to make enough credits to pay everyone back and not be in hock for the rest of my life?"

Sandy smiled, "I wouldn't worry about that kind of stuff. We make a lot of credits." She found two of the outfits that she could wear and they both looked very nice. The others would be taken back later. Max got home as Betty's shoulder length blond hair was being combed out. He walked in and Sandy smiled. "What do you think, Max?"

Max looked in and smiled. "Wow, Betty you clean up real nice. You look like this girl I picked up in a Charms just the other day."

Sandy laughed and asked "Her hair, up or down."

Max smiled. "I think down."

Sandy nodded. "I do too."

They went to the club and found a table. The full kitchen wasn't open. They would make more money selling quick stuff. Max asked Betty if she would like to dance. Betty was a little scared. "I don't know how."

Sandy smiled. "Max is a good teacher."

Betty smiled. "I don't have a choice, do I?"

Max said. "There is always a choice."

She didn't want to do this. "Ok, slowly."

On the dance floor Max told her about the interview. "Bill will be by tonight. He is going to want to dance and talk to you. Be straight up honest with him. I don't know Bill that well in some areas." He paused. "If he gives you any crap about…"

She smiled "I'll tell you."

They danced a while longer before she asked "If a person had four credits that they wanted to bet on Ironman to win how would they go about something like that."

Max smiled. "They would bet one credit on each of the people to win. The odds are better and it's a sure bet. Your one credit should bring back about eight. If you bet four on Ironman and he wins, four will bring you seven. And you could lose." He tried to explain but she wasn't getting it. It didn't make any sense. If this was true then why didn't everybody do it? Max told her most people were not too bright. They laughed. He smiled. "We're going to make a pool and you can put in your money." She thought that was a good idea. The song ended and they went back to the table.

Sandy told him. "Max, that guy came by and he'll be back."

Max nodded "Ok, how much are we going to bet?" They pooled the money and counted it out. "99 credits,"

Max started to make up the one credit but Bill walked up. "How much…"

Max spoke. "Hey, Bill. We have 99 so whatever you think you can stand."

Bill smiled. "Put me down for twenty-one. I like round numbers."

He counted out the credits as Sandy asked. "How did you know we were going to bet like that?"

Bill laughed. "There is no other way to win." Bill added. "I'm expecting a guy named Warren. You'll know him when he comes in he'll look very out of place. Please bring him over to the table."

As a second thought he added. "He may want to get in on your pool."

Bill smiled. "So, this is Betty. Would you like to dance?"

She sort of smiled. "No, but being scared to death never stopped me before."

He laughed and held out his hand. She took it and they went to dance. Bill must have done something right because Betty started laughing. They danced two songs before they came back to the table. Bill nodded. "She's good." He excused himself and went to find Warren. Max handed her an ID card for the Einstein. "Welcome aboard."

She smiled, looked at the id and saw 'and daughter Brandy' printed on the bottom. Anyone could see she was happy and trying to not look too excited. "Thank you."

Bill called Max over and told him that professor Kidling was doing growth experiments on the children on the ship and he could get Betty's daughter on board as crew. "It'll make things a lot easier." Bill saw Warren at the door and waved him over. "I'm going to get him away from her as soon as possible before he calls me Captain."

Warren came over and Bill introduced him. "Warren, do you know Max? This is Warren." Max shook hands with him.

Warren was pleased to know Max. "Nice to meet you Max, I have heard a great deal about you."

Max nodded, "Nice to meet you, Warren."

Bill added. "Warren was a trainer in the fight game. He is going to watch Ironman and see if he can help him before the next fight." With that Bill and Warren went to find a seat closer. Warren didn't want in on the bet.

When Max got back to the table he explained that Bill had other obligations. Sandy took his arm. "That's nice. Let's dance." As they danced Max explained about Warren and Sandy laughed. He also asked. "Do you know a Professor Kidling?"

She said. "He's the one who keeps tabs on all the kids."

Max asked. "Will you talk to him and get a request for Betty's daughter?"

Sandy agreed. "Yeah, I'll get the information when I get back to the table."

The man came for the bets and Karen told him. "I want to bet a round and I have 120 credits." The guy didn't say anything just took the money, handed her a slip, and went to the next table.

They had snacks, talked and danced until midnight. There were a lot of familiar faces in the bar. The fight started at midnight and it was a bruiser, twelve minutes until one of the fighters threw in the towel. He couldn't go on; he barely made it off the mat. The second fight was far stranger. James had drawn a boxer. He stood face to face with the boxer. The boxer punched him in the face at will for the first three minutes. It wasn't pretty and it didn't look good for the Ironman. The tide turned after four minutes was called. The boxer was tiring. Ironman's head wasn't snapping back as far when he was hit. At the five minute mark Ironman hit the boxer, for the first time. It was an upper cut and the boxer took two steps back and fell to the mat. Ironman waited for him to get up and he did. Now the fight was on. The boxer was now at a clear disadvantage. Ironman wasn't hitting as hard as he could. He was just messing with the man. He was careful not to hit him hard enough to knock him out. After several minutes he got tired of beating the boxer. One huge blow from bottom to top put the man to the mat and he wasn't getting up this time.

As Warren passed Max on the way out, he was talking. "He needs a lot of work but he's just a bull." Bill took Max to the side and angrily told him. "You tell that boy the next time he better not be messing around in the ring, get the job done as fast as possible." Max felt the same way. This was a fight, not a place to settle a personal score or indulge one's self. He didn't approve of what James had done. He found it to be cruel and mean. But more than that - he could have lost.

Betty became Mouse that night; she couldn't wait to collect the bet. She took the slip and went to collect. The line was short but her old boss and one of the girls from the cleaners were just behind her. Her old boss seemed full of himself and more than a little condescending. "Got you a winner Jack?."

Mouse shook her head. "I was hoping I would never see you again."

He got mad. "Don't talk to me that way, sooner or later they're going to send you back to work."

Mouse wasn't going to do that. "I'll kill myself first, you stupid piece of shit." Her old boss started to yell. James was making his way back to the table. But instead he started over to the impending fight. Max was on his way as well.

James arrived first. "Want some help Mouse?"

She had an evil smile on her face. "I think I can take care of it." Max arrived. She was pleased that he was there but she had it in hand. "I got it Max."

The girl liked to run everybody down. "No wonder she never liked you, look at the real men she can get."

Mouse put the slip in her pocket and hit the girl in the face as hard as she could. The girl's nose crushed under the power of the blow. The man started to help but James popped him in the face and he went down. Mouse took out a lot of hate on the girl before she turned to the man. Before she stopped kicking him she was crying. James asked calmly. "If you're done; can we get a drink?"

She laughed and kicked him one more time. "I have to collect our winnings first." She collected the twelve hundred credits and they went back to the table leaving the two on the floor. These clubs are on the fringe of government control, nothing was going to be done about the fight.

Mouse kept thumbing through the credits. "I have never even seen this many credits." The winnings were split and they had to get back to the ship. They all had duty the next day, hell, in four hours. Mouse got to show her ID to the guard. It made her very happy. She stopped by Max's quarters on the way home and picked up the cleaned uniform. Sandy showed her to her quarters and they said good night.

The next morning Max had business with a man who could get him real jewels for Sandy's ring. He planned on Sandy going with him. He told Mouse to start the mapping of the blanks in the ship. He had some hull charts to help but they were not reliable. He gave her a box and told her if the box didn't fit through then the area wasn't suitable. "Take a sandwich with you and meet me in my office somewhere around 1300."

Max left the office about nine and picked up Sandy. They went down town, 'if you will,' the trading for the jewels was long winded. It took a lot longer than Max intended and cost more than they thought it should have, but they got what Sandy wanted. Max was late by the time he got back to the office. He shouldn't have taken Sandy with him. She would have loved the ones he picked out. It was just that there were so many that she couldn't decide. He would get over it, and she's very happy. He stopped by admin and picked up the papers he was expecting.

Mouse was in his office. She had poured herself a cup of coffee but had dozed off in his chair with her feet on the desk. Max couldn't help but smile. "JACKS, what are you doing?"

She flew out of the chair yelling as she came to attention; "Sorry, SIR." Max started to laugh. She realized it was Max. "Damn it Max."

He pointed toward the door. It was open. She should have been paying better attention. "Sorry Sergeant Dent."

He closed the door and laughed. "Sorry Mouse, I just couldn't resist."

She was still a little shaky. "You nearly scared me to death." They laughed.

Max asked. "How far did you get on the mapping?"

She took a sip of her coffee. "That's cold. What time is it?" Max told her he was about a half hour late. They both got a hot cup of coffee. She told him she had found several rooms, "a large room, well several large rooms and they will be hard to find unless you know the way." She pointed to the map and made the corrections. She asked. "When do I find out what is going on?"

Max smiled "Tonight. But for now I have some things for you to do."

He asked her to have a seat. "Ok…" He put a paper in front of her "Sign that. It's accepting assignment to the Einstein as a sweeper, grade private and Level eight. It explains that the pay will be delayed for two weeks until the official paperwork comes down. But you are to wear the rank effective now. It also explains that you will be required to pass the security augment test. I have uniforms in that bag for you, any questions?"

She asked. "What about my daughter?" Max pushed another paper in front of her. "This is a release for your daughter to be examined by a Professor Kidling. He is doing an experiment on the children on the ship." She started to get a little upset but he continued. "Don't worry, he is monitoring their growth. He checks their weight and height once a week and blood once a month. He's doing research on the growth of children in space compared to Earth. There is a school where she can stay when you're on duty, no charge. She will be considered a part of the crew as far as benefits, uniforms and all."

She smiled. "Am I dreaming?"

Max laughed. "No, you were doing that a while ago when you were sacked out in my chair." She smiled as she signed the two papers. Max handed her another. "This one is for the family quarters where you are now."

She was surprised. "They're nice; I didn't think I would get to keep them since there is a second bedroom." She smiled. "Brandy will love that."

Max separated the papers and handed her the ones she needed for the promotion and the ones for Brandy. "You have the rest of the afternoon off, to take care of this business. I need you back by 1900, you and Brandy - dinner in my quarters." He added. "I'm not even going to ask the next question." He handed her a thousand credits. "You'll be in flight for nine months no stops, no chance to spend credits. Get what you need and pay me when we get to the next pay day."

She smiled. "I knew you were going to offer and I was going to say no, but I didn't think about how long it was going to be." She took the credits. "There's not any interest on this is there?"

Max just shook his head. "No, just the credits back." Max smiled. "You have to be in uniform when you leave the ship. So, you better get going." She smiled. He added. "Oh yeah, we got Brandy's size from the place she is staying. You might want to take a uniform for her."

She laughed. "She'll love it."

Max smiled. "Her pass and grade is noted on this new ID, she is a Level ten research assistant." Betty went to get ready.

CHAPTER FOURTEEN,
BRANDY

Betty, well Mouse, wanted to hurry but couldn't help but stop and look at herself in the mirror. The uniform was a light gray, Level eight; it had collar brass that told everyone she was a private. The right sleeve was orange and had a black stripe around the cuff, which made her job a sweeper. The left sleeve was dark blue, security augment. She wasn't wearing the badge which meant she was in training. She left the ship at 1420. She was going to catch the bus to the Anderson child care unit. It didn't matter that it was late because she wasn't going to take Brandy back there today. She was going to take her to their new home; their first home.

The guard at the end of the dock was a familiar face, it was Frank. He joked. "Wow, do you look nice."

She asked "Do you think so?"

He assured her that he did. "It's good to have you aboard, Jacks."

She smiled "Thank you" and went to catch the bus.

She didn't catch the bus. She decided to take the transport that was waiting for a fare. She asked the driver "How much to the Andersons child care unit?"

He called in and told her 4 credits and "I'll need it in advance."

She handed him a ten. "I'll need you to wait when we get there."

He took the ten "This will keep me waiting for two hours if you think you're going to be longer it's one credit for twenty minutes.

She handed him another ten "I'll need a ride back to this area." She cautioned him with impending death if he left without her.

At the child care unit, Brandy was sad. The closest thing she had to a friend, Hanna, had went with her Mother. Hanna's mother had signed intent with a man who was taking them to Earth. Brandy had seen a lot of things in her few years at this place. The worst was the gray uniforms. Mother or father would get a job on a starship and would have to leave their child behind. It would seem like forever before they would come back for the child. The Sisters knew the gray uniforms would leave a child without a parent and them with less credits to run the unit. They could not understand why a parent would do such a thing.

Brandy was very sad for another reason. Yesterday Mom didn't come by to see her. It was the same day that Hanna left and she was all alone the whole day. She knew it would be four more days before she would see Mom again. Mom could only come by on her day off because she couldn't afford a place to stay and make the trip to the unit each day to drop Brandy off. She often worked late and the unit would be closed and she couldn't pick her up. The unit wasn't a bad place but it was a cold place. The kids were mean, and the Sisters were overworked. They didn't have much time to do more than just take care of the children. The food was not good and Brandy looked forward to the day when Mom would come by because they could go to the café and get a hotdog with a spoon of chili on it. She smiled just to remember the taste.

Betty watched out the window of the transport as it passed the café where she and Brandy would get something to eat. The chili that Brandy loved was such an extravagance, but she loved it so much. She remembered how she would save it for the last bite so she could taste it longer. She thought to herself that maybe today she would buy a bowl for her. It was a whole credit but she thought she might be able to afford it.

The transport pulled into the gate and was greeted by the Sister. "What can I do for you today?"

She smiled. "Hello Sister Barbara, I'm here for Brandy."

The Sister waved them in. She was a little mad at Betty. She knew that Brandy was going to be abandoned so Betty could make more money, so Brandy could have a better life. "Brandy needs a mother, not what she is going to get." It was apparent that the rest of the staff felt the same way by the less than warm reception Betty got when she went into the building.

The classes were looking out their windows; a transport was a big deal. Somebody rich was coming to visit. The gray uniform was announced almost with horror, "It's a gray." The scary words echoed through the rooms. Nothing good ever happened when a gray came to the unit. Somebody was going to be left behind for a while until a parent could come back to get them. They hoped it was one of the parents who had left their child coming back to get them. But it was a gray and not another color, when parents come back they are not wearing a gray uniform.

When the phone rang in the classroom and no one was expecting a parent to return. It meant to the kids that a parent was going away and someone was staying. The Sister reluctantly answered the phone. She knew when she sent the requested child to the office that child was going to be heartbroken.

Every child was waiting for the name, they were all scared. The Sister tried to smile "Very well. I will send her to the office." The boys were relieved but the girls were not. The Sister hung up the phone. "I'm sorry Brandy, but your mother would like to see you in the office." Brandy was devastated, Mom would never do this. She didn't even notice how bad the rest of the children felt for her. On her way to the office she decided to be brave. "Mom wouldn't do this unless it was for the best." She was almost in tears when she walked into the office. She put on her 'I am happy face' "Hello Mom."

Betty squatted down and said "Come here baby."

Brandy ran to her, she was going to be brave. "This is not the day you visit."

Betty smiled. "No, I had to work that day but my new boss gave me the afternoon off to come get you."

Brandy asked "How long can you stay?"

The answer was interrupted, by one of the Sisters "These papers are all in order."

Brandy couldn't hold it in any longer. She started to cry. She knew for sure now. Mom was in a gray uniform and had brought papers. She was going to leave.

Betty picked her up. "What's the matter baby?"

Brandy pleaded through her tears. "I don't want you to go."

Betty tried to reassure her. "But we have to go. I've already signed the papers."

Brandy asked "How long?"

Betty almost laughed "Well, I'm not planning on ever coming back." Brandy started to cry and Betty couldn't get her to stop.

The Sister smiled. "I don't normally get involved in these things. But Brandy thinks you are going to leave her here and not come back. When a parent comes into the office in one of those uniforms it usually means the child is going to be left alone for a while, you just told her you were never going to come back."

Betty smiled. "I'm so sorry baby. This isn't like that. You are going with me."

Brandy slowly started to sob a little less and then she asked the Sister. "Is Mom just trying to make me feel better?"

The Sister smiled. "According to this paperwork you and your Mom have been assigned to the science vessel Einstein."

Betty told her. "I have a bag for your stuff. I think we should go pack. I have a surprise for you."

The Sister took Betty to the side and asked. "If you don't mind, would you take her back to her class so she can pick up her things? Something like this would give the other children hope, there is so little here."

Betty smiled. "I have a uniform for her. Would you like her to put it on first?"

The Sister was giddy. "That would be very nice."

The Sister took Betty and Brandy to the dorms so Brandy could get her things. Betty asked the Sister. "That ice cream wagon, does it still come by?"

The Sister told her it did. "Yes, but it doesn't stop long. He doesn't get a lot of business."

Betty asked "How much do you think it would take to buy each of the children an ice cream?"

The sister was hoping she guessed right. "The ice cream is a tenth of a credit and we have fifty-eight students. So I guess almost six credits."

Betty gave the Sister a fifty credit slip. "Could you see that everyone gets one? I would like to donate the rest to the school." The Sister was very pleased. "That is a month's pay for most that use this place."

Betty smiled. "I have a very good job, now." She looked toward Brandy. "And we are going on a starship that will not dock for nine months."

The Sister took the fifty. "I'll go make sure he stops."

Brandy took the bag and went to get her stuff. There was something in the bag and she took it out. "Mom there is something in this bag."

Betty smiled. "That's the surprise." Brandy took the uniform out of the bag. "Oh, it one of your uniforms, why is it pink?"

Betty had a slight smile on her face. "I don't think I can fit in that uniform. I think maybe it's yours." Brandy's eyes got so big that it made Betty laugh. "And you need to put it on so we can go."

The Sister met them at the door. She said to Brandy. "Oh my, you look nice."

Brandy was pointing to the emblems. "See, I'm going on the Einstein."

The Sister addressed Betty. "The wagon will be here in about ten minutes." They followed the Sister to Brandy's classroom. Brandy went into the room. She was very happy to deliver the news. "Guess what. I'm going to live with my MOM. We are going to live on the Einstein. That's a starship." She added "and this is my uniform." The Sister in charge of the class laughed and smiled. Brandy got her stuff and was ready to go when the ice cream wagon was allowed into the yard. An announcement was made that Brandy Jacks was going to the stars with her mother and that everyone was invited to have an ice cream, free.

Betty wouldn't let Brandy have a lot of ice cream. She told her she had another surprise and she could have another ice cream later. They were thanked for the gifts and they were on their way. Betty told the driver to take them to the café where they ate on the days they were together. Brandy was smiling. She was going to get to show Ruth her new uniform. Betty told the driver that they were going to have something to eat and it would be a half hour if he wanted to get something. "But you wait. Do you have enough credits?"

He smiled "Yeah, yes."

They went into the café. Ruth was behind the counter "Have a seat and I'll be with you in a second." It was clear that she didn't recognize them. A short time later she came around. "Do you know what you want; the chili is the best on station."

Brandy asked. "We know Ruth; don't you know us?"

Ruth smiled. "I do now, Brandy. What are you wearing?"

Brandy smiled big. "My uniform, Mom got a job on a starship."

Ruth smiled. "Well, I'm happy for you, Betty." She was a little quieter about the next question. "Does Brandy get to go with you?"

Betty smiled. "Yes, there is a professor on board who wants to study the growth patterns of children in space, so Brandy is assigned as a lab aide."

Ruth smiled and was more up-beat. "I'm very happy for the both of you." She smiled "So what can I get you today?"

Betty smiled "We would like two bowls of that chili and crackers."

Brandy smiled "And root beer."

Betty changed the order "Two root beers, please."

Ruth smiled. "This new job must pay better than the other."

Betty smiled "a lot better." They finished the chili and then had ice cream. When they left the café Brandy was rubbing her full belly. "Mom, that's the best food I ever had"

They found the driver and he took them to the office where Betty used to work. She wanted to get the few things she had in her locker; mostly she wanted the pictures of Brandy. She was cleaning out her locker when one of the girls came into the room. She laughed. "So, I guess Jacks finally got caught again. I knew that girl was no good and the security force would be by sooner or later to pick up her stuff."

Betty turned around. "No, I joined the security force and I have been investigating this place for months. You guys have no idea how much trouble you're in." She didn't say much more. She just took her stuff - and Brandy - and left. It was all she could do not to start laughing. But she made it to the transport. He took them back to the shops.

The ship was within walking distance from the shops so Betty let the driver go "How much do I owe you?" He told her she had one and a half credits coming back.

She smiled. "Just keep it and thank you for the day."

He was excited. "Thank you lady, and if you ever wave at my cab I'll stop."

They stopped at as many shops as they could on the way back to the ship. Betty told Brandy that they were going to have dinner with her boss and didn't want to be late. It was six thirty when they got to the ship and a simple flash of an ID got them on board. The guard at the entrance smiled "Did you have a good day, Mouse?"

She smiled. "I sure did Frank. Oh, Frank this is my daughter, Brandy."

He smiled. "Well, I want to tell you she is a beauty in that uniform."

Brandy asked Frank if he was the only guard. "You're always here."

He laughed, "No, I just give them breaks. You just happen to pass through when I'm here."

They went on board and Brandy asked "Who was that?"

Betty told her. "I'll be working with him in security."

Brandy stopped. "You're a policeman."

She smiled. "No, security; it's different from police." They got to their quarters and went inside. Betty said. "Brandy, your room is this way."

Brandy smiled. "I have a room."

Betty was still smiling. "Yes, now get a shower and put on some of your new stuff. We need to hurry." She didn't want to put on any of her new stuff. "I'm going to wear my new uniform." Betty told her she still had to take a shower and there was another uniform in the drawer. Once the uniform was off, and the shower taken; she decided to wear something else. They were ready by five minutes of seven and walked down the hall to Max and Sandy's.

She knocked on the door and Max yelled "It's open." She opened the door and they went inside. Max was putting on some music. "Hey Mouse; is that the most beautiful child in the world you told me about?"

Brandy was still a little upset. "I look better in my uniform." They laughed.

Sandy was finishing some of the food in the small kitchenette. "Max get her that thing that Bill brought."

Mouse sounded a little disappointed. "Bill's not going to be here?"

Max told her "He had to work, but he left this for Brandy." Max handed Brandy a teddy bear as big as she was.

Brandy wasn't sure about the thing. "Thank you, what is it?"

Betty laughed "It's a teddy bear."

Brandy smiled. "What's that?" Did you ever try to explain a teddy bear?

Although Max and Mouse tried, it was Sandy that did it best. "A teddy bear is your friend. He goes with you to dreamland and protects you from bad dreams. He makes you feel better when you're sad. He is anything you want him to be. He is always there and will do anything he can to make you feel better."

Brandy smiled "Does it have to be a boy?"

Sandy said. "No, but mine is…" She looked up at Max "His name is Max and I got him when I was eight."

Brandy got the wide eyed look she could do so well. "They grow up to be people?"

They laughed. "No, they'll always stay the same." Sandy continued "Max got me the bear when I was eight and so I named it Max. Max the bear helped me through some hard times. I would hug him and somehow I felt close to the real Max."

Brandy was ok with the deal and the bear. But she didn't really know what to do with it. "So I should name the bear Bill because he gave me the bear." She wrinkled her nose up and sort of smiled, "Who's Bill?"

Mouse laughed, "If you want to name the bear Bill then you can but you don't have to."

Brandy nodded, "I don't want to name it Bill. I'll think of another name."

Mouse smiled. "As far as Bill goes, I'll introduce him later."

Dinner was fried chicken, grandmother's chicken. Brandy wasn't really interested in the chicken or the potatoes or the gravy or the corn. She watched her plate and the other people eat. Sandy asked "Don't you like chicken?"

Brandy smiled. "It don't look like chicken."

Sandy smiled "That is what chickens look like, the other stuff is chopped up chicken and then pushed back together."

Mouse requested. "Brandy, you don't have to eat it but I would like you to taste the food." Brandy was very reluctant to taste the chicken so she took a very little bite. She chewed it slowly, although she had not bitten off enough to chew. It was almost enough to make you laugh. It wasn't long before she was eating a little more and then more. She finished her plate and was sitting quietly.

Sandy asked. "I have a wing left would you like to have it?" She nodded. Sandy went and got the chicken for her.

Brandy smiled "It don't look like chicken either, but it smells good." She took a drink from her glass. "That's good, what is it?"

Sandy replied "It's orange juice." They talked a while longer and then Sandy went to the kitchen and brought back a plate for each of them with a slice of chocolate cake. Brandy didn't ask what it was, she just ate.

After they finished Betty and Sandy cleared the table. Max offered to help but was sent to the sofa. Brandy went with him. Betty said to Sandy "Are you two planning on having kids?"

Sandy smiled "Six."

Betty laughed "You'll change your mind after the first one. Getting them in is fun but getting them out, damn, that's not fun at all." When they went to find Max and Brandy; she was sitting in his lap and he was telling her the story of Cinderella. He was about half way into the story when Brandy went to sleep and he stopped. Sandy insisted "Well go on."

Max laughed "You're kidding, right."

She told him. "I have never heard that story."

Mouse shook her head. "I haven't either, so what happens?"

Max smiled. "That story is hundreds of years old. I can't believe you have never heard it." They were not going to let it go. Max took a deep breath and finished the story. The girls were almost crying.

Sandy smiled "That a very nice story."

Mouse nodded. "It really fits my situation too; doesn't it?"

Max laughed. "I don't believe this." He lay Brandy down on the sofa and went to get the stuff for Mouse. He gave her the package and told her to read the instructions. "Make sure you know how it works." Meet me in my office at nine. "That'll give you time to get Brandy into Professor Kidling's group. They're expecting her."

Mouse decided it was time to go; and Sandy volunteered Max to carry Brandy to bed. Mouse wouldn't have any part of it. She was looking forward to caring for Brandy so Max carried the package.

When Private Jacks got to A S Dents office the next morning she was unusually quiet. She had a donut and coffee but acted like her mind was somewhere else. Max noticed and asked if she was all right but she just assured him everything was good. Max and Mouse went to get a shuttle. They were going to be about an hour away from the port at a sub unit. It was a half hour into the flight when Max decided that he had enough "Mouse, what in the hell is wrong with you?"

She didn't say a word but he could see her start to get madder and madder. He knew it would come out in a minute. When it did she was almost yelling. "I don't like to be played a fool Max. It really PISSES me off."

Max had no idea what she was talking about. "Mouse, you are going to have to tell me how you are being played a fool."

She started. "That is a damn incubator you gave me last night and I just can't believe we are going to hatch chickens on a starship. We would never get away with it and I would find myself kicked out of the force and back doing some crappy job and trying to make ends meet for me and Brandy - with no help. So just what are we going to do, make some kind of drug? I'm not going to do that, not a chance. I am not going back to jail." She stared at Max, "not for drugs. I would never get out. They would put Brandy in a care unit and that is all she would ever know."

Max smiled. "Well, I hate to tell you this."

She started again. "I do have a choice Max. I would have to give this up but I do have a choice."

Max was almost laughing. "Mouse we really are going to hatch chickens on a starship. We'll have the protection of the Captain. We'll get away with it because he wants us to raise the chickens and in space he's king. And he is also on the Admirals list."

She didn't know what to say but when the breeding farm came into sight. She was surprised "You're not lying; we really are going to hatch chickens."

Max laughed. "Now we are not going to make all the credits in the world, the Captain won't let us but we are going to make enough to spread around."

She started to laugh "an Admiral?"

Max nodded "on the list."

She laughed. "I won't have to meet the Captain, I hope. I just can't talk to people like that."

Max smiled. "You might even have to dance with him." Mouse just looked disgusted.

They landed and took a short tour before picking up the eggs, 4000 to eat and 200 to hatch. The fertilized eggs were almost as many credits as the others. But who wants someone else horning in on his business. It was a cash deal; thirty five hundred credits. Mouse later figured that was five years pay for her. They started back to the ship and Max asked Mouse to fly the shuttle for a while. She didn't know how. Max knew that and that was why he wanted her to fly the thing. She did better than Max the first time he flew. He landed and they began to move the eggs. Max went back to his office and left Mouse to take care of the eggs.

He had a half dozen messages for Private Jacks from Aide Brandy Jacks. He read one of them and then made a call to admin.

Mouse came by after she had placed the eggs as she was told. "Am I at lunch?"

Max told her that she needed to go by admin for some paperwork and then pick up Brandy. "She wants her charms, all the other kids have them and she wants hers."

He laughed. "You guys have to get some charms or Brandy said she is going to die."

They laughed. Max told her, "Set up the incubators tomorrow"

He paused to think. "I don't think we'll put the eggs in until after we launch."

She told him "As long as it's within ten days."

Max told her to take the rest of the day and she left. She signed out and went to see if she could get Brandy's charms.

CHAPTER FIFTEEN,
THE NEW LIEUTENANT

Four days later the day started bad and didn't get any better. The fight was tonight, the new Lieutenant arrived, and last but not least, a media crew arrived on station. The crew was here to film the presentation of the awards to the members of the crew who saved the ship from the cascade. It's to be filmed and then released after they left port.

The Lieutenant didn't check in at the ship but everyone who mattered knew she had arrived. Her name was Carol Anderson; she was in her late twenties and was sure she's behind in the game because she hasn't made Lieutenant Commander. The fact was she wasn't behind except by her schedule. She brought with her a Sergeant with eighteen years in grade named Mason Black.

Mason was Max's nemesis in his training years. He was a hard unreasonable man. Max didn't hate him but he really did not like him or the way he did things. The last member of the crew was a Private Harriet Smith, all one had to do was lay eyes on her and it was clear she was an old school Mouse. This was an inspection team.

An old school Mouse was a mouse who had been kept secret. The Captains of the old school were against the black market or at least didn't want to know about it. In fact, Bill was the first

Captain that Max had met who recognized how important the black market was to morale.

But deep space is a new world and Mouse has a mouse charm on her left arm in the personal area to prove it. She said that the charm maker was more than a little surprised when she asked for it. But deep space is proving to be very different from normal duty. Max got Mouse the small arms, and security badge added to the security Charm even though those two skills would be completed over the next few days.

The media crew was just a pain in the ass. They wanted everything and they were always in the way. The best thing was that they had stepped up their schedule because of the fight. They wanted James before he took a beating. As a result, the awards were presented in a private room and wouldn't be released until the ship left dock. The promotions would take effect at the time of presentation.

A lot of awards were to be presented to a lot of people because of the cascade event. The most important were the ones that were presented to A S Dent, Professor Aide Lieutenant J G Sandra Dent and Captain William Holt. The Cross of Congress is the highest award that can be presented to a member of the force. The Star of Congress is the second top award. A career is made if you are nominated for the Cross of Congress but only got the Star of Congress. Bill could attest to that - he would now be wearing both. Today there would be three of each awarded. It is a major media event. While Professor Aide Lieutenants James and Karen House and Professor Commander Larry Kent would receive the nomination award, the Star of Congress, it was Max, Sandy and Bill who saved the day. Max had never even seen a person who had either of the awards except Bill who is charmed with the Star already. They are very rare.

The promotions were strange. They all had to change jackets on their dress uniform, because of the level change. Bill would wear a different stripe on his sleeve. Even though he would still be a Captain; he would somehow outrank all other Captains not on the Admirals list. Max had to don an officers jacket with his new ensign bars, Sandy's new jacket was so much different that the other couldn't be changed. She would have an entirely new jacket. She would remain a Lieutenant J G, but with a lot more power as a Professor.

They were Charmed on the spot as the media filmed the event. The entire event was not to be talked about. Charms for the Cross of Congress and its companion the Star of Congress, are placed on the back of the right hand. There would be no hiding these charms. They were told to wear civilian attire until the lock down for the launch.

The fight that night found the new Lieutenant and her party at the club early so they could watch everyone arrive. The Lieutenant preferred to be called 'sir' even though she was female. The Sergeant liked 'Sarge' and the Private was Private. They were better friends then their conversation would infer. They were mainly watching for the troops assigned to the Einstein. Sarge's job was to help read the charms. The private was looking for the black market players. The Lieutenant was to help find the officers.

Mouse was the first one they noticed. Private said matter of fact. "There's your Mouse." She began to read, "Forced to enter, scrubber then sweeper then private, security badge and small arms." She read "She's assigned to the Einstein, that's your Mouse." She added "And a very well equipped Mouse she is." She smiled. "She can go anywhere on the ship, no questions asked."

Sarge laughed "Look at the mouse charm on her left arm."

The Lieutenant smiled "She must have a very powerful protector to have that charm."

CC3 Mike Hall and his intended, Louise, came in the door while Mouse was still looking for her party. Louise, one of the scientists, knew Betty from the school that Professor Kidling ran. She had a son in the class. Louise smiled a kind of fake smile but a smile. "Hello Betty. I didn't know you liked this sort of thing."

Betty smiled. "Yes, I do, but I'm hoping to find someone here tonight and con him into dancing with me."

Louise introduced her husband. "This is my husband Mike. He might know the person you're looking for."

Betty was a little ashamed. She didn't know much about this guy. "Well, I don't know where he works. I don't really know his last name but his first name is Bill."

Louise smiled. "Bill Holt."

Betty smiled. "I don't really know but he's about six feet and medium build with grayish hair and the deepest eyes."

Mike smiled. "Well, I don't know about his eyes but he will be here. Are you Mouse?"

Betty smiled. "Yeah, do you know Max?"

Mike laughed. "Mouse, I'm happy to meet you; and yes, everyone knows Max."

Louise smiled. "Well, Mouse, how nice; I would like to talk to you about a little something that I'm having trouble finding."

Mouse smiled. "I'll do my best."

The new Lieutenant was a little shocked. "I'll be damned; you guys are looking at a full Commander socializing with a Private." The Private at the table smiled "A full Commander. Now that's some protection."

Bill walked in with Warren and Ironman Jim. Ironman spoke to her. "Hey Mouse, come out to see me kick this boy's ass?"

She smiled. "No, I came out to see you get yours kicked." He laughed.

Private didn't miss the name "Mouse - God, what gall."

Bill smiled. "Why don't you two guys go find a table before they're all taken?" Sarge said "Did you see the Star of Congress on that guy's hand."

Private said. "Yeah and the Cross and Star on the other guy's hand."

The Lieutenant added. "It gets worse. He's an Admiral selectee."

Private said under her breath 'an Admiral.'

Sarge grinned "And worse, he's the Death Dealer, her friend, the guy with the star is Ironman Jim. He's fighting tonight for fleet honors, Ironman Jim."

Lieutenant smiled, "Brute force and political power. This is going to be a very bad trip."

Betty asked Bill to dance. He smiled "You're a bold one." He danced one dance and then had to go help the Ironman.

The Lieutenant smiled. "We got big trouble."

The Sergeant started to laugh "more than you can imagine, two more Crosses of Congress and a Star just walked in the door. I thought those things were nearly impossible to get." He added. "And one of the crosses is attached to Max Crash." He laughed out loud when Max waved to him. He waved back "God, we are in trouble. Max is a convicted five time killer. When he turned eighteen and his prison time was up; he was trained by a force so special you won't find it in any book."

Max brought Sandy, Karen and Mouse over to meet Sarge and his group. "Hello Mason, it hasn't been anywhere near long enough."

Karen smiled. "Carol, I could say the same about you."

Sandy laughed. "Damn, it is Carol the snitch."

Karen was sarcastic, "Now, now, she was just doing her job."

Sandy was smiling when she told her "There will most likely be a fight in here tonight other than the one in the ring and I'll be looking for you."

The Lieutenant didn't like her tone. "You can't threaten me, I outrank you."

Karen backhanded her and she went to the floor.

Sarge started to step in but Max stepped between them. "That fight can start right now."

Karen smiled. "There isn't any rank in here and you know the regulations have to be followed when we get back to the ship."

Bill, Mike and James were quick to the encounter. A number of others from the Einstein moved in the direction. Bill was very commanding "You children play nice. I don't want my new people beaten too badly before they get aboard." Bill helped the Lieutenant to her feet. "It is a strict ship but out here anything goes. And know this; there will be no repercussions for anything that happens here when we are back on the ship." The two groups separated.

Private smiled. "You two make nasty enemies."

The Lieutenant said. "Yeah, that girl, that 'star' carrying Lieutenant, once tried to kill me. I don't know that for fact but I sure believed she did. It was never proven that she poisoned my roommate but she did die."

Sarge said. "Did you notice Max and Sandy? They're both charmed with Crosses. The hearts on their arms say they're married. Max took the rap for a double murder that most believed was carried out by his girlfriend at the time. I think her name was Sandra, and one of their Lieutenants," He looked at the other two. "I don't remember his name, but they called him Stickman." He paused. "What do you think the odds are of that being her?"

The Lieutenant smiled, "Sandra was very sweet on a guy she said was in prison. But that was when they were eight or nine wasn't it?"

Sarge nodded. "Sure was."

Private laughed a serious laugh. "So this time we are up against real killers not just maybe killers. They have childhood links, heavy protectors and brute force. This is going to be tough."

Two guys with security charms came in and looked around the bar. Max was sort of watching for them and told Sandy. "I'm going to go buy those guys a drink and see if they want to join us."

Sandy asked. "Do you know them or are you just picking up strays again."

Max told her they were the two new security guys he had requested. And yes, "I do know one of them, the Sergeant." He smiled. "How long has it been since you saw Stickman?"

She laughed "I really thought he was dead."

Max nodded. "Nope, he's sitting over there." They excused themselves and went to see their friend. Max told Sandy that he had found him on a roster to be transferred. I wanted him and they wanted rid of him and his mate."

She asked. "He has an intended."

Max smiled. "Well, it's the guy with him. He sort of likes guys."

She laughed "So that summer he wasn't chasing me. He was chasing you."

Max laughed. "I don't think so, we were just eight." He slowed his walk and almost stopped. "You don't need to go nuts on this, ok?"

She smiled. "Max, he was our friend and he may still be and I don't care who he is sleeping with." She laughed, "As long as it's not you."

Max walked up to the table. "You guys assigned to the Einstein?" The Sergeant said, "Yes, sir." Max smiled "There is no rank here."

The Sergeant stared at him a second or two "How long you had that scar? I only ask because I used to have a buddy that had one almost like it."

Sandy moved into view. "He used to wear an eye patch too."

Max smiled. "It's been a long time, Stickman."

Stick started to laugh. "I haven't been called that in years. Max, are you responsible for us being here?" Max nodded. Stick introduced Larry. "This is my friend Larry."

Larry nodded. "Hello."

Stick smiled. "Larry, this is Max and Sandy."

Larry smiled. "Oh my god, they're real; not something you made up."

Max asked them "Why don't you guys join us at the table over there."

Stick started to say no, but Max assured him. "Whatever is between you two is your business. I have a two man room for you and that is where all this should stay." Larry smiled an unsure smile. "That's a better deal than we've gotten anywhere else."

Stickman agreed and they went to sit with the group." They had to pass the table with Sarge. Max made it a point to address Stickman when they passed. "So Stickman how was your last assignment?"

Sarge said after they passed. "Looks like the whole gang is back together."

Stick noticed the deliberate 'introduction' as well. "someone you wanted to intimidate?"

Max laughed, "Yeah,"

They ordered snacks and drinks as they caught up and just talked. Bill came by and danced with Mouse. Max introduced Stick. Bill smiled. "It's been a long time."

Stick didn't know what he was talking about. Sandy smiled. "He has pictures of us together when we were eight."

Stick nodded, "So I guess we're about to do this thing. Whatever it is?"

Bill smiled, "If one believes his dreams of The Mist."

The fight was an unknown number of five minute rounds with five minutes in between. Bets could be placed at any time before the match started. They were also taken between rounds. It would go on until one fighter either couldn't or wouldn't continue. Both fighters went off at five to four odds. The trick to making a lot of credits was to pick the round or find a fool who would bet with you outside the odds. That is usually a member of the crew of the other ship and you might not be able to collect if you do win.

Ironman was not as a strong starter. So bets on him winning in the first round would be easy to get at high odds. Max had been watching Warren and James work together. He had also talked to James or Ironman. He was going to try to take the fight in the first round. Max felt that James was just playing with the other fighter because he wanted to fight. Max got Stick to lay two hundred credits on Ironman to win in the first round; he got 10 to 1 from the club. Larry placed another fifty credits on Ironman Jim because Stick told him to. "Max doesn't play to lose."

Mouse got Max to dance with her. Max asked. "What can I do for you?"

She laughed. "Why did Bill have me bet 300 credits on James to take this fight in the first round?"

Max laughed "It's a real gamble but I believe he is going to take it in the first."

She wanted to be sure. "But it's possible I could lose if I made a bet like that."

Max smiled "likely."

The dance was finished and she went to make the bet. The fight started. James was hitting harder and more often and it was looking good. But it looked like the credits were gone. There was less than a minute left when Karen started to really yell. "Quit fooling around and get it done." It was unlike her to yell about anything.

Sandy asked. "How much do you have on this round?"

Karen blurted out, "500." They were laughing when the upper cut sent the man almost into the air and he was out. There was twelve seconds on the clock. He had to be down for ten for it to count as a knockout. His corner was yelling and screaming but their man was in dream land. The fight was stopped, the bell rang, "and the winner IRONMAN JIM."

Everyone was yelling and screaming. Sarge said. "Well ladies, you just saw a fixed fight."

The Lieutenant smiled. "I don't think it was fixed, but it was well read."

Everyone cashed in; Mouse ran into her old boss who was there again. He was much nicer. "I see you did well."

She smiled. "Yes, very well." He didn't matter any more. Mouse just walked by him and went to find Bill. They spent the next few hours together.

The next day was the last open day at the station; the ship was on skeleton crew. Mouse was out trying to get the last of what she wanted. She repaid Max and had enough credits left to buy an acoustic guitar. She had wanted one for a long time and it was going to be a long trip. She was going to learn to play. Sandy was at the same store looking for a guitar for Max. She noticed Mouse. "You and Bill have a good night?"

Mouse smiled. "Not as good as I hoped." Mouse could be extremely frank. "Is he married or something? He's not too old for things to work is he?"

Sandy laughed. Mouse seemed a little disgusted. "Well, he was a gentleman and that's not exactly what I was looking for."

Sandy wasn't sure how to approach this. "You know there are a lot of problems for him to be involved with you at all. Maybe he's just trying to save both of you a big problem."

Mouse was short and a little loud. "Well, how bad can it be? He's not the Captain of the damn ship, and he is involved in the black market so why can't he be involved with me?"

Sandy was standing there in awe. "You don't know?"

Mouse questioned "What; know what?"

Sandy smiled "You did read the charms on his arm, didn't you."

She smiled. "I'm not very good with those and I was too busy looking at his eyes."

Sandy laughed. "You need to learn to read those charms. Bill is my uncle and the Captain of the ship and on the Admirals list."

Mouse didn't say a word. Sandy smiled "And I think he is just as taken with you as you are with him. But this is a very difficult situation for the both of you."

Mouse was concerned. "I hope he doesn't think I was… well, just because he is the Captain."

Sandy smiled. "I'll make sure he doesn't think that."

They talked a while longer before they got to why they were there. The cost of the two new guitars was almost as much as a used karaoke unit that came with two used guitars and a lot of other things. They decided to go together and buy the unit. The package was a little larger than they intended so they took the two guitars out and had the rest put in the hold. It wasn't any problem; Max was a big cheese on this ship not to mention Sandy's uncle, the Captain. When Sandy wanted something she got it, besides the package was cleared by security - Private Parks.

Max had stayed on board the ship to tie up a few loose ends; he was as ready as he was going to get for this trip. He had lunch with the Captain and Mike. It was a quick sandwich because they all had a lot to do. There were the last minute shipments that would have to be cleared, but they were all above board. Some of the new crew additions were checking in. Stick and Larry checked in and Max showed them their room. He told them they were free for the rest of the day but needed to be on board by 1700.

The surprise was a power unit technician, a Corporal Luanne Le'Beau; she was not expected, but welcome. Max was cleaning a vent in his office when she entered. She said. "Hello, I'm Corporal Le'Beau; I was told to come by here and I would be shown to my quarters." She paused a second and said, "I hope you work here; there isn't anyone in the outer office."

Max introduced himself as Max, and told her to put the records on the desk. He was dirty and he asked. "I need to finish this, do you mind waiting a minute?"

She set her bag down. "Could I ask some questions about the ship?"

Max said, "Tit for tat."

She wasn't expecting the response. "What?"

Max laughed. "I'll answer one of yours and you answer one of mine."

She laughed and it didn't seem like something she did often, "OK."

Max smiled and went on with what he was doing. "There's coffee and cookies over in the corner if you want?"

She went to get some. She asked "Do I need to pay for these?"

Max said. "No, they're contraband; we have to dispose of them. You first, what would you like to know?"

Her first question was about the ship. "Is it a good place to work or one of those tight ass rides?"

Max laughed "On the surface it's a tight ass ride. Everyone is expected to do their job without being asked. But this is a deep space flight. The more you get to know people, the looser it gets."

She asked. "So, the officers aren't that strict once you get out into space?"

Max answered, "Nope, not as long as you do your job the best you can."

Max asked. "How about you? I can smell that black market perfume even over the smell inside this vent."

She noted. "I think we all do a little black market. But I bought this at the station and I'm not going to sell it; do you think that'll be all right?"

Max started to crawl out of the vent. "Hand me that other cleaner and those towels." She handed him the cleaner and he polished the vent as he came out.

She asked. "What do you do on the ship? I see you have some personal charms. Your sleeve slid up when you reached for the cleaner. The double hearts stand out."

Max smiled and as he put the vent cover back. "That's my wife's idea. Not that I minded. Are you intended?"

She smiled "I was. But it ran out and he didn't want to sign another one... I did."

Max smiled "I'm sorry, it must be tough when that happens."

She smiled. "I thought you said you were; no you said wife."

Max smiled. "Yeah, Sandy, she keeps me from going nuts."

She wondered "So you two have been intended for a long time?"

Max laughed, "No, we were only intended for a short while. We married for life a few weeks ago."

She was surprised "Really I never knew anyone who did that."

Max nodded. "I've known her since we were eight, she says she loved me then, I know I did her. Then we were apart for years until we were assigned to this ship. She's a professor in the lab areas." Max added. "Let me get out of these coveralls and I'll show you to your quarters. As he changed behind the screen, "How many power units have you pinned?"

She said, "Four, were you on board when they had the cascade?"

Max laughed. "Damn right, it was scary." Max came out from behind the screen. "I didn't get a chance to shake hands with you before." He held out his hand. She shook it. She had a very blank look on her face. "You're not a scrubber are you?"

Max smiled. "I am today. Betty is off ship."

She turned his hand. "That is the Cross of Congress isn't it?"

Max still wasn't happy about the promotion, "Yeah, they made me take that and if that wasn't enough they promoted me to Ensign."

She stepped back. "I'm sorry to be so… sorry sir."

Max smiled. "What I said about the ship is true; do your job to the best of your ability. You'll become part of the family and you'll not get any crap from anybody who counts."

She said, "Yes, sir."

Max told her. "Now, next rule, when I'm not in uniform I'm Max."

As they were leaving the office, Frank yelled. "Max, I need your John Henry on these load forms. Your wife bought something and Mouse signed it in; but there isn't any room in your hold."

Max looked at Luanne "How much stuff do you have?"

She said, "Not very much."

Frank was already doing the paperwork. "I could assign her a four by."

Max asked. "Would it be alright for me to store whatever that is there for a while."

She didn't care. "I guess."

Frank said as he was leaving. "I'll take care of it." He turned; "Big spaghetti dinner tonight in the chow hall, it's one of the things they can cook."

Max smiled "My wife already told me that we are going."

Frank left the room. Max informed her. "While we're at it, the doors on the ship close at 1800, no one off and the only ones that get on, are the ones we pick up from the brig."

She nodded. "I have all I need."

They went to find her a room. "All we have are two man rooms but I don't think you will have a room mate." As they walked down the hall the Lieutenant and her people were coming to take control of her domain. Max said "You know that stuff I told you about the officers being ok, well the exception may be coming down the hall and she's our boss. She likes to be addressed as Sir." They stopped and exchanged introductions. The Lieutenant was nice enough but wanted to see Max; or A S Dent "as soon as you are finished." Max asked if he could show the Sergeant and Private to their assigned quarters. He was told that they could find them later. They walked on toward the room.

Stick and Larry came out of their room. Max spoke. "Stick, Larry this is your new neighbor, Luanne Le'Beau."

They said hello, Max could see that they were in a hurry so he let them excuse themselves. "We have to get some stuff and get back on this boat before 1700." They were in a big hurry.

She wondered. "Am I being treated special, only one in my room?"

Max nodded. "There are four other females assigned to this office and this set of quarters. One is a Lieutenant; she is assigned to officer's quarters. The other has her daughter aboard; she is assigned to family quarters. The other is assigned to another room. I have one more room and you get it."

She questioned. "But those guys; the Sergeant out ranks me..."

Max said in a very flat tone. "I would like for you to just leave that alone."

She shrugged and then. "Ok, if that's what you want...oh, I see - not a problem."

Max showed her the room. "It's all yours. You'll have the Private and the Sergeant assigned to those quarters there and there.

The Private seems ok, the Sergeant's ass I would like to kick; so if he gives you any problem just give me a call." He told her he had to go.

She said. "Thanks."

He nodded, "Oh, you may not know but the chow hall is a Charms club after 2100 most of the time. Today that is going to start at 1700 so people can get to know each other." She asked if she needed to be in uniform to get to the chow hall. He told her "yes, but you can take your jacket off at the door if you like. Most people don't; they roll up their sleeves."

Max's leadership style was questioned often but as the Captain put it. "I believe that if he asked one of his people to walk into certain death - the man would be walking before he finished asking."

Max started back to the office, Frank was just coming out the door and stopped him as they met. "Sir, Lieutenant Dent wants the stuff she had put in the hold moved to the chow hall."

Max asked. "Do you have authorization to put it there?"

He said. "Yes sir, the CC3 signed off on the move but I'm to get a counter signature from you." Max signed off on the move. He didn't know what it was but he knew Sandy and it wasn't going to be bad. He did ask if Frank knew what it was and was told no.

He walked into the outer office and then knocked on the Lieutenant's door. "You wanted to see me sir."

She said. "I want you to report."

Max couldn't do that. "I'm not in uniform, Sir. And I'm under headquarters orders not to put one on until tomorrow, this hush-hush thing about my promotion."

She said. "What promotion is that A S Dent?"

He smiled shyly "I have been promoted to Ensign as of yesterday but headquarters wants it kept quiet until we launch. I'm under orders not to wear a uniform until then."

She typed into her computer and waited. She was getting disgusted. "Come in Ensign Dent, close the door behind you and have a seat." Max went in; closed the door behind him and had a seat. She said. "I need to speak frankly, I have a job to do here and I intend to do it."

Max asked. "Are we talking about security?"

She was taken back. "What else would we be talking about?"

Max smiled. "You said you wanted this frank."

She said "go ahead."

He smiled. "Everybody on this ship knows you are an administrative spy. If you do your job as well as it is supposed to be done they'll cut this ship up in little pieces and make bullets out of those pieces; so they'll have projectiles to fire, when they stand the entire crew up against the wall and shoot us." She got out of her chair and turned so he couldn't see her face. But it wasn't long before she started to kind of heave. Max thought she was crying. "Are you alright sir?"

She couldn't hold it any longer she started to laugh. "They think it is going to be that bad."

Max asked. "We are still being frank, right?"

She said, "Yes."

He continued. "It's always that bad. Haven't you ever looked back to see what happens when you leave. We have all been through this crap before. It's not about the Job. It's about doing it by the book and sometimes that just doesn't work in the real world. You have to make decisions in seconds based on what you think will keep you and the crew alive and to hell with the book."

She smiled and shook her head. "I don't think you can back up that statement, Ensign."

Max was serious. "Ok, let's look at the cascade. If we had gone by the book this ship and the crew would be dead. Those damn power units are junk and they go critical at least once a week. We have submitted hundreds of requests for the manufacturer to be held to higher quality specifications but nothing is ever done."

She sounded a little mad "And you went by the book and got them shut down, that is your job."

Max smiled. "Did you read my report?"

She had the report in front of her she picked it up and sort of waved it at him. "Yes, I did." She started to read. "The technicians were able to slow the power unit crash long enough for the computer to shut it down. This was a by the book operation." She paused before continuing a little madder. "I'm quoting Max."

Max started to laugh. "Would you like to see the report I sent, it's in my office." She began to back pedal. "Ok, I'm sure there has been some editing but, yes I would like to see that report."

Max went for the report and was back in a few minutes. "You can have that copy."

She sat in her chair. "Do you mind, I would like to read this?"

He stood to leave "Not at all, would you like some coffee?"

She was taken off guard. "I can't ask you to do that."

Max said. "I volunteered."

She said "Thank you."

He asked. "Do you use cream or sugar?"

She smiled. "You have cream and sugar?"

He laughed. "Yes sir. We buy it on the black market."

She didn't know what to think by this time. She said sarcastically "Sure, two sugars and maybe some Pecan Sandies while you're at it."

Max smiled. And waited for her to look up, when she did he said. "I think chocolate chip is what's open. Do you want me to open the Sandies?" She shook her head, in a disgusted; leave me alone, kind of way. He smiled, "I'll open them."

She sat for a while before she started to read again. She thought to herself. "Surely he doesn't have any Sandies and he would never give me anything that would prove that he's dealing black market.

The coffee pot was empty, so Max made coffee. The Private asked if she could help but he was ok. "Nope, I got it." He excused himself and went to the bathroom. When he returned the coffee was ready. He poured two cups, picked up a sleeve of Sandies and went back into the office. She just motioned for him to sit, never taking her eyes off the report. He set the coffee in front of her and opened the cookies. A few minutes later she lay the report down and picked up a cookie. "You stuffed shoes into a power unit and they changed your report to say you slowed the power unit down." She started to laugh. "Good cookies. But surely you haven't sent hundreds of requests…"

Max told her. "I gave you access to a copy of a file on my computer; its called requests.hlp. It has the reports from the other 18 power unit failures as well."

She was becoming unsure of herself. "I thought there were only two."

Max informed her. "No, there were eighteen, plus one bad power unit. If that one had failed, it would have blown. The safety recovery mechanism was bad." He smiled "and the shoe fix was yet to be discovered."

It was clear that it was just too much for her to take in. Her boss had lied to her "Damn." She asked "What are we going to do now, now that I know what is happening?"

Max thought for a while. "I think I will have that nasty smelling cheese on my spaghetti."

She was lost. "What?"

He shrugged. "There is nothing I can do about it. Some Admiral or Senator or whatever has been bought by the company that makes these power units. We are going to get these bad power units until something horrible happens; now back to the cheese. There is a spaghetti dinner in the charms club tonight, well, the chow hall. It starts at 1700 and I'm supposed to meet my wife. Why don't you guys; now that you know the score, come up and get to know the people you're about to destroy."

She said "Do you think we would be welcome? And what should I do about the power units?"

Max laughed. "Why wouldn't you be welcome, you haven't hurt anyone, yet. As far as the power units go; I would try to tell them the truth about the power units but I wouldn't be surprised if nothing is done."

She smiled. "Yes, I have. I have hurt a lot of people, like Karen and Sandra." She wondered why she was so at ease with Max.

Max smiled. "Sandy and I talked about that last night and we decided that if you were a nicer person she and I might not have ever found each other again. So while she still doesn't like you; I don't think she's looking to kill you. Karen on the other hand is very, very mad. She wanted the assignment to the Dawson that you took."

She was having trouble deciding if she would go to the dinner or not. Max smiled. "Carol, at some point in time you're going to have to just let go; do your job and don't be the spiteful bitch you have practiced being for years. And remember there is not always something wrong."

She was not amused by him calling her Carol. She sat and stared at him "And now is a good time, why?"

Max said "Because they don't hate you yet. They just think they're going to."

She laughed. "You present an interesting point. Maybe we'll come by the club. There is no rank right?"

Max told her "It usually starts at 2100 but tonight it starts at 1700."

Max was in line with Sandy when the outsiders got there. They were close to the end of the line. He had already talked to Sandy and they went back to the end of the line. Max smiled. "Hello Carol, Mason and I believe its Harriet."

Mason smiled "Do you think that is going to help, Max?"

He smiled. "Yeah, I think it is going to help you do your job and not be an ass; but I may be wrong."

Carol smiled. "I decided to try this a little different than we usually do. Thank you for inviting us, Max." They got their spaghetti. Max chose the Alfredo sauce for his.

It wasn't the friendliest of tables with all the enemies. But they made it through dinner. Mouse and Bill danced a couple of times but they were careful and he danced with Sandy and Karen as well. Mouse got Max to dance with her. Bill even got Carol out on the floor. Brandy was a talking machine, all through dinner she never closed her mouth and it was always full of spaghetti. Luanne and Frank even had a dance. There was no liquor served aboard ship, but it was a good night anyway.

Sandy unveiled the karaoke machine when the night started to slow down. She made a brief statement before saying. "I hope everyone enjoys the machine; Now Max, how about a few songs?"

Several people started to clap. "Come on Max, I want to hear that fighting the law song."

Carol smiled. "You sing too?"

Max smiled, "Only if I have too." He went up to the stage. The people who had heard him sing were cheering him on. Max kissed Sandy on the cheek and whispered. "Damn you." She laughed. He took a minute to see how the machine worked. "Ok, for the kids." A few false starts, a brief statement that it had been a long time since he tried this sober. Then The Magic Dragon came out in good tone.

When he was finished he said he was going to sing a little song for his new friends. He sang "Be Happy." Several people wanted to try their talent. Stickman and Larry did a version of wiping out, Max joined in with the guitar. The old songs are a fixture on a ship. Most people had at least heard of them and they can be done *a cappella*. Mouse smiled "Is it alright if Max helps me with my guitar? He's very good."

Sandy laughed "You would have to ask him but I don't care. And save us all some grief and don't tell him how good you think he is. He might start to think the same thing."

Mason smiled. "I remember when he started trying to play that thing. I think he did it just to make me mad." He thought for a minute and added. "He did a good job." They laughed. Mason smiled. "He's gotten a lot better." Somebody was playing with the machine until 0200 when the Captain closed the place down.

The next day was spent gathering up strays. There were three, a cook and two cargo handlers. The last of the fresh supplies were loaded aboard and at 1800 the ship moved to orbit position. It would be in position to launch in nine hours. Everyone was supposed to be closing everything down and securing it. It was a busy time. No one had a lot of time to fool around. Max and Sandy had so much contraband in their quarters that it was packed too tight to shift. Brandy was complaining about her room being full. They suspected that everyone else had a lot of extras in their rooms as well.

CHAPTER SIXTEEN, THE LAUNCH

An hour before launch the call came for everyone to go to the launch room. That, in this case is about half of the chow hall. It has strong enough 'tie downs' for the chairs to stay in place as the ship launches. This was old school for the crew, they had done this before. This is done for more than one reason. The main one is a roll call; it's far easier to have just enough chairs. If one is empty then something is wrong. If you don't have enough then something is very wrong. This type of launch has been done many times. It's standard for the Force. The ship would power out and line up with its next destination and fire the power units. It's always a little dangerous and it is always a little rough.

Max was making a final inspection of the fire control power units. He brought Luanne with him. "When I came aboard the Lieutenant didn't invite me along on this little inspection, I didn't like it."

Luanne smiled "So you thought I might like to see the inspection."

He nodded. The power unit room was isolated so Max got on the phone to do the computer checks "You good up there Sandy?"

She answered, "Yeah, everything is good; too good, it's a little scary."

The call was made to the Captain, "It's a go." He told them to find a seat and enjoy the ride. Luanne noticed a fire axe hanging on the wall in a frame with a brass plaque. "Boy, do I remember polishing the one at training over and over. Do you have any idea why we had to polish that thing at training?"

Max admitted that he had no idea, "But I sure polished it a lot." They went to find their seats.

The launch was worse than usual. The ride was very rough but after two hours they were at speed. The Einstein was on its way to Gamma station on the other side of the Kuiper belt. But that was several months away and they needed to find out what was going on in the power unit room. The launch was too rough; anyone who knew how it was supposed to work knew that something wasn't right. Sandy had grabbed Max's arm, she confessed later that she thought it was going to blow.

The Captain even came down, none of them could find anything wrong; but something was. Power unit maintenance looked for days and never found anything. Max was certain he had missed something. Sandy had run the computer logs so many times that she could see them in her dreams. Max even got past his problems with Mason enough to have him take a look at it. He came up with "One of the main power units is getting out of sync with the other three." It was a good theory and one that no one had thought of, but how would you check such a thing. He told them a story about a power unit set "When they were just starting to use them in sets. Whatever happened, that test ship took off like a bat out of hell. It was under full acceleration until it was so far away that we couldn't track it any more." He paused, "Never saw it again."

Max asked, "Did it blow?"

Mason shook his head, "Just don't know. After that they started to put accelerator control boxes in them.

Sandy was getting upset. "I have checked it half a dozen times."

Max smiled, "Me too."

Luanne asked Mason wonderingly and sort of off the cuff, "Do you know why we have that axe hanging on the wall?"

He laughed, "I don't know the real reason; it's just always been there." He laughed louder. "I sure made old Max polish it a lot of times." He paused and then added in a more sober tone. "Sorry sir."

Max started to laugh. "That kind of messes with your mind doesn't it?"

Mason nodded, relieved that he wasn't mad about it. "It sure does sir."

Mouse caught them in the chow hall three days after the launch and the fruitless search for the problem. She got her lunch and went to sit with them. Max smiled. "Mouse we haven't been avoiding you."

She was eating, and leaving little doubt where Brandy got the bad habit of talking with her mouth full of food – she began to speak. "I'm happy that things are starting to settle down. Did you ever find out what was wrong?"

Sandy shook her head. "No, everything looks right but something is wrong."

Mouse finished her lunch and was opening a candy bar from her pocket. "Well, I hope you find out what it was because we have a hundred and sixty-eight babies in the oven. We lost thirty two in that rotten take off."

Sandy smiled. "Max, you will tell me what she is talking about, right?" Max assured her that he would.

The Captain was close enough to hear, he joined them with his coffee. "I heard that comment about my take off." Mouse laughed. The Captain smiled. "Max, I'm going to order a stand down on the power unit problem. I just hope when it does it again we can stop it, whatever it is." Max agreed. The Captain asked Mouse "and how are the children?" She told him they were just "baking away." It was clear to Max and Sandy that the Captain and Mouse had gotten closer during the time they had been searching for the power problem.

The power unit crew was happy to get the chance to get a good eight hours of sleep. Sandy insisted on knowing what Mouse and Bill were talking about. Max told her that there was a hundred and sixty-eight eggs in incubators and about a hundred and twenty should hatch into chickens in about twenty-six days. She started to laugh, "Max you beat everything I have ever seen. Does Uncle Bill know?"

Max smiled, "You heard him ask about it at lunch."

Two nights later Lieutenant Anderson went to find the Captain. She was told, in confidence, by one of the operators in operations that he had gone down to see Private Jacks. "I don't know the room number…"

Lieutenant smiled. "I do." She went to the elevator and started toward the quarters level. She was a little mad that a Captain on the Admirals list would risk his career over the friendship of a Private. She hoped it was just friendship. Surely he wasn't dumb enough to get involved with her. The regulations would destroy him even if she was willing. He was still the Captain and there would be enough of a question to destroy his career. The elevator stopped two floors above the quarter's level and Private Jacks got on. She spoke. "Lieutenant Anderson, what brings you out so late?"

She asked. "Are you on duty?"

Mouse smiled. "I finished about twenty minutes ago. Are you working?"

She smiled. "Sort of, I'm looking for the Captain."

Mouse said. "He's in my quarters." The Lieutenant didn't say anything before Mouse rephrased. "Oh, that sounded bad. They gave the kids shots today for childhood diseases and I didn't have a sitter for two hours. He volunteered."

The Lieutenant was relieved "Good, I thought it might be more than that."

The elevator stopped and they started toward Mouse's quarters. Mouse asked "We would be in a lot of trouble if it was more than that wouldn't we?"

They stopped and Carol took a deep breath. "The regulations are there to protect lower ranking troops from unwanted attention. Now I can just watch you two and I know that's not what's happening. But the regulations won't see it that way. Just the hint of you two getting more involved would be very bad. They would destroy both of you." She paused. "You're pushing the envelope as it is."

Mouse was sad. "If it was just me that would lose I wouldn't care but … well."

When they went into the quarters Bill, the Captain, was giving Brandy a pony ride as he crawled around the floor on his hands and knees. She was giggling with glee. Mouse laughed and then Carol started. Mouse was a little loud, "Ride'em cowboy."

Bill was a little embarrassed. He got up pretty quickly. "I wasn't expecting you for a while and not with company."

Brandy giggled. "You got caught; does that mean your 'dig-na-tee' is gone?" It was a new word for her and she was trying to remember it.

He laughed "I'm sure that these ladies will keep the secret and my dignity will be ok."

Mouse smiled. "I thought you were going to put her to bed?"

He confided. "I wasn't sure how and besides how often do you get a chance to bruise your dig-na-tee."

They laughed and Carol smiled. "I have never been on a ship like this in my life." Carol added. "I need to talk to the Captain about something important."

Mouse nodded. "Well, I need to get this cowgirl to bed."

Bill smiled. "Betty we'll be going."

She smiled. "Thank you and I hope you had a good time."

He smiled, "It was interesting." Carol told her good night and she and the Captain left.

In the hall going to the elevator the Captain asked "Is it the Captain you need help from?"

She said. "Yes sir. This is an official request."

He said. "Ok, Lieutenant what can I do for you?"

She was a little hesitant. "I need you to do a full back up of the computer system, an 'A-one total.'"

He nodded, "That'll take over four hours." They got on the elevator and started to the command floor.

She grimaced. "I need it now. We are the only two who know it has been requested. I need very much to walk into operations, call the place to attention, move everybody out, close down all information flow and run the backup."

He sort of asked. "You know you can have that done anytime, given your job on the ship."

She sort of smiled. "I know and last month that's what I would have done; times change." She paused. "I have the codes we'll need." She added. "I hope that this is just an exercise in backup but I think it is a lot more."

The Captain wondered. "Commander Mike Hall is on duty tonight."

She nodded, "I know, he's ok."

The Captain realized this was serious, "You're looking for a certain thing aren't you; not just what you can find."

She said quietly, "Something I hope I don't find." The Captain felt better about the deal. She was onto something or thought she was. She was not just looking for something to write up.

The Lieutenant went into operations first and as the Captain walked thought the door she yelled, "Captain on deck."

The crew in the room came to attention expecting the usual 'as you were' which they didn't get. The Captain ordered them to "go to the chow hall and wait." As the crew filed out of the room the Captain stopped Mike. "Commander Hall, I want the doors closed and locked and all data links in or out closed, now."

The Commander was wondering what was happening. "Yes sir." The crew was out the door and it was locked. The links were severed and then the Captain tried to ease the tension. "Mike, you know Carol, we want an 'A-one-total' backup." Mike looked nervous and the Captain told him. "Someone may be in trouble Mike, but it's not us, so relax."

He was happy to hear it. "Louise will be pleased."

The codes were loaded and the backup started, four and a half hours later it was finished. Two copies were made. The Lieutenant took one of the copies and the second was placed in a safe in the Captain's office. She nodded. "Thanks, I need to say that this isn't a trivial thing; if I'm right it's bad and if I'm wrong we just wasted four and a half hours. I hope we have wasted our time." She went to a special operations room to go over the data she had just received. The Captain stayed in operations. Commander Hall went to get the crew from the chow hall. When Commander Hall returned to operations with the crew, the Captain went to his quarters.

The next morning, Sandy had to be at the lab by five to check the progress of her experiment and begin the next step. Max went to work. There wasn't anybody in the office when he got there. He started coffee and went into his office to try to catch up on the paper work – the never ending paperwork.

Stickman came by a while later; he told Max about the operations room mess the night before. Max was interested but guessed he would find out what was really going on later. Stick told him they had a few problems with security while the power unit crew was trying to find out what was wrong with the power units, "People were scared and they did some stupid things." Max asked if they were malicious. He told him only three "Those reports are on your desk, the rest are in the folder marked stupid." Max laughed.

The Lieutenant walked into the office, "As you were."

Max asked, "Things going better?"

She took a sip of her coffee and then. "I think this honesty stuff works. I have more solutions to problems that we never knew existed. It's great." She added as she looked around the office, "I started some more coffee, I got the last cup." Max unlocked his bottom drawer and handed her the Pecan Sandies. She laughed,

"I looked everywhere for those damn things." She opened the cookies. "You know that vent over there is very clean. It would be a good place to hide contraband." Max laughed.

She took a bite of one of the cookies. "Did Stick tell you about the three malicious reports?" They nodded. "I think we need to go easy on two of them, but that guy who wouldn't stop. We took him back to his quarters a dozen times. But he was back at the shuttle bay doors as soon as we left him alone. He was trying to break into the shuttle bay and he did a lot of damage. If we had wanted to get to the shuttle we couldn't have for two days. It took that long to get the doors fixed." Max asked who it was and was told one of the new cooks, "He's just scared to death."

Stick noted. "He's in the brig and seems to like it there." Max sort of smiled.

Max asked if the other two were in the brig.

The Lieutenant wanted it done. "Yeah, but I think I'll let them go with time served." I will need another officer to sign off on that action, before I send my recommendation to the Captain."

Max admitted. "I haven't read the report but, Stick what do you think?"

Stick agreed. "Well, we have already talked about this; and I agree. They both hit me pretty hard but they backed right off. They knew they had messed up."

Max hoped. "Will it get some of this crap off my desk?" They both laughed and assured him it would. The Lieutenant found the right papers and Max counter signed the works. While he was signing the Lieutenant went to get coffee, she brought back three cups. Max smiled. "You have sure relaxed."

She smiled. "Thank you."

She looked at Stick. "Sergeant, I need to talk to the Ensign, alone."

He stood, "Yes, sir." He left the room.

She told Max "The information that you gave me about the power units started me thinking. I started to look into the problem and last night I took the first steps toward trying to fix it. What

I found is locked in my bottom left desk drawer if I don't get this done. If something happens to me, finish what I started."

Max was a little distressed, "Is it that bad?"

She nodded, "It may be a big problem with big important people involved." She paused and then added. "Max, that's all I'm going to tell you. If I'm wrong then the only one I'm hurting is me. I haven't looked all the information over yet but what I have found so far is scary. I'm almost certain that what I have found is real."

Mouse was checking on the eggs or babies when Harriet spoke from behind her. "Well, I finally found your lair."

Mouse was a little startled but tried not to show it. "What are you doing here?"

Harriet was a little sad, "I was hoping it would just be something simple contraband but cooking drugs is more than I can let go."

Mouse laughed. "I'm not cooking drugs."

She was very serious. "Then what are you doing?"

Mouse smiled and sort of childishly. "Hatching chickens so we'll have eggs to sell in three months."

Harriet didn't believe her. She looked inside one of the incubators. "Are you telling me the truth? God, I think you are." She started to laugh and then they both started laughing. Harriet grinned. "I refuse to write a report that has anything about hatching chickens."

Mouse smiled. "Good, there are cokes and candy in the fridge if you want."

Harriet smiled. "Can I get you one?" Mouse accepted and Harriet starting telling war stories about her first days as a Mouse. They both had a good time.

Life on the ship was normal for the next few days. Well, almost, Max did a lot of talking to Mason about the control unit. He dug up every bit of information he could find on the incident that Mason remembered. They went over the reports and he had Mason try to translate them from the management language to the truth. But it was all just guess work. Sandy was becoming upset because he couldn't leave the problem alone.

Carol dropped in on the Captain in his office. He could guess why she was there and he really didn't want to know what she had to say. He invited her in. She put a folder on his desk. "Could I have a cup of coffee please?"

He asked. "Am I going to need one?"

She nodded, "If you have a little of Kirkland's best whiskey you might want to add it to the mix."

He sort of smiled, "That bad." He asked his aide to bring two coffees.

Carol informed him. "That's my findings; the information, the proof, and god help us I believe the why. I don't want to let it out of my sight. If you don't mind I'll just sit here and drink my coffee while I wait to see if you think I'm anywhere close to right."

He agreed and told his aide when the coffee was brought; "I'm unavailable until further notice. Twenty minutes later the report was starting to be alarming. He called for more coffee, "Bring the pot."

He finished the report in about an hour and wanted to check the information a little closer. "I'm going to get my copy of this data; I just need to be sure."

She told him. "Please, please I don't want to go out on a limb all alone on this one."

He laughed. "If what this is inferring is true I don't want to be out there alone either."

When the entire report was read and comprehended he sat back in his chair. "I have some Kirkland's in the bottom drawer, if you want."

She grimaced. "I guess you agree."

He sighed. "Yeah, whole heartedly; and I don't like it."

She was pleased that she was correct but hated it at the same time. "I think I'll pass on the drink; I feel a little sick."

He felt the same way. "I understand; if you don't mind I would like to have Mike do a little more checking before we continue. I'll tell him that reports are not getting to headquarters intact and ask him to go over the logs, comparing them to the paper work. Let's see what he thinks."

She sighed. "Ok, just make sure that he knows it is not to be shared with anybody but us."

"Agreed" was the return by the Captain.

Fifteen days into the flight, and the day the CC3's report on the report was due; the first power unit failure of this leg of the flight, occurred. For the new crew members it was a very tense time; to hear about facing death was one thing; to do it was another. The old crew was accustomed to the danger, as accustomed as one can get. The danger was always present. They knew that if that power unit blew it was all done. They trusted the power unit crew to do the very best that could be done. They also knew that they couldn't do much to help. The Lieutenant was becoming keenly aware of the death threat hanging in the air. She was more than a little nervous. She was getting a very close view of what goes on in a life or death situation. She realized that if Max and Luanne didn't have the attitude that they did, the ship would be in big trouble. Luanne pinned the power unit while she and Max were discussing how bad the power units were. Sandy was joking with them from the computer control area. The Lieutenant's only comment was that something that dangerous should not be so common place. She was scared but Max noted to himself that she was a lot madder than she was scared. The chow hall continued to serve lunch.

CC3 Hall asked for another day before he gave his opinion on the report, "The power unit failure is going to give me more information." He was given the time with a hearty ok from both parties. "We need to be very sure about this."

The next day he walked into the afternoon meeting with the Captain and the Lieutenant. He was given her report and asked to review it. He had two hours to justify his thoughts with her report.

Two hours later, the three met in the Captains office. Mike handed each of them a paper. "I'm going to say a lot more than is on that paper but that is how I decided and what I found. Plus the points I'm going to cover." They didn't read the paper but waited for him to speak his mind.

He started. "First, I agree with most of the report except for four points. The first point is that the…" He took a deep breath and blew it out slowly. "CC2 Adams could not have pulled this off by herself. She would need help. The final stage of the report process is a review by the sender and a signature on a document that states 'the original contents have not been changed enough to change the meaning of the report.'" The Captain started but he was asked to wait. "On every flight that I have ever been on the CC4 has always been the sending authority. On this flight it's the CC5, CC2 Dawn Adams' intended, Mark, is the sender. That is not normal but it's not wrong either." He sighed, "CC5 Mark Adams has to be as guilty as his intended. It just can't happen any other way. This morning at 0600 Max turned in a report on the power unit failure yesterday; that's two hours early. It has to be reviewed and sent within two hours after it is received.

When I stopped by operations a few minutes ago; CC2 Adams had not started the process. I looked at the records and tried to find the paper work. I asked her about the report; she told me that she had the job in hand and I should enjoy my down shift. I didn't see any paper on the power unit problem. It has been seven hours and it has not been sent. I verified that the last thing before I came to this meeting."

He was not happy to continue. "Second, the one power unit report that was sent with CC2 Adams signature was at a time when CC5 Adams was sick and not on duty for three days. Something that makes this seem a little odd is that they always pull the first shift, that's the shift that sends the messages out unless there is an emergency. They have two boys and it would seem that they might at sometime have a problem and have to pull separate shifts. The shift they work is not considered a good shift but it is the one where messages are processed.

A few weeks ago, before we got to Beta station one of their boys, Randall broke his finger. They both stayed on shift and didn't go check on him. That was a day when a power unit error report had to go to headquarters. That report wasn't sent. Another time the other boy, Franklin, hurt his ankle and both of them took off. There were no power unit problems pending." He looked at them and tried justify the actions. "But all that might just be me."

"Third - and this really sucks. There are several reports that are sent without change or editing, one of those reports is the thirty day power unit status report. These reports have the Captain's signature and are to be sent as is; even if a word is misspelled. They have all been edited, by CC5 Mark Adams." He sighed. "The number of power unit failures has been changed."

"Fourth and last is more of an observation than anything else. CC2 Dawn Adams' family name is Dorcell; as in daughter of Franklin Dorcell Electronics Corporation." He paused. "I do a little stock trading and Dorcell Electronics is the parent company of Johnson Reactors. Their big money maker is the D123 Beta power unit. That's the one we're having so much trouble with. It has some kind of 'small' problem on Earth but in space it becomes a much bigger problem. They are working on the problem but don't want everyone to know about it. I think it would break the company." He added, "The government contract can't be canceled unless the power units can be documented to be bad."

The three of them sat for a few minutes and didn't say a word. It was a lot to take in, two 'command and control' officers conspiring to keep very dangerous power units in operation for credits and put their children and themselves in death's path to do it. None of the three could believe it. Whatever compassion they might have felt for the two was gone.

It was Mike who spoke next. "I guess that you two have come to the same conclusions." They nodded, 'Yes.' The entry of the report into the official records and the yes votes by at least two of three officers for formal charges to be brought against the Adams' was next; before anything else could be done. The indictment was confirmed and officially recorded as three yes votes. The Captain was next. "Commander Hall on my authority I want the Adams' removed from the access list effective as soon as we leave this room. Lieutenant Anderson, the Adams' are to be confined to quarters, a guard posted at the door, and above all I want them to have no access to the computer. Their children are free to move about the ship." He continued after the 'yes sir' "Let's keep the charges a secret from everyone but the Adams' for their own safety." He paused, "They are to have 'NO' access to a computer. If they want to send a message, then clear it through me." He added, "This sucks. I've known them both for years."

Mike agreed, "Amen to that."

Carol commented. "You know, I have never had to be part of the disciplinary action. I don't like it."

The Lieutenant told the Captain that she wanted to call two law enforcement officers to the outside of the operations room. "When they get here I would like for you to send the Adams' to lunch. As they leave operations my officers and I will intercept them and take them to their quarters; very quietly. I hope." Mike assured the Captain that all computer access to and from the quarters would be locked down.

The Captain didn't like this business. "I'll follow in five minutes to read the charges. This just sucks." The call was made to law enforcement. When the officers arrived outside the operations room they contacted the Lieutenant and the show started.

It was a quiet operation and the Adams' were taken to their quarters with little or no fuss, although several people saw the 'arrest.' The word spread quickly. The Captain arrived at the quarters as he said he would. Dawn was mad. "Bill, what in the hell is happening?"

He began. "Commander Dawn Adams…"

She slumped down seated on the floor, "god, and formal charges."

The Captain started again. "Commander Dawn Adams it has been found by the required three member committee of your peers that you have maliciously made changes to official reports that could have resulted in the deaths of your fellow crew mates. It is further alleged that these actions could have contributed to the death of the crews of other force ships and the destruction of those ships. Therefore; you are charged with conspiracy to commit murder, and murder, both crimes can be punishable by death." He turned to Lieutenant Commander Mark Adams' and repeated the charges as Mark stood quietly. When he had finished he asked if they understood the charges. They told him they did and he handed them the required folder that contained the information, the charges, the evidence and the conclusions of the peer board and the members of the peer board.

The Lieutenant ordered a search of the quarter for any weapons, any electronic or other device that might be used to contact anyone. The Captain told them they were relieved of any Command and Control authority and they were confined to quarters. If they wanted to go to the chow hall for meals a guard would accompany them. Other wise the meals would be brought to them. Their children would be allowed free access. "Any violation of these rules and you will be transferred to the brig and the children placed with a family on board the ship."

After the official crap, the Lieutenant went out into the hall to post the guard and give them their instructions. Bill told the Adams.' "Dawn, Mark, I hope this all works out in your favor but with the evidence in those folders I had no choice." Bill and Mike left the quarters. As they walked down the hall the Captain informed Mike. "You're CC2 for now, move everyone up and fill the two gaps."

Commander Hall noted. "Captain there are only two other officers on board that are in the command line of Command and Control."

The Captain added. "I know, give Carol CC8 Law and Max CC9 Security. And I know that requires a Lieutenant J.G. grade so take care of that too."

Mike understood, "Ensign Dent to brevet Lieutenant J G, yes sir."

The Captain went to his office to file the report with higher headquarters; he was not going to be guilty of the same thing that the Adams' were suspected of doing, even though it couldn't be to the same degree. The message went out at 1743 the same day as the charges were read. The Captain was a little sad to press the send button. The feeling was felt throughout the operations room. The operations crew didn't know why the charges were filed or just what they were but they knew the Adams' were going to be tried in a military court when the ship reached Gamma Station. That's eight months from now. They were going to have a long trip.

The earliest a return message could get back to the operations room was six hours, it usually took twenty four. Seven hours and twelve minutes later the answer arrived. It was just one sentence, 'Return to Beta Station.' Within the hour the Captain gave the order to begin the turn. He knew it would take twenty days to get back to Beta. A few hours later another message came in; it read 'the Einstein will be met by a fast transport in five days at the location stated below. The prisoners will be transported to Beta Station to await your arrival and a formal hearing.' It was confusing. The location was not in a direct path to Beta station. It also informed the Captain that he would not be getting replacements.

The ship was a buzz with talk of the news. Neither Max nor Sandy had heard anything about the problem until they went to work. The Captain called a meeting of the Command and Control Board. The invitation to attend the meeting was not unexpected to Carol. She knew how these things worked. But

Max had a large problem with even attending a CC meeting. It was short notice and Max and Carol had little choice. They entered the meeting room and sat in the guest chairs waiting for the meeting to convene. The Captain entered the room and it was called to attention. He put them at ease. He admitted, "first order of business, I'm two members short on the CC board. Lieutenant Anderson you will assume the post of CC8, the seat is there and the job is law enforcement. Ensign Dent, you will assume the seat of CC9 as a brevet Lieutenant Junior Grade in charge of security to include power units control.

The assignments and the brevet promotion were strictly administrative; they are noted in your record but that was about the end of it. Well, except for the required collar brass, and a great deal more authority. The brass was presented to them and they put it on their uniform. Max didn't like the deal. He was already in charge of security, and he had Carol to hide behind if something went wrong. She in turn had the CC8 of law enforcement/ security to hide behind. The appointment to CC made them the department heads and now they were responsible.

The meeting was brief and to the point, they were told in general what had happened and what the new orders were. They were not told any specific information about the Adams case. They were told to dismiss any inquires about the case and to discus it as little as possible. They were adjourned at ten fifteen.

Max went to the chow hall, he asked Carol if she wanted to join him and she accepted. "Yes Lieutenant."

He smiled a very crooked smile. "I wish you would just call me Max."

She questioned, "Well, aren't you proud?"

He nodded. "I guess but, somehow I can't help but think I stole this."

She smiled. "I know what you mean; I have always wanted to be part of CC, but on my own merits, not like this."

They got a snack and had a seat. It wasn't long before Sandy showed and came to sit with them. Max was surprised. "I thought you couldn't get away till two."

She smiled "Am I welcome?"

He smiled wide, "Of course, it's just that I would have come by for you if I had known."

She interrupted "That's alright. What can you tell me about the Adams?"

Max told her. "I'm to avoid the subject but I don't know much anyway."

She stared at him, "Max, are you CC9?"

He smiled although he wasn't comfortable with the idea, "Yeah and a brevet Lieutenant J G as well."

She laughed. "Ok, I ll believe you don't know much because you don't lie but you wouldn't tell me anyway because you aren't supposed to." She could tell by the way Max had told her about the promotion that he wasn't comfortable with the way things had happened so she cut him a lot of slack.

Max told her "sorry." She made sure he knew she was very pleased with his new position on the ship. She congratulated Carol on her appointment to CC8 and could tell by the response that she felt the same as Max about it. But what she really wanted to know was about the arrest and they weren't going to tell her. So, Sandy told them what she knew and suspected they didn't confirm or deny any of it. But she knew Max if she had been too far off the mark he would have told her so to stop any destructive rumors. As it turned out she knew as much as Max did; except for the drop off instructions.

Sandy had to go back to her experiment She kissed Max and rose to leave, "Congratulations anyway." She held his hand as she walked away and let it drop when they could reach no further.

After she left Max asked Carol, "What do you think about this off course drop point?"

She laughed. "I don't like it."

Max smiled "Kind of sounds like a trap; or maybe an attempt to cover something up doesn't it?"

She smiled, "Those are my thoughts but I have a suspicious mind." Max smiled and told her he was going to check out the ship that was going to pick up the Adams. She smiled, "I'm going to do that too but if you want some of the heat that's coming - welcome."

He laughed, "I'm going to start the inquiry. I'll let you know what I find out."

She told him she had to go make a schedule for the guards, "I'm short on men. Can I use a few of your security guys? I'll post them with a law enforcement trooper."

Max didn't have a problem with the assignment "Just don't leave them hanging." He added. "We should look at activating the security and law enforcement augments." Carol agreed. As Max added, "Mouse is sort of deep into something..." Carol stopped him. "I'll cut her a lot of slack."

They walked back to the security office. The Lieutenant would move her office to Law Enforcement and Max would take her office. They decided to pair off a security man with a law enforcement man for a while until the pickup at least and maybe a while after that. It was just more efficient and safer, two different types of training in one place. They decided to activate the augments, security and law enforcement. They both knew that the more visible police the better.

Sandy was back at her lab and her friends wanted to know if the rumors were true. What did Max say? Did he tell you anything? Sandy smiled. "He wouldn't say." She paused, "but he is a brevet J G and," she almost laughed "and CC9." She was very proud of him.

Carol took Mason with her to the law enforcement side. He had been working both until now because it was one branch. With the appointment of Carol as CC8 and Max as CC9 the office split. Stickman was senior Sergeant by almost two years and in line for Mason's position on the security side. He didn't want it and talked Max into letting Frank, Mason's second, continue on the job. Max didn't have a problem with the assignments; Frank was next in line. Frank wasn't near the field man that Stick was; not to think about how messed up things were going to get if Stick tried to run an administration office. It just meant a little paper work; Frank took care of the paper.

It took three days for the new system to start to gel. Max was having trouble getting information about the ship through official channels so he went through the back door. He contacted a roommate from the old days; he was as crooked as they came, knew something about everything and owed Max big. He ran a little bar at Beta station, ok, a heroin den and brothel. The message traffic was slow and Max made the call outside of official channels; it came back the same way. It was coded in an old code that was used by such people.

The code had never been broken and Max knew the secret. He decoded the message and went to find the Captain, on the way he stopped by to pick up Carol. She wasn't in her office but was in the chow hall – it was on the way. She was having a cup of coffee with Harriet. She looked up at Max, "Chickens?" He laughed and sat down uninvited; handed her what he had decoded.

She read it and stared at Max. "How did you get this? I have been trying for days and nothing." Harriet knew when she wasn't needed and excused herself.

He said. "We need to see the Captain." As they walked into the office the Captain was mad about something. He told them to come in and close the damn door.

As the door closed he started to rave. "I can't get a damn thing on that ship. All I get is it's top secret or need to know and all kinds of crap like that." Max handed him the paper. He was not in any kind of mood. "What is this?"

Max told him. "The ship is the Franklin; it's on a test flight. It is a Johnson Reactors test ship."

He started to continue but the Captain still a little pissed. "I can read it, three Admirals and two Senators. Where did you get this information?"

Max was a little shy, "Some people call it the smugglers channel."

Bill laughed, "I should have guessed that you would know where that channel is located. How good is this information?"

Max assured him, "I got it from what I consider a very reliable source. I would bet credits that it is true. The question is do we have a choice, not to turn over the Adams?"

The Captain didn't think they did. "We just have to cover our backside, because they are going to try to cover this whole thing up."

They decided not to worry about something they could not do anything about. The Captain started to put the information out about the arrest to everyone he knew, Max had given him the names of the VIP's on board and he put them in the message. The Lieutenant and Max did the same thing. None of them thought it would do much good, but you do what you can. If the information was spread out enough then maybe it would reach someone who might do something about it.

CHAPTER SEVENTEEN,
BETRAYED

At the appointed time and place the Einstein arrived and within the hour the Franklin arrived. The crew of the Einstein was on edge. This was not normal and in spite of their misgivings the crew welcomed the VIP's aboard. They didn't bring any security. They did bring some technicians to secure information from the ships computer, a full A-one back up of the Einstein computer system. When the back up was finished and a brief review of the information was completed, transfer documents were signed and Einstein security escorted the prisoners to the Franklin.

One of the Einstein's law enforcement officers was concerned that the boys were not with them. He was told that the boys were already aboard. It seemed wrong but when both parents and a guard on the other ship tell you something; then you have to believe them or at least accept what they say as true. Carol tried to get them to take the prisoner from the brig; they refused. One of the many VIPs was talking to the Captain for the entire time they were aboard. Sometimes it seemed that they were almost pleading with him about something.

Security was tight, and a little confused, neither Max nor Carol trusted any of the members of the other crew. Security teams were watching everyone who boarded the Einstein like the proverbial hawk. The Captain limited the number that could be on board. That is what Stick had been told to do; check everything twice. Max knew Stick was a good field man and he would be able to tell this might not be all it seemed although he couldn't tell him outright what was happening.

When the ship departed with the Adams everyone took a deep breath and sort of relaxed. All except the law enforcement officer who had asked about the boys; he couldn't get it out of his mind. When he was relieved from duty; he went straight to the Lieutenant. He asked her if they could check the Adams' quarters. He explained why. The Lieutenant wasn't quite sure if it was necessary but she had come to trust her men. They went to check. It also wasn't going to hurt anything.

What they found surprised everyone. The quarters seemed empty and except for some mess, it seemed ok. The guard was more determined than Carol and insisted on looking a while longer. He was looking in the back of the room. Carol turned to face him; her back to the door. She told him he could look as long as he wanted but she was going to go back to the office. He turned to face the door behind her. He pointed, "Lieutenant, one of the boys is at the door." She turned and saw the boy.

The boy wanted help. "They tied my brother up and put him out here, I'll show you."

They followed the boy Carol asked. "Why didn't they tie you up?"

He started to cry, "I ran away. They were going to take me with them and leave my brother here." He sobbed out, "I don't want to leave my brother." They went to an unused room, used their security override to open the door and found the other boy. The Captain was called.

They tried to contact the Franklin about the boys. They didn't have any luck. If they were being received; the Franklin wasn't answering. After talking to the boys Bill called Max. "I believe this ship may have been sabotaged. I don't know how or where – FIND OUT." The alert went out to all offices – it wasn't that discrete, the search started. The people who worked in an area were told to report anything out of place.

The search went on for hours. There were a lot of suspected items but they were just out of place. Nothing dangerous was found. The Captain was still certain that something had been done. The ship sent out a distress call. For the next twenty four hours the ship was allowed to drift. There was a lot of traffic and occasionally they would pick up another ship but none of them answered the distress call. The transmitter must not be working – FIX IT. The Captain didn't want to touch any of the controls. He didn't want to take the chance that any action would doom the ship. He asked Mike if he thought he was just being paranoid. Mike smiled. "I might be going a little further than you are; so no, I think this is just, prudent."

Bill was also waiting to see if the Franklin or any other ship would come to their aid. But even he knew that sooner or later, he would have to do something. He called a meeting of the CC and tried to get all the advice he could; then he started to give orders. Max had suggested that if he was to try to destroy the ship he would use the power units. He wanted to shut all of them down. The Captain ordered all the secondary power units shut down, that left only two up and running, plus main power and the operations unit. He ordered the maneuvering rockets to fire and moved the ship to launch position for Beta station. The ship began to turn and slowly, slowly moved to the line for Beta Station. The Captain ordered the ship ahead slow; everyone on the ship was holding their breath. The ship began to move ahead and pick up speed. Three hours later they reached maneuvering speed. The crew was starting to breath easier until, "Captain, the secondary power units just started to come back on line."

Max knew the power units system better than anyone on board. He should, it was his job. Sandy was a close second and they went to work. Luanne knew the power units system almost as well. Max ordered her to shut everything down. She was quick to the work. Three secondary power units, each of them provided start power for six other power units. Those four power units had to be shut down manually in a way they could not be reactivated by the computer. The team, Max, Sandy, James, Kent, Karen, Luanne, Bill and Mason started shutting down the power units, as they shut them down they manually changed switches; these power units were not going to restart without manual intervention. They scurried around like insects on a hot plate, as they ran from one power unit to another. The worst part was all the people who were scared to death. They were in the way and made the job a lot harder. They somehow knew this was different.

The CC2, Mike, called the power units team over a secure channel and informed them that there was a virus in the computer. "We are trying to shut it down and we are not having much luck." The computer continued to degrade while it was up, so it was shut down. It wouldn't shut itself down so they 'unplugged it.' Alarms started to sound all over the ship. It was at that time that Max realized some of the alarms had been disabled by the computer. None of the remaining power units would shut down and they started to fail. Mason was very busy so the Lieutenant took Stick as her second and they had her men running interference between the power unit crew and the other people on the ship. They were actually doing some good. It seemed like hours before things started to calm down; but it was less than fifteen minutes start to finish. All of the secondary power units were down. If even one of the power units failed it would be all over. The Einstein would have been no more.

There wasn't any time for the power unit team to rest. They had to make checks on the two main power units. Mouse was almost frantic. "I need generators NOW to run the electric heaters." There were none not in use. Harriet remembered some emergency fuel type generators in the hold. There was a shipment of settler survival packs in the hold. They would have fuel type heaters and fuel which also produced a small amount of electricity. Max was very busy and told Mouse to just take what she needed. Incubators don't use much power but the room they are in must be temperature controlled to some degree. The heaters in the incubators will only warm the incubator a limited number of degrees. The room had to be kept warm. She and Harriet took the heaters and went to take care of the babies.

The power unit crew looked at the readouts on the main power units and did not like what they saw; the levels were slowly rising. Both of them were going to fail. The recommendation was made to the Captain that they shut down the main power and run off the power generated by the propulsion power unit set. It would slow the failure. It was well known that unused power generated by the power units was a problem. It's the main reason they failed. The control boxes were supposed to fix the problem. They may have helped but they didn't fix the problem. However, some other considerations had over ridden the removal of all but one or maybe two of the power units from each ship. It was beginning to become apparent that the consideration was so the Force would buy more power units. The Captain told them that he wanted the main power units shut down. Then he powered the propulsion power unit a short time; long enough for them to get up enough speed to coast to Beta Station. Then he ordered everything shut down. The trip to Beta Station would be uncomfortable but "we will get there."

There were tense moments until the propulsion power unit was shut down. They were happy they were running on batteries. The next several days would not be comfortable but they will now reach Beta station. The ship just wasn't meant to run off batteries for days. The solar collectors would provide some help; everyone hoped it would be enough.

James and Karen took the boys. They didn't really know the Adams but Karen knew the boys and James didn't mind. Gravity and all other ship functions were turned down to a minimum and the crew settled in for a cold few days. Mouse found several heaters and took them to help with the babies. They were not electric and each day someone had to fuel them. Brandy and Harriet helped keep them fueled. Brandy loved going to work with her mother. She got lost several times in the space between the outer and inner hull and thought it was great fun. It was cold and a lot of the crew spent most of the time cuddled up to someone they cared about.

Two days into the flight and five days out of Beta station; one of the propulsion power units rebooted for unknown reasons and started to fail fast. It was running power to the other three propulsion power units and they began to fail almost as soon as they fired. The ship changed course unexpectedly. There was a lot of confusion. The failure wasn't spreading out like last time. This time the whole show was in the propulsion room.

The call came at a very inopportune time for Max and Sandy. Let's just say they were deeply involved – almost done. "DAMN, DAMN and double Damn!" was repeated a lot as they dressed quickly in warm clothing shivering in the cold room. When they got to the propulsion room, most of the power unit crew was already there. Mason arrived seconds later, Bill and Luanne were looking at every possibility. Max and Mason joined them on the floor and Sandy went to the control room. Professor Kent, James and Karen weren't having much luck either.

A power unit can't be pinned until the safety mechanism starts to drop; then you have about seven minutes. And not to mince words, that's a lifetime. Sandy had her hands full in computer control. Max, Bill, Luanne and Mason were going to help pin the power units. They didn't get seven minutes. When the safety mechanism started to drop it dropped fast, too fast to pin. It was going to blow in ninety seconds, at most. Max looked at Sandy and yelled "I love you." She gasped, "Oh my god! I love you Max, Max do something."

There wasn't time to get anything between the contacts. The contacts were going to touch. They were going to die. Max yelled. "If I'm going to die I have to know. Bill, trust me and order the engines to full." Bill told Professor Kent to power engines to full. He announced over the speaker system. "Brace yourself for launch, now." The engines started to wind to full and were ready to fire. All four propulsion power units were back on line. Max got the fire axe from the display. "I hope you're sharp." The axe was sharp and Max cut the wires to the control module with one blow of the fire axe. To Max it seemed the axe was placed there by fate, or maybe that lady, The Mist. It had always been there, waiting for it's time. The axe hit the floor hard after going through the wires. It sounded like the starting gun of a great race as the electric shorted and popped.

The engines kicked hard and no one was ready. Throughout the ship the members of the crew were slammed into the walls and pinned by the force of the acceleration to the back wall of compartment they were in at the time. Anything that was not tied down was thrown toward the same walls. They waited to die, thinking of how their life had been. They waited for the explosion. Max had always heard that you never hear the explosion that kills you. He wondered about that, as he passed out from the gs. He thought of Sandy.

Sandy was pinned, by the acceleration with her face on an inspection window in the computer control room wall and she could see Max but he couldn't see her. As his eyes started to close she started to cry. "Don't leave me Max, god, I love you." Max's lips moved and although she couldn't hear him she knew he said. 'I love you Sandy.'

CHAPTER EIGHTEEN, THE FLYING DUTCHMAN

When Max woke he was surrounded by heavy fog; not only the fog around him but the fog in his head. He stood slowly and realized that the fog only came up to his knees. Where was he; was he dead? Had the ship blown? Where was Sandy? Other people began to stand; one of them was Sandy. She was facing the other direction. Max laughed and in an effort to lighten the moment. "I thought it was only 'until death do you part.'"

She turned and laughed. "Well, maybe we can renew our vows saying until it is all over." She laughed as she hugged him. Others started to stand.

James walked up to them "This is strange isn't it?"

Karen laughed. "So this is it. The thing we're all so afraid of, death."

Bill came up with his arm around Mouse and carrying Brandy. He said. "I guess all that military stuff is done."

Mouse smiled. "Now, if we can find a bedroom."

Someone laughed and then said "There won't be time for that here. You are going back shortly." Sandy and Max remembered the voice. They had heard it long ago but it was unmistakable. Max asked. "Will we remember this?"

The person who they could only sort of see laughed. "Yes, Max, you'll all remember this." Everyone looked in her direction.

She continued as she slowly took form. Sandy smiled when she recognized the lady in her dream from the cave. She told Max, but he already knew. Bill recognized her as the lady from his room at the hospital.

Stick smiled, "hello Granny." It was the name he caller her when he was small and slept in the trunk. She smiled and touched his face.

Betty smiled. "You, you're the one who handed me Brandy after she was born." The Mist smiled.

She, The Mist, continued "You will all remember this. There is a great evil that exists in the universe. It is not a person, but an idea and I want it gone. It is greed and inhumanity. There will be a great war and you will do many inhuman things in the pursuit of honor. Remember it is to serve a greater good. This crew will become the caretakers of what remains. This crew will be my sword; to destroy the old ideas and start to help the most human of humanity. I believe you will do a much better job than those who have gone before."

She paused. "Eighteen of you will not be returning." She smiled and quickly added. "But don't worry; I have work for you here. I've need of a few guardian angels to watch over my army. Keeping up with the rest of you will be their job." She laughed. "I think they are going to have a very tough job."

She turned slowly as she spoke. "The rest of you are going on a wild adventure in which I plan to recreate the elder A'chant race of man. For all their failings they were honest and forthright. They said what they thought and meant what they said. They also knew when to stop. Some called it honor. This crew has honor and we are going to spread it all over the universe once again." She smiled. "Sandy do you remember that last impossible dream - your majesty, queen of the universe and her king the great Warlord Max of the Royal house of Dent. What do you think of that Max?" Max thought she might be 'a little nuts' He didn't say anything.

She turned to Mouse. "Goddess, I will give you the destiny that I promised when you entered this world. The Deathh Dealer stands at your side already." A brief pause and she continued "Bill or Death Dealer as you choose; you are about to meet an old enemy that took everything from you many years ago." Her face hardened and she almost spit the venomous words. "I want them utterly destroyed. Not a single one is to escape." She softened somewhat and added. "There will come a time, as it always does, when it is time for peace. All of you will know when that time has come. Until that time there can be only war."

"Stick, if that is what you wish to be called. You are the most level minded of my leaders." She smiled, "Try to keep them headed in the right direction." She took Brandy's hand. "And you, my little one, are going to make your parents and me so very proud."

She started to talk to the group again. "I say to the rest of you. Think back, I have selected each and every one of you. Think of the time you almost died. Think of the time when a decision was forced upon you that you wouldn't have chosen. I was there and I brought each of you to this place and this adventure. You are the royalty of an empire that does not yet exist; always live honorably or I will keep you when you come to me in death." She sounded very serious. "Now, it's time to get started; if you would exit through the door over there." Those of you who are to stay with me will simply not go back to the ship with the rest. I should say to those going back that when you get back to the ship you will be in a great deal of pain." They started to file through the door. She added. "The ones who are staying just find a place at the round table and I will be there soon to start the meeting."

The closer Max got to the door the worse his feet and arms hurt. Sandy was starting to feel the pain as well. He woke on the floor of the power unit room pressed against the wall with his legs on the floor. His legs fell to the wall yielding to the gravity when he moved. His feet hurt. But gravity was being applied to keep him on the wall.

The ship was creating gravity by acceleration. Max guessed at least two maybe three gravities or Gs; he could still move and breathe but it was difficult. He saw something move above him. It was Sandy. She had crawled over and was looking through the glass safety window that was now the floor of the room above. She smiled and turned on the intercom. "I think I broke my arm."

Max laughed "I think you lost an eye too. I can't see out of my fake eye either." Bill groaned. "That's because the elder race of man were a bunch of freakin' Cyclops." They laughed but were in pain.

The ship was in great disarray. The way a house would be if it was turned on its side without securing the contents. It was something from the apocalypse mind set. The rooms were all just eight or ten feet wide but they had really tall ceilings. It didn't take long for the scientists to figure out that the ship was traveling through space at a steady acceleration rate. Which in turn caused 3.1 Earth gravities (Gs) to press the crew against what was the back walls, but now was the floor. It was difficult to move and breathe. The human body just wasn't made for this kind of gravity. A pair of socks now weighed three times what it did before. The average five pounds of clothing a normal person wears now weighed fifteen. It was difficult to just move and to stand and walk took a lot of effort. If Max got on a scale in this gravity his weight would move it to over eight hundred pounds. And yet everyone was able to move, slowly and with effort but move. The Mist had to have something to do with this.

All of the crew had been injured in some way. Everyone had damage to one eye, some both. Brandy and twelve others had lost both eyes. The furniture fastened to the wall, that used to be the floor, was a strange and dangerous sight. It made a good ladder to move through the ship. It was best to stay close to what was the floor but is now the wall. It gave access to the door that was now halfway up the wall or on the ceiling. The strangest was the doors that opened in the now floor of this room and ceiling of the one under it. They had to be careful. They stayed out of the hallways; which were now deep shafts.

Mouse and Harriet combed as much of the hull as possible for any problems they knew had to be there. They found plenty and a maintenance man named John Gentry stepped up to the plate and made as many of the repairs as he could. He made some he wasn't sure of; but he was all there was to help – he was healthy other than the missing eye. The space between the outer and inner hull was crossed with braces and made a very good ladder to most parts of the ship. New stair wells just had to be mapped out. But that would have to wait Mouse's current concern was the eggs.

She and Harriet went to check on the eggs. They found them in a lot better condition than they thought they would. However some of the incubators had slid into some very small places and were a lot of trouble to check. It would be impossible to get them out until the eggs hatched.

Mouse couldn't help but think back to The Mist. She was looking at a miracle. She had just been involved in a miracle. Brandy really had been born dead and The Mist had already brought her back. She and everyone on the ship had been given another chance to live by... Is the Mist a god? No, not unless you think of a god in the way the Greeks did; a god that could be talked to and would answer." She didn't believe The Mist was a god but she did believe she was very powerful and on their side. That didn't change the fact that the chicks could be monitored but what was going to happen when they hatched, if they hatched. She smiled, "Of course they're going to hatch. We have to have them."

Max's feet were burnt on the bottoms where the electricity grounded him through the axe handle to the floor; his hands had almost no feeling in them. His feet were bandaged and he was told to stay put. He didn't. He found a large pair of boots that his bandaged feet would fit into and kept going. Sandy was limping around; her left arm was in a splint, it was most likely broken. She had to turn her head to see to the left. Everyone on board had some of the same injuries. The most dangerous in the heavy gravity were the cracked or broken bones. If the cracks or breaks were in the ribs then it made it even more difficult to breath. The other breaks were nearly as bad; the bone protects the structure of a limb. A break could cause the loss of a limb if not carefully monitored.

Max and Sandy took control of the crew. Bill and a team he selected from the more healthy who could climb tried to find out what was happening to the ship. Doris had her hands full with the medical problems, all of which seemed to be emergencies.

Max and Sandy made sure that the people got what they needed. Some of the choices were difficult but they did their best to do the right thing. Max started to look for survivors who couldn't make it to the hanger, the place they were gathering. It had a twenty-five foot ceiling before and now had a twenty-five foot floor with an eighteen foot ceiling. Everyone was helping but Stick was for the most part in control of securing the area. He reported to Max but Max would have none of the reporting. He told Stick to take care of security "I have other things to do." Stick told him he didn't like being in charge.' Max laughed and told him "Tough shit." They laughed for a second and then another emergency called.

Sandy organized a triage unit. She did the best she could without much training to determine who could wait and who needed to see Doris now.

Doris took charge of the medical problems. She worked the staff and anybody she could draft until they could work no more. Then she asked for more. She got more.

No one on board moved too fast, too far, or too long at a time. After all, a hundred pound person now was a lot heavier than their muscles were used to moving.

Max found a little boy who had a foot missing. He stopped the bleeding and took him to Sandy. Doris looked at the wound and told Sandy to clean and dress the wound; "try to be sure it doesn't start to bleed again."

Brandy was sitting in the corner, whimpering, where Bill had told her to stay. She was scared and she couldn't see. Max put the boy next to her, "Brandy talk to this boy. His name is..." Max was at a loss. The boy said. "Sam, but I like to be called Hank."

Brandy said. "I know Hank."

Max nodded. "He has lost his foot, you guys talk. The worst is over." Brandy nodded and told Hank that he could tell her what was happening "because both my eyes are gone."

The rumblings throughout the ship didn't testify to the worst being over. Some hours later the ship had settled into steady acceleration and they began to get used to the gravity. It had only been a short time and they were just not moving that well.

During the emergency a lot of short cuts had been taken just to keep people alive. Although most people wondered if they even could die now and it helped to keep them calm.

People began to find something to eat and drink. The field rations were not so bad in an emergency. People began to find their loved ones and settle in for some sleep. Mouse was curled up with Brandy and Hank, or Sam. No one had claimed him. She had her head on Bill's leg as Bill sat on the floor with them. He told Max and Sandy to get some rest. The Adams boys were hiding in a corner.

As everyone settled in; it was the first Max had time to think about himself. He realized his feet hurt very much. Max with Sandy's help went and sat with the Adams boys. It was a scary time and sleep didn't come easy even though they were exhausted. The boys and many others were unable to sleep. A damaged small guitar was close. Max picked it up and played as best he could. He sang softly, more of a hum. The Captain looked to see him and then dozed off.

Sandy woke from sleep. She tried to wake Max but he wouldn't wake. She looked and saw the guitar was stuck to his hand with dried blood. Sandy started to cry. Doris was close. "He's all right, I just checked him."

Sandy sniffled out "Are you sure?"

Doris said. "Yes, he played until a short time ago. Although I think he's been asleep for a couple of hours." She smiled trying to reassure Sandy. "He's a bloody mess but he is just asleep."

Mike struggled over. "Bill, we need blankets. Are there any in the hold? Do you know?"

Max said, "Section 4, hold 6 a, four hundred and fifty. I'll get them."

Doris could hold him down. "No, you're not. Somebody else can get them. I'm going to redress those feet."

Harriet was close. "I know where that is. I'll go."

Mike said. "We'll need a few people to transfer them up." Bill told him where some tie downs that could be used as ropes were located.

Mouse sat up. "I'll get'em." Doris smiled. "Not until I wrap your foot; it may be broken. I don't think it is but in this gravity I don't want to take any chances."

Bill started to move. Doris said. "I need you here. We have made a serum that these people need to take. It has some things in it that they will not want to take, but they need it or this gravity is going to kill them."

Bill asked "What?"

She smiled, "A lot of steroids, the ones that can hurt you. But they've all got some kind of break or crack and it has to heal fast or it is going to be a big problem."

Bill told Mike to draft Stick. The boots had to be cut off Max's feet and for the next two days he lay on his back. He told Sandy where things were and she passed it on to whoever needed the information. He knew who could fix whatever needed fixing. He and Sandy had no problem getting things done. The Captain took a team to the control room and started to try to get back to normal. Mouse did what she could to find any problem in the hull. Her foot was broken and it was put in a splint. She and Harriet took control of the hull. She kept the foot wrapped. The incubators were doing their job and they would soon know if the eggs were going to hatch. Stick kept the peace.

They 'drafted' a cook and a cargo man who were small enough to help. Harriet was just too hard to say so it was shortened to "H." She seemed pleased to have a nickname. John, the maintenance man and the crew members who had volunteered to help him were at Mouse's call. They welded and enhanced and repaired what she wanted so it would be stronger. H and John's intended chased supplies. Brandy was made to leave the hull several times. Mouse was afraid she would get hurt. Brandy just wouldn't stay out. Brandy reasoned that it was dark in there anyway and she couldn't see 'so what's the big deal.' More that once she was called on to help in small areas where neither Mouse nor H could get. At first Mouse was terrified for her but it soon became almost normal. "Don't touch anything Brandy; just hold your hand above it and see if you can feel the heat." Brandy being blind helped in this case.

The ship was finding a new norm. Doris let the Captain know that she was transporting a large number of computerized eyes for military use on Gamma Station. They were top secret and going out for field test. She was willing to use them for the crew. She explained it was an updated version of the one Max had. They were designed to be placed on a brace and the electronics would then interface with brain. Doris saw no reason why the eye couldn't be placed in the now vacant eye socket. She wanted to try the first one on Max. It turned out to be a close fit and took very little modification to install the eyes in the human eye socket. Who knows, that may be what the military had in mind in the beginning.

Now that things were calmer the dead had to be dealt with. James, Karen, Mason and Professor Kent were among the dead. It was hard. Sandy told Max how alone she felt as they held each other. It was a sad day when the bodies were put into the freezer. The thought of them being guardian angels held little comfort.

The service was too long and too sad. The realization that these people had to pass to the Mist because of the greed of the Adams was enough to piss them off.

A week later the crew were all recovering nicely and most had their eye or eyes replaced with the computerized ones. There were some hold outs, they believed it was unnatural. They were not the ones with both eyes gone. The eyes looked a little weird. There was no lens to cover them. Doris hadn't thought about that when she put them in the human head. She would work on a cover so they wouldn't be so strange looking. But now you could see the machine inside the eye socket. The camera aperture would move as it focused. Brandy had two and thought it was funny. She laughed as she watched herself in the mirror. She told Bill she didn't care what it looked like. She could see and that was all she cared about. She smiled. Besides everybody else has one. Mouse was having a lot of trouble keeping Brandy out of the hull. It seemed to draw her like moth to a flame.

CHAPTER, NINETEEN, A NEW NORM

Ten days into the runaway flight the Captain was ready to share some of his hard decisions. Mouse told Sandy that he had been moody and seemed just mad. The call came to Max; it was CC2 Hall, "Lieutenant Dent, there is a CC meeting at 1300, please bring Private Parks with you."

Max asked, "What's happening Mike?"

Mike laughed, "Nothing and everything - just be there ok?"

Max told him he would. That was two hours away. He called Mouse and told her to get cleaned up; there was a meeting she had to attend. It wasn't long before Carol came by. She leaned on what used to be the floor while standing in the new doorway that had been cut. She sipped her coffee. "I guess he decided what he's going to do. I just got a call too."

Max nodded. "He has to fill the CC board doesn't he?"

She said softly as if she was happy not to be making these decisions, "Yeah, at least seven members. He has another thirty days to fill the rest. I wouldn't want to be the one to make those decisions. He has to redo the whole board to suit this new situation. It's going to be a mess for a while." She asked as a second thought. "Did Sandy get her transfer approved?"

Max sort of smiled. "Haven't heard, and I'm not sure how I feel about her working for me."

She wondered. "What did you recommend?"

He shook his head. "I didn't, I talked to Bill about it. He said he would work it out. You know, what's best for the ship?" He added. "Mike asked, no, ordered me to bring Mouse with me to the meeting."

She sort of smiled. "I expected that. She is the logical choice but it is going to look bad."

Max smiled, "You mean with him and her shacked up now." They laughed.

Carol was about to laugh again. "Shacked up, we thought they had died in there. Doris checked on them the third day." They laughed and she asked. "Well, are you ready to see what is going to fall out of the magic box?"

Max laughed. "I'm getting real damn tired of that magic box." They stopped by to get Mouse. She wanted to know what was going on but they could honestly tell her that they were not sure.

She asked "Is Bill going to be in a better mood after this?"

They laughed and Max said. "I hope so."

Carol smiled at her and Mouse looked embarrassed. "We didn't know it had been two days." They laughed. She just shook her head. "It didn't seem like two days."

The meeting was a closed door deal. The room had been rearranged and the furnishings moved to the wall. Private Parks, Ensign Sandra Dent, Sergeant Van Smyth and Corporal Gentry were guests; they didn't know what was coming. The rest of the board was almost sure they were going to become part of the board. They had all sat in those seats before. The Captain came into the room; it was called to attention. The 'at ease' was given and "be seated." He was hesitant to start. "Well, I'm happy that you could all come to this meeting; even if it was an order."

He paused for a laugh but only got a snicker. "I know you want to know what's happening. I'm given by the regulations a wide range of powers in a situation like this. They are badly written and open to interpretation. I don't think that anyone ever expected them to be used. So this is what I got out of them and this is what we're going to do. I'm going to activate my promotion to Admiral. We are going to be in a 'small town' atmosphere for a while. What I mean by that will be discussed tomorrow at 1300. Be here." He paused. "The crew will need someone they can come to with problems. I'm going to try to stay out of the business of the board and be more of a mayor, of sorts. Now, don't get me wrong I'm still in command of this ship. I will sit in the meetings and will have my say; when I please. By regulation that makes me the CC0. Now I am going to sit down and turn the meeting over to Captain Mike Hall, CC1." Bill was already wearing the Admiral rank.

Mike was already wearing the Captain rank. He started. "First I have to say that brevet promotions are permanent after you have worn them for five years. That is what the regulations say. That information will become important soon. There are also rank requirements that are attached to these positions." He paused. "So, Commander Warren Lawrence will be the new CC2, he has moved from Lieutenant to Commander. CC3 is another of the positions that helps make policy. It is a command position. The position should by rank go to CC7 Doris Baxter, but, she is needed very badly in her position. She has requested to remain as medical and experiment control. She will be moved however to CC6 Lieutenant Commander Doctor Doris Baxter from the rank of Lieutenant. That leaves CC3 open and we have talked new Commander Carol Anderson into taking that position."

Max looked at her. She already knew what was going to happen. She had a say in it. Mike continued. "CC4 as the head and CC5 as the second are going to run the everyday business of the ship, they are responsible for everything that is the everyday life on board from power to security. The top three have a choice, the rest of you don't." Everyone laughed a nervous laugh. "CC4 is, he smiled and they almost laughed. CC4 is now Commander Bartholomew Dent. CC5 is now Lieutenant Commander Sandra Dent; Sandra would you move to the table please. The new CC7 will be taken by now Lieutenant Albert Van Smyth as security and law enforcement, Stick would you please move to the table? The last two positions," He looked over at the two sitting nervously in the gallery. "CC8 is responsible for the integrity of the ship. They will check or have checks made on the hull as often as necessary and insure that such repairs as necessary are made, quickly." Mouse sunk down in her chair just hoping it would go away. Mike continued. "The CC8 position will be covered by now Lieutenant Betty Parks; Betty would you take your place at the table. The CC9 position will make repairs as requested. He will also have control of the maintenance department. The CC9 position will be covered by now Lieutenant J G, John Gentry. John, please move to the table. That concludes the official meeting for today."

He handed them the new rank pins and smiled. "This is going to be a big job and I believe there are going to be some real adventures. Just do your best. I've already seen what you can do or you wouldn't be here." He paused. "The official Charmer for the ship is now Professor Lowell. No questions today think about them and we have packets for each of you with your new duties and requirements Please remain for your formal paper work." The meeting was over. There was still a lot to say, and questions to be asked - it just didn't need to be on the record.

Mouse found Bill and asked, "How much did you have to do with this?"

He told her "Nothing, you will be doing the same thing you have been. I couldn't have anything to do with promotions of my soon to be wife, my niece or her husband. It would have looked bad."

She said. "I'm scared to death." Max and Sandy came to talk to Bill.

Sandy asked, "Why us?"

Bill said. "I only recommended, but you two make a good pair and it is going to take that and more to get done what you have to get done. Besides like I told Mouse, you are already doing what is being asked of you." He smiled, "You might want to know that all the decisions we made today were board unanimous."

John approached Mouse, "I guess you are my boss now. I need to tell you that I'm not an engineer I just welded what they told me to weld and stuff like that."

Mouse smiled. "We'll figure it out together or we'll all die."

He smiled. "I'm not sure which is more frightening - I kind of liked being dead."

The room started to snicker; it was the first relief from the tension since they entered the room.

Mike said. "I did too, John." Everyone laughed. John told Mouse quietly. "I always wondered what it would be like to have someone on the board know my name. - It's scary."

Mike got their attention. "Everyone, I'm not going to announce these promotions until tomorrow. However you are wearing the rank so tell whoever you want. I'm going to put out a memo saying what they are and tell everyone to find a way to be useful. It'll be handed out tomorrow while we are in conference. Don't forget to get your paper work and get up to admin and have yourself charmed. It's important and an order, so go now." They opened the door and most of the remaining crew of 87 - were waiting. They wanted to know. Max told Carol she was scum for not telling him. She just laughed and told him how difficult it was for her to not tell.

John's intended was not shy about asking him if he was in trouble. He laughed. "Yes, big trouble."

The members of the board laughed. Mike slapped John on the back. "You are a funny man, good to have you aboard." John's intended was a Corporal in the chow hall.

He said. "I have to go to admin and be charmed. I have been promoted to Lieutenant J G and made CC9 over maintenance."

She put her hand over her mouth, "Oh my."

Brandy was at Mouse's feet. She picked her up. Brandy asked. "Is it scary mommy?"

Mouse said, "Very."

The charming took two hours. It took another hour for Mouse to get her uniform right. She went to see Max. When she walked into the office Max yelled, "Officer on deck." Betty almost jumped to attention before she realized it was her, and then the people in the office started to clap. He had done the same thing to Stick earlier. She smiled. "Thank you."

She went into the office and Sandy asked if she would like coffee. "Yes, please."

Max asked if she had read the stuff in the packet. "Yes, I guess it'll be H. But how do I hire two augments? Where do I look?" She added "I would talk to Bill about all this stuff; but it's kind of weird."

Sandy tried to help, "It should be pretty easy for you. Your main requirement is size. After that you just have to talk to them and see if they'll fit in your world. Stick has the same problems. He needs trained or trainable people."

She nodded. "You're right. Did he promote Luanne?"

Max nodded. "Yeah, Luanne, he promoted her to Master Chief."

Sandy sort of smiled, "He said Larry was going to be mad but Luanne has training in Law, Security and Power units."

Max added, "Did you see your office? It's a mess, but it's yours." They made their way across the cat walks that now crossed the hallway to the office across the hall. Max had set the desk up in the inner office and found a chair. He smiled. "That's all I had time to do."

Mouse started to laugh. "Are you guys as dumbfounded as I am about this deal."

Sandy said "Yeah…" Max nodded and Sandy added. "We'll get past it. Just act sure of yourself and then come by our quarters and we will have a large drink. They were laughing when H came into the area. She was puzzled and looked as if she had something to say but not now. Max and Sandy made their way back to their offices. They knew Mouse had business with H and they needed to be alone to discus it.

After they left Mouse said. "See if you can find yourself a chair and have a seat." Mouse went behind the desk and sat down. H asked as she scooted a chair up to the desk. "What did I miss?" Mouse told her there was a big meeting today and the new CC board was formed. H smiled, "I thought that was commander's brass they were wearing; but I didn't believe my new eye." She sat down.

Mouse didn't say anything about the Lieutenant bars on her shoulders. H's mind was somewhere else. "They were just giving me some advice and showing me my desk. She took the paperwork out of the packet she was given. "Private Harriet Smith, I am authorized to promote you to the rank of Master Chief and the position of my second. Do you choose to accept this promotion?" She paused. "I hope I did that right."

Harriet smiled. "They made you a Senior Master Chief, Are you kidding?"

Mouse told her "No, H, they made me a Lieutenant and CC8. I don't know if I can do this job or not but it sure would be nice if I could count on you."

H smiled. "And Chief, a Master Chief, I never thought I would see Sergeant."

Mouse laughed, "Never thought I would see corporal." The chief ranks were between officer and enlisted and seldom used. Anyone who held a chief rank was respected on both sides of the officer-enlisted line.

Harriet stood and saluted, "Happy to be aboard, sir."

Mouse returned the salute. She handed Harriet the rank insignia for Master Chief and said. "Good to have you aboard; now the first order of business is to sign these papers and to get this office space cleaned up. Then we get to hire two more people."

Harriet smiled, "There is one more thing. She went back to the door and came back in with a small box. She opened the lid and said. "They've hatched; over a hundred of them. They're not walking to well in this gravity but they are all over the ship. They seem to just jump. And they are in places I can't even reach."

Mouse started to laugh. Something struck her as very funny. H didn't quite know what to say. Mouse was able to calm herself enough to say. "My first crisis in office is the ship's hull is infested with chickens." They were both laughing when Brandy came into the office. "Max said you were in your new office." She paused and the ladies tried to pull themselves together.

Brandy wondered softly. "What kind of bugs have you got in the box?"

Mouse said. "They're not bugs…" She thought for a second. "How did you know there was something in the box?"

She said, "I can see them in the red. There are four of them and they have feet made like this." She drew the track in the dust.

Mouse questioned. "How can you see that?"

Brandy smiled, "You just blink two times real fast and the things turn red."

H tried it. "She's right. The eye changes to infrared when you blink twice."

Mouse tried and smiled. "That is just strange." They explained to Brandy that what she was seeing was heat.

Brandy said. "When you blink three times the colors float around. What's that?" They tried that but didn't know what they were seeing.

H sort of laughed. "Did these things come with a manual? Brandy, how do I get back to normal?"

Brandy laughed, "Mash your teeth together." Mouse laughed. "I don't believe this." But it worked.

Brandy asked "Can I see the bugs?" H let her look in the box. Brandy smiled with delight. "They are not yucky at all. Can I hold one?" Her hand was in the box before they could answer; she scooped one up and was giggling as she cuddled it. H smiled, "The kids are members of the crew aren't they?" Mouse nodded yes but didn't grasp just what she was saying. H added "They're a lot smaller than we are."

Mouse thought about it for a short while and then bit her lower lip. "Well, it is an emergency of sorts. But, I think it would be best to ask their parents first." She smiled. "Let's go talk to Max. Brandy put the chicken back and bring the box."

Brandy was surprised, "That's a chicken!"

Mouse told her "Yes, a baby. It's called a chick."

They went to see Max. His response to the idea was. "You want to do what?"

Sandy was playing with the chicks. "They are so cute."

Max teased her. "For goodness sake you are a Lieutenant Commander and that is food."

She couldn't help but laugh. "They're still cute. Here Max hold one."

Max shook his head. "Not unless you got some salt."

Brandy made a 'yuck' sound. "We should shave them first."

Max laughed. "I'm going to have to run this by the top 'four.' He was chuckling and asked Brandy if she thought they should cook them first.

Sandy noted. "Look Max,-- we are more or less asking for the Adams boys, Brandy, and Mike's boy."

Brandy said. "Philippe, his name is Philippe." The other three children were Billy, John Gentry's son; Levi, Doris' daughter, and the boy Sam. He's the one who lost a foot. We'll have to find out who took him in and if he's well enough to participate.

Max asked "Are the tunnels safe?"

Mouse laughed out loud. "No, but they're as safe as any other place on this piece of crap." She put her hand over her mouth, "Don't tell Bill I called his ship a piece of crap."

Max laughed and shook his head in disbelief that he had even asked such a dumb question. "You're right and I won't."

They started to make the calls. Sam was with a cargo man named Dan and his intended Sheila, a cook. The ones that Mouse had drafted before; both were trained in the handling of hazardous waste. They were friends with the boy's mother who had died in the launch. Mike and his intended were willing to go along with the deal.

Doris didn't have any objections; "As long as they are as safe as possible and Levi is driving me nuts wanting to help." She even corrected herself, "I know that's a stupid thing to say; but you know what I mean. This thing is not safe."

Bill told Mouse that "It sounds like a very good answer to the problem." The board gave the idea thumbs up over the phone. After all, the kids were for the most part children of the board. They wanted to help in any way they could. The parents gave permission for them to help Mouse, not fully knowing what they would be doing.

Mouse talked to John Gentry in person. He smiled. "Billy will be very happy to help." Billy was all smiles at the prospect of something new to do. The approval took place over the phone because it was hard to move around. The last child was Sam; Mouse and Brandy went to see him personally. The boy opened the door walking on his new foot. He was getting around just fine. Brandy said. "Hi Hank, nice foot and I like your eye. It looks so much like mine." They laughed. They were invited in and got right to the point. They were walking on the wall and there just wasn't much room for anything but a mess. Dan and Sheila Grant were small, that's why she had drafted them to do the hull inspections.

"Welcome to our home, sir." Sheila was apologizing for the mess.

Mouse said "Thank you. I would like to talk to you about changing jobs and your new son. And everything on this ship is a mess. You should see my office." It turned out that they were both overages now. There wasn't much for them to do after the runaway. They would be happy to be reassigned to hull integrity. When she asked about Sam they were a little surprised, but gave their permission. They were told that a meeting would take place in an hour across from the security office, in her office.

The meeting brought all the players. It was a little overwhelming for everybody. Lieutenant Parks was running the meeting and the Captain of the ship was there. She closed the door and said. "Hello, I'm Lieutenant Betty Parks. Most of you know me as Mouse and that is what I prefer. But this is an official meeting so it's Lieutenant Parks. I'm going to address the children first. This is a secret meeting." The kids were instantly quiet. "We don't want anyone to know what is going on for a while. It is very important that you tell no one." The kids were all nodding and said they would keep the secret. Max was standing by Mike. Mike asked quietly. "What's going on? I thought this was just about hull integrity." Max smiled and whispered. "They've hatched and escaped. They are all over the ship."

Mike nodded not fully understanding. It was a second later that he snickered and quietly left. He could be heard in the hall laughing. Shortly he came back into the room.

Mouse said rather flatly. "You got it under control now, Captain?"

He smiled, "Yes, Lieutenant; thank you for your patience."

Doris was a little short. "I have other things to do if this is some kind of joke."

Mike said. "No, this is serious. It's funny but it is very serious. The survival of this ship and its crew could depend, no, does depend on the success of this mission."

Max started to smile. Mike started to choke back a laugh. "Max, please don't start."

Mouse took control, "Why don't I just tell them what is going on?" She had the attention of all. "How do I start this?" She took a deep breath and began. "As you all know the Einstein has a large black market operation." H smiled. Mouse looked at her "Don't you start." She continued, "as I was about to say. When we started this mission the market intended to have eggs available for the entire flight. To do this they brought aboard eggs that would hatch and then those chickens would start to lay and thus fresh eggs for the entire trip would be available."

Mouse started to smile and Max started to laugh followed soon by Sandy and Mike. Mouse tried to stop but when H started Mouse just said it. "They've hatched and they are all over the ship." Mike laughed out "We're infested with chickens." The rest of the players started to understand what was happening. They smiled and then laughed, even Doris laughed.

It took a while before things got back to where they could be talked about the chicks and even then the thought was funny. Mouse tried to be serious. "We need these chicks alive. We don't know how long we are going to be out here. They may become very important as a food source." She paused. "Now this is the very serious part. I have the power to draft any person in the crew to help me secure the hull. That is read, in this case as get the chickens out of the hull space and to safety. I want to draft your children."

Mike said. "Any way this comes down; it is a secret until you are told different."

Sheila asked. "Are these chickens dangerous? I've never seen one alive."

The box was passed around and the children were allowed to hold them. There was some talk about safety but as all had to agree, no place was safe. The meeting broke up about a half hour later. The children were all allowed to stay. Sheila and Dan stayed and were told about their new jobs, and their new rank. They were made aware of the functions of the new eye. The hunt would begin in an hour.

Mike complemented Mouse. "Let me do this right. Lieutenant you are doing a great job in a strange situation, a very strange situation."

Mouse smiled, "Thank you, sir"

After a brief training course on how to hold and catch the fragile chicks the children were ready. They were split into four groups. Mouse, H, Sheila and Dan took a squad; Brandy and Sam went with H.

It took most of the night to catch the chicks and some surely got away. Sam found a place in the hull that was hotter than it should have been. The hull plating was a bright red through his eye. He reported it to H and H to Mouse. Mouse called John and the procedure to have a possible breach repaired was established. Just like that. Mouse had to write it up but that was another task. She would have to talk to Max about just how to do that.

Mouse got four hours sleep before the 1300 meeting the next day. Everything went very well. Brandy and the other children had gotten about six hours sleep. They had been dead tired. Chicks are hard to catch and the fourteen hour ordeal had taken its toll on the kids. After two hours two of the squads sat out for two, they sort of worked in shifts after that, two hours on and two hours off. Mouse thought it should have been four hours but the kids were just getting used to the gravity and so were the adults. Everyone knew that when all was said and done this was about the ship. The kids knew it and they were perfect little soldiers. But they were sure happy to see the mission finished.

The CC board meeting was more informative today than the day before. Things were more or less what passed for normal. Mouse reported the hot spot in the hull found by one of the kids. Bill interrupted. "We're going to call them the Mouse Brigade."

Mouse smiled "It was found by Sam of the Mouse Brigade." She wondered why it was so easy to report to the CC. It didn't take her long to realize the reason, she knew every member of the board as people. She knew she drew a line between the human her and the new officer; her. It was easy to be relaxed with people you knew and understood.

John reported that it was fixed and that it had not recurred, but should be watched. "I believe it is a pressure point from the speed and design of the ship. I believe it may occur in the same place in a circle around the ship." He seemed relaxed. Mouse knew better; but he could put on a good public face to cover how on edge he was. The very relaxed atmosphere helped. It was all first names until something had to be decided and then it became official titles. It was just the way Max operated in his office.

Mouse reported that she was planning on reinforcing the areas that were expected to fail; but not if it meant an excessive use of repair material. She instead was going to watch the area and only patch when it was necessary and long before it became a problem. Mike agreed and informed them "The Mouse Brigade is to be awarded the 'letter of hero' for their work last night and from now on they will be referred to as 'recruit' with a promotion to level nine. That is if the board has no objections?" He waited for no votes but got none. "The hull is going to be a major problem through out this flight. Those children are going to be our life line." There were no objections. He added that the adults would be awarded a letter of appreciation. "A letter will be placed in their records. We don't want to step on the new recruit's ego." Mouse and John smiled. It wasn't a problem.

Mike nodded. "OK, let's get down to other information. This is the way it stands now. The engines will not burn out for three and a half years, maybe a while longer. I'm told by the scientists that I would be insane to try to shut them down. I guess I'll believe them. The ship will not slow until at least that same amount of time. It is estimated that we will be traveling somewhere around light 40 to light 45 when the engines burn out. Given the rate at which we slow that should give us average speed over the next seven years of around light thirty." He laughed, "Now, Professor Mills provided that information. For those of you who don't know him he's a very exacting person; so for him to not be able to pin this down to anything more exact than five light years, give or take should tell you just how deep we're in trouble."

He paused a second before he continued. "We have rations for eighteen months, maybe twenty if we're careful. Those chicks are the most important things on this ship. We must keep them alive; or we don't stand much of a chance. They'll provide eggs and more chicks for food. They must be protected; and they will get enough to eat." He paused again and rubbed his chin. "The worse news is that we can't even begin to try to repair the ship until after it slows to below light speed. We have to go outside the ship and you don't do that at light speed. When we reach engine burn out the gravity is going to switch back as we slow. The wall will become the wall again. Watch how the ship is modified. We are going to have to switch back to artificial gravity sometime in the next three or four years."

Max informed the board that the settler packs "Have seeds in them and we might be able to grow some kind of plants." Sandy was the expert in that field and she asked for Doris' help. "I know I can make them grow but I might have to do something that could make them poison." Carol thought it was funny given her last experience when she believed Sandy had tried to poison her. Doris agreed to help She didn't want the crew poisoned. They were assigned to check into the possibility of growing the seeds.

Mike added. "We are about to have a very big pinning ceremony with the kids. Before that happens I'm going to tell the crew what I just told you. I'm going to try to sugar coat it as much as possible." The meeting ended with "There will be a pinning ceremony on the lower flight deck in an hour. Make sure that the kids are there. We plan to charm them right then: and we have their new uniforms. They're gray with brown sleeves. They will each get four charms, promotion to recruit, Mouse Brigade, and the Letter of Hero; Sam will also receive a discoverer letter for finding the possible breach; a red stripe will be added to the letter if he finds another hot spot. It's not our plan to start a competition but the more excited the kids; let's make that 'new recruits.' The more excited they are about finding the breaches the better off the ship. The fifth red stripe turns the four before it into a cluster and the charm can contain four clusters." Let me add the Cascade charm has been extended to them as crew. Let's get these new recruits to the lower flight deck in uniform in fifty minutes." He laughed "Phil is probably already ready to go. He knows something is happening."

The new recruits were dressed in their pink uniforms when the meeting began. The meeting was called to order. "Attention," then "as you were." The Admiral made the announcements about the new board and made sure the rest of the crew knew who to contact for what. Then he turned the meeting over to the new Captain.

Mike informed the crew of their plight. The adults were very concerned about food. They were told about the possibility of the seeds and told that they would be kept informed. The kids were no longer the least bit concerned about what he was saying; they were bored. But they perked right up when he picked up a chick from a box sitting on a table. "This is a chicken; or will be in a few weeks. It will lay eggs and later, after a flock is established, be a protein source. These little guys and the seeds will get us through after the first year. We may get tired of chicken but we'll have food."

He took a deep breath and added "Last night a major operation was conducted to get these guys out of the hull. It was carried out by some very specially qualified members of the crew. It's a new special hull Maintenance group." He paused. "Attention to orders" The room came to attention. "The following crew will report to the stage. He began to call the names; each name was preceded by 'Level ten research assistant.' As he called the names the kids walked to the stage: Samuel Pickle, Randall Adams, Franklin Adams, Brandy Parks, Philippe Hall, John William Gentry, and Levi Baxter.

The kids were told where to stand and to remain at attention. Captain Hall continued. "Each of these Level ten Research assistants is promoted to level nine recruits." They all smiled in spite of being at attention." They will also be listed as part of a new hull maintenance group that will be known as the "Mouse Brigade." When they thought he was done everyone cheered.

The Captain held up his hands to get quiet. "We're not done yet. Recruit Philippe Hall you will report." He picked his son because he knew that he knew how to report. Philippe snapped to just like the little solider he was. "Recruit Philippe Hall reports as ordered, SIR." The Captain read. "Attention to orders. Recruit Philippe Hall, for heroism under very dangerous circumstances in the rescue of essential ships property and the safe return of that property that could mean the life of fellow crew members; you are awarded the Letter of Hero." The medal was pinned to his little chest that seemed to swell to twice its size as the medal was pinned on by his father.

The rest of the new recruits took a page from Philippe as they reported. Mouse was so proud of her new Mouse Brigade. She believed every one of them deserved the Letter of Hero but when Brandy's turn came she was overwhelmed. Her four year old baby was getting a Letter of Hero and she damn well deserved it.

The call to report for Sam was last and the second medal for the discovery of the hot spot was presented. You could see the eyes of the new recruits. I want one of those. They handed out the letters, the charm certificates and the new uniforms. Sam was so happy; "Now I can toss this pink thing."

As the charming started everyone talked. Mouse bent down to look Brandy in the face. "Congratulations Brandy." Brandy sort of gritted her teeth, she was embarrassed; and said in a soft yell. "Mom - stand up!" Mouse stood and Brandy said, "Thank you Lieutenant Parks." Mouse smiled. Brandy waited a second and added. "Mom, can I go see the rest of the 'Mouses.'" Mouse smiled, "Of course Recruit Parks. You are dismissed." Brandy didn't think it was as funny as Bill and Max did but went to talk to the rest of the Mouse Brigade. Max told Mouse and Bill "We have created monsters." Mouse didn't doubt it but she was so proud.

They laughed but Mouse remembered just how happy she was to be promoted to private just a few months ago. Now her daughter was the same rank that she had been... it seemed like a lot longer ago than it was. She had been stuck in that dead end job for two years, now she was happy. She was about to marry the love she thought would never come. She was a Lieutenant and going to marry an Admiral, and eighth from the top to command a starship and she never had to sleep with anyone; well that she didn't want. She had good friends that she was going to die with at any moment. She had a very important job. And now Brandy was a very important part of her work and not just her life. She smiled. Some very proud parents left the meeting with some very, very proud new recruits with newly charmed sore arms.

Sam had already found a place to change into his new gray uniform. Brandy saw him and smiled. She remembered how much the kids back at the center hated to see a gray uniform. She smiled as she looked down to see the gray uniform that she was holding. She left to find a place to change.

Over the next few weeks the ship began to fall into a routine. The chickens were going to live. Doris commented that their drumsticks were really going to be big. They were walking well in spite of the triple gravity that they had not expected when they hatched.

Doris and Sandy had gotten a good response from the seeds in the settler packs. They had some small plants. That meant the people would have food. The plants also helped with the air quality. Everyone had settled into their new rank and the general structure of the new Command. Several of the Mouses had added either the Letter of Discovery or a red stripe for finding a second hot spot.

The computers were going to be booted soon and there would be some functions. Sanitation was almost in hand, and the water supply was not contaminated. It was checked every day. With the aid of the steroid concoction that Doris made; the crew was moving almost as well as they did before the gravity problem. Doris told Bill off the record that she believed The Mist had something to do with how well it worked. "It should have taken a year even with the drugs for us to be able to move this well in this gravity."

Max was clearing the release of the guy in the brig; Stick was tired of messing with him. Everyone had a new eye or two, although it was a little sad. The wide eyed look that Brandy was so good at was gone; now it's just the machines.

It's been two months since the Einstein started its runaway flight. Today is a day of celebration; Mouse and Bill are going to marry. A full dress military marriage, no one said but Max suspected that it was because the Mouses wanted to wear their dress uniforms. Larger adult uniforms had been collected so the new uniforms for the Mouses could be made. A number of the Mouses had added red stripes to their Discover Charm. It was becoming very apparent that the hot spots were going to be a continuing problem. They were also occurring in a circle around the ship, just as predicted.

There was going to be a big party with a lot of food compared to what they had been having. It was a time to relax. The ship's company had done very well, they had become a family. Each had their work to support the village. The crops were to a point where they could be left alone for a while. The chickens were doing very well; everyone was ready for them to 'lay an egg' but that was some weeks away.

The wedding was a grand event. Betty was married in her dress uniform to Bill in his dress uniform and all seven Mouses attended them in their dress uniforms. Max in his dress uniform gave her away. It was a sight to see. They took vows that their marriage would last until 'The Mist keeps us.' After they were pronounced married, by the Captain, they called Brandy and asked "Brandy Parks do you wish to call this man Father and change your name to Brandy Holt." Brandy smiled. "Yes sir, I do." They were pronounced a family and the party began. They had no idea how many of the things they did that day would become tradition.

It didn't take long before the first of those traditions started to appear. Randall and Franklin came to Max and Sandra and asked to be adopted. They also wanted to take new names. It didn't take much discussion to understand they were serious. Max and Sandy agreed. They could make the declarations at the next meeting of the ships company in a few weeks. Their mother had often read them the story of the founding of Rome and they enjoyed the story. Randall chose the name Romulus Randall Dent, and his brother chose Remus Franklin Dent. Sam Pickle also chose to be adopted. He would change his name to Samuel Pickle Grant.

During the next meeting the adoptions were professed in front of the entire crew, to a grand round of applause, they approved. Later that afternoon the charmer made some frantic calls; the Mouses were in his office and they wanted charms. The parents went to see what was going on. Max and Sandy arrived about the same time as Doris. What the Mouses wanted was a charm that reflected their house. Brandy argued that she was a member of the crew and could request a charm if she wanted. She seemed to be the leader, or inciter, of the group or at least the one who talked the loudest. Mouse told her that was true to a point but "What kind of Charm do you want." Each of the Mouses wanted a charm that read 'House of' their surname. It was decided that it would be permitted but that the 'house' members should have some say over what it would look like. The charming was delayed for a week.

It was a few days later that Max set out to complete a mission before it was too late. He had been trying to get something done all day. Every time he tried he was interrupted in some way. But now he wasn't going to let anything else get in his way. Max had a special problem and of the remaining ninety-six crew; there was only one who might be able to help him. He went to see Doris to see if she would act as a go between. It was her job but he wanted this off the record and … She asked a few questions and then sent him to see Professor Morris. She called and informed Professor Morris that he was assigned to a special project. "I don't know what he wants, he's being vague." After Max left her office she did note that it wasn't like Max to be that evasive.

CHAPTER TWENTY,
FOOD AND FORWARD
MOVEMENT

Max went to see Professor Morris. Professor Morris' specialty was cloning. He was a happy man and was in a good mood when Max came into the office. "Doris called down and told me I was working for you for a while. I hope it'll be interesting."

Max laughed. "You can count on it being that." Max told him that what he was about to ask was to be attempted in earnest without any crap and "Its top secret." No one is to find out; "If it doesn't work it'll make us look very silly. I don't want the crew to get their hopes up and it doesn't work." The professor told him it sounded intriguing.

Max started to laugh as he closed the door. He handed the Professor two bags and told him he wanted him to clone the contents. The Professor opened the bags one by one and started to laugh. He could barely contain himself. In the end he just laughed. He asked Max if he knew anything about cloning. Max told him he knew some about the process. The Professor told him that what he was asking could not be done. "It's impossible." He laughed as he told Max "You can not clone a pig from a slice of bacon or a cow from some ground beef." He also cautioned max that there probably wasn't a live cell to work with in either of the samples. Max smiled and told him he was going to try.

Everyone on board knew that Max was just not to be messed with; so the Professor tried to calm the situation. The Professor assured him it just couldn't be done. "The best I could hope for is to grow a big piece of pork or beef if there is a live cell to work with."

Max smiled. "Wouldn't that be good enough?"

The Professor laughed and thought for a minute. "You are a very interesting man Max; and you are right. I'm not saying I can do it but I'll try."

Max told him if he needed help he could get all he wanted; but that was the last of the base material."

Max and the Professor agreed to keep the project secret. "We don't want to get the crew's hopes up and it fail." The Professor told Max over and over that the chances of success were one in the highest number he knew, maybe worse. But he wanted credit if it worked and no blame if it failed. Max was happy to give him anything he wanted.

Every thirty days or so, Bill had a birthday party. Sweets were controlled and there was always a cake. Morale was always higher after the party. At the fourth such event, Doris took the stage. She had become responsible, as the doctor, for the food distribution and nutrition. She had everyone's attention as she began to speak; the smells in the air were not field rations. "Now, today we are each going to get two special treats, in addition to the cake. The first is we have enough eggs for everyone to have one, boiled is the best way to distribute them. We hope the chickens continue to produce eggs. Therefore we want the shells back."

Brandy asked why. Doris smiled. "Well, the chickens need the shell so they can produce new eggs." Sam asked if they ate the egg shells. Doris nodded, "Yes, we crumble them up and they eat them."

Phil asked how they picked out the right parts to rebuild the egg "and how does the chicken know which egg parts are hers?"

Levi started to laugh, "You guys are so dumb. The chicken just needs the calcium the egg shell is made out of to make a new egg."

The Mouses gave her a dirty look and Brandy said. "Well, why didn't you just say so?"

Romulus added. "We've never even seen an egg before and neither have you Levi, miss smarty pants.

Levi yelled at him. "At least I know about calcium."

Brandy was yelling too. "We all know what calcium is, Levi. It's what bones are made of."

The kids were getting out of hand and before long it was impossible to know who said what but when Brandy made a fist and busted Levi in the mouth it had to stop. Levi picked herself up off the floor and charged Brandy; the fight was on. The other kids got into the act and the parents were trying to separate them without much luck. Bill yelled "Mouses ATTENTION."

The Mouses stopped and were breathing hard. They were still mad. Mike laughed. "I like that."

Mouse smiled. "It's nice. Just yell attention and it all stops. We should have put them in the military a long time ago." Max agreed it was better than turning on the suppression water. The Mouses were still standing at attention. But they were also still steaming mad.

Bill told them that they were responsible for the clean up after the dinner. They were not happy about it but they were going to do it. He put them at ease and told them they would behave as soldiers. He seemed to cut his remarks a little short; Max wondered why. It was as they ate he would find out that Bill was about to laugh and he was starting to feel a little sorry for Levi as she tried to sniff the blood back up her nose. He thought Billy was going to cry but he noticed the big red mark that resembled a fist by his good eye. He had just gotten hit in the eye. Doris gave a little quick medical attention before she continued.

Brandy and Levi sat with arms crossed staring at each other as Doris smiled and got back to business, "Now that the floor show is over let's get back to the eggs. In a few days we plan to divide the crew into thirds. This will allow for one third of us to have two eggs each every third day. Then the process will start all over again. The second surprise, which most of you have guessed is that we have vegetables." She pulled a cloth off the table uncovering the vegetables. "On a sad note we made the decision to sacrifice four roosters. So today you will be served a vegetable chicken stew." She laughed. "And we won't have to eat those damn field rations." Everyone laughed and waited for their turn to pick up their delicacies. Some days are just better than others.

Brandy and Levi were talking and playing again. In fact all the Mouses seemed to be having a good time as they talked and laughed at their own table. Max smiled, "A good fight always brings friends back together."

Doris shook her head, "I mean they were fighting too; not squabbling like kids but a real fist fight." She looked at the others present and added. "I never acted like that."

Stick said dryly "I never did either." Max and Sandy started to laugh. Doris looked at Sandy waiting for an explanation.

Sandy smiled, "You don't want to know." Everyone knew the three had been friends for a very long time and had heard stories but to Doris this just confirmed that some of them might be true. Bill didn't say a word; he had heard all the transgressions of the three from his sister Carol. He just smiled.

Several uneventful months later the crew had settled into a false sense of security. It was easy to do. They weren't flying the ship and for the most part all their needs were being met. They also seemed to have some of the things they just wanted. It was easy to be lulled into this fake security; well, if you disregarded the fact that the ship could crash into something any second. Professor Sheldon told them that Einstein believed that wouldn't happen. The theory put in lay-man's terms said that as you reach the speed of light your atoms just pass through the spaces between other atoms of solid objects. It was evident to Sheldon that his audience thought he was crazier than a loon. Most of the crew reasoned that they would likely be killed in an impact and never really know about the crash. When such things were discussed the Mist and her plan for them was always discussed. Most believed that she was guiding the ship and it wasn't going to crash into anything.

The ship was operating on a strange type of schedule. Time had started to run together. In what was passing as the afternoon of a day it became apparent that they were still in other dangers that wouldn't kill them. One might say the crew had a day of awakening. Max and Sandy were trying to make a work list; it was getting more difficult with several of the women on board being with child and having some special needs. Sandy jumped to her feet. She grabbed Max and they ran to a vent opening. Max didn't hear anything until they got closer. Levi was screaming at the top of her lungs. The scene at the vent opening was chaotic. Romulus and Remus were off duty but they pushed their way through the crowd and into the vent. Levi needed help, now. Soon after, as Levi continued to scream, but not as loudly; Brandy started screaming. Mouse and H pushed their way into the vent with their sidearms ready. All got quiet and the crowd waited for any sign from the group.

Larry and Stick had arrived and were heavily armed but they couldn't get too far into the vent. John Gentry squeezed into the vent to see if there was something he needed to fix.

The laughter that started to echo down the vent wasn't what they expected. When Mouse emerged from the vent she was laughing. She couldn't even tell the tale. Levi wasn't laughing; in fact she was mad because she was embarrassed about the way she had reacted. "I flushed a wild setting hen and she had chicks. It was scary. She came right at me." She was flapping her arms and hissing. Everyone was laughing with relief that they were safe and Levi could tell a good story. Brandy told her that was still no reason for her to step on her hand and it echoed out of the vent. Brandy and the rest of the group emerged from the vent laughing. The relief was nice and the story was very funny. Brandy wanted to know if Levi was going to have a chicken charm added to mark the event. "NO' was the loud answer. As time went on it would get much funnier as it was told over and over.

Everyone being safe didn't change what had happened. Something had to be done. This crew wasn't really trained to cope with the things that were being thrown at them. The chickens had again brought a problem to light. It's no wonder that the chicken is so highly thought of by the crew. Mike and Bill walked off by themselves and after a few minutes of private talk Mike addressed the crew. "There will be a meeting of the CC in an hour." He looked around at the crew. "If you have any ideas about how this or any other potential problem could be lessened then we want to hear about it. Members of the crew; see one of the CC board members if you have something productive to add that will lessen a problem."

It wasn't long before the crew was informing the board members about some things that they thought needed changing. They had all kinds of fixes to things that might happen; for the most part they didn't apply to this case. However the solution to this could affect the other problems; so taken as a whole - it was somewhat helpful.

Doris and Professor Hays had a very long talk. He had a very good idea. It solved several problems. She hated the idea but it was a very valid solution. She would bring it up and if they wanted to hear she would bring him in to present the idea. She would also make her reservations about the idea known before he was heard.

The board met without talking about any old business. They just got to the problem at hand. Mike asked them to make note of anything other than the business at hand for the next meeting. "Ok, anybody got anything?" No one answered.

After a while Sandy started. "I got an earful about a lot of things but I don't think any of them will take us toward fixing this hole." The group agreed that most of the people thought it was just a matter of training. The board had to agree but they needed something to work with. What kind of training was needed? Max told them he was asked why phones weren't put in the hull for the Mouses to use. It was at least an idea. But how would it help? Communication was the answer.

Stick argued that he had never been in trouble close to a phone. "I had to rely on the communication devices I was carrying."

John agreed, "We need to find some kind of two way device for the Mouses to carry into the hull with them."

Mouse interrupted. "We can't have them getting stuck in there. We go through some places that we just barely fit. I sure wouldn't want to be carrying something on a belt or a pack." Everyone agreed the communication fix was the best of the ideas.

Mike smiled. "Doris you're very quiet."

She nodded. "I think I know how to do this but I sure don't like it." She had everyone's attention. Bill told her to spit it out. She nodded. "Professor Hays believes he can modify the eyes to be a communication device."

Sandy asked, "So what's wrong with the idea?"

Doris took her time answering but did. "The communication would be routed through the computer. As a result we would be able to access information at all times." She stood and started to pace. "I'm afraid that we would become dependent on the computer and stop thinking for ourselves."

Mike smiled, "I think that could happen too."

Warren spoke, "Could someone put something into the computer that would maybe brainwash us?"

Bill agreed "We would have to find out how to stop a brainwashing program."

Several of the board members looked at him. I guess he felt he had to say something else. He assured them that he was very concerned about brainwashing, "the possibility will be fixed or... let's just fix the possibility."

Mike nodded, "I agree, the whole idea is scary."

Sandy noticed that he was looking at Max as he spoke. She looked up at Bill and he was looking at Max as well. He was very serious.

It seemed the cure had as many problems as the disease. The board voted to – check that; this was not a vote, the board made suggestions and Mike decided what we were going to do. We would hear Professor Hays' pitch tomorrow at 1300. He told us to think about the problems and to ask questions. "Because right now I don't see a better idea and we need to do something."

Max told Sandy as they walked toward home that the, "Eye deal is going to be something that is going to be voluntary. It just won't fly any other way."

Sandy nodded. She agreed. "We'll hear the Professor out; but right now I'm just not sure what I'll do if I'm given the choice."

Mouse and Carol were walking in front of them and stopped. As they caught up Mouse asked. "Is this brainwashing thing real?"

Max just nodded, "Scary real; I've seen it." He paused, "Hell, I've done it." Phil came running up. "Max, Dad and the Admiral want to talk to you."

Max nodded, "Thanks, Phil."

Phil was off in a run again "I got duty." Max excused himself to go to the meeting.

Mouse said after he left, "I didn't think it could really be done." Sandy, Carol and Mouse continued toward their office. Carol added, "I have a very high clearance and I have never heard anything about a working program."

Sandy smiled. "You know Max has had some training on a lot of things that are not in the book."

Carol nodded, "Mason told me about the same thing; but he wouldn't say just what."

Mouse let out a breath. "I bet Bill and Mike both know something – and Doris seemed very concerned about the possibility." Sandy noted that Doris was a doctor and some of her research was in controlling mental impulses. So the mentally ill could be helped. They all agreed that Bill and Mike were high enough in rank to be part of the secret. Doris' reluctance was just more proof. The three really hated to admit that in this case two and two were adding up to five. Brainwashing is possible.

The next day at 1300 all were assembled in the conference room and Professor Hays had the floor. He seemed a little nervous. He made his spiel. It amounted to little more than what they already knew. He did not address the brainwashing issue. In fact when Mike asked him about the possibility he didn't believe that such a thing was possible. The board members, all of them, were not going to let the "improvements" on the eye go without some kind of security.

Hays tried to explain but it went over everyone's head. He had to be cautioned to explain in terms that the entire board could understand. He tried to explain about the eye having four unused channels and about piggy backing a signal. What he said was about a third technical jargon, a third understandable and the rest just gobbley-gook. When he was finished Mike told him the board would have to talk about his proposals. He left a paper packet for each member of the board. Mike told him "Thanks and we will get back to you as soon as we can."

Mike and the rest of the board sat quietly for a while before he spoke. "We need a computer expert, other than Professor Hays."

Bill nodded and said. "I noticed Stick asking some very good questions. I didn't understand most of the answers so, what do you think about this deal?"

Stick was almost embarrassed. "I didn't give away any secrets and it was hard to ask questions given the restrictions but, I got all that info from Larry. He's really good with computers. In fact he... well he has computer security conviction on his youth record from when he broke into some government office computers."

The board didn't seem upset. Max laughed, "Well get his ass down here. Maybe he can explain this." Sandy laughed; Bill and Mike looked at each other. Doris added, "I think that's a good idea." Everyone seemed to agree. Mike called a brief recess and Stick went to find Larry.

At 1500 Larry was very nervous and waiting, hoping to be able to answer the questions. Stick had only told him generalities and he had to be made aware of just why he was needed. He thought for a minute and then started. Stick was right he knew how computers worked and he hadn't been trained in them so he spoke English. Everyone understood what he said and what he thought the solutions were. The mud was getting thinner; some of the mud was getting easier to see through.

He couldn't speak for the eye modifications but computers could be modified to separate anything. He talked about just setting up the eye for communications through a separate circuit in the computer and it should be easy. He added that it should be easy to separate the training mode and keep only what we wanted. He started to say something about a memory hold in the eye itself but... Mike stopped him. "The board has to talk some more about this new development but I would like for you to attend the meeting at 1300 tomorrow." Larry agreed and left.

Mike was shaking his head, "We need Larry in charge of this eye thing." Doris agreed, "I don't mind playing second fiddle to him. He knows a lot more about this than I do." The discussion took the crew to a new way of doing things. Larry needed to be in charge. A suggestion was made that he be promoted for the project. It was more of a too-bad-we-can't. The meeting broke up a few minutes later.

Mike told Warren and Carol to stick around. "We need to talk about something."

Carol shook her head and said to Max. "I'm not looking forward to this. I'm not sure I agree with what I think is coming."

Max smiled, "I have heard it a hundred times —what's best for the ship."

She smiled, "Yeah that's my problem; my opinion and what's best for the ship don't agree."

Stick, Max, Sandy and Mouse walked back toward their area together. Stick asked Max, "Do you know what they are talking about?"

Max shook his head, "The eye thing, yeah maybe about half the time." The statement got a slight laugh all the way around because they were in the same boat on the eye.

Stick clarified, "No, I mean with Larry."

Max nodded and answered. "I think they may be thinking about doing something that has been done since the run away." Sandy added that she did too. Mouse told them that she was where she was because she was good at her job.

Max agreed and Stick smiled, "Do you think they are going to put Larry in charge of this thing?"

Max nodded and Sandy smiled. Mouse nodded, "That's what it looks like to me too."

Max added, "If we can make brevet promotions to a job why can't we make brevet promotions to a project?"

Stick laughed. "He's not going to like this new development."

Luanne came down the hall and smiled at the group as she stopped. "I have those nasty little Mouses in the brig."

Max laughed, "What now?" She was a little mad, "They were fighting again. I had to cuff Brandy. That girl is a hand full."

Mouse laughed, "Tell me about it."

Max nodded. "Let's go talk to them."

The story was simple Levi had told Brandy she would take her duty and she didn't. Remus had told Sam he would take his duty. Levi and Remus were busy with a card game and lost track of time "We forgot." Max, in-an-aside, told everyone to go along with him. He was a lot madder at them than he appeared. He yelled at the Recruits and told Brandy and Sam they were going to be tried for dereliction of duty. He looked at Remus and told him he was ashamed of him. "All of you Mouses are going to have a little time to think about this – three days in the brig for fighting."

Brandy was right in his face. "We deserve a trial before you can do that." Mouse told her to "Back off, Recruit." Brandy looked at her mom; she knew Mom was madder than Lieutenant Holt.

Max nodded, "Ok, if that's the way you want it. I'll see the Captain about a Court Martial." He smiled "Meanwhile you can stay right where you are – in the brig. You will be released for duty and then return." The Mouses were the quietest they had been for days. He said very harshly. "Is that understood?" He got a Yes Sir from all but Brandy. He asked her again. "Is that understood Recruit Holt?" It took a few seconds before she replied and she was steaming mad; "Yes sir."

Phil and Billy had duty and they were sent to that duty. Mouse commented when the group was alone away from the Mouses that she was just too mad to deal with this right now. Mouse told Luanne that she would have the duty schedule sent down so she would know who had duty.

Luanne told Stick she was going to need a couple of more people. He nodded. "I guess we can activate a couple of augments."

She laughed. "There isn't any augments on the damn list. We're going to have to train some."

Stick smiled, "We should train the entire crew."

Max smiled, "That is a very good idea."

They were right about a brevet promotion to manage a project. Larry was made a Lieutenant commander in charge of the eye upgrade project. He didn't like the idea but it didn't take but two days to know he was going to do a good job. Professor Hays was yelling at Doris and she told him Larry was in charge of the project and he would talk to him. Professor Hays was mad. Larry was a problem – he knew as much as the professor did about the computer.

The board saw a need to take the brevet project promotions a step or two further. They believed this was not a single case and it would be needed again. It was to this end that they developed a dual rank system. The left side of your collar was your rank. The right was your operating rank as to a certain project.

The Mouses had been in the brig for three days and only released for duty. Max went down to see them. They were all sitting very quietly. He told them that he had come to see who they wanted to represent them at the court martial. Brandy spoke first, "Can I just plead guilty of being stupid and get this over?"

Max shook his head "It's too late for that."

Remus nodded, "I told you."

Max smiled. "You guys really messed up." The group kind of as a whole agreed. Their parents had made that clear over the last few days when they came to visit. Max smiled, "I think your best choice to represent you is Louise Hall." Phil was quick to answer "Mom, but she'll know I'm in jail."

The Mouses laughed, Sam told him he believed she already knew. "She's come to visit you twice."

He nodded, "Yeah, I guess she does. But it's still weird."

Max smiled, "Would you like me to ask?" The general consensus was yes – even Phil agreed.

The court marshal wasn't that big a deal. Brandy and Sam defended themselves with "We had made arrangements with other Mouses to take the duty but we should have checked to make sure they took the duty." The story was confirmed. The truth was told and now some sort of justice had to be administered.

Mouse had already declared that every change on the duty schedule would be approved by herself or H. It would be noted on the duty schedule and initialed by all parties.

Louise did a very good job of defending their actions although she never said they didn't do the things of which they were accused. She made the point that there just wasn't much for them to do as children. It wasn't said but it was understood that the adults had just been lying around making babies and leaving the children to find themselves something to do.

The fighting was excused with 'time served.' Sam and Brandy were found guilty without comments of the court. They each received the black frame on their record and added to their charms. Sam thought it was a bad thing, Brandy remembered the black frame on her mother's arm and Max's. She smiled, knowing she was now a criminal, just like her mother. The only thing she regretted was that her time in grade was taken along with Sam's. Neither she nor he would make private second until three months after the rest of the Mouses. By far the worst of the 'justice' fell to Levi and Remus. They had broken their word and it wouldn't be forgotten by their peers. The court couldn't do anything to them but they knew just what everyone thought of them.

Max was glad the whole thing was over but now he had to find something for everyone to do. He started the augment training including the Mouses. Bill wondered if it was a good idea to teach someone to fight who liked to fight as much as the Mouses did. Man started to teach music. Brandy was very interested, so was Mouse. Sandy started an exercise program and all members of the crew were required to attend one of the exercise programs every other day.

Things were settling in to a new norm. The Mouses and several of the others were looking forward to blade weapon training in two weeks. Brandy could talk of nothing else; the only thing that could be better was small arms training in six months. Mouse really questioned the sanity of giving Brandy a firearm.

The eye project continued, Larry was doing a very good job and expected the first prototypes to be ready in about a month.

Sandy was with child as was Mouse. It was scary.

Max was surprised but hopeful when Professor Morris asked him to come by the lab. They walked to a secluded part of the lab and the professor handed him a lump of meat. "I don't know if it is safe to eat; but it is growing." Max was pleased. "I'll have Doris check it for safety." Professor Morris wasn't letting it out of his sight.

Doris was doing a crossword when they went into the office. She spoke to them and they put the container with the lump of 'pork' flesh. "We want to know if this is safe to eat."

She opened the container. "This is pork?"

The professor sort of smiled "Maybe."

She tested the meat as they waited and found nothing unsafe. "How much of this do you have?"

The professor told her he had several lumpers that weighed four or five pounds, and a few bumpers that weighed two or three pounds. The beef doesn't grow as fast.

She shook her head in disbelief "Where did you get them?" Professor Morris was reluctant to tell her but he did. "I cloned them from a slice of bacon and some ground beef. I called the pork, lumpers and the beef, bumpers."

She laughed. "I'll be damned." She wanted to do more tests now that she knew where and how the meat was grown. It was a week later when Doris told the professor that she thought the lumpers and the bumpers were safe to eat. He forwarded the information on to Max. They began to try to make bacon out of the lumpers. There would be a learning curve. Doris wanted enough meat to make a meatloaf for the monthly party. The Professor was happy to give her all she wanted; it was starting to get out of control.

Mouse found a great deal of comfort in her guitar. She and Brandy were having a very good time learning to play. Max helped then with the notes and the rhythm. The new Mouse and Brandy were getting acquainted. They were getting better with the guitars every day. Mouse was getting bigger every day. It wouldn't be long before she wouldn't have a lap to hold the guitar. The karaoke machine was used every day, some days all day. The books and stories in Max's head were being transcribed to paper. The simpler games like checkers and a deck of cards were being produced; the board games would be a while longer. Word games were very big with the adults and the kids. Singing groups and bands were popping up every day; some of them were very good. There always seemed to be something to do.

The new specs for the eyes were presented to the board on schedule. Larry had done a great job. The eyes were capable of communicating with each other with little chance of brainwashing. He had built a personal storage memory unit into the eye that only the user could access. The eyes could also access the computer through a filter program that Larry said would catch repetitive uncalled for information. Repetitive information is the way brainwashing works. The user may not be aware of the information. They just began to accept it as fact, which caused them to react in a way the brainwasher wanted. He had the thirty extra eyes ready. They could replace the first ones and the ones that were removed could then be updated. In six weeks they would be ready to replace the remaining eyes.

That left a question; "Who would get the first thirty?"

Mouse asked that the Mouses be given first opportunity to volunteer. "They need to be able to communicate easily because of their work." The request was reasonable but the board would not allow all the Mouses to get the new eye at one time. They still believed that brainwashing could be a problem and didn't want to put all their eggs in one basket - so to speak.

Mouse would get three eyes. She asked H to volunteer for one and offered the other two to volunteers of the seven Mouses. Of course all the Mouses want the new eye. Mouse knew they did but when she asked for volunteers she only got three, Sam, Brandy and Levi. Remus was quick to pull Levi's arm down. "We owe them and we talked about this." It was clear to Mouse that Levi really wanted to volunteer but she didn't. Sam and Brandy got the eyes.

The eyes were replaced and over the next month the board became satisfied that the chance of brainwashing was a chance they had to take. Larry had done a great job and was very happy to go back to his old job and rank. Now that everyone equipped with one of the fake eyes was going to get one of the new eyes; the full function was starting to be known. The computer had linked to them. They acted as communication and information centers. Soon everyone had one of the fake eyes and could be reached at anytime. Files were set up in the computer so classes could be taught as the wearer slept. They had their own private storage area in the eye. It was working very well.

The new lumpers and bumpers had added several things to the menu. The chili was the best thing that had happened for Brandy in a while and the first batch was served on her fifth birthday. She ate too much.

Some part of the crops was ready every week. The harvest was ongoing. The crop harvest had nothing on the harvest to come. It started late one night. Max was lying next to Sandy. He had his hand on her immense belly; he didn't know how she got around the ship with this baby getting so big. The little monster had to come out sooner or later. Max was starting to doze when he heard the baby crying. He woke very quickly. Sandy turned and was half awake. Max asked. "Where is the baby?"

She smiled, "Right where he was when I went to sleep. The little monster will not leave." The crying baby was yelling at the top of its young lungs. Max smiled and asked if she heard the crying, she smiled and told him she did.

They went to look for the baby. Max was in a hurry but Sandy kept waddling slowly along. When they looked into Doris' hospital she yelled. "Please, not you too." She had two babies delivered and five mothers-to-be doing their best to become mothers tonight. Over the next three months all 32 women who were expecting gave birth to healthy babies; 15 boys and 17 girls. When it was Sandy's turn, she did her best to be brave; but she screamed a lot. Max seemed to feel every pain. He wondered why anyone would deliberately do this.

When their son was born, Max and Sandy both understood what it was all about. He was so small. Sandy didn't quite agree, but he was small. Max took his son, their son and walked around the ship showing him to everyone who would look. Bill had his and Mouses daughter; she was born the day before and it was a good thing it was a girl because they got the babies mixed up. Mouse had named her and Bill's daughter Billie Ruth Holt. Sandy insisted on naming theirs after Max. Max had to take Bart back to Sandy after a while; he couldn't figure out a way to feed him. If he hadn't had to give him back he wouldn't have. Sandy and Max had several discussions about a name; Max really didn't want him to be a 'junior.' But Sandy did and she would most likely get her way. Max gave the baby back to Sandy. Sandy said. "Well, is he Bartholomew Allen Dent Junior?" Max nodded "Yeah, Bart. But let's make it the 'II' not junior." Sandy smiled and agreed.

For the next two and a half years the ship sped along producing three g's of acceleration gravity. The crew was more or less a family; and lived in a village environment. Sandy had given birth to another child, a girl, who they named, Nicola (Nikki/Sissy) Dawn Dent. She was six months along with a third. But times were about to change. They were approaching the tipping point; gravity was going to shift sometime soon.

The population of the ship had increased to 153; just under half were less than three years old. The Moures were three years older; Brandy was the youngest at seven, Romulus at ten was the oldest; Remus was nine.

CHAPTER TWENTY-ONE, THE TIPPING POINT

The time of the tipping came and went without causing any major inconvenience; almost. They had prepared well for everything they could think of from storing extra food to a baby being born in the couple of days of weightlessness. The weightlessness was great fun although a little sickening. The children enjoyed the change like playing in the first snow of winter. The problems that they had not considered came to light as the gravity in the ship was restored. The people were used to living in a three g world and they wanted the gravity turned up. They found the one g world to be strange; and the babies could jump out of their cribs. The other was much more of a problem – the water supply was contaminated.

Most of the contamination would be filtered out by the crops. They would be safe to eat. The scope and type of contamination combined with the failing filters could cause major problems for people. It was easy to make the water drinkable by adding a small amount of easily produced grain alcohol; that was and wasn't the problem. Several of the crew considered alcohol a very bad thing. The fact that it would have to be given to the children as well made for some loud and stupid arguments that were just out of place. They had no choice; except to die. Mike got tired of the crap and made the great decision. "Water will be turned off at all locations and will only be available at the water bar. If you want alcohol added then ask - if not, then die. This meeting is over and you idiots can do as you wish." A number of the people wanted to argue about the alcohol. But they knew it was the only option and accepted the judgment.

There is always a hold out and this time it was a scientist named David Goodwin, and his wife, Val. David was the man who tried the hardest to convince the rest of the crew not to drink the alcohol laced water. They had a two year old son and Val was expecting. Doris came to Max and told him that this was the dumbest thing she had ever been involved in and she never thought she would say this but, "We need to take their child; force Val to drink the alcohol laced water until she gives birth and then to hell with the parents."

Max agreed. Sandy was consulted and then the board. The loss of the children was something they were not going to chance. Max, Sandy, Stick, Larry, Mike and Bill all went to see David and Val. David still wanted to argue; they didn't. He was told just how it was going to be. "You don't have to drink the water. But, your son will and your wife will until she gives birth. Then she can quit if she chooses." He was told that he would die if he didn't drink the alcohol laced water but it was his choice.

Max added. "I'm sorry David but we can't have this zealot like behavior on the ship."

Doris told him that it was his life. "But you will not be allowed to take others with you. That is especially true if they are not old enough to understand."

The boy was having a screaming fit. He wouldn't let anyone touch him. That is until Larry picked him up. The boy calmed down and laid his head on Larry's shoulder. David wouldn't say a word. But at the risk of losing her children Val did. She told them that David was an alcoholic. He was scared to think of the way he used to be, and never wanted to go back. The group had little choice but to empathize. David was convinced, after a long talk and urgings from Val, to give it a try. It was a big deal, no one wants to die but there are worse things one can do. David's secret was out in the open now and the crew would watch him and help him, without passing judgment, everyone hoped for the best. The boy was returned to his mother and the Goodwins went with Doris to be checked out.

It was a few weeks later that Max saw Stick and Larry talking to Mary and Joan; two lady scientists who embraced the same gay life style as Stick and Larry. It was a strange sight.

Max and Doris worked on a solution to the water problem. A course of action was decided and they began the work hoping for the best but not expecting too much. The work was slow and any mistake could put them in worse shape.

Max had other problems as well; the alcohol laced water was being abused. It was hard to say who thought of it but a sugarless flavoring was being added to the water. The water had become a drink with the red or green powder added. It was very good with a lot of ice. However, more than the required amount of alcohol was being added to the drinks. The Mouses were drinking a lot of water or Jewels as they called them; a lot more than they needed. Sandy was trying to work out a way of rationing the water claming they were short on drinking water and everyone should try to help. She developed a system of chits where people got a number of chits each day and they should try to limit their water consumption to that amount. She explained that the alcohol combined with the filters could only do so much and drinking water was short. Drinking water was the only problem since other water was pure enough for how it was being used. The crops were not affected. The lie seemed to be working and the alcohol abuse was reduced.

Max was in his office going over the repairs of the water system; it was not going well. Sandy came by and asked him to guess what her surprise was. He laughed and guessed that she was pregnant again. She laughed and told him she would like to get rid of the one she was carrying before they started another. Max laughed. She sat down on the corner of the desk and told Max that she had a request for larger quarters a few minutes ago and was thinking of putting them in the guest quarters. Max asked her if that wasn't a little large for a new couple. Do they have children? She smiled "No, but there are four of them."

Max couldn't place a group that had four in it. "Alright, what's going on?"

She laughed, "Stick requested the quarters for himself, Larry...." She started to smile "Mary and Joan." She laughed. "It a strange group but I think they want children, and they are not going to get any the way they're going."

Max shook his head. "How is Bill going to take care of this?" They laughed and both were just happy that they were not the ones having to deal with the possible social problem. Sandy approved the request with Max's go ahead but it had to go to the board.

The monthly gathering was in a few days and whatever was going to happen was going to happen then. Bill took the stage and asked if anyone had a declaration. He knew some did. Declarations were the way things were brought to the 'village.' I guess village is the best description. During the monthly meetings people just came up and declared things, like marriages, the intent to have a child or just about anything that would affect the village.

The group came forward and declared that they were forming the House of the Four Winds. They stated the members and the purpose, "to function as a family and raise children; while retaining our own life choices." No one knew what would happen next. The approval of the crew was not required but it would make it easier. Max started the applause of approval and the vast majority of the crew followed. You could see the relief and happiness as the House of the Four Winds was accepted. The smiles replaced the anxiousness on their faces. It was a very happy celebration. Alcohol rations were changed for the day.

Sandy gave birth to another baby girl; they called her Starlene. They searched for a middle name but nothing quite fit. They settled on Starlene Marie Dent. Sandy said she was going to have six babies and, well, some people are just too stubborn for their own good. She was pregnant again in six months.

Not to try to explain but the House of the Four Winds was blessed with two children over the next eleven months; and the ladies were pregnant again in less than four months. The two boys were called Albert and Lawrence. As time went by it did seem strange that Albert looked a lot like Larry and Lawrence looked a lot like Stick. Sandy even asked Max "What do you think they do, just go to bed and all of them have at whoever?" Max laughed but he wasn't interested in guessing. That's about all I care to say, except; the children were loved by all members of the House of the Four Winds.

When you are on a runaway space craft small things make the news. The occasion of the birth that took the total population to two-hundred and fifty was one such occasion. She was a beauty from the House of the Winds. She was named Sun Nebula; a lot of the children were being named like that. Sandy had given birth to a set of boy-girl twins and she was pleased that the child she was carrying would be her last. What she was not happy about was that Bart would be four in two weeks and he was already asking about joining the Mouses. His friends were allowed to join when they turned four and he wanted to join too. Sandy knew she didn't really have a choice. She didn't like the idea of her baby joining the crew.

Mouse had the same problem a few weeks before. Billie would turn four the day before Bart. The enlistment wouldn't take place until the next gathering; two weeks away. It was one of those things that just had to be, a rite of passage from child to a member of the crew. The bigger problem they had not considered - the eye. The computer eye that every member of the crew had; it helped them with their duties. It had become a necessary part of being in the crew.

The problem had already started when the oldest of the ships younger generation had joined the Mouses. They couldn't communicate with the other Mouses. The solution was to mount the eye as it was intended on a mount worn on the head. The ones who had the eye attached in this way couldn't get all the benefits of the technology. It was a growing point of anguish for the Mouses. Another problem was the lack of eyes. New ones were being designed but not too quickly.

The younger Mouses themselves solved the problem with a blood pact. Bart and Billie had just entered the Mouse brigade and were reportedly the ones who hatched the plan. Donny Hall may have encouraged them. It was late in the sleeping time when Levi woke Doris. "You better get ready Mom; we can't find the new Mouses."

Doris asked about half asleep. "Do you think something is wrong?"

Levi nodded, "We tried to talk them out of it but you know how stubborn a Mouse can be." Doris looked at her questioning. Levi said softly "They've made a blood pact; all of the younger ones are going to punch out one of their eyes so they can have the implant."

Doris was up and making calls on her eye. The crew and especially the parents were quick to start a search for the younger Mouses. They didn't find the Mouses until they started down the hall toward the hospital. They each had blood running down the side of their face and a smile that went from ear to ear. Bill nodded, "Fix them and we need to talk about the eye being a part of the induction to The Mouse Brigade. The punched out eye had to have hurt but the joy the younger Mouses were feeling made them laugh and talk, disregarding the pain. Doris didn't have enough eyes to go around, she was one short. Brandy volunteered one of hers for Billie. "I can't have my stupid sister going around with an eye patch." Billie hugged her. She told her "stop doing that in public. I'll just get one of eyes that couldn't be upgraded until a new version has been made."

Doris told Bill that she might need Larry back to run a project to build new eyes because they didn't have any of the old ones left.

"Not a single back up." Brandy asked sort of franticly. "Please tell me I'm not going to have to wear an eye patch."

Doris laughed, "No Brandy, I have one that can't be upgraded to replace yours for a while."

It was another six months before the new eyes were ready. Three new Mouses waited not so patiently for their turn to have an eye implanted after they were inducted into the Mouses. It was now a rite of passage. Doris hated the idea but 'For the good of the ship' with the parent's permission and the insistence of the new Mouse.

The operations went well.

CHAPTER TWENTY-TWO, SUB-LIGHT

The world passed slowly in the small village mode until the day the ship dropped from light speed. The instruments were useful for the first time in over seven years. The command crew took a while to remember how to use them. The Mouses, who numbered one hundred and fifty and represented almost half the population of the ship, were in the hole as fast as they could scramble in; the hull was a major concern. The seven older Mouses were in command and shouting orders to their respective group of Mouses.

The parents loved their children, this new generation of beings that they had created. They worried. Max and Sandy had five of their children involved in the operation. Sandy told Romulus and Remus to watch out for their brother and sisters. Bill and Mouse had four, counting Brandy. Willy, Bill and Mouse's third, had only been a Mouse for four weeks. Brandy smiled as she took her sister's hand, "I'll watch out for her." She then looked down at Willy, "Now, get in that hole." She smiled at her sister "MOUSE." Willy smiled and ran for the hole. Her sister Billie was waiting at the entrance of the hole, "This way recruit." Willy smiled, "Yes Sir."

Every parent worried until the Mouses began to emerge from the hull. They had cuts, bruises, and a few burns but they were alright. Willy had found the only breech and it had been patched easily but her ego was bigger than she was. She was looking forward to being awarded that letter of Discovery and maybe a letter of Hero.

It took two weeks for the scientists to get an idea where they were and it was not good. They placed the ship based on the stars and their position relative to the ship. They had no idea where but somewhere two-hundred and fifty light years deep into unknown space, given the earth as the center of a clock; somewhere toward the one o'clock position. They were headed for a large star, it was pulling them in and they had no brakes. By their calculations Sandy's child would be born and two months old when they would all burn to death.

There was still nothing that could be done. The people accepted their fate and went along with life trying not to think too much about what was in store for them. Surely the Mist had a plan. Sandy was a little sad as she gave birth to what she had hoped was her last child. She told Max as she held the baby boy. "I'm going to name him Maxwell II, I like it. It is a shame that he will not grow to be a Mouse."

Max took the boy around to see everyone just like he had the other five; a proud father. Bill smiled as he tickled Maxwell's nose. "I have news Max. We are not going to hit that star."

Max asked. "Why not, what's happened?"

Bill told him that they were going to hit a large asteroid in about two weeks; "I haven't told many people. They know they are going to die and I think this just changes the timetable."

Four days later they started the ten day countdown. Those ten days were very strange.

Day one: They continued as normal. They had game night; and a chili supper. Brandy ate and drank too much and would be asleep and useless for the next few hours. They were very careful not to speak of the impending doom; but everyone now knew. There were jokes and music and dancing. Several of the Mouses added awards. Willy got her letter of Hero and Discovery.

She insisted on Brandy presenting them. The older Mouses were presented with long overdue Sergeant's stripes.

Day two: It was officially announced shipwide that they were not going to hit the star; a ship was on an intercept course. "It will be here in eight days."

Max asked Bill why he had told them it was a ship. Bill laughed "Because it is, Max. It's damn big, but it is a ship." Sandy and most of the crew were sure that the Mist was going to save them.

Day three thru seven; someone watched the ship every minute. It was headed straight toward a point in space that the Einstein would be in at the same time.

Day eight: the Captain announced that the ship was not responding to calls and there wasn't any reason to hope that the ship had any better control than the Einstein. "We believe it is a runaway; a Flying Dutchman just like us. In any case we're going to hit that ship."

Day nine: The mood of the crew was grim. It was announced that the Einstein was going to hit and roll down the side of the larger ship. "The other ship will reach a point in space first and the Einstein a few minutes later. The speed of the Einstein and angle of impact will make the hit very hard. If we hit just right and it is as big as we think and we survive the hit there is a good chance that we will roll down the side of the larger ship. This will change our course. We will miss the star; we will be a very safe distance from that star." Everyone was feeling very good. It was the first chance they had to survive in months, or years. Some believed the Einstein would go into a sustained orbit around the star. It was something the Mist might do.

Day ten: three hours from impact, the crew moved everyone and everything they thought they might need to an inner room and hoped for the best. The crew was counted. The walls were padded; the Mouses were 'in.' The crew had what might be the last meal of their life.

A half hour before impact everything that could be put into the hall was removed from the room. There was no need to have things flying around in the room. The doors were secured and the crew secured themselves as well as they could. They sang songs until the Einstein slammed into the larger ship. It was a very hard hit. The Einstein rolled down the side of the ship slamming into things. Billie yelled "That hull is going to be hard to fix." For some reason it was very funny. They had survived the impact. The screeches of the ship on ship contact were the sound of buckling medal. The gravity was gone and the belts and ropes that they had tied themselves down with were all that held them in place. The door buckled and everyone knew it was over. The ship slammed hard into something and they could feel that it had changed course as the gravity returned. They were traveling with the other ship; maybe they had been rescued.

There was no lights and no sound; none. Bart asked. "Are we dead?" Sandy laughed. "I don't think so; dead isn't like this." The roar went out from the darkness. Their eyes began to adjust to the light from the partially opened door. They were glad to be alive.

Max smiled. "I don't believe this shit."

He heard Stick yell. "I don't either; but I'll take it." He woke his two day old son he was holding and smiled.

The next they heard was The Mist. She was laughing. "I just want you all to know that you all died. But since I was going to bring you all back I let you enjoy the ride." Max couldn't help but laugh. She told them that they had passed all of her tests and now it was time to start "your great adventure."

Bill laughed. "What have we been having the last seven years?" She told them to be careful and enjoy the new ship. "The next test is to see if you can learn to fly your new ship."

The older new sergeant Mouses took the lead through the small opening in the door and brought back jacks so the door could be opened enough for the rest to get out. There were several large openings in the hull. Whatever atmosphere was outside of the Einstein was safe. They left the Einstein for the first time in seven years. They exited into a large hanger. Bart looked at the Einstein and said. "So that's what it looks like from the outside." Everyone laughed who heard him.

There was a lot of work to be done before they could explore the ship. They had to make sure they had a place to go in case this went bad. They closed the outside door to the hanger. It was a hand crank and it took a while. Whatever fortifications could be made they made them; as they salvaged the contents of the Einstein. After a week they decided to start investigating the new ship. No one had come to look for them so they had to begin to explore.

CHAPTER TWENTY-THREE,
THE SHIP

The technology and design of the new ship, their new home, was beyond words for a poet engineer. The Einstein was one of the larger Earth ships of it's time and yet it was dwarfed by the unbelievable size of the hangar bay in which it had come to rest. Dozens of ships the size of the Einstein could be housed in this one compartment.

The crew had watched this ship for as long as it was safe before taking shelter. They waited until there was no doubt it was on a collision course with the Einstein. The ship covered the entire viewing area. There wasn't even a frame of stars. It was like they were approaching a planet. It was much, much, much larger than the Einstein. The crew knew that this square room with slick metal walls where they had come to rest was just one compartment of the massive ship. This was but one tiny room on something that must be as large as a planet or at least a moon.

How many more rooms are there? What are these walls made of? The scientists provided a range of options and scientific gobbledygook as to what type of metal the walls were, but they really had no idea. The only thing they could be sure of was there was a human sized door in the center of the back wall. The door in itself gives some testimony to the size of the previous owners. The fact that a security force had not come bursting through told them that the ship was vastly undermanned or not manned at all.

That being said it didn't change a thing. The tension in the air could almost be cut with a knife. Everyone believed that they were supposed to take control of the ship. After all The Mist told them the next test was to learn to fly. That suggested that the ship was not manned or to be taken. This was a learning opportunity.

Several things troubled the CC board. Given the facts as they are at this moment; this ship may not have any life other than themselves on board. What happened to the life that had to have been aboard at one time? Was it a disease, a plague that they could catch that killed off the other crew? Were they slaughtered by unknown beast or beasts? Are they still here; they, the beasts and or the others? What other tests does The Mist have for them?

Bill couldn't help but think of the eighteen that The Mist had kept before. Is she going to keep more of them as they died? Would she send them back? Did it matter that they had already died – is it two or three times now. Each time they came back was just gravy. They should be dead. They were dead. They may be dead. This could be the after life. The most vexing question was now that The Mist had the children does she need the adults?

He paused as his thought took him to the ninety-seven people the Einstein had on board when the runaway started. He smiled as he thought about the seven Mouses and the other seventy-eight people on board. There were thirty-nine females and thirty-nine males. They had all coupled and married. Some of the couples were very strange.

H, the older shy Mouse top Sergeant, had found love with Sheldon. He's a very out going professor and is seven feet two inches tall. They are an odd looking couple as they walk down the hall. He smiled as he thought of H standing tall at four foot eleven looking even shorter as they walk side by side. Their triplet girls are now three years old running around their legs playing. It's enough to make anyone smile.

Carol fought so hard not to fall in love with the cook, Harold, from the brig. He smiled as he remembered her yelling at Harold as she gave birth just a month ago to the fourth of their children. He also remembered her telling everyone after the first child that she was never going to have another.

He couldn't help but smile as four Mouses ran by him. They had started with seven Mouses and now, he believed there are one-hundred and fifty-three with seventy-four more waiting until they turned four to join the Mouse brigade. That led him to the thought of Doris and how she told him she felt like Frankenstein when she removed an eye from the new Mouses. But even she agreed it was better than having them put their own eye out so they could get a computerized one.

Stick that had taken over security and ran it like it had to be perfect all the time; most of the time he succeeded.

Larry was so much help in so many things where the computer was concerned.

Mike and Warren ran the ship as well as Stick did security. They too tried for perfection all the time.

Max and Sandy, he doubted the community would be in the excellent shape it was in now if it were not for them.

He guessed that everyone else was reminiscing somewhere along the same lines. He needed to think about this a while. The kids had to be considered this time. The kids, the Mouses seemed more appropriate. They are not really children and haven't been for a long time. They are seasoned members of the crew. Brandy is eleven. Romulus is almost fourteen. They are not children and Romulus and Remus are too big to be Mouses. The Mouses are to a man a well seasoned crew with scars from various wounds and medals and charms for selfless acts to prove it. They are Charmed as crew because they are crew. Over the next months more of the children will demand admittance into the Mouses. His daughter B'Linda was so happy that she is alive and would soon get to be a Mouse, a member of the Crew. No doubt her mother, as well as he, was happy she would see her fourth birthday. Her mother,

Mouse, commander of the Mouses had such problems ordering the children into the dangerous hull. B'Linda will be the fourth of their children to serve under her. The thought of the crew was a chilling thought, the Mouses all of four years old when they join the brigade, what of them, were they now destined to become more – warriors, maybe.

His chain of thought changed, the bay is large enough for the crew. They could live here for a long time. Maybe until after the children have children. We have a lot of room to farm and grow families. There is even room for some kind of permanent village.

The other side of the thought came harshly into his mind. What if there are others on board and they are coming to see who has just boarded their ship. Would they have a choice but to fight? What would The Mist do if they just made a home here? Is it an honorable thing in her mind? This isn't going to be easy. He needed more input. He needed to know what people thought. He asked Mike to call a meeting of the CC. It wasn't much of a meeting. He just called the members to the side and asked them to talk to the people. "Find out what they think. We'll meet in a few days."

He knew and wondered if the crew knew that there was only one way to proceed – like it or not they had to go through that door. It was two days before all the yelling and discussion stopped. There was only one choice that made any sense. They needed to know what was on the other side of that door. The meeting of the CC didn't happen. It wasn't necessary. The opinions of the crew were all the same. "Open the damn door."

It took some time to get the door open. The electronic lock was the easy part, strange as it looked it wasn't very difficult to pick. Mouse had it open in less than a minute. However, when the lock clicked open the door didn't move.

The sliding door had to be pried open. There was pressure on the other side and it was dangerous to continue the work of opening the door. However, no one wanted to stop. This was a necessary evil and had to be done. It was the only way to proceed; they needed to know what was on the other side of that door. It was more than just security it was the nagging thorn of curiosity in each and every one of their brains.

The door was slow moving; just fractions of a centimeter with each prying effort. It took a lot of effort and several hours before the door came out of the locking frame. Max noticed that everyone was shocked by the sudden snap. He wondered if they were as surprised as he by the nothing that happened after that. There was no escape of air or burst of pressure throwing them to the back wall. It was a non event, a very scary and welcome, non-event.

It was almost twenty hours later that the door slipped again under the continued prying and opened a crack wide enough to get a flat hand through. No one volunteered, Sandy was there and she pushed her hand into the crack and hit a solid invisible wall with the tips of her fingers. The wall started where the door stopped. The wall was the pressure on the door. The invisible wall on the other side didn't allow the hand to pass the back edge of the door. It was solid. Whatever the wall was made of it was pressed in on the door after it was closed.

They looked into the area on the other side. It was semi-clear like a thick glass and began to become more opaque somewhere out there. They could see into the hall but the increasing distance caused the view to be more and more distorted. The turn in the hall made it impossible to see any farther. They needed the door open further. One of the scientists said it was like someone had filled the hall with a clear plastic.

In about an hour a hydraulic jack opened the door about half way; but it wouldn't move any further. The door was warped out of it's glide path by the pressure on the other side. It was like the plastic was slowly easing into the room. You couldn't see it move but the pressure on the edge of the door seemed to be increasing.

The scientists were given a crack at the invisible wall. Max suggested that they start working on a way to close the door just in case. The suggestion was quickly turned into an order by Mike with full agreement of the board. The Mouses and maintenance began to try to weld things to the door to push it back closed. They were not having a lot of luck and decided to try to bolt something to the door. Both groups were very good at their work.

The older Mouses believed they could weld air to steel and not have a leak. Some of them swore they had while trying to keep the hull together on the Einstein during the last part of the trek before the crash. The welds didn't work. Nothing would stick to the door. They couldn't get it hot enough. The final answer was a fifth rate chance and it just didn't seem likely it would work. But the door was cleated with a barbed piece of angle iron. The jack would be placed at a forty-five angle. This would push the door back into alignment; hold the cleat in place plus push the door toward the closed position all at the same time. It was at least an option; but not a very good one.

The scientists were like kids in a candy store. They didn't know what this new wonder was but they were going to find out. The first thing was to find out what it wasn't; in order to do that, you need a piece of it. They couldn't even get scrapings.

It didn't take long to find out it was solid. But it wasn't. It was moving very, very slowly according to the laser measuring devices. It was also harder than their hardest tools. You could pound on that wall with anything you chose and it didn't make a mark. The medical lasers didn't do anything but overheat – themselves; not the door.

It was with great hesitation that Bill decided to shoot it. He didn't think it would do any good and it was dangerous. The bullet might just bounce around or it might make a hole in the hull. It was a last chance before they had to go through the wall beside the door. Not that anybody thought that would work either. He didn't get any objections from the board. They were very frustrated.

Bill took aim and fired. He wouldn't let anyone else do it. Everything had been secured and several hull patch kits had been found. The Mouses were ready with welders and steel patches cut from the Einstein. They didn't know if they could weld them to the hull or not. Everyone was holding their breath when he shot. The shot bounced of the invisible wall and several other walls before its energy was spent. It didn't hurt anything. Max was smiling as the Mouses began to peek up from their positions of cover. Their faces told of their excitement. They were laughing and starting to chant "Do it again." They were disappointed when Bill refused.

The bullet didn't punch a hole in the outer hull. It was the best result they could have hoped for outside of affecting the wall. You couldn't see where the bullet hit the wall. They were at a loss. They also now believed that they couldn't go through the wall.

It was three days later and people were just staring at the wall. There had been a lot of settling in after the shot at the wall failed. Some believed The Mist would show the way as long as they kept looking. The wall didn't seem to be moving any longer; careful measurements confirmed that as fact. No one had any idea how to get through.

Sam turned out to be the hero of the day. The Mouses were playing a game of 'king of the circle.' They liked it very much and played as often as they could.

It's sort of like king of the mountain and sumo wrestling combined into one. It's a very rough game. It often got out of hand and the Mouses would wind up in a big brawl. But it's just a game to them. Although they were sort of on even ground with each other; a normal human would have been killed in the playful mêlée. It's almost always stopped before someone got mad enough to pull a weapon. They usually were made to put their knives away before the game started.

Bill remembered when they chose to give the Mouses the knives. It was after Levi was 'assaulted' by the wild chicken. Oh, that was funny. He smiled as he remembered the chicken and then frowned as the thought of the knife fight the Mouses had gotten into. Several of the Mouses had been cut by one of the others before cooler heads could stop the melee. Brandy had even cut Bill, her father, once when he tried to stop a fight. She was very apologetic but it didn't matter. Bill described it as trying to break up a dog fight. The Mouses lost their knives for a while and it was only with the promise that they would stop cutting on each other that they got them back.

In this case the weapon hurled at Remus by Sam was a hamburger. It clipped him on the side of the head and parts of it slammed into the invisible wall. "Hank, (as the Mouses called Sam) I will kick your butt for that." They 'played' a while longer before it was stopped. Billy Gentry had drawn a knife he wasn't supposed to have. He just as quickly put it away. Max just shook his head, "I'm sure glad we didn't give them side arms." Sandy laughed but had enough of the fight for today.

The loud noise woke her baby and she didn't like it. "That is enough, Mouses Attention!!!" The Mouses fell into a line and stood at attention. She addressed the group as Max and Bill snickered. "If you little... little Mouses can't play quieter I am sure I can find some duty that you will not enjoy. Like cleaning the deck." She turned and paused a minute before she turned back to the group. "IS THAT UNDERSTOOD?" It was like they all spoke at once, "Yes SIR, Sorry SIR." She told them to play cards or something. "Yes sir." They were released.

Doris was the first to notice the wall was starting to take on a whitish color and she thought she saw something move. She walked up to the wall and watched. Others noticed her almost trancelike state as she watched the wall. She pulled a piece lettuce from the burger off the wall. The wall moved. She was sure this time and rather alarmed "I need some help over here!"

It didn't take long after that. The front part of the wall began to change to a whitish shade and to move slowly; not as a wall but as a creature. Arms and legs began to form from the mass. Mike ordered the door closed; that took a little time as the cleat slipped twice and had to be repositioned. The door didn't go back in its facing and therefore didn't lock. They had scrambled to secure the door as quickly as possible. But a number of the creatures that had awakened moved into the hangar. They were small, four feet tall, slight of build and grayish. Some were killed outright until one of the four year old Mouses killed one with his bare hands.

The creatures were no direct threat. They were easily killed and didn't fight back. There were only three of the creatures left alive in the hangar at that time. Sorrow over killing without cause began to sweep the crew. They had been concerned and had acted rashly. They were ashamed that they had acted so harshly. The creatures were watched as they began to scavenge for some of the green plant material. The Mouses thought it was almost fun, like having a new pet. They fed the creatures the unusable green plants from the Einstein. That is all they would eat, the green plants. It didn't take long for the real threat to be known.

The Mouses had lost interest in the creatures after about an hour; they were boring. The three creatures hadn't stopped eating since they entered the hangar. They continued to forage for green plants as they got greener and larger. One of them started to scream; it got a lot of attention as the crew watched it split into seven small creatures, leaving little of the original accept a heavy leather like skin. The small creatures began to eat and started to get larger, the other two creatures split into seven creatures. This was very alarming. This is what filled the ship choking out all other life and then they went into hibernation when there was no more to eat. The three that had been allowed to eat, were now twenty one. It didn't take much to realize that they were going to do the same thing again.

They were ordered killed. The creatures screamed at the touch of a human. The smell of their flesh burning from the touch was like warm cinnamon. It smelled very good. They were killed never the less.

Mylissa, a three year old, tried to save one of the cute little creatures. A tug of war started over the creature with her brother, a young Mouse, who wanted to kill it as ordered. In the battle the top of the creature's skull was ripped off; brain matter was splashed on the two who were battling. Some of the bystanders got brain on them as well. A two year old boy started to pick up pieces of the brain and eat it; as boys of that age do. He seemed to really enjoy it and searched for more. He was of course stopped. One of the Mouses on a dare ate some of the brain. He liked it, it was sweet. The children were stopped until Doris could determine if it was safe.

Doris asked the Captain to restrain the living creatures and not feed them until it could be determined if they were a food source. It took two days but she declared it safe, nasty but safe. The tale of the taste had spread quickly and before long the door had to be opened again; not to get to the sweet brain but to clear the hall. The brain was just going to be an extra. The hall had to be cleared if they were going to leave the hangar. It was thought the green plants would bring the creatures back from their hibernation to a waiting death. It was true but the Mouses had plans for the creatures other than instant death.

The door was opened. The green plants caused several more of the grayish creatures to slowly awaken. They did not have to be lured. They almost ran into the hangar. The door was closed again with ease now that the pressure was removed. One of the creatures was killed. Bart pushed his thumb into it eye and pulled back the top part of the skull. His sweet tooth was hurting and he wanted something sweet to stop it. He tasted the brain and it was nasty, it tasted bad. He spit several times on the floor trying to get the taste out of his mouth. Doris knew what to look for this time and determined quickly that it wasn't safe. The adults were poison.

Through the day and many mistakes they found that the creatures had to be green to be eaten and that the younger they were the sweeter. The Mouses referred to it as getting ripe. You fed a creature and waited for it to divide. The kids, the Mouses and some of the adult crew were like vultures waiting for the parent to split. The creatures were named in much the same way.

The strategy was to segregate a few at a time, get them ripe and kill the creature by laying open their skull and have the sweet snack afterwards. Just before the door was opened the Mouses would start to chant 'Seg-ley.' It became the creature's name. The remainder of the adult body, mostly the hide, could be used for clothes. What remained was not edible in any way. Except for the three small orbs that formed as the creature decayed. They were very sour and highly valued by the Mouses who fought over them. No one really noticed; the Mouses fought over everything. The 'corpse' – the small amount of the original creature that was left would dry to a tar like substance in a few hours and as it decayed it was like a room freshener; it smelled good. It all seemed like a cruel joke. The Segley were the perfect prey for an army of children.

The slow process of clearing the hall continued for several days. Doris had determined that the brain of the Segley was a well balanced meal. Something like biscuits and jam with a protein pill. The orbs were full of vitamins and minerals. Some of the adults wouldn't taste the brain until Doris did. She confirmed the stories that it was sweet and then they wanted their share. The hides which were soft and easy to work made a very good cloth substitute.

The Segley were being dealt with and their caste in this world was established; they're food. It was time for the next problem. The supplies were starting to be a problem. The crops were starting to grow again but there would be a short time when there would be no crops. The Segley would have to take up the slack. The kids and the Mouses thought it was a very good idea. Segley brain was better than carrots anytime. The chicken flock had suffered. The loss of this season's chicks which were just eggs when the crash happened caused a shortage of chicken protein. They would live past the problem and the chicken population would increase back to normal very soon.

Doris reported to the board that other things were happening and she believed that the Segley brain was the cause. The children who were eating the most Segley brain were showing no signs of gravity sickness and they were stronger and faster than they were before. She suggested that the adults eat more Segley brain. Sandy smiled. She liked the sweet treat and would have no trouble eating her share. She was mashing the jam- like brain up and feeding it to her baby as well.

Doris told the board that it didn't change the fact that the crew was in trouble. The situation was getting serious. Water was short, not just drinking water, but water. The filtering system was working; it just didn't have anything to filter. A lot of the water was lost in the crash and the air just doesn't have enough moisture in it for the distillers to get a lot of water out. They had to find a source of water and be very careful to recycle what they had. The conscious effort to recycle urine was one of the answers. Stick told Max that he felt like an animal eating brains and drinking piss. Mary, one of his mates, told him to never, ever say anything like that again where she could hear him.

The CC and everyone else believed there had to be fresh water somewhere on the ship. The Mist wouldn't leave them here without water. They just had to find the answer to the puzzle. They had to pass another one of her tests. This time Doris wondered if she would help or just start over with another group if they failed.

There was only one way out of this hangar. They have to be going the right way. "We'll just have to work faster." It was decided to close up all the greens except for some bait; and just go on a killing spree. They opened the door and the green that they were using for bait began to do the trick. The Segley started to wake and thus could be killed. The creatures were allowed to ripen and then the killing started. There was no shortage of ripe Segley. It was nasty, noisy work. The creatures had a shrill scream and when they were touched they screamed like someone had poked them with a hot poker. Doris would find later that was just about the way it was. The living creatures were affected by the salt in the human skin as a human would be by sulfuric acid.

The screams were almost enough to burst one's ear drums. When one Segley started screaming the others followed whether they had been touched or not. The ones giving 'birth' were screaming just as loud. It was a three day massacre. The hallway was still not clear.

Even the strongest sweet tooth was satisfied. Everyone was tired of killing so they took a break. One could only guess what effect the massacre had on the kids and the Mouses or for that matter the adults. Not all the Segley were killed, some were saved to breed new food. It was two days later that the screams were heard again. Max wasn't first to the scene but he wasn't alone. Bart, his oldest, had caught one of the caged Segley and fed it till it burst. He and his friends were having a picnic and the Segley was dessert. Max couldn't help but feel a chill as he watched his two year old daughter pull off the skull cap of one of the Segley and giggle as she ate the brain. They were just food and the Mouses and the younger ones were all going to be warriors. They had watched them butcher the chickens. It dawned on him that death is a way of life for a warrior and these children are warriors.

Most of the equipment on the Einstein still worked to some degree for several weeks but one of the meat keepers malfunctioned and the crew had to have a feast in order to save the meat. It was a welcome change. The kids were even tired of the sweet brain of the Segley as a steady diet. The major thing that stuck in the minds of the crew who noticed was that everyone now liked their steak very rare.

The clearing operation lasted weeks longer than expected. The water problem was solved, temporarily by the liquid in the Segley brain and the rare meat. It was still a problem but not to the degree it was two weeks ago. They worked in four hour shifts as they cleared the ten foot wide hallway. As they cleared the hall it seemed to refill and push forward; fortunately at a slower rate than they were clearing. However, the day came when they broke through.

The wall was gone and they could see a short distance into the dark hallway. They were able to walk down the hall for the first time, it was dark and they didn't go far without a light but... The scientists were able to get a look at something more than ten feet from the door. At last they had cleared the hall. They were so pleased. The cheers went up from all as the news was shared. Doris was very happy. The moisture in the air increased and allowed the dehydrator to make water.

It wasn't long before a few Segley came down the hall looking for the green plants. They were easily caged and kept for food.

The crew could, after three weeks of hard work, go through the door and not encounter a horde of hungry Segley. Doris could only guess the effect all the extended killing of the Segley had on the children. The Mouses were issued side arms and given the run of the hall. They entered into a dark hallway using the infrared and lowlight aspects of the eyes. As they investigated they found that the hallway passed through a court yard about three hundred feet down the hall. All the doors entering the hall were closed. The size of the ship escaped them for a brief moment but soon they realized; they hadn't cleared the ship – just one hallway. The hallway was four thousand feet long, ten feet wide and had doors on both sides with a central courtyard about every eight-hundred feet.

The courtyards were about four-hundred feet square and in five levels of about twenty feet; each level had a circle of two story buildings set back leaving a walkway of about twenty feet between them and the rail that looked down into the square courtyard. The doors were not evenly spaced suggesting rooms of different sizes. Everyone knew the doors had to be opened. What could be in those rooms? Segley was the most often guess.

But until there was better lighting the doors would remain closed. The crew and the board had enough surprises.

There was some investigation of the square or Roanoke Colony as Bill called it. In spite of the historical connotations the name Roanoke Colony brought to mind of a lost colony, the name stuck.

It was another first of many new traditions for the crew. It would carry over into their everyday life and the way they thought.

The crew began to claim the quarters and set up homes, in the first courtyard. There were no lights unless they were brought with them but they didn't care. Once the Segley were removed the new quarters were very nice. The furnishings were nice and comfortable. They liked the way they were designed. There weren't many Segley in the quarters and with the help of a few friends the chosen quarters could be cleaned of them in short order. You could even have a party at the same time. Then you helped them clean their quarters. The current order told them not to clean the floor level. These two story buildings on the first floor were not to be used for quarters. They were going to be the village center.

Roaming Segley weren't much of a problem but a guard was posted just like in the hanger, everyone took a turn. A few Segley did wander through but not many and the unexpected sight of them in the night was a lot more frightening than their presence. The ones that wandered around in the dark were just herded into an enclosure to be dealt with the next day.

The lighting problem was conquered a few days later when the power panel was found. They said it didn't look much like a power panel and that's the reason it took them so long to find it. The scientists found it several hours before they figured out how to restore power. But, once the power was on the job of cleaning the closed rooms was next and it had to be done. This left only the water supply problem to solve.

The two story buildings on the base level of the village were shops. They were made different with an in-ordinate number of windows opening to the square. They couldn't see through the windows and they wondered; what was in those shops? People began to guess. They laughed as they guessed Segley but quickly added and maybe some very nice things.

The lower rooms of the two story shops were stuffed with all kinds of things. The items found were Segley and items from unknown and exotic places. Just what most of the items were, no one was real sure; but they tried to guess. It made for a fun afternoon. Many of the items were claimed by members of the crew. The Captain told them to make note of their claims but everything had to be cleared before it left the shop it was in at that moment.

The technicians came to the conclusion that the village was self-contained. They traced the electric back to a main supply and were able to turn the water and all other necessary things on as well. The village was functional at last. They believed the rest of the ship was most likely dark and Segley infested.

The doors leading to what were most likely hallways on the other five floors were closed off. There were five to seven other doors off the main court, depending on the floor you were on. When they were opened the hunches were proven correct - they opened into hallways. The Segley were not gone from the ship. Every door opened revealed more.

The rooms off the four upper level hallways were more apartments. They were an efficiency type with just three rooms, a bedroom that doubled as a living area, a small kitchen and a bath with a tub. The two areas on the first floor that were in the hallways to the left and right of the shops, on parallel hallways, might have been offices.

The apartments on the four floors in the main square were made for a large group, family if you will. There are sixty apartments on each of the four upper floors that opened onto another court yard; enough to house the crew. Each of the apartments was two stories and had the recurring central courtyard theme. The second floor of the apartments had twelve bedroom suites and the lower was a very large living area. The efficiency type apartments in the halls were one man units or maybe a couple. There was enough room for the entire crew to have private quarters or live in the family units. Some chose both - there were quarters to spare.

The two compartments on each side of the hangar were defense batteries. They had small windows where you could look out into space. The Mouses were very concerned; they didn't like holes in their hull. They kept watching them very closely.

Max didn't like the idea of windows in what looked to him like a defense battery. There was no mistaking guns and some kind of fighter. It occurred to Max that this was a village and they were responsible for the defense of this part of the hull. It was their job. After he voiced his opinion it seemed reasonable to most of the crew.

Within a few days the entire area was working, water, lights and sewage. They found a bath house with spas, steam rooms and a swimming pool depending on what you wanted. This place was made for human comfort. It was nice to hear the children laughing as they played in the water. Most of the crew didn't know how to swim. They had never seen that much water in one place. It didn't take long for them to learn. The shops were cleaned, the items in the shops removed for further study and labs put in them.

There were several shops left and Bill declared them open to be claimed as a business. The first shop in Roanoke village was a restaurant. The chow hall people who started the place preferred the term over chow hall. Preparation of food was their job on the Einstein. It was now going to be their contribution to the village. It was what they wanted to do. It was a logical step. By the same reasoning other members of the crew continued to farm and others to clear the hall. The village began to function much the same way it had for the last seven years.

The Mouses had a lot more time on their hands; this ship wasn't about to blow at any second. The hull needed far less attention and they were bored. When Mouses or Warriors are bored; there are fights. Max and Sandy opened a Charms club called 'The Rat's Nest' in one of the shops. It was decorated with parts of the Einstein. The crew needed a familiar place to blow off steam. The Mouses really needed a place to blow off steam.

The Einstein was slowly being salvaged; every piece of it. The parts that couldn't be used were turned into keepsakes, rings and necklaces and the like; small and not so small pieces placed in a secret box or storage areas so the owner could go back and remember the Einstein.

The larger parts, like the Karaoke machine, were moved to The Rat's Nest. The stoves and other restaurant supplies were moved to the new chow hall (sorry, restaurant) although it was being called 'The Soup Kitchen' with good reason. They always had soup, stew, chili and Pinto beans. The crew liked these types of one dish meals. It's what they had eaten over the last seven years. There was a lot of variety and each member of the crew had his or her favorite. It was once noted that Brandy could eat a gallon of chili in one setting. It was an exaggeration of course, but not by much. The breads were baked on the second floor of the restaurant. Everyone had their favorite bread, from Max's cornbread that he couldn't eat without, to the soft white bread that the majority of the crew preferred.

The baker who had made the black market doughnuts opened a sweets shop. Sandy had already started to cultivate plants like sugar cane and sugar beets that there hadn't been room to grow in abundance on the Einstein. Here she had plenty of room. Soon there would be more sugar than they could eat. Segley brain was very good but nothing was better than candy, chocolate candy. Cacao beans were grown on the Einstein but not many were shared. It was more of an effort to keep fresh seeds or live roots in some cases for possible future use.

The scientists worked to understand the working of the new ship and the shops began to fill. Stick took one for a police station and turned the second floor into a sort of brig. He hoped he would never need it but it's best to be prepared.

Doris took one for a medical unit and converted the upstairs to a hospital. She had no doubt she would need it sooner or later.

Professor Morris took charge of growing and controlling the Lumpers and Bumpers. Doris just had too many things to do now that everything had to be tested for one reason or another.

The restaurant was the main user but anybody could sign for the meats that wanted them. There was more than enough to go around. Morris would also take charge of the chickens and eggs when there was enough to go around.

The hangar was converted to grow things. The chickens seemed pleased to be in a larger area. Their eggs were being left alone for the time being and several of them were setting again. A new crop of food would soon be available. The crew was now in the same position as they were a month ago; well, they would be as soon as the crops started to produce. The stores they had put back just in case they had a crop failure were going to take them to the harvest with ease.

Doris had developed new eyes with the help of Larry and an engineer named Dean. The shortage was over and now the Mouses who didn't have a computerized eye wanted one. They were told that they wouldn't punch their eye out and if they did they still wouldn't get one. Dean was very close to a mount that would place the eye on the side of the head and allow it to be tied into the computer system just like the others.

It was time to move forward. Documents had been found that told them they were on a floor somewhere between the tenth and the thirty-fourth floor. That is what it looked like in the drawings, given the scale it was hard to tell. Further exploration would start soon.

CHAPTER TWENTY-FOUR,
TIME TO EXPLORE

Most of the crew volunteered to help search the ship. Seven adult members of the crew were accepted to explore the ship. The seven older Mouses were paired with them and promoted to Sergeant second and issued long-arms to go with their side arms. Two of the younger Mouses finished out the unit, forming seven, four person exploration units. Mike decided to call them Scout units.

That was the birth of the first thru seventh Scouts. The Scout units grew to five members each before the end of the week; four just wasn't enough to do the job. The larger of the Mouse volunteers were put in the units because of the heavier work the unit was expected to do. They were told to explore the ship, try to stay out of trouble and turn in nightly reports to H.

The older of the smaller Mouses were put in charge of newly developed Mouse units one thru twelve which consist of ten Mouses each. The leader of each unit was promoted to Sergeant. They had to submit nightly reports to Mouse. It became very cumbersome, very quickly. Mouse didn't have time to deal with twelve different people bringing her reports and neither did H. The rank of Administrative Sergeant became necessary. The Scout Sergeants Seconds were watched carefully by the board as well as the new Mouse Sergeants. They tried to make the decision without them knowing they were being tested.

After a week the board met. They tossed the entire board structure out. They had little choice; the old one just wouldn't work under the new conditions. The board had to be reformed and so they may as well develop a Rank structure to better deal with the current situation at the same time. The board had to be formed before any other decisions could be made.

The members of the board were even in question. After two days of long and sometimes loud discussions Captain Mike decided that the board would remain with a few changes. The board would now consist of him and his second, Warren. Carol accepted the position of City Manager with Bill, the Mayor as her boss. She was the Mayor's voice on the board. Bill wouldn't be part of the board any longer. It was his idea. Doris continued to serve as medical but wouldn't take direct experiment control. She would train a second who would not be on the board, Professor Kidling. She reasoned that he was the most level headed of the scientists. The new position would help him in the current growth pattern experiments. She also reasoned that it was becoming very important with the new babies being under three gs all the time. He would be happy to watch them more closely.

Further changes brought Mouse to command of the Scouts and as her second H would have the Mouses. John Gentry would take over Maintenance without Mouse to run to for help. Stick would take over Security with Law Enforcement falling under him to Luanne. Max was assigned Training and Sandy control of the farms.

The new jobs caused some problems but after a few days the boundaries were set. Max was training the watch personnel hard and cutting them very little slack. The rest of the crew was pressed into service as augments to the defense batteries. He hoped he could with the help of the scientists, figure out how they worked soon.

It took another meeting of the board a week later to address the rank structure. The Mouses and the Scouts were the main interest which brought H and Mouse into the picture. H was to be promoted to Ensign and given command of the Mouses. Mouse as a Lieutenant would take the Scouts and command of the two groups. The vote of the board was next and it was serious business. Who in the respective group was going to take charge as their seconds?

The vote for the 'Command Sergeant First' slot of the Scouts turned out to be very easy. The board had been watching them for weeks and they all came to the same conclusion. Mouse hated to vote for Brandy, it seemed a little wrong for her to vote for her daughter but that's what she did. Mike started to read the papers containing the name in the secret ballot.

He opened the first paper, "Brandy Holt." The second ballot was opened and then the third and all the rest — "Brandy Holt." Mouse was very pleased that she had the Mouses with her daughter as her second. The members of the board agreed Brandy was her second and as odd as it looked it was still the way it was. Brandy was second in charge and that was all there was to it. Mike commented that he agreed "She sure is just like her Father. He took charge of the East Coast armies back in his day and Brandy has taken charge of the Scouts." Mouse smiled, she started to correct the error in Brandy's parentage but decided not to; Bill was her Father. He had raised her since she was four and she acted just like him. She would also be in charge no matter who the board put in charge. Mike smiled. "Ok, Brandy is promoted to Command Sergeant First and she can name her own Second with consent of Mouse." The board sort of laughed as they said together "so say we all." The joke was not going to stay a joke for long, 'so say we all' became the term for agreeing with everything.

The Mouse units were another story. There wasn't a front runner like there was in the Scouts. The list was narrowed to four names because those four names were all on the list more than once, Nikki Dent had three votes but it wasn't considered a majority. Max and Sandy were asked if they voted for their daughter. They told the board no, they didn't believe she took the work serious enough. Mike told them they were just blind to how good their daughter was at her job. They would watch some more before the promotions were announced. The Command Sergeant First slot in the Scouts was Brandy's to keep or lose. The Command Sergeant First slot of the Mouses was Nikki's to win or lose. The promotions would be made official and the respective promotees would be told at some time in the near future.

In the meantime Max kept the pressure on the crew to train.

The quandary of the guns in the battle platform had been solved. The battle stations were passing as much as a game as they were training aids. The laughter echoed through the ship. It was very pleasant. They were enjoying firing the guns at the targets that could be launched from the ship. It was great fun even though Max made them log three hours a day on the guns.

The Scouts opened more doors every day and made their reports. H would be happy when this ended. She was very tired of all the paperwork. The Mouses turned in their reports every day. Nikki brought her report to H every day, on time. Max and Sandy were starting to think they might have misjudged Nikki's devotion to duty.

The older Mouses were trying to get the fighters in the defense area to work and one day they had a breakthrough. One of the fighters launched with Billie, Bill and Mouses oldest daughter, in it. She's six. She was scared and screaming. Mouse went to see what was wrong with her baby and when she opened the hatch it was discovered that Billie thought the fighter had launched; that she was in space. Max got in the fighter and after a while Billie was able to remember what she had done. Max tried it but it didn't work. By this time the entire crew was watching. Sandy suggested that maybe the hatch had to be closed.

Max closed the hatch and pressed the buttons. He heard himself scream as the fighter launched. After a few seconds he laughed. "You guys have got to try this. It feels like I'm in space in a fighter but I know I'm still in the control area because I can hear you talking. He tried to learn how to fly the thing. It was a lot like the shuttles but much faster. He was getting better. He turned it so he could see the ship. He told them it was huge and then he started to count. "There are lights on the twelfth section. Turn them off so I can see if it's us."

They scrabbled quickly and the lights went out. Max told them that the light had just gone out. "We are on the twelfth section of the ship. It looks like hundreds of sections below and the size of this thing is unimaginable." Max simply opened the hatch and the fighter shut down. The Mouses who were tall enough to reach the controls and everyone else took full advantage of this new toy. Target shooting and then it was discovered that the fighters really shot; when a passing meteoroid was unexpectedly destroyed. These were real fighters, the guns were real guns. This was not a game it was a defense battery, with training aids. It didn't matter, the Mouses who were tall enough and the Scouts; were in space, alone, in a fighter. They could not have been happier.

It didn't take them long to discover the outer limits of the craft. If you got too far from the ship the fighter ceased to exist. It was very annoying. The guns would only reach about half as far as the fighters and they would not target the fighters. The Mouses tried; children will be children.

Max took his training duties very seriously. He had drills every time he thought no one expected them. It was a big mess. Sandy was sort of mad at him. The rest of the crew was ready to choke him to death. The scientists ignored him once when he called for a drill using the system, "Battle stations." They didn't come. They had discovered an auxiliary control area and they thought the discovery exempted them from the attack drill. It didn't and when Max got through with them; well let's just say it probably will not happen again.

It was almost a month after the discovery of the auxiliary control room when the frantic call came in the middle of the night. "Battle stations now, Battle stations, repeat BATTLE STATIONS NOW." Sandy started to yell at Max for waking her and the baby. It was then that she realized he was sitting up in the bed next to her. He waited for a second. The call came again even more frantic than before. "This is the Captain of the Watch, I have incoming hostiles. This is not a drill. Confirm launch Scout one and two. Get your freakin' asses down here now." Sandy said to Max. "That's Nikki." Max was out of bed and headed toward the defense bunker. "She does have the watch." Sandy was close behind with their baby. They heard as they got close to the bunker, "confirm launch Scout six, Scout seven – Mouse four open fire as soon as they are within range of the guns."

Max asked Nikki, "What happened?" She was almost yelling. "I saw them and tried to make contact; just like I was told. They fired on us and I ordered Battle Stations."

The incoming crafts blasted right through the fighters and continued toward the ship. The pilots of the fighters were out and manning a gun. The wave of ships just passed right by, firing at the ship but not slowing.

When the battle was replayed it was determined that they needed a lot of training. The pilots and the gunners told stories of the ones they almost hit. It was a big relief that the crafts just kept going. Bill told everyone that they were the same type of craft that took out his entire force back in the war. He was very pleased that no one was hurt or killed.

The board used the incident to start the promotions. Max and Sandy voted for Nikki this time. She had taken command with no hesitation. She deserved the Command Sergeant First slot.

The board called for a general meeting at 'The Rat's Nest.' It wasn't that big of a deal; they did this sort of thing often. This was just the first time at the Charms club and in the square of Roanoke. Everyone knew there would be some business discussed and then there would be a lot of food and drink.

Mouse and Bill were talking to Brandy before they went to the club. Mouse said to Brandy. "Brandy, there are going to be some changes tonight and I need to know who you think should lead the Scouts."

Brandy shrugged, "You're doing ok. Are they thinking about replacing you?"

Mouse shook her head, "No, but they want me to have a second and H is going to take the Mouses."

Brandy nodded, "Me. But I don't guess they would go for that with you in command."

Mouse smiled, "I never thought of a Scout but maybe. But I don't know how the board would react to you being that person."

Brandy nodded, "I guess it would be pushing it."

Mouse thought for a few seconds, "If I could get a Scout do you think Bart would be ok?"

Brandy smiled, "Bart's ok but he's a little young, he's not one of the older group and I think they would resent it. I know I would."

Mouse nodded, "You may be right but who would you choose if you were in command and needed a second?"

Brandy smiled. "Hank, he's always been there for me and that's who I would pick."

Mouse smiled. "I'll look at his record." She smiled. "I know him and I like him but I would need to see what's written in his record." Mouse laughed, "Nikki really took over during the attack, didn't she?"

Brandy laughed, "She sure did. I didn't think she had it in her but she was really barking out the orders. She'd be a good choice for H." They arrived at The Rat's Nest and went inside.

The board sponsored party at The Rat's Nest got off to a good start when Captain Mike walked in the door - "JEWEL." Everyone looked at him. He said. "That means I'm buying the first round right now." The amount of alcohol per Jewel wasn't changed but they didn't count them either.

Before the first round was half gone Mike took the stage, drink in hand. "Well, this is sort of weird. This will be an update on what's next to come. First I want to say a very loud THANK YOU to the ones who fought in the battle the other night."

Everyone was shouting and he continued. "We got our asses handed to us on a silver platter but we were in the fight for a little while. The best thing is no one was killed and nothing was really destroyed. We came out smelling like a rose." He laughed, "Our pants won't stay up because we have no asses but we did well for our first encounter." Everyone was cheering.

He calmed the room and added. "Fortunately we have a trained fighter pilot in our company and he is going to set up a training course so the pilots will have some idea of what to do once the Captain of the Watch calls Battle Stations. Now, don't get this wrong, Max did a very good job of training you pilots and gunners to take action and Nikki did a great job of getting us in the battle". He paused. " But we need training badly in fighter tactics. The Death Dealer is going to train the pilots."

Bill stood and smiled. "And that is just what we're going to do - deal death to anyone who attacks us." He started to have a seat but stopped. "We might even pick a fight or two." Bill smiled "Chug. That means to finish your drink. We are about to be called to attention. They drank the drinks and slammed the glasses down on the table making a lot of noise.

Mike took the stage, "Please come stand on stage as I call your name. Master Chief Harriet Sheldon, Chief Luanne Le'Beau, Sergeant Second Brandy Holt, Sergeant Nikki Dent."

Nikki smiled and said to Brandy as they walked toward the stage. "Do you know what's going on? I was just doing my job last night."

Brandy smiled, "Relax, believe me, they don't yell at you in public so this is a good thing."

Nikki smiled, "You mean not like my Mom yelling at me about my freaking language."

Brandy nodded, "I wondered if you were going to get away clean."

Harriet joined them on stage. Luanne had already arrived. Mike smiled, "Attention to orders." The four snapped to attention. "Remember, you are at attention." Professor Sheldon was already headed for the stage. When he arrived Mike continued, "Chief Sheldon, due to a reconfiguration of the board, you have been promoted to Ensign in command of the Mouses." Carol came up next to her and smiled as she handed Sheldon one of the ensign bars. H didn't know what to say. She was almost in tears as Carol smiled, "Congratulations H. This is a long ways from where we came but I'm happy to serve with you." Sheldon smiled as he said; "now maybe my sister will shut up about our level difference." H smiled.

Luanne's husband, Frank and Stick, her boss, walked out on stage. Luanne just tried not to fall down. She knew she was about to be promoted. However, she didn't expect it to be to Ensign. She looked a little green around the gills.

Mike smiled at Brandy. Mouse and Bill came out on stage and helped her with the new stripes –Command Sergeant First Class; Mouse told Brandy "You're right. You should be my second and now you are." Brandy looked at her Father as he said. "Congratulations Command Sergeant First Class Holt. They stepped back a half step and together, "We're very proud of you." Brandy was just about to cry. She had only made Sergeant a month back and they just handed it to her. This was a big deal.

When Max and Sandy walked out on stage Nikki was starting to hyperventilate. They talked softly to her telling her how brave she was the night of the attack. Max told her to hold it together a while longer just like she did the night of the attack. "Command Sergeant First Class Nicola Dent."

The promotions were over and it was time to party. Max yelled "Jewel'" and the crowd responded "Jewel." Everyone had another drink in their hand very soon after the call. This one was on Max.

The newly promoted all went for a talk. They had the jewel in their hands before they were told the bad news. They had to pick their second. Mike told Brandy and Nikki that there was a set of Command Sergeant Third stripes in the envelope and they could give them to one of the other Sergeants. "I need to know now who you plan to draft."

Brandy smiled, "So that's what the conversation was about today." She nodded, "Hank."

Mouse nodded a yes and Mike smiled. "Done, Hank it is."

Mike turned to Nikki, "I guess you heard all of that. Do you know who you will draft?"

Nikki smiled, "Yeah, I was thinking about it ever since this afternoon when Mom sort of set the stage for all of this.

He smiled. "So who?"

Nikki smiled, "Donny."

Mike asked, "Who did you say?"

She repeated "Donny, your son, Donald Hall."

Mike nodded, "that's who I thought you meant. Are you sure? He's sometimes…"

Nikki smiled. "He always there and he does a great job." Nikki smiled, "Would you like to help me pin the stripes on him?"

Mike nodded. "Yes and let's get Chief Grant up on stage to help with Hank's stripes."

Brandy walked on the stage and Hank yelled, "Nice stripes. What are you going to do now, make a speech?"

Brandy smiled "Chug." They drank their drinks and Mike yelled "group attention, Sergeant Samuel Grant please come to the stage." Samuel started to the stage and Mike spoke again. "Sergeant Donald Hall please join us on stage." The stripes were presented and then the party really started. Max and Bill both yelled 'Jewel' about the same time. Everyone got two drinks.

Bill got everyone's attention, "The Mist came to see me earlier; she said we were safe here for a couple of days and to have a good time." He laughed as he added, "She said she might join us."

When she did appear it was next to Bart, he smiled and offered her an extra drink he had, "Hi Misty, it's nice of you to join us without someone being dead." He realized he had said the wrong thing almost immediately. "Oh, I'm so sorry. I meant no disrespect. She laughed took the drink and yelled "chug."

CHAPTER TWENTY-FIVE,
THE BEGINNING

Three months later at the monthly meeting the findings of the scientists were announced. They believed they could fly the ship. They believed a lot of other things as well. They would have to be tested. One of the things to be tested was a folding technology.

The test proved them correct and the crew was informed that they could be home in about sixty days. It wasn't greeted with as much enthusiasm as expected. Max and Sandy along with their group of friends and their children had already decided that they were going to stay with the ship. They were not going back to Earth to live. They knew others who felt the same way. What was a surprise to them was that every member of the crew felt the same way.

This crew was going to stay with the ship and live out their lives in space. Even the hard core Earthers who had resisted some of the changes were going to stay with the ship. One of them said it best. "We are no longer Earthers; on Earth our children would be freaks. We have robot parts and are just too strong to be put in a group of humans. Our children and everyone on board, every member of the crew is a trained warrior. We would be freaks on Earth. They, the children and we will have a much better life in space. It's where we belong now. This ship is huge. We can live here for generations." The applause was very loud.

The meeting did several other things after they decided to stay aboard. It was suggested that from this day forth that they refer to themselves as Einsteinee. Bill dubbed the ship the Bismarck. "Because we are going to become the target of the universe and it is best for us to remember that any ship can be destroyed; no matter how big and bad it may be." It was accepted "so say we all" and the people, the crew, the Einsteinee ate their first meal on the ship. The Bismarck was now their world. For dessert they feasted on sweet Segley brain.

You would think that was the end of the story but it's not. The Mist joined them and told them "Now that you have decided to be a part of space; I have many things that I would like for you to do. I will protect you and show you many wonders. I will expect you to wage war on the Segley. They must be destroyed." She smiled, "Along with their masters - but we'll save them for later.

She gave them a setting for the fold. The fold took them to a planetary system that consisted of two Suns and three planets that orbited them in an ellipse that was squeezed together in the middle; something resembling a figure eight without crossing in the middle. The planets were not stable and the seasons would take some watching to decide how they worked. The gravity also varied between 1.8 and 3.0 earth gravities. It was guessed that neither of the habitable planets was habitable year round, but, if you lived on a space craft; and you only visited the planets; it was an acceptable place. That is if you could handle three Earth gravities like the Einsteinee.

It was the beginning of the Empire:

year one

month one

week one

day one

hour one

minute one

and second one

of the Einsteinee Empire.

NEXT

BATTLE STATIONS

THE EXPANSION OF THE EINSTEINEE EMPIRE